PRAISE FOR GAYLE ROPER'S

Summer Shadows

"Once again, Gayle Roper shows herself to be a master at creating compelling characters."

NANCY MOSER, AUTHOR OF *THE SEAT BESIDE ME*

"Gayle Roper has combined her special brand of wit and wisdom to weave a highly entertaining tale with just the right touch of mystery. I'm already looking forward to my next visit to Seaside."

DEBORAH RANEY, AUTHOR OF *BENEATH A SOUTHERN SKY*
AND *A VOW TO CHERISH*

"Suspenseful drama, sweet romance, and breezy seaside setting...Gayle Roper's *Summer Shadows* is ideal for summer reading."

DEANNA JULIE DODSON, AUTHOR OF *IN HONOR BOUND* AND
TO GRACE SURRENDERED

"Gayle Roper's interesting characters, not to mention heart-swelling romance and heart-racing suspense, will keep you turning the pages of *Summer Shadows* long after you planned on turning out the light!"

LISA E. SAMSON, AUTHOR OF *THE CHURCH LADIES* AND *WOMEN'S INTUITION*.

Spring Rain

"*Spring Rain* is a heartwarming love story that doesn't shy away from tackling tough subjects like homosexuality and promiscuity. Ms. Roper handles them with grace and compassion, never compromising the hope-filled truth of God's Word while giving us a bang-up tale of romantic suspense!"

LIZ CURTIS HIGGS, BESTSELLING AUTHOR OF *BAD GIRLS OF THE BIBLE*

The Decision

HOLT MEDALLION AWARD WINNER
which honors outstanding literary talent

REVIEWER'S CHOICE AWARD WINNER
from Romantic Times *magazine*

"If you're looking for a contemporary mystery with wit and romance, Gayle Roper is the author you've been waiting for."

"*The Decision* packs a powerful punch as Gayle's endearing characters come to terms with love and reconciliation. Set in Lancaster County, the author's attention to detail shines in her portrayal of the Amish people. *The Decision* is one of the best novels I've reviewed to date."

"*The Decision* combines gripping suspense with heartwarming romance, and a touch of humor besides. You'll grow close to Jake, Rose, and their families, share in their pain and frustrations, and exult with them in their victories from the first page to the last. A wonderful book!"

Novels by Gayle Roper

The Decision
Enough!

SEASIDE SEASONS:
Spring Rain
Summer Shadows
Autumn Dreams (June 2003)

THE AMHEARST MYSTERIES:
Caught in the Middle
Caught in the Act
Caught in a Bind

Summer Shadows

SEASIDE SEASONS BOOK TWO

GAYLE ROPER

Multnomah®Publishers *Sisters, Oregon*

SUMMER SHADOWS
published by Multnomah Publishers, Inc.
© 2002 by Gayle G. Roper

International Standard Book Number: 1-57673-969-4

Cover image by David Bailey Photography

Unless otherwise indicated, Scripture quotations are from:
The Holy Bible, New International Version
© 1973, 1984 by International Bible Society,
used by permission of Zondervan Publishing House
Other scripture quotations:
Holy Bible, New Living Translation (NLT) © 1996.
Used by permission of Tyndale House Publishers, Inc.

Multnomah is a trademark of Multnomah Publishers, Inc.,
and is registered in the U.S. Patent and Trademark Office.
The colophon is a trademark of Multnomah Publishers, Inc.
Printed in the United States of America

For information:
MULTNOMAH PUBLISHERS, INC. • P.O. 1720 • SISTERS, OR 97759

Library of Congress Cataloging-in-Publication Data

Roper, Gayle G.
    Summer shadows / by Gayle Roper.
        p. cm. — (Seaside seasons; bk. 2)
    ISBN 1-57673-969-4
    1. Accident victims—Family relationships—Fiction.
  2. Mothers and daughters—Fiction. 3. Hit-and-run drivers—
Fiction. 4. Widows—Fiction. I. Title.
    PS3568.068 S86 2002
    813'.54—dc21

                                              2002000327

04 05 06 07 08—10 9 8 7 6 5 4 3

For Anne, Dave, Don and all the others who made
my Seaside summers so special.
Thanks for the wonderful memories.
And Don, thanks for introducing
me to Chuck. Who knew, huh?

—⁓—

With special thanks to Julee Schwarzburg and Karen Ball
for their excellent editing and encouraging support.
I am most fortunate.
Abby would like to thank Vicki León for her books *Uppity
Women of Medieval Times* and *Uppity Women of the Renaissance*.
They were a great inspiration.

—∞—

Sing to God, sing praise to his name,
extol him who rides on the clouds—
his name is the LORD—and rejoice before him.
A father to the fatherless, a defender of widows,
is God in his holy dwelling. God sets the lonely in families.

PSALM 68:4–6A

One

ABBY STARED UP the flight of stairs and mentally kicked herself. The rigors of climbing to the second floor every day hadn't seemed such an overwhelming challenge when she talked to the realtor over the phone. All Abby had paid attention to was "on the beach," and that made up her mind for her. That and her desperate need to escape.

Idiot, she muttered under her breath, though even now "on the beach" tempered her self-criticism to a mild reprimand rather than a blistering diatribe.

Sighing, she grabbed the banister and began the arduous trip up the outside stairs to her new second floor beachfront apartment, pulling herself from step to step, trying to ignore the pain. After all, there was a time not too long ago when it would have been much worse. She gritted her teeth and "pushed through."

How she hated that phrase.

Her physical therapist had yelled it at her for months. "Push through, Abby," Helene always called. "Push through. You can do it. I know you can." Easy for Helene to say as she stood there on two strong legs while Abby with her damaged hip and leg tried to climb one step, then two, walk the length of the room, then back, dripping with sweat and almost retching from pain.

Because Abby had no choice other than a life of immobility, she had pushed through, crying as she pushed. Three times a day, then twice, then once. Then three times a week, then twice, then once, she had pushed through the torture known as physical therapy. As a result she walked without a cane unless she had to be on her feet for a long time or had to traverse an uneven surface.

Tipping her mental hat to Helene, she continued to climb the stairs to her new apartment, step by straining step. She couldn't help smiling. Sometimes such small things were really momentous victories.

"Excuse me, but just what do you think you're doing?" The deep voice was cold, the question accusatory. "This is a private residence."

Abby gripped the banister to steady herself and turned. Even looking down from her vantage point halfway up the stairs, she could tell he was one big man. He was also an irate one. His mouth was pressed thin, and his dark eyes shot sparks. His hands were fists on his hips. In each fist he held a messy sheaf of papers that fanned out on either side of him like a stiff tutu. Abby could see handwritten corrections in bold, black marker scribbled about the typing. She must have disturbed his work, and he didn't appear to handle interruptions well.

It was sad, his surly attitude, because otherwise he was really quite impressive. A beautiful fallen angel, she thought, struck with a flight of imaginative if theologically incorrect fancy, an angel who lacked civility. She sniffed the air in curiosity. All the supernatural, Peretti-type novels said she should smell the brimstone if he were indeed a fallen angel, but she didn't catch any hint of sulfur in the clean sea air.

"Well?" he prompted, his fair hair falling across his forehead. The sun struck it so it looked like a gleaming golden halo. He was too handsome by half.

She lifted her chin and straightened her shoulders as she tried to remember his original question. Neither fallen angel nor grumpy man was going to intimidate her. She backtracked mentally from her image of an angel and brimstone through impressive and irate to— She grinned. What was she doing here? That was the question. She even knew the answer, not that he deserved it.

"Marguerite de la Roque," she said. "Without the moral baggage."

He blinked. "Well, Marguerite, I repeat, what are you doing here?"

"My name is not Marguerite. She has been dead for several centuries."

He looked understandably bewildered.

"She sailed from France to Canada in 1541, the first European woman to reach the New World. Like her, I am embarking on a great adventure. I am moving to Seaside today." *To my New World full of promise.* She smiled brilliantly at him.

"I hate to tell you, but you're hardly the first woman to reach town," he said dryly. "And, I'm sure, not the last. Now why are you here? Climbing these particular steps, I mean."

A loud woof brought her gaze to the dog that stood at the man's side. The rottweiler stared at her, his brown eyebrows pulled together in an unblinking frown that matched the man's.

Great. Steps, a grumpy neighbor, and an ugly monster besides. Wait until Puppy sees him. She'll have a coronary on the spot.

"I'm Abby Patterson," she said, remembering at the last minute to look at the man, not the dog. "I'm not trespassing. I'm renting the second floor indefinitely."

"Oh." He looked nonplussed, and she was irritated enough at him to enjoy his discomfort. "You're not coming until tomorrow."

She shrugged. "Change of plans." If ever she'd uttered an understatement, that was it. But how could she possibly explain to this glowering man that coming today was her private Declaration of Independence. Her own giant leap for mankind. Her personal strike against tyranny as she raised the banner signaling the belated liberation of Abigail Lynn MacDonald Patterson, aged twenty-nine.

She waved the keys she'd gotten at the realtor's. Then she turned her back and continued her climb. She was surprised to feel the wood vibrate beneath her feet. She looked over her shoulder. Both the golden man and his monster dog were ascending her steps. Her *private* steps.

She reached the small landing at the top and turned to him, her back against the sturdy wooden railing. He stepped onto the landing too, followed by the monster. Talk about crowded.

"What?" she asked, voice abrupt. He and the dog unnerved her standing in the tight space with her. As a result she gave him her frostiest stare to prove she wasn't bothered by his nearness. It was just that he loomed, sort of like her father did.

He stared at her, every bit as frosty as she. It was a wonder snow didn't fall on this strip of New Jersey beach in spite of the balmy mid-June temperature. "I'm Marsh Winslow."

She was so busy wishing he would back up onto the porch, which ran across the width of the building, and give her breathing room that it took a minute for the name to register.

"You're Marsh Winslow? My landlord?" Abby was appalled. She had to share the house with this snarling, ill-tempered person? She glanced down. And his monster dog?

The dog nudged his master's hand for all the world like he wanted to be introduced too.

The man looked at the monster, his face softening into a smile. "This is Fargo, the wonder dog."

"I've got a cat," Abby said, staring at Fargo with distaste. He was so big. "Puppy."

Marsh Winslow blinked again. "You have a cat and a dog? I thought you only had a cat. That's all we agreed on in the lease."

This time she blinked. "I do."

"Er, you do what?"

The man couldn't even follow a conversation. "I do have just a cat," she patiently explained. "I'd have told you if I had a dog." She glanced at Fargo. "They're hard to hide."

"But you just said you had a puppy." Fargo nodded his agreement. "They're even harder to hide."

"I said I had a cat named Puppy."

"A cat named Puppy?"

It was his quick look at the dog that made her angry. It was like the two of them thought she was playing with less than a full deck. It was too much like the way her parents had looked at each other when she told them about her new job in Seaside.

Well, contrary to public opinion, she was not an idiot. Her mental deck was a full fifty-two cards, carefully shuffled and ready to play.

"I suppose naming a dog after a city in North Dakota makes more sense?"

Her landlord scratched his ear like he couldn't believe he was involved in such a foolish conversation. Fargo sat, lifted his rear leg, and began scratching his ear too.

Fleas? Both of them?

Marsh took a deep breath, the kind you take when you are putting up with someone who has tried you to the limits. "I, um, I need to apologize if I sounded a bit abrupt," he said abruptly. "I didn't realize who you were."

She looked at him a minute without reacting. He didn't appear sorry. His mouth had the puckered look of someone who'd just swallowed something extremely sour or someone whose mother had forced him to apologize countless time when he didn't want to.

"Don't let it worry you," she said, waving her hand regally in the air. "You couldn't have known." Having dismissed him, she turned ninety degrees to look out over the beach and the ocean. "It'll be a case of Isabella and Ferdinand."

Fargo woofed in question as Marsh said, "I beg your pardon?"

"Isabella and Ferdinand." She again waved her hand to shoo him away.

"Of Christopher Columbus fame, I assume? You're Isabella and I'm Ferdinand?"

She nodded. She was Queen Isabella dismissing the diminutive Ferdinand—except that Marsh Winslow was anything but little and he didn't seem to realize she'd dismissed him. Still, if they could work out a policy like Isabella and Ferdinand did, they'd probably manage all right. As coregents of Spain, Isabella ruled Castile while Ferdinand ruled Aragon. She would rule the second floor, her Castile, and Marsh the first, his Aragon. If such an arrangement allowed the royal marriage to survive, certainly it would allow the two of them to coexist through the summer and beyond.

"How many miles to the horizon?" she asked suddenly.

He blinked at the change of topic and glanced quickly at the water. "I haven't the vaguest idea."

How was he able to convey with just the tone of his voice the idea that she had asked a foolish question? "Oh. I just thought you might know, living here and all."

He answered with icy cool. "I bought this house three months ago. I have lived here a total of one week thus far."

"Oh." She watched the gentle surf roll onto the sand, a covey of quick-footed sandpipers darting just ahead of the advancing waves, then dashing back to search for food before the next comber came. The gloriously radiant sun bathed the scene, making her squint against the glare in spite of her sunglasses. It was all she could do not to hug herself with delight in spite of her grouchy landlord.

A place at the shore, right on the beach in the southern part of the island that was Seaside. When she'd driven over the Thirty-fourth Street Bridge onto the island just a few miles south of Atlantic City, she'd greedily inhaled the tangy, salty air. She felt like she was coming home though she'd never before been in Seaside longer than two weeks at a time. Still, the feeling of rightness reinforced her belief that she'd made the correct decision in deciding to settle here.

From the top of the bridge she looked down on Egg Harbor Bay. In the marshes she saw a great white heron standing still as a statue, its plumage brilliant against the deep green of the swaying grasses. On a slim strip of beach outlining an islet of shrubs and grasses sat at least ten cormorants, their snaky necks stretched to the sun, their wings spread wide to dry.

Then she'd driven into Seaside, turned right on Central Avenue, and found 4311. Her new home. Her new porch with nothing between her and the sea but the wide strand of soft, golden sand.

When she and her parents had come to Seaside through the years for vacations, they had always rented the first floor of a house that stood three blocks back from the beach. Financial considerations had forced that rental.

As a child, she had thought everyone lugged chairs, umbrellas, towels, toys, rafts, and bottle upon bottle of suntan lotion to the beach every day only to tote it all back every evening, all sandy and sticky, tired and grumpy. One day it dawned on her that people actually lived in the houses that lined the beach. These fortunate few got up each morning, had breakfast on their big, wide porches, and stepped off their decks right onto the sand. They went back to their houses for gritless lunches, then walked back onto the sand for the rest of the afternoon. They even played on the beach in the evenings after the lifeguards went off duty or sat on their porches and watched the waves.

Nothing was more thrilling than watching the waves, nothing, and it was like they belonged to the people who lived right on the beach. They could watch no matter the weather. Even on a wild, rain-soaked day, they could sit inside all dry and cozy, observing the temperamental sea slapping the sand, waves crashing in fury, spume flying.

Now here she was with her own porch right on the beach. She could eat breakfast on her own deck to the music of the purling sea. She could sit beneath her own awning and watch the sun jewels dance on the ceaseless motion of the water until she was glutted on the sight. If she wanted to, she could lie on her chaise and listen to the waves sigh and break all night long. When the weather turned, she could enjoy the ferocity, the violence, from behind her floor-to-ceiling windows. And she had only to step from the walk beside the house onto the sand, then cross the lovely cream expanse to stand in the cool green water.

Three cheers for insurance settlements.

"Let me show you around the apartment." Marsh gestured toward the door just behind him on the landing.

Abby glanced at him. "That's okay. You needn't bother."

She knew she sounded less than gracious, but he hadn't exactly been the warm and welcoming host. Besides, she wanted nothing more than to be alone. She was bone tired. She ached from head to foot, and she needed the bathroom badly. She gave a perfunctory smile. "I'll be fine."

This time he took the hint. With a brusque nod, he started down the steps. "Let's go, Fargo."

The dog threw her one last look before lumbering off in his master's wake.

Abby turned back to the view, telling herself it was all right that she was uncharacteristically unfriendly. She had a good excuse. Sitting in the same position for five hours had played havoc with her hip, making the muscles tighten, the nerves scream. Add to that the tension of traffic and the fact that she was essentially a runaway, and she was stressed. It was perfectly understandable that she was brusque.

But she was free!

Two

WELL, SHE WAS free until tomorrow afternoon. Then Len and Hannah MacDonald, full of love, concern, and advice that she did not want to hear, would pull into the drive behind her car.

She cringed as she thought of her parents' well-meaning but highly pointed comments when they would arrive.

"Abby, my dear." Her mother's voice would be heavy with hurt. No one did hurt better than Mom. "When I found your note, I felt pain as if a knife had pierced my heart. You ran away. You left without us." A tear would appear. "I cried on your father's shoulder all night."

Right.

Then they would look askance at the staircase. A whole flood of comments would gush forth like a geyser exploding, playing, drenching everything nearby, attempting to drown Abby's independence. After ticking off all the problems, Mom would switch to that overwhelmingly compassionate tone she used when she wanted to comfort or correct Abby, a sound that grew more cloying every time Abby heard it until she thought she'd scream.

"You can't stay in this place, sweetheart. You simply can't. You can't deal with the stairs." And she'd pat Abby's cheek with her slim, well-manicured hand and say in her loving, infuriating way, "I'm so sorry. I know this meant a lot to you."

"Don't worry, kitten," her father would say, his voice too hearty and avuncular. Apparently he thought that if he acted like the glass was half full, she'd automatically agree with him that all was rosy. This in spite of the fact that her glass was totally empty and had been for far too long. "We'll just break the lease and find you another place somewhere." Then he'd pause and give her his father-knows-best look. He'd rub his hands together and say, "I suggest that you just come home with us, baby, and we'll take our time and plan more carefully."

By which he meant, "Come home with us, and we'll make certain that you never leave again."

But she couldn't go home. She knew that with absolute certainty deep in her bones. She'd die if she went home. Her spirit would suffocate under the loving, smothering burden of their affection and concern.

She sighed. How had she come to feel such resentment toward these two people who loved her more than anyone else in the world? She knew they wanted only happiness for her. She shook her head. The root problem was that they reserved the right to define what happiness should be for her.

A loud bark drew her attention. Fargo was standing beside her car, staring in the open back window. He barked again.

The snarl that followed would have done credit to a jungle cat. Fargo backed up a step, then frowned with menace.

Uh-oh. Puppy.

Abby grabbed the rail and began as rapid a descent as she could manage. By the time she reached the bottom, Fargo and Puppy were engaged in a verbal war that reverberated loudly in the narrow space between this house and the one next door. Apparently the animals were going to get along as well as she and Marsh.

"Puppy, shush!" Abby hissed through the car window. The black-and-white cat lay crouched in her carry cage in the middle of the backseat. Her ears were down, and her fur stood at attention all down her back. "It's only a dog. Granted he's quite large, but he's only a dog."

Puppy was not convinced. She let out a shriek guaranteed to raise the dead. At least it roused Marsh Winslow.

"What in the world?" He stood at the edge of his back porch and stared at her. This time he had papers in only one hand.

"Call off your dog," Abby ordered. "He's scaring my cat."

"She doesn't sound scared to me."

Abby pushed at Fargo. "And you, you monster, get away from my car. You're drooling all over it." She stared with disgust at the saliva sliding down the shiny paint.

"Here, Fargo." Marsh rattled his papers. "Here, boy. Let the poor kitty alone."

Abby slitted her eyes and stared at Marsh. Was that laughter she heard in his voice? Or sarcasm? His face was a bland mask, but she was sure he was enjoying her distress.

Fargo gave one last bark, then padded to Marsh's side where he sat, tongue lolling, the picture of innocence.

With a snort, Abby turned to Puppy, who was muttering to herself as she turned circles in her cage. Abby opened the car door. "It's okay, baby. The mean dog's gone. Don't you worry. Mommy'll protect you."

Abby thought she heard a snort from Marsh—or maybe it was Fargo—but she didn't look their way. She slid in beside Puppy and poked a finger into the cage. Immediately the cat rubbed herself against it, purring sweetly.

"Good baby," Abby crooned. "Sweet Puppy. Let me take you upstairs where you'll be safe."

She grasped the handle on the top of the cage and, Puppy in hand, slid awkwardly out, hauling herself upright by pulling on the car door. When it started to close because of her weight, she lost her balance and fell backward. She let out a little squeak as she landed sitting on the edge of the backseat.

Instantly Marsh was there. "Are you okay?"

"I'm fine, thank you," she said with as much dignity as she could manage. "I'm fine." She looked into the carry cage. "So's Puppy."

Marsh gave a stiff little nod and stepped back as Abby climbed successfully out of the car.

Puppy lay in a boneless heap in the cage until she spotted Fargo standing behind Marsh. She stiffened, hissed, and spit while Fargo growled deep in his throat.

Marsh looked at the dog. "Stop that." Fargo glanced up, gave a final growl, and collapsed. He laid his great head on his paws and watched Abby carry the cage to the stairs.

She grabbed the rail and began to pull herself upstairs once again. She'd reached the third step when Marsh said, "Here. Let me."

Something in his voice got her dander up. Maybe it was the you're-an-idiot-I'll-save-you condescension. Maybe it was the me-strong-male-you-weak-female attitude. Whatever it was, she looked at him as he stood beside her, hand outstretched for the cage, and said quite clearly, "No, thank you. I can manage quite well by myself."

He drew his hand back and looked at her with a raised eyebrow. She stared back. No one was going to pity her or talk down to her just because she limped. No one. She had to put up with it from her family because there was no way to get rid of them, but by George, she didn't have to take it from anybody else, not even a landlord.

She turned from him and continued up the steps. Puppy and the cage thumped against her hip, getting heavier and heavier by the second, but she ignored the discomfort and kept climbing. Finally she reached the top, and it was a good thing. Her leg was trembling.

She went to the door and let herself in, using the key the realtor had given her. The pride she felt as she walked into her own home more than compensated for the staircase. She dropped Puppy onto the sofa and unlatched the carrier door.

Puppy was out in a flash. Then she froze as she realized she was in a new place. She hunkered down and looked around suspiciously.

Abby sat on the sofa and, leaning over, ran her hand from Puppy's head to tail several times. "This is your new home, sweetheart. Isn't it beautiful?"

Puppy slithered from beneath her hand and across the floor to the TV. She looked behind it like she expected Fargo to be hiding there. She moved to the overstuffed chair and circled it. Then she jumped up onto it, sniffing and patting.

Abby smiled and went into the kitchen. She needed to take a muscle relaxant and fast. She rooted in her purse until she found her vial of pills.

"Don't leave home without it." She dumped the contents in her hand and grabbed a relaxant and a pain pill. She swallowed them, then sat on the edge of a dining room chair and kneaded her sore leg and hip.

Puppy came up to her, butted her shin, and whined.

"Uh-oh." Abby got to her feet. "The litter box."

Sighing, she returned to the car and pulled out Puppy's litter box. She took it to the bottom of the stairs, balanced it against one hip, and grabbed the rail. The top seemed miles away, tired and sore as she was. But she had to prove to herself that she could manage here, and she had to prove it today. Tomorrow her parents would be here to undermine her.

"Abby, dear girl," her father would say. "You have come so very far, but you aren't the girl you used to be, and you never will be." Then he'd smile lovingly. "But we love you just as you are. We count it a privilege to take care of you."

Well, she was sick of being cared for! She was going to manage on her own even if it killed her. If Jimena de El Cid, widow of the famed Spanish warrior, could defend her own castle from the Moors back in the late 1090's, Abby Patterson could climb a flight of stairs today.

Halfway up the stairs she felt the litter box begin to slide off her hip. She imagined little granules of litter flying all over the place, messing up Marsh's neat and tidy steps, to say nothing of depositing a couple of unsought treasures where someone—probably Marsh—was likely to step on them. Well, she wouldn't give him the satisfaction of finding her unable to do simple tasks.

Calmly she stopped, steadied herself, and set the box back against the top of her hip. When she reached the top of the stairs, she felt like she'd just climbed Everest. She grinned all the way to the kitchen where she placed the box on the floor beside the refrigerator.

Puppy immediately padded over and climbed in.

"Life goes on," Abby said. "One point for me."

And, oh, but the small victory was wonderful.

The pain pill and the muscle relaxant were kicking in, so Abby decided to survey the apartment rather than collapse. All in all, it was larger and brighter than she'd expected.

The living room took up one half of the front of the house,

looking out through great floor-to-ceiling panes of glass on to the sea. The other half was a dining area with sliding glass doors that opened onto the porch. The kitchen was directly behind the dining area. A central hallway ran from the living room toward the street with two bedrooms opening off each side.

Abby immediately chose the large yellow-and-white bedroom on the left as hers and the cozy pink-and-white one on the right as her sewing room. The others could be guest rooms, though she couldn't imagine anyone wanting to stay in the violently purple room that had an honest-to-goodness lavender shag rug. She bet her parents would like the relaxing room done in soft greens and beige.

I hope the mattress is lumpy enough so they won't want to stay too long.

She was promptly smitten by guilt that poured over her like a vat of boiling oil poured from the castle wall onto the attackers below.

She sighed at her disloyalty. *Oh, Lord, I don't intend to be so mean. I'm sorry. But I don't want them to stay too long. Thank goodness Dad's not retired yet and has to go home to work!*

Another vat of guilt poured over her.

The apartment came furnished, and though Abby wouldn't have picked the plaid beige-and-blue sofa with its sturdy nylon upholstery or the recliner in an equally tough beige-and-blue tweed, the living room was homey and comfortable. The kitchen was all white, and she decided that a couple of colorful pot holders and dish towels would give personality to the otherwise sterile room. She'd also take down the white valance and replace it with one in some pretty floral print.

But her main concern at the moment was food. The refrigerator was bare of even ice cubes. She filled the white plastic trays with water and slid them in the freezer. She took another pain pill and lay down for a rest, forcing herself to use her bedroom instead of the porch on the theory that she'd sleep better if she didn't hear the waves. She managed to sleep for about fifteen minutes. Then she stared at the ceiling, grinning, for fifteen more.

Now she had to get some food. When she ran away this morning, she'd left while her mother was at the food store getting everything she deemed Abby would need. Then Hannah MacDonald planned to spend the afternoon making delicious dishes so Abby wouldn't have to worry about what to eat until she decided to come home. Meatloaf, casseroles, macaroni and cheese, spaghetti sauce, chili—there was no limit to the woman's plans.

Too bad she never asked Abby if she wanted all that food.

Ironically, she did. Her mother was a wonderful cook, much better than Abby. And when she started her new job as children's librarian at the Seaside library, she'd be more than happy not to have to cook dinner every night.

But tonight she did have to take care of herself. She found the phone book in a kitchen drawer and looked up the local Acme. She was at Forty-third and Central. It was on Eighth. No big deal.

As she drove slowly along Central Avenue, she noted that the town was still off-season quiet, especially here at the southern end of the island where the summer people stayed. She passed several new homes squeezed between the more typical two- or three-story rectangles. The new homes were invariably built on pilings with nothing but a garage at the first floor level, a protection against a hurricane's surging tides. Above were two living-area levels with interesting windows even here on the street side of the houses. She wondered what these places looked like from the beach. Probably glass, glass, and more glass.

She turned on a country-western station and cranked the volume. No one yelled, "Turn that terrible music down, Abby!" Not her parents, not her husband. She sang along with Faith Hill at the top of her lungs.

The light at Central and Thirty-fourth was red, and she slowed. A little girl in pink overalls skipped up to the opposite corner, her stride awkward as she worked to hone what was obviously a new skill. Her ponytail was caught back in a pink scrunchie, the same shade as her overalls, and it bounced with every skip. Her mouth moved, and she was obviously singing to herself.

What a cutie! Just like Maddie in a few years.

No, she caught herself. Just like Maddie would look right now. She always forgot that Maddie wouldn't be two anymore. Three long years had passed. She would've been five, just about the age of the pixie in pink. The barb of bereavement twisted in her heart and her vision blurred.

The little girl on the corner looked at the stoplight, saw she had the green signal, looked both ways as an extra precaution, and started across Central Avenue, skipping and singing.

At the same time a car roared down Thirty-fourth Street, trying to make the light before it went red.

"Idiot," Abby muttered as she reflexively grasped her wheel more tightly. But she was safe. She wasn't in the intersection. No one could hit her. No one could hurt her.

At the last minute the car flicked on a left turn signal and squealed around the corner onto Central.

Abby screamed.

The little girl in pink never had a chance.

Three

$\mathcal{M}$ARSH SLID INTO his red Adirondack chair on his porch and sighed with pleasure. He couldn't imagine things turning out any better than they had. He stared across the beach at the ocean. The haze of a humid June day caused the horizon to blend with the sea, and a couple of ships miles out in the water looked like a pair of misty toys. Much closer to shore a catamaran sailed by at a snail's pace in the sluggish breeze.

He studied the pair sitting on the catamaran. Maybe he should learn to sail now that he was a shore resident. He'd enjoy flying across the water on a pair of those sturdy hulls with their colorful sails puffed out with wind. He, of course, would be wise enough to sail only on days with brisk breezes.

Buying this house had been a major financial commitment, but he didn't regret it for a minute. The realtor with whom he'd worked had been wonderful, making it possible for the whole process to be handled long distance. Marsh hadn't actually seen the house except in pictures until he arrived for the summer last week, a full two months after the April date on which he'd signed the sales agreement.

But the pictures hadn't lied. His new house was exactly what he wanted, the perfect place to hide from the world and write. Granted, the furniture that came

with the place left a bit to be desired, but he could live with con-
flicting plaids until he found time to replace a couple of the easy
chairs.

His tenant had arrived a day early, leading to a most interesting contretemps, but with that misunderstanding behind him, he
relaxed. A children's librarian, her rental form had said. He
thought of Doc Forbes, the librarian at the seminary where he
taught. If Abby were anything like Doc, she wouldn't say a word
all summer.

Which was fine with him. Silence was what he'd paid all that
money for, was what he craved. Silence and privacy.

He shimmied in his Adirondack chair, marveling again at how
something that looked so uncomfortable could be just the opposite. He stretched out his legs, resting them on the second rung of
the porch railing in front of him. Just beyond the railing the low
dunes began, sliding gracefully into the flat beach which in turn
slid into the sea. He breathed in the tangy air, laced his fingers
behind his head, and looked up.

*It doesn't get any better than this, God. Thanks! You have been
more than gracious, and I am most appreciative.*

He looked at his dog, who sat staring at him from his resting
spot under the picnic table. "Happy, Fargo?"

Fargo woofed, a sound Marsh chose to hear as affirmative.
"Me too."

He reached to the table beside him and picked up his laptop.
He'd spent the last few hours finishing a hard copy edit of his next
book, *Rocky Mountain Midnight,* due out in October, just in time for
the Christmas trade. The corrected galleys were all packaged, lying
on the table by the door, ready to overnight back to his publisher.

Now it was time to move on to his next project, the one he'd
come here to write. He booted the laptop and went to the file
called Frost Spring, the preliminary title for his work in progress.
He had to squint a bit to follow the cursor in the outside brightness, but the porch above gave enough shadow that he could
manage. He'd already adjusted the brightness level to get the most
he could from the machine. So what if he had to squint a bit. No
weak cursor was going to send him inside. Writing on the porch
while listening to the sea was a major part of his dream.

He began to type.

Randall Craig looked up at the woman with a frown. She sat atop her horse with ease and authority, her back straight, her heels down, her hands loose on the reins. Though she wore a split-leather skirt and a cream Stetson, her boots were eastern with laces up the front, her saddle English.

Bridle trails back East—that was doubtless the extent of her riding experience. Greenhorn. More trouble than she was worth in spite of her air of competence and her heart-stopping beauty.

"I'm sorry," Craig said. "This is private property." He didn't bother to tell her that it was soon to be the site of a range war too. "You'd best go back to town."

The woman looked at him with barely concealed contempt. "I am aware of everything about this property."

Well, she wasn't aware that he was foreman. Anyone who knew anything knew that by now. So what did her ignorance say about her and her claim to knowledge?

She was slim—too slim—fine-boned, and regal. Her black hair was pulled back into a knot at the nape of her neck, and her great black eyes reflected the sun in two small spots. Her skin was creamy and pale. She was far and away the most stunning thing he'd ever seen. He was very thankful he'd never set eyes on her again, once he got her turned around and headed back to town.

Marsh stopped typing and stared at that last paragraph. It was the third time he'd tried to write it. Once again he'd described that irritating woman upstairs. He closed his eyes and saw Abby Patterson, all skin and bones and glowing black eyes. Even the coolness between Craig and Marguerite—now where had he gotten that name?—was a replica of the frost between himself and Abby. Too weird.

He reached for the delete key, then hesitated. He'd leave it for now. It'd be easier to make changes later when she wasn't so much on his mind.

Snotty, irritating, fascinating woman. Silent woman.

"Can you tell me your business?" Craig asked.

He watched her face freeze with disdain. "My business is certainly not your business."

He felt his temper spike and struggled to control it. "If you're riding this road it is."

"Are you telling me that a person cannot ride this road?"

"We've been having some trouble around here. The road is open only to those going to Frost Spring Ranch."

"And those going there are only those you approve?"

He smiled with one corner of his mouth and dipped his head in acknowledgment. Where had she learned haughtiness? She could give a queen lessons.

She eyed him like he was a worm left too long in the sun and urged her horse forward until its nose almost touched his chest. He had to admire her nerve, foolish though it was. It took more than a horse knocking into his chest to move Randall Craig.

He reached out, running a gentle hand down the animal's forehead, patting him softly on the cheek. The horse whinnied its approval. Craig smiled up at the woman. It was time to try diplomacy.

"This is a fine horse. Someone knew what he was doing when he bought it for you."

Her dark eyes flashed with anger. "I selected this horse, not that it's any of your business. I am more than competent at recognizing and obtaining good horseflesh."

Uh-huh, I'm sure you are—or at least you think you are. "Well, ma'am, you shure done good with this here boy. I bet you might could teach me a thang or two."

She rolled her eyes at his sudden transformation into the uneducated cowboy and urged her horse another step forward. One more, Craig knew, and he'd be forced to step back.

"Please get out of my way." When he didn't move, she ordered, "Now."

"Go back to town where it's safe, Miss—?" He waited for her name, but she did not offer it. He took hold of the bridle. If she wouldn't turn on her own, he would turn her himself.

"Unhand my horse," she hissed.

"Look, Miss," he began in his most reasonable voice.

"Don't *look Miss* me." She glared, red flags flying in her cheeks. "I'm going to Frost Spring Ranch and nowhere else."

"Marguerite! Margie!"

They both looked toward the ranch house a half mile down the road. A young girl in braids was running toward them, her arms waving, her face wreathed in a smile.

Craig frowned as the haughty princess became human. Her smile was luminous as she waved wildly back. "Addie! Oh, Addie!"

A chill settled around Craig's midsection. "Just who are you?" he asked, his voice abrupt.

When she looked down at him, the haughtiness was back in full force. "Frost," she said, her voice and demeanor as chilly as her name. "Marguerite Frost of Frost Spring Ranch."

Craig closed his eyes and sighed. When he woke up this morning with Snelling's gun barrel at his temple, he should have known it would be one of those days.

Marsh's hands stilled as he stared at the screen of his laptop. Now where had Snelling and the gun come from? Even more basic—who was Snelling? Did he have a first name? Did he live locally, or was he some kind of hired gunslinger? How was he involved in the coming range war?

And what was Marsh to do with this twist in the story line?

He laid his head against the back of his Adirondack chair, staring out at the blue sky. He lowered his legs from the railing, stretching them out in front of him. Fargo rose and nudged his hand. The dog always sensed when it was safe to bother him. Marsh absently scratched the animal behind his ears. Fargo moaned and laid his great head on Marsh's thigh.

One of the wonderful things about writing fiction was the sense of surprise when people like Snelling, whoever he was, showed up on the pages. Now all Marsh had to do was figure out the secret of the man's identity. It was undoubtedly rattling around somewhere deep in his subconscious.

Okay, God, he thought, *help me figure out who Snelling is and why he had a gun at Craig's head. In the meantime, I'll check my e-mail.*

He minimized his text and went to his AOL screen. He made certain his modem was connected, then clicked on all the right icons for automatic mail. In a moment, he had a filing cabinet of letters to read, and his phone line was open again, not that he was expecting anyone to call. Still, he tried to keep it free until he had a second line brought in.

He loved e-mail. Every day he talked to people all over the country, often all over the world. Courtesy of the Internet, the narrow life of a writer/academic broadened exponentially even as he sat on his deck in New Jersey or hid in his office back in Ohio.

He glanced down the list of messages, checking who had sent them. Maybe there'd be something from his agent about that new series he wanted to tackle—Trails of the West, generational stories of the Strong family that took place on the great pathways to the frontier, on great waterways like the Erie Canal and the Ohio and Mississippi Rivers, on land trails like the Oregon Trail, the Overland Trail, and the Santa Fe Trail. So far three houses had expressed strong interest. He shook his head at the wonder that he might be the object of a bidding war.

Who'd ever have thought!

It was because of the TV movies made from two of his earlier books and the knowledge that the third one was now in preproduction. With Rick Mathis as the lead in both and signed to do the third, *Shadows at Noon,* the publishers smelled money, big money. He grinned, looked out at the beach, and took a deep breath of salty air. The money smelled very good indeed, if more than slightly briny.

He stopped scrolling his messages at one from rickmathis.com. He clicked it open with anticipation. He liked this actor who played his heroes with a world-weary attitude balanced against a strong moral and ethical core. The fact that Rick was also the producer of all the films helped protect Marsh's high standards for plot and character.

At first Marsh hadn't been sure how he'd like working with

Hollywood. He'd heard horror stories galore, but he was willing to take the risk of writing the screenplays from his novels so he could exercise at least some control over the content. Rick had not only agreed to Marsh's participation but had encouraged him in it. Because Marsh had admired Rick's work in his weekly series about a cowboy named Duke Beldon, he was predisposed to trust Rick.

"I like the moral core of your heroes, and I don't want that quality lost," Rick had said. "I don't see that kind of integrity in a lot of material today."

"I write from a Christian worldview," Marsh told him. "Sometimes Christian things are spelled out, like when a verse is quoted or a doctrine is debated. Other times it's more subtle, but everything I write is seated within the framework of the Bible."

Three years ago Rick had said, "Yeah, whatever. I just know I like it." Today he was a believer in Jesus, trying to be real in the land of make-believe.

> Hey, guy!
> I just finished reading the latest version of the script of *Shadows at Noon*. Almost good. The director and the studio honchos didn't wreck all your hard work too much. Did they ship you a copy? I'm coming to see you so we can rassle this thing through. Besides I want to see what a New Jersey beach house looks like. I've become so California that it's hard for me to believe there's another ocean. Sunday, dude.

Marsh smiled. Sunday. The day after tomorrow. If he didn't stop to rewrite, he could get Craig and Marguerite another chapter or two along before Rick got here. Then the fun would begin as he and Rick ripped apart the script of *Shadows at Noon,* then put it back together again. He never ceased thanking God that he worked with a producer and star who valued words as much as action, who loved the sound of a good phrase.

He closed Rick's letter and scanned on down the long list. His smile tightened when he came across his father's address. At one time his mother had been the family correspondent, keeping the three of them connected. She had died many years ago, a fact that Marsh still had trouble grasping. When Dad had remarried four years ago, his new wife understandably didn't correspond much with her grown stepson. Now any messages came directly from his formidable father and made him—what? Uncomfortable? Defensive? Angry? He shrugged. Pick any negative emotion and you were on the money.

Marsh clicked the message open. Might as well get the bad news over with. Then he'd be free to enjoy the rest of his correspondence, especially ChiLibris, the novelists' loop that he loved so much. Talk about great conversations! These writers were some of the most interesting people he'd ever encountered, thoughtful as in full of thought.

> Marshall,
> So you have bought a house at the New Jersey shore. I find that very interesting. We'll be up to visit you next week. I want to see whether you've made a wise invest-ment.
> Dad
> Senator Marcus Winslow
> United States Senate
> Washington, D.C.

Marsh stared at the screen, trying to determine what about the note irritated him most. Was it the Marshall? Dad was the only one who called him by his full name.

"A name is given for a purpose, Marshall, and a nickname destroys it by rendering it weak. As no one calls me Marc, so no one shall call you Marsh."

Well, no one called Dad anything but Marcus, not even Marsh's mother, but everyone called him Marsh. He couldn't stand Marshall. It made him feel like a western lawman.

A thought streaked across his mind. *Is that why I write Westerns?* He shifted with discomfort. Hadn't he chosen Westerns because of his love for history and the chance to ponder the good guys and the bad guys outside the formal trappings of academia and the treatises on theology and philosophy that ruled most of his life? Surely he didn't owe his father this clandestine career?

That is, if it stayed clandestine after Dad discovered Rick Mathis in residence. The very thought made Marsh shudder. He'd just have to make Rick disappear on Tuesday. He'd understand. He knew all about Marsh Winslow aka Colton West. In fact, he was one of only three who knew: Rick, Marsh, and Bettina Harley, Marsh's agent.

Marsh wanted it to stay that way with an intensity that never failed to surprise him. He glared at the computer screen as his father had glared at him for years. Look at that full signature: Senator Marcus Winslow, United States Senate, Washington, D.C. As if he didn't know who Dad was.

Even as he understood that the Senator had set an automatic signature for all his electronic correspondence, it still irritated Marsh that he couldn't turn it off for a personal message to his own son.

But by far the most aggravating thing was the last line in the message: *I want to see whether you've made a wise investment.*

Translation: I don't trust your judgment.

Translation: I want to know where you got the money to buy an oceanfront property.

Translation: What are you up to this time that will embarrass me?

Wouldn't the good senator just die if he found out? Marsh Winslow, holder of a Doctor of Ministry in practical theology and a Ph.D. in philosophy, tenured professor at Tyndale Theological Seminary, holder of the James Goodwin Chair of Practical Theology, son of Senator Marcus Winslow, wrote Westerns under a pseudonym and was making a small fortune by doing so.

And just like that, Marsh knew who Snelling was. He was the overbearing cattleman whose property adjoined the Frost Spring Ranch and who was trying to control all water rights. He wanted to make the whole valley jump at his command. Mr. Frost, ill though he was, was unwilling to jump.

Marsh minimized AOL and pulled up his text screen. Fargo, schooled to the ways of a writer, lifted his head from Marsh's leg and slumped to the floor. Marsh began entering ideas and questions as fast as they came to him.

Why was Snelling himself in Craig's little cabin at the edge of the small spring lined with cottonwoods? Wasn't he too important to be there? What had Craig done to rile the man to the degree that he risked such actions? And, my, my, my, did Craig resent Snelling, not only for trespassing on his little patch of heaven and for hurting all the ranchers in the area, but also for catching him off guard.

The small spring that burbled not far from the cabin door gave the ranch its name. It wouldn't suffer if Snelling dammed off the Anasazi Creek, the major source of water that flowed down from the Sangre de Cristo Mountains of New Mexico on the way to the Pecos River and eventually the Rio Grande. However the spring wasn't sufficient in size to water anything except the people who lived and worked on the property. The Frost Spring cattle needed the water of the Anasazi as did the cattle and people downstream. That was only one of the reasons Craig was determined to help Mr. Frost stand up to Snelling, though as yet Marsh had no idea what the other reasons were.

How would Marguerite react when she saw the cabin under the cottonwoods? Marsh knew that Craig had built it with his own hands and was fanatically proud of it. Marsh nodded. More conflict between the two. Maybe Craig had built it on her favorite spot by the spring, and she resented his usurping her space. How dare he, she'd think in true queen-of-the-realm fashion.

What would happen when she saw the faith her father put in Craig? The more Mr. Frost's health failed, the more Craig was the de facto authority at Frost Spring. Marsh grinned, anticipating the trouble he could develop. Even though Marguerite had been back East for several years at school, she'd assumed things would stay the same until she came home to change them. Was she about to be surprised!

Marsh rubbed his hands together. He loved it when a story began coming together.

The phone rang, making him frown. He'd been at Frost Spring Ranch with Randall Craig and Marguerite Frost in the year 1890. Now he was back on his porch, staring at his flickering laptop screen. He waited for the answering machine to pick up to hear who was on the phone. Whoever it was, it'd better be good, breaking into his world like that.

"This is Memorial Hospital calling for Marsh Winslow."

Four

At THE WORD *hospital* Marsh forgot all about Marguerite and Craig.

"We have an Abby Patterson here who gave us your name as her next of kin."

What?

"She is unable to drive herself home. Would you please come for her at your earliest convenience? Come to the emergency entrance."

Marsh rushed to the kitchen and lunged for the phone. "What's going on here?"

"Is this Mr. Winslow?"

"Yes. What's wrong with Mrs. Patterson? Why is she at the emergency room? Was she in an accident of some kind?" He thought of her limp. "Did she fall and break something?"

"I'm sorry. I don't know what her problem is."

Like you'd tell me even if you did know. "I'll be there as soon as I can."

He ran outside, grabbed his laptop, shut it down, and rushed inside to drop it on the couch. Fargo followed him in and looked at him in question.

"You can't come this time, guy."

Fargo snuffled his disappointment and collapsed with a thud.

"Don't whine. It's unbecoming. It's not my fault

they don't let dogs, especially giants like you, into the emergency room."

Fargo looked unconvinced.

A half hour later Marsh sat in an uncomfortable green plastic chair in a little curtained cubicle, staring at the woman lying on the hospital gurney. He'd known she was thin—no, make that skinny—but he hadn't realized how truly small she was. She barely lifted the sheet. She looked so pale and frail and defenseless that he had to watch her chest to make certain it was rising and falling. One arm was outside the covers with an automatic blood pressure cuff and a finger clip to monitor pulse attached. A drip of some kind flowed into the needle taped to the back of her hand.

It was disconcerting to see her like this. She'd been so fiery, so forceful back at the house. She'd all but ordered him and Fargo off her porch—and he owned the house! Now she was small, helpless, and needy. Every protective instinct he had was on alert. He wanted to pick her up, to somehow shelter her.

He knew that he had to have a scene where Craig saw Marguerite when she was physically and emotionally vulnerable. As he knew Abby would be much distressed if she knew he saw her as fragile, so Marguerite would resent Craig for seeing her that way too. Then he'd even things out by having Craig come to the end of himself somehow. He'd be in a difficult spot, and Marguerite would rescue him. Except she wasn't physically strong enough for an action scene. How about a secret? Secrets were always good. She could find out Craig's secret and help him come to terms with it. All Marsh needed to do was figure out this secret, a secret Craig would go to great lengths to protect, just as Marsh protected his.

His eyes settled on Abby. Just like that, fictitious Craig was forgotten in the face of her reality. How had she gotten her limp? Was it congenital, or the result of an accident of some kind? At least the ER nurse had assured him she hadn't hurt her leg today. They hadn't told him what she had hurt in spite of his frequent inquiries, but if he was patient, he was bound to find out soon enough.

Dear God, lying here unconscious she looks more child than woman, except for the lines that fan out from her eyes. Please be there for her, giving her Your comfort and peace.

He'd been sitting beside her for fifteen minutes before she

blinked, her eyes unfocused for a second. Then he saw panic flare when she realized where she was. She pulled her other arm out from under the sheet and threw the covering off. Frantically she tried to rise, threatening the attachments on her arm. The pole holding the IV bag tipped, and Marsh made a grab for it, steadying it.

"Sam?" Abby breathed. "Maddie?"

He stood and leaned over her, placing one large hand over her small one, the other on her shoulder. He pushed her back down with gentle hands. "Easy, Abby, easy. Everything's going to be just fine."

She looked at him a minute without recognition.

"It's me, Marsh." He smiled.

"Marsh?"

"You know. The big black dog. You live in my upstairs apartment."

She blinked several times. Then her eyes stilled and she nodded. "Marsh," she repeated. "Fargo."

"Right." A burst of relief rushed through him at her recall. "Fargo."

A nurse brushed the cubicle's curtain aside and peered in. "Did I hear you two talking?"

"Sort of," he said, ever the stickler for accuracy. "She whispered. I spoke."

Abby eyed him strangely, then turned to the nurse. "Where am I? How did I get here?"

"How do you feel?" the nurse asked. She checked the instrument readouts just behind Abby's head.

Abby lifted her unfettered hand to her forehead. "I think I feel fine." She hesitated. "At least as fine as usual. What happened to me? Why am I in a hospital? Am I hurt?"

When the nurse didn't respond, Abby turned anxious eyes to Marsh.

"You're fine," he told her, squeezing her hand.

She didn't argue with him, but it was obvious that she was confused. "I feel fuzzy."

"Sedative hangover," the nurse said as she pinched off the IV and pulled the needle from the back of Abby's hand. She pressed gauze to the bead of blood that rose and snugged a Band-Aid over it to hold it in place. "It'll pass in no time."

"Sedative?" Abby turned her hand over, grasping Marsh's as she stared wide-eyed at the nurse. "Why did I need a sedative? I just went to the grocery store." She looked at Marsh. "Didn't I?"

Marsh nodded, patting her shoulder with his free hand. "I heard you leave."

She frowned, concentrating, looking into her mind for answers. "But how did I get from there to here?"

A policeman stuck his head into the cubicle. "Can I talk with her now?"

"She's all yours." The nurse busied herself disconnecting the instruments that had monitored Abby's vital signs.

Abby struggled to sit up, and Marsh took her arm to help. She swung her legs over the side of the gurney, swaying slightly.

"Dizzy?" asked the nurse.

Abby shook her head. "Not really. Just confused."

"I'm Greg Barnes." The policeman held out his hand.

She took it. "Abby Patterson."

Greg turned to Marsh. "Mr. Patterson?"

He shook his head as Abby flushed. "I'm Marsh Winslow. Abby rents the upstairs half of my house."

"Ah," Barnes said. "So tell me all about it, Mrs. Patterson. Describe it just as you saw it."

Abby stared at the cop, her face white, her eyes haunted. "Describe what, Mr. Barnes?"

He cocked his head. "You don't know what I'm talking about?"

"I'm sorry, no." She shivered and rubbed her arms. "The last thing I remember is leaving the house to go to the Acme. Then I woke up here."

"When you left home, were you driving?" Barnes asked.

"Yes." Abby seemed certain of that much. "I drove down Central Avenue." She turned to Marsh. "Didn't I?"

He smiled. "At least you started off on Central. You had to. The house is on Central."

"Central and?" Barnes asked.

"Forty-third," Marsh said. "4311 Central."

Barnes nodded and turned to Abby. "And then?"

Abby stared at him, stricken.

Barnes sighed. "Mrs. Patterson, we desperately need your help here."

"I want to give it, believe me. I just don't remember anything between leaving the house and seeing Marsh loom over me."

"I didn't loom," he muttered. "I never loom." His father loomed.

"You loomed."

"Ah, Mrs. Patterson." Barnes called her back to the issue at hand.

"What happened that I don't remember?" Abby asked, dark eyes wide. "I didn't hurt anyone, did I? Tell me I didn't hurt anyone!" Her voice shook as she gripped Marsh's hand so hard it hurt, like it was a lifeline to save her from drowning.

"Easy, Mrs. Patterson." The policeman held up his hand to stop her jumping to conclusions. "You didn't hurt anyone."

Her shoulders slumped in relief and Marsh thought he heard her mutter, "Thank You, Lord."

"Do you remember stopping at the traffic light at Thirty-fourth and Central?" Barnes asked.

Abby stared at her lap, eyes narrowed in fierce concentration. Her free hand moved in little circles, like she was telling herself to hurry up and get with it. With a look of frustration, she shook her head. "Nothing."

"You were at the light when the ambulance crew arrived."

"Ambulance? But I'm not hurt, am I?"

Marsh, the nurse, and the policeman all shook their heads.

"So who is?" Abby rubbed her hand down her leg and winced.

"What?" Marsh asked.

"Easy," said the nurse.

"I am hurt." Abby opened her hand and looked in disbelief at the four red slashes traversing the center of her palm. Marsh turned the hand he held over. There were four slashes across that palm also. Slowly she closed her hands, and Marsh watched in fascination as her fingernails matched up with the slashes.

"I did this to myself?" Abby stared in disbelief.

"You were clutching your steering wheel so tightly the police had to pry your hands loose," Barnes said.

She was shocked. "But why?" she whispered.

Barnes looked at Marsh. It was obvious he didn't want to

answer her question. Marsh moved a little closer to Abby, like he could protect her from the unpleasant news, whatever it was.

"You were the eyewitness to a hit-and-run, Mrs. Patterson."

"What?" Her voice was stark, more a breath than a word. Marsh wouldn't have thought it possible, given her pallor, but she paled even more. Her eyes filled with tears.

"Who was hit?" Marsh asked when it became obvious that Abby's emotions rendered her speechless.

"A little girl named Karlee Fitzmeyer."

"A little girl?" Abby cried. "Oh, dear God, please, no!"

Marsh started at the unexpected and terrible anguish in Abby's voice. Certainly he expected distress but not at this emotional level. The nurse and Barnes looked at her in surprise too.

"She's going to be all right," Barnes hurried to say. "The car swerved and almost missed her. It was more like it sideswiped her, sort of tossing her out of its path. When she fell, she broke her arm. Besides brush burns, that's about it."

It was obvious Abby hadn't heard any of the policeman's explanation. She dropped her face to her hands and shuddered. "Maddie! Oh, Maddie, baby!" There was a keening sound of such deep pain to her near whisper that the hair rose on Marsh's arms.

"Who's Maddie?" Barnes asked Marsh.

"I don't know. I only met Abby today."

"Mrs. Patterson." Barnes's voice was loud, firm. "Mrs. Patterson, Karlee will be fine. And that's Karlee, not Maddie."

Abby continued to sob.

Marsh and Greg Barnes looked at each other, at a loss about what to do.

"Maybe she knows Karlee?" suggested the nurse.

"But she just moved here," Marsh said.

"Do you know Karlee Fitzmeyer?" Barnes asked.

Abby didn't answer, couldn't answer, but she did manage to shake her head no. Marsh watched her weep and ached for her.

"Abby?" He slid an arm around her shoulders. He could feel her trembling. She turned into him, grabbed fistfuls of his shirt, and hung on. "Shh." He stroked her back. "Shh. It's okay. It's okay."

"Did she die?" Abby asked in a cracked voice, her face still buried in Marsh's chest. "Is she dead? How old was she?"

"She's got a broken arm and brush burns," Barnes repeated,

his voice soothing. "That's all. Her life isn't in danger. She's very fortunate."

"Thank You, God," Abby muttered, her voice quivering with emotion. Slowly her trembling eased, then stopped, and her breathing returned to a normal cadence, though she remained with her cheek resting on Marsh's chest. "Thank You, thank You, thank You. Not Maddie."

"Who's Maddie, Mrs. Patterson?" Barnes asked.

"My daughter," Abby whispered. "She's dead."

Marsh felt another great shudder pass through her and wrapped both arms about her. How did you offer comfort for what was obviously such an immense hurt?

"Hit-and-run?" asked Barnes.

"A man trying to dial a cell phone ran a stop sign."

"Were you driving?" The policeman's voice was gentle.

Abby pulled away from Marsh and shook her head. "My husband. He's dead too."

Marsh flinched.

"How long ago?" Barnes asked.

"Three years last month. May 12."

"How old was your daughter?" Barnes's eyes were kind.

"Two."

For several minutes no one spoke. Marsh found himself staring at Abby's bent head, wondering how so fragile a person could survive such pain.

"It's important that I remember so that you can catch the driver who hit that little girl, that Karlee, isn't it?" Abby asked in a tired voice.

Barnes nodded. "It would be a great help. We'll pursue other avenues of investigation, of course, but there's nothing like an eye-witness account."

The ravaged face Abby lifted to Greg Barnes tore at Marsh's heart.

"But what if I never remember?"

Five

WHERE HAD SHE come from, that little girl? He had turned the corner like he'd turned millions of corners, and there she was, right in the middle of the road. What in the world was she doing there?

He could feel himself still shaking as he remembered. Adrenaline surge. It was a wonder the steering wheel wasn't vibrating in his hands. Instead he forced himself to focus, to keep himself centered.

Concentrate!

Drive!

Get away! Get away! Get away! Fast!

He ground his teeth, torn as he was between fury and relief. He was furious with that little pink girl for the trouble she was causing him. It couldn't have come at a worse time for him personally. So much was at stake. On the other hand, he was relieved because he didn't think he'd hurt her badly.

He had swerved to avoid her and almost succeeded. When he glanced back in his rearview mirror, he saw her somersault through the air, but she hadn't gone far or high. She'd be all right in the long run.

You hope.

"She'll be fine!" he shouted at his conscience.

Which was more than he could say for his car. In the process of saving her bothersome little life, he'd smashed the car's right side to a pulp scraping along the vehicles parked against the curb. The screaming whine of metal scraping metal raised goose bumps, even in memory.

He knew the right front fender was pressing against the tire. It pulled as he drove, forcing him to wrestle with the wheel. But he could still drive.

He had raced around the block, over the bridge, off the island, and away from the scene as fast as he could drive.

No one knows, he assured his jangled nerves. *There's no way anyone'll ever know.*

He took big breaths, trying to slow his breathing before he began to hyperventilate. He inhaled slowly to the count of fifteen, pulling the air deep into his diaphragm. He held the breath for fifteen, then exhaled over the same count. By the third time, he was dizzier than ever, gasping for oxygen.

Where was a paper bag when you needed one?

As he tried to calm himself, his mind raced with one big question: What should he do now? He couldn't go back and admit guilt. Even the thought made him nauseous. He swallowed against the bile that rose in his throat.

If I went back, I'd always be the one who hit and ran. He shuddered at the loss of face such a situation would mean. *No, I won't do that to myself. If there's one thing I've learned in all my bootstrap pulling, it's never admit you're wrong.*

He thought of Johnny McCoy. He'd laugh himself silly before spitting a chaw of tobacco. "You're no better than me, hotshot" he'd say when he could catch a breath. "Under them fancy suits and that fancy-dancy car and that superior education you got yourself, you're still a no-good Piney. Always was and always will be, no matter how you try to forget. You can't rewrite where you come from."

Yeah, well, he wasn't willing to let family heritage control his destiny. The very thought chilled him all the way to the marrow, even in the heat of this sunny June day. There was no way on God's green earth he was going to be like Pop, sleeping away his life, letting Mom earn what little money they had. On days he was feeling kind, he wondered if Pop had narcolepsy, he slept so much. On the 364 other days of the year, he hated Pop.

Forget Pop. Forget McCoy. What are you going to do?

He ran his hand over the steering wheel and fondled the tan leather seats. He loved this car; he really did. It was absolutely gorgeous and handled like a dream. Some psychiatrist could probably have a field day with his affection for a piece of metal and machinery, but it was a symbol of how far he'd come.

He sighed. It had to go, of course. It was too damaged in too telltale a manner. He hadn't come this far to throw everything away over his sloppy, sentimental attachment to a piece of metal. He scowled out the window, furious all over again at the bad hand life had dealt him.

Stupid little girl!

Okay, so the car had to go. But how? Where? That was the trouble with living inside the law these days. He wasn't used to thinking like McCoy anymore.

At the thought of McCoy, the answer—obvious and inevitable—leaped to his mind. The Pine Barrens, that 1.1 million acres that covered much of South Jersey. Deep. Secret. Impenetrable. If what they said was true and the Mafia got rid of all those bodies there, why couldn't he get rid of a car?

He'd laugh if he weren't so upset. Here he thought he'd never find a plus to being raised in Atsion, in the Pines. Hard as it was to imagine, everything he'd hated as a kid was going to save him as an adult.

Six

ABBY WALKED TO Marsh's car with hardly a wobble. She thought she was doing very well, considering. Apparently Marsh didn't agree. When she veered just a smidgen to the right, he grabbed her elbow.

"I'm fine." She pulled her elbow free and proved herself a liar by lurching to the right again. If only she didn't feel quite so woozy.

"Yeah, you're fine and I'm Santa Claus."

She closed her eyes for a minute. A sarcastic caregiver. Just what she needed. He made Helene, the sadistic PT, look gentle and loving. Why had she ever given the police his name?

She grimaced. The answer to that one was easy: She didn't know anyone else in Seaside except Nan Fulsom, her soon-to-be boss at the library. She had rejected calling Nan as soon as she thought of her. There was no way she was going to get to know Nan while lying flat on her back on a hospital gurney, all woozy from drugs. It was not the way to begin a strong professional relationship.

Not that she actually *knew* Marsh, not like you know people you call in times of trouble. In fact, all she knew about him were his name and where he lived. And that he owned a monster dog named after a city.

"Have you ever been to Fargo?" She put out a hand to steady herself on a red convertible.

"What?"

She nodded, feeling like he'd confirmed her original opinion of him. "I didn't think so." She lurched to the right another time.

With a sigh that would have done her mother proud, he took her arm again. This time when she tried to free herself, he tightened his grip.

She glared at him. "Please let me go." A shallow acquaintance like theirs meant that she didn't care a fig whether she fell flat on her face in front of him, irritating man that he was. Of course she'd prefer not to do so. Some modicum of dignity and decorum was always desired, especially after the way she'd sobbed all over him mere minutes ago.

She glanced at his shirt and saw a wet amoeba-shaped patch over his heart. It'd take some doing to recover her self-respect after the pathetic scene that had caused that watermark. She tilted her head to look at his face—he was one tall man—and saw the unfocused glaze in his eyes. Instantly she recognized boredom and preoccupation. Just when she was remembering how nice he'd been when she drenched him, he checked out. Still, she'd take his ennui over her parents' smothering any day.

She shuddered at the thought of their reaction to her hysterical amnesia. That's what they'd called it in the hospital. Hysterical amnesia. Given what they had told her about her condition when they dragged her from her car, hysterical seemed a good if scary adjective. Should Mom and Dad hear of it, they'd probably sedate her, bundling her back to Scranton in an ambulance before she even blinked. Their cotton batting would suffocate her once again.

Even the thought of it made her pull at the neckline of her T-shirt for a decent breath.

"You can't tell my parents," she blurted.

He stopped, blinked, and looked at her as if he were trying to figure out who she was. "I can't tell your parents what?"

"That I have hysterical amnesia."

He gave a nod. "It'd scare them."

"No. It'd imprison me."

The bored look disappeared, but the look he gave her wasn't much better. Clearly he thought she was several cans short of a six-pack.

"They would coddle me and love me and make me nuts. They have ever since the accident."

"They care."

She agreed. "While I appreciate it, they go about it in a way that's killing me. That's why I'm here, you know. In Seaside, I mean, not here at the hospital. I had to escape or die."

He looked at her, eyes narrowed in thought. "Parents."

That was all, just the one word, but the way he said it caused her to wonder about how he got along with his parents. Given his chirpy little personality, she wouldn't blame them if they stayed as far from him as they could. It was probably a case of the more they stayed away, the more sarcastic he got, and the more sarcastic he got, the more they stayed away, ad infinitum. When he grasped her elbow again and began towing her along at a fast clip, she couldn't decide whom she felt sorrier for: him or his parents.

When Marsh pulled her to a stop beside a dark green Taurus, she put out a hand to steady herself. You'd think after all the medicines she'd taken over the last three years that she'd be better able to tolerate them, but no. She still got loopy so easily. She hated it.

"Do you like your parents?" she asked.

Marsh looked at her, eyebrow raised.

She frowned. "I'm fine. Tipsy on Tylenol with codeine but fine."

He grunted his disbelief, opened the door, and held her arm while she slid onto the seat.

"Buckle up," he ordered and slammed the door.

What a charmer.

They drove home in silence, but she noticed that he didn't drive down Central. He went down Bay until they reached Forty-third Street, then cut across to Central. Did he follow that route because he thought passing the accident scene would upset her or because it was quicker? She wouldn't have thought him so perceptive, so sensitive, but maybe he was.

As soon as they parked in the driveway, she climbed out of the car before he had a chance to come help her. Then she had to lean for a moment to get her balance. She looked past her steps to the beach, past the beach to the sea. She smiled. In spite of her recent ordeal and her present company, she wouldn't trade being here for anything. She was surprised at how much this place already seemed like home, staircase, grumpy landlord, and all.

She walked to the stairs without a single lurch in any direction. She took a deep breath and began the upward trek, her knuckles white from grasping the banister in a death grip. If the second floor had seemed a long distance before, it looked miles away now. Her bad leg was throbbing and her sedative hangover was still making her dizzy.

If Madame Guyon could handle all the terrible things that happened to her and still believe God was in control, so can I. Abby pulled herself up another step. *At least I don't have a terrible husband and mother-in-law making me miserable. I also won't be spending a good portion of the rest of my life in prison as she did.*

A strong hand gripped her elbow, making Abby jump in surprise. Marsh stood beside her, a look of patient martyrdom on his face. More than anything, she wanted to shake him off, but she knew that would be foolish. She needed his strength now, just as she'd needed his comfort back in the emergency room. Was there such a thing as independence?

Silently they labored up the steps. At least she labored. He never even took a deep breath. When they reached the porch, Abby forced herself to smile. "Thank you for your help. Thank you for coming to get me. You've been very kind. I'll be all right now."

He raised that skeptical eyebrow again but said nothing except, "Um." He turned and ran nimbly down to where Fargo sat waiting. Abby watched the reunion between man and beast with amazement.

For Pete's sake, dog, he's only been gone an hour. Suddenly she wanted Puppy to greet her like she had been missed.

"Hey," she called to the cat who lay curled on the one porch chair in the full sun. "I'm home, slightly wounded but otherwise well."

Puppy twitched an ear but didn't move.

"Yeah, I'm glad to see you too." She dropped onto the chaise and lay back with a groan. She closed her eyes. Sometime later she awoke with a jerk, her heart pounding wildly, though she couldn't remember what had scared her. She sat up and looked around. Where was she?

Recognition came quickly. Seaside. Her apartment. The hit-and-run accident.

She shivered. Was the little girl really all right? They said she was, but was she? Maybe they just told Abby that so she wouldn't have hysterics on them. She wished she had thought to see for herself before she left the hospital.

She rose, walked to the railing, and looked out over the beach. The lowering sun cast long shadows of the houses across the sand. She glanced at her watch. 7:15. With the longest day of the year less than a week away, it'd still be light for quite some time. She loved the long days of summer.

The water demanded her attention. She watched the waves roll in, breaking white with spume, mildly disgruntled to be reaching shore and the end of their journey across countless miles of open water. Their muted grumbling made her think of the man downstairs.

She looked down over her porch rail. There he sat, leaning back in a red Adirondack chair, feet on the second rung of his railing, golden hair muted in the shade cast by her porch. He had a laptop computer in his lap, and he was typing like crazy.

Not that it was any of her business, but what in the world was he writing? She realized with a start that she had no idea what he did for a living. She tried to imagine him as a salesman or an engineer or a CPA. Nothing seemed right. Maybe he was independently wealthy and played the stock market on-line all day. After all, the typical man couldn't afford a place on the beach. The costs were prohibitive. Why, the hurricane insurance alone would more than break the bank of the average person.

Then again, maybe he had a large family and got lots of e-mail which he was answering.

Deciding that Marsh Winslow's career path was not an issue worth wondering about, Abby went inside. She felt more alert, less dopey than when she'd come home, but still she stopped in the bathroom and splashed cool water on her face. It cleared the last of the cobwebs, though not her memory's fog. In her bedroom she grabbed her cane with the four prongs at the base and pulled a fleece jacket over her T-shirt. The sand and surf were calling.

It was wonderful to walk directly from the pavement that ran beside the house onto the sand. She ignored Marsh sitting on his porch, Fargo lying at his side, as she slowly made her way over the gentle dunes. The prongs at the end of her cane sank into the soft sand until the horizontal plate they were attached to rested flat on the ground. Her bad leg tended to drag as the sand pulled against it, and the uneven, shifting surface made the cane necessary for balance. She didn't mind. Walking difficulties were simply part of her life.

She kept her eyes fixed on the sea, on the constancy of the grumbling waves, the never-ending pattern of ebb and flow.

"Mightier than the thunder of the great waters, mightier than the breakers of the sea—the LORD on high is mighty."

Remind me over and over of that truth from Your Word, Lord. Remind me!

The soft grains of dry sand gave way to the packed sand that the tides kissed daily. The walking immediately eased, and she put her cane down. She stood at the very edge of the water, watching the waves throw themselves at the shore, their energy driving them forward until there was nothing left but the tiny wavelets that licked the tip of her shoe.

But there were always more waves and then more still. They never gave up. Their strength was beyond comprehending, their quest to eat the shore unremitting. And they were winning. Ask anyone who knew anything about the ocean. If it weren't for the unceasing efforts of man as he pumped sand from the ocean floor onto the beaches to replace the sand eaten by the relentless tides and the ferocious storms, barrier islands like Seaside would gradually diminish until nothing was left.

She closed her eyes for a minute, breathing deeply, savoring the sea air, feeling her spirit revive. The Lord was mightier than both the sea and the men who tried to circumvent it. Little girls got hurt, sometimes little girls even died, but God was mightier than any and all difficulties.

She had to believe that, or there was nothing.

She turned to walk along the water's edge only to have her solitude broken by a pair of little boys who ran, shrieking for joy, across the beach and up to the edge of the water. The smaller one, a little tyke of four or five, was so excited to be on the beach that he ran in circles, waving his arms and yelling for the sheer bliss of it. His older brother looked at Abby.

"We just got here," he explained. "We're staying for the whole summer." He pronounced *whole summer* with an emphasis that Abby understood completely.

"Me too." She smiled. "Sounds like forever, doesn't it?"

He nodded. "We never stayed that long before."

"Me neither."

"Just a week, you know?"

She nodded. "Two weeks tops."

"But Dad got rich. Now we can stay and stay and stay."

"Sounds wonderful to me."

"Is your dad rich too?"

Understanding that he meant her husband, not her father, she shook her head. "I don't have a husband anymore."

He nodded. "Neither does my mom." His young face looked sad for an instant, then brightened. "But I still got a dad."

"I'm glad." Divorce, Abby thought, fascinated by this little fount of information.

"Me too," he said, his floppy brown bangs hanging over his eyebrows. "Do you live near here?"

"Right up there." Abby pointed.

"That's where we live too," the boy said excitedly. "We live in the white one with all the glass."

Abby nodded. She'd admired the remodeled house next door to Marsh's with its wide decks and modern windows. "I live on the second floor of the house to the right of yours, the one with the awning."

The boy squinted. "The old green-and-white house?"

She smiled. "The old green-and-white house."

The little guy came to stand by his brother. Sand covered his dimpled knees and a streak of grains ran down his left cheek. He pulled on his brother's shirt.

"Walker, we're not supposed to talk to strangers," he stage-whispered.

Walker looked down at him, condescension dripping. "Come on, Jordan. She's not a stranger. She's a neighbor."

Jordan peered at Abby from the safety of the far side of his brother. "If she's not a stranger, then what's her name?"

"My name's Mrs. Patterson," Abby answered, delighted at the

child's logic. "Your mother gave you good advice about not talking to strangers."

"Told you."

"Shut up, Jordan. Go build a castle or something."

"Come with me." He tugged on Walker's shirt again. His eyes slid beyond Abby, and she could see his interest stir. He pointed down the beach. "Who's he?"

Abby turned to see a man with a white ponytail sticking through the opening at the back of a baseball cap. He was waving a metal detector back and forth. "He's looking for things people have lost in the sand," she explained. "His machine shows him where they are."

"Yeah?" Both Jordan and Walker were fascinated. "How's it work?"

"I don't really know, but somehow it registers metals. I think he finds mostly money." Abby smiled at the little boys.

"I want to see," Walker said.

Jordan grabbed his brother's Flyers T-shirt. "We can't. He's a stranger too."

Walker looked at his brother with exasperation. "You listen too good." But he didn't pursue the man.

Abby sighed with relief. Strangers were always a risk.

Walker pulled off his sneakers and socks, then walked cautiously into the shallows, letting the little waves roll over his feet. He didn't seem to feel the pain that by rights should be shooting up his legs from the cold water. What was the temperature of the sea this early in the season? Low sixties? Abby shuddered at the thought.

Jordan stared, bedazzled and bothered by his older brother's daring. "Walker, Mom said no."

Walker looked toward the houses. "Mom's not watching. She'll never know unless some little twerp tattles."

"I'm not a twerp," Jordan defended. "I don't tattle."

"You'd better not. That's all I can say." The older boy turned back to the water.

Jordan sighed deeply, for all the world like a mother who doesn't know how to handle a recalcitrant child. "You'll be sorry, Walker," he muttered, dropping to his knees, his back to the water. If he didn't witness the disobedience, he could make believe it wasn't happening. He began to mound handfuls of sand.

"Don't you go in any farther than your ankles," Abby said. Once a mother, always a mother, even with someone else's child. "It's too dangerous." And this child was too independent.

Walker nodded absently. He bent over to study a shell rolling back and forth in the waves.

"I mean it, Walker. It's too dangerous." Abby's tone, the same she used to quiet little people at StoryTime, brooked no nonsense. Walker recognized her authority; with an unhappy face he backed out of the water.

"Thank you." Abby smiled to show there were no hard feelings. Walker sank down beside Jordan and began digging. He wouldn't look at her.

I do have a way with men, don't I? With a wave to Jordan she began walking south. She took a deep, invigorating breath. The dependability of the sea and the ordinariness of two little boys had made the world steady on its axis once again.

Lord, these tilts. Why? Why, if You're mightier than the sea, since *You're mightier than the sea, do You let the world go crazy? That little girl—why?*

Seven

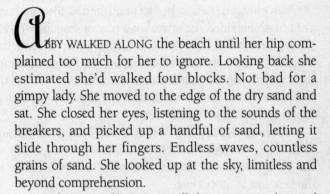

ABBY WALKED ALONG the beach until her hip complained too much for her to ignore. Looking back she estimated she'd walked four blocks. Not bad for a gimpy lady. She moved to the edge of the dry sand and sat. She closed her eyes, listening to the sounds of the breakers, and picked up a handful of sand, letting it slide through her fingers. Endless waves, countless grains of sand. She looked up at the sky, limitless and beyond comprehension.

God was so obvious, yet all the questions she tried to contain, the uncertainties and doubts about His care, about life, about pain, about Maddie and Sam, washed over her once again. They threatened to sweep her into what she called the Sea of Heresy, a place where good little Christians who dared to doubt were swamped and drowned.

I'd never have survived these past three years without You. I know that. I also know You love me. The Bible says so. But I don't understand why You let such unloving and hurtful things happen. I believe in You, Lord. I do. But please, Father, help my unbelief. Don't let me drown.

She stared at the horizon, her eyes unfocused, her mind in free fall as questions tumbled. How far away was the horizon? Was it always the same distance when you looked out to sea, or did the distance vary from vantage point to vantage point? What about the waves? She watched them foam and froth. Why did they advance and then recede? Why didn't the ocean keep coming and inundate the land? She knew there were answers in the pull of the moon and the rotation of the earth, but why did the earth rotate and the moon pull at the sea to begin with? Why was the sand here on the Jersey shore so soft? How did the Gulf Stream that warmed these waters come to be?

Lord, while I wonder about the unanswerable questions of life on one hand, I see Your might on the other. So with all that power, why?

She was not surprised when she heard no answer.

She pulled herself to her feet and started the trek back. A strident noise heralded the arrival of a pair of seagulls who landed on the sand mere feet from her. One held food in its beak; the second lunged for it. Soon they were tugging on the same scrap, half in each beak. With a sudden movement one tore it out of the other's mouth and launched himself into the sky. The second gull gave chase, screaming in raucous fury.

Limping slightly, Abby shook her head at the disappearing birds. They reminded her of too many boys and girls who came to the library, fighting for their own way, their own choice of books, the best seat at StoryTime.

They also reminded her of herself and her demands that God explain Himself. Sighing at her audacity, she drew even with the man holding the metal detector, the one who had so fascinated the boys. He was digging a hole in the sand with a little red beach spade. He reached in the hole and withdrew something.

Abby couldn't resist. "What did you find?"

The man turned to her. She saw his shabby sweater and faded, stained jeans, his gray ponytail and shabby Phillies cap, and she wondered about him. Then she noticed the huge sparkling chip in his left ear and the slim gold watch showing through the unraveling cuff of his left sleeve. A diamond stud? A Rolex? Now she really wondered.

"I'm Abby."

He bobbed his head in greeting. "Clooney."

"As in Rosemary?"

He looked pained. "As in George."

"Ah. Of course. Forgive me."

He grinned, holding out his hand. In the palm sat a gold link bracelet with sand clinging to it.

"How lovely," Abby said as she inspected the design of the links. "I've never seen one quite like it before. I wonder who lost it?"

Clooney shrugged. "She'd never have found it if she'd looked all day," he said. "Besides, it's been here for a long time. Look at the way the sand has attached itself to the links. I'd say it's been here since last summer."

"And it's still shiny?"

"Real gold doesn't tarnish."

"How sad for someone to lose such a beautiful piece."

Clooney held it out to her. "Why don't you take it? Let it be worn by a pretty lady again."

Surprised and a little uncomfortable at the offer, Abby put her hands behind her back. "Oh, I couldn't."

"Sure you can. It's mine now, and I can do with it whatever I want. If I want to give it to you—" He shrugged. "Well, why not?"

Why not indeed. She leaned closer and studied it. The craftsmanship was excellent, the links designed like little shells that fit into each other. She reached out a finger and traced the lines of one shell. "Very seashoreish." Very tempting.

Clooney grabbed her hand, making her jump. He set the bracelet in her palm. Then he closed her fingers over it. Without a word he picked up his spade and detector and walked off, swinging the machine back and forth, back and forth over the sand.

Abby stood there a moment, staring after him. Then she looked at the bracelet. With her forefinger she reached out, carefully brushing grains of sand away. What should she do? Run after the man and insist he take the bracelet back?

Yes, she should.

She turned to follow him, but he was gone. She blinked. She knew he'd just walked off the beach. She also knew that she could never move fast enough to catch him, especially with the broad expanse of soft sand to be crossed. Sighing, she slipped the bracelet into her jacket pocket. Maybe she'd see him another day.

As she approached what she'd already come to think of as her beach, she saw Jordan standing at the water's edge, staring out to the horizon. He was a cute little guy with his cowlick à la Alfalfa from Our Gang. She wondered what he'd think of her talking to Clooney, a stranger. "Hi, Jordan."

The boy didn't move, didn't seem to hear her. He was like a setter on point. She followed his line of sight and went cold. Walker was bobbing up and down with the waves.

If he were mine, I'd tan his hide! Going in the water alone!

She laid a hand on Jordan's shoulder. "Has he been in there long?"

Jordan turned a worried face to her. "I don't want to be a tattletale." His voice quivered.

"Don't worry." Abby smiled. "You don't have to tell. I've seen." She raised her voice. "Walker! Come out of the water this instant!"

Walker didn't turn. He just kept bobbing on the gentle waves.

Whatever had possessed their mother to let them come down here without checking on them? They were just too small to trust. "Walker! Come out of the water this very minute! It's not safe to swim alone."

Still Walker didn't turn, and a terrible realization prickled its way along Abby's synapses. Walker wasn't touching the bottom.

She toed off her shoes and pulled off her jacket. She moved into the water as quickly as she could. Its chill struck to the marrow as she waded ever deeper. "Hold on, Walker! I'm coming."

A wave broke against her stomach and threw her off balance. She staggered back, almost going under. She flailed about until she regained her balance, then pressed on. The water was chest high by the time she reached the boy. She grabbed his hand and pulled him to her. His lips were blue. When he wrapped himself around her like a little monkey, she felt his shivers.

She began the long walk back to shore.

"Are you all right?" She held him close with one arm about his waist while she used the other to keep her balance. A wave surged forward, lifting them and moving them toward shore.

"I knew somebody'd come," Walker said. His teeth chattered like castanets, but his voice was steady. "I asked God."

Abby blinked. She was the answer to his prayers? "I'm glad I was here when you needed me."

"Me too." He smiled, his white teeth a sharp contrast to his blue lips.

She put him down as soon as they reached shallower water. He splashed to shore beside her. Jordan stood at the water's edge, jumping up and down and cheering. Behind him Abby saw Marsh running across the sand with Fargo, ears flying, loping behind him.

"Never again by yourself," Abby said as she took Walker by the shoulders. She knew she was ruining his vision of her as his rescuer by becoming a lecturing adult, but there was no choice.

The boy studied his blue toes and didn't respond. He shivered convulsively under her fingers, and she knew hypothermia was a real concern.

"Walker, look at me."

"What do you think you're doing, woman?" Marsh yelled as he drew near. Jordan stopped jumping around to stare open-mouthed at the red-faced man who jerked to a stop beside him.

Abby ignored Marsh. "Walker."

The boy's lips drew together in a tight line. As if she needed more proof that he was an independent kid who didn't like being told what he could or couldn't do. Finally he looked at her.

"Never again alone," she said. "I want your word."

"You could have drowned out there," Marsh yelled.

"Calm down," Abby said. "As you can see, he's fine."

"Not him! You!"

She frowned. "I was fine. I'm a very strong swimmer. Now be quiet a minute. I'm talking to Walker." Her command lost some of its force when she shuddered with cold.

Marsh glared at Walker. He opened his mouth to lambaste the boy, but Abby spoke first. "Do I have your word, Walker?"

When he still didn't respond, Marsh roared, "If she hadn't come along, you'd still be floating off to Europe, boy!"

Abby flashed Marsh a look. His kid skills were pathetic. She turned back to Walker.

For the first time Walker looked scared. He moved away from Marsh and closer to Abby. "Don't tell my mom," he whispered.

Abby raised an eyebrow. She knew a bargaining tool when she heard one. "Then give me your word."

"Okay."

"Okay what? Say it."

"I won't go in the water alone."

"Ever again." Marsh coached none too gently.

"I won't go in the water alone ever again," the boy repeated to his feet.

"Me neither," said Jordan, his little face serious. "It's too cold."

Abby smiled and ruffled the little boy's hair. She turned to Walker. "You two go home. It's dinnertime. And Walker, take a hot shower as soon as you get there. We don't want you getting sick."

The last she yelled at the running boys as they streaked across the broad beach to their house. She grinned after them as a great shiver took her.

When she turned to look for her shoes and cane, she found Marsh glaring at her.

"Are you crazy?" he yelled.

She blinked at him. "What's your problem? Everyone's fine."

"I heard you screaming. I looked up and saw you plunging into the sea. I saw you lose your balance and almost go under. I know the temperature of that water. No one in her right mind goes in when it's that cold."

"Just little boys who are too independent for their own good."

"Yeah, well, it took me a minute to spot him."

Abby sat and shoved her wet feet into her sneakers. "What did you think? I was suicidal?"

He didn't answer. Instead he became very busy retrieving her cane from where she had dropped it earlier.

Abby stared up at him openmouthed. Even when she'd been her most depressed, no one had thought her a danger to herself. "Why you—"

"Yeah." He raked his fingers through his hair. "I am. Whatever it is you're thinking. But you scared me to death." He gave her a sickly grin. "I mean, where else would I find a renter for the whole summer?"

"Very funny." But she couldn't help smiling back. Much as she hated to admit it, from his point of view things must have looked very strange, especially if Walker's little head wasn't easily seen. Okay, so he had run to her rescue. She had to give him full marks for that. But he was still grumpy.

When he held out a hand to help her rise, she took it. Squirming around like a beached fish as she tried to stand was the last thing she wanted to do in front of him. Once on her feet she grabbed her cane from him and turned toward the house. She shivered hard enough to make her teeth chatter as water dripped from her clothes.

"Where's your jacket?" he barked.

"What?"

"Your jacket. When you left, you had a jacket."

So she did. She rubbed the goose bumps on her arms as she looked vaguely around. "There." She pointed to the water's edge where it bobbed in the incoming tide.

He grabbed it and wrung it out. "Here."

She took it, holding it away from her. It drip-drip-dripped, making little indentations in the sand. She started in surprise when Marsh pulled his own sweatshirt off and dropped it over her head.

"Arms," he ordered. She obediently pushed first one arm, then the other through the sleeves, trading her wet jacket from hand to hand.

"Thanks," she muttered as she pulled the sweatshirt close. It felt warm and wonderful.

"Um."

They reached the powdery sand, and Abby began her slow traverse. Her hip hurt like fury where Walker had kicked her when he wrapped his skinny legs about her, and the chill licking at her had tightened the muscles further. She hadn't limped this much in months.

As she took a step, a shaft of pain slashed through her hip, across her lower back. She grimaced, pausing to let the agony recede. In spite of her best efforts a slight groan escaped.

Marsh heard and stopped too. Instead of the "poor baby" treatment she was used to, he sighed. "This is ridiculous. You'll be in a wheelchair and have pneumonia before you get home."

He turned to her, lowered one shoulder, and hit her in the stomach like a tackler would the quarterback, though probably not as hard. He wrapped an arm around her legs and straightened. Next thing she knew, she was hanging over his shoulder in a fireman's carry, her head bumping his back with every step.

"What do you think you're doing?" she yelled as soon as she recovered from the shock of his move.

"Saving you from yourself."

She braced her hands on his waist and pushed herself away from his body, holding on to his T-shirt. She found herself nose to nose with a confused Fargo. "Nice dog." She gave him what she hoped was a conciliatory smile.

Fargo sneered.

Abby sneered back. "I'm not hurting him, you idiot animal. He's hurting me."

"Like I care."

For a blink of a second Abby thought Fargo had spoken. Then the rumble of Marsh's back under her hands registered. "Put me down!"

"Yeah, yeah. In a minute."

"I hate to hang upside down. It gives me a headache."

He didn't bother to answer, just tramped over the sand and onto the paved area beside the house.

"I'm getting you all wet." She almost felt guilty.

"I'll dry." He began climbing the stairs to her apartment. Her cane, dangling from her hand, bumped against each riser. She was struck by an overwhelming urge to use it in a sharp swat across his bottom. It would be nothing less than he deserved for man-handling her like this.

Fortunately for both of them they reached the landing at the top of the stairs before she had time to act. He bent and dumped her off as unceremoniously as he had picked her up. When she rocked on her feet, he steadied her with a grip on an elbow.

He glared at her. "You take that shower you told Walker about."

Shivering uncontrollably, she glared back and nodded.

He turned to leave.

"Thanks." She was pleased at how ungrateful she sounded.

"Um," he replied. He really was a great conversationalist.

"When I'm warm and dry, I want to go get my car." Now where had that come from? It was like some little demon in her wanted to make his life as difficult as she could.

He stopped. "Tonight?" His disbelief and reluctance were obvious.

Perversity ruled. She looked at him as haughtily as she could. "Tonight."

He grunted. "Eight-thirty."

Fargo, watching with a frown from the bottom of the stairs, woofed agreement.

Abby waved a weary hand and went inside. Puppy raised her sleepy head from the sofa where she was snoozing, her eyelids at half-mast. She yawned, showing Abby her tonsils.

"I saved a kid's life just now." With a burst of pleasure, Abby realized that was absolutely true. She was a real-life heroine, sort of like the Old Testament queen Esther. Granted Esther saved the lives of many and Abby only saved one, but she knew she, too, had been born "for such a time as this."

Puppy, uncaring and unimpressed, yawned and was back asleep before her chin hit her paws.

"Thanks for the affirmation," Abby muttered. "You sure know how to make a woman feel good."

As she walked past the phone, she noticed the message button blinking. Without thinking, she stopped and hit play.

"Abby, how could you?" Her mother's soft voice filled the apartment. The sorrow and hurt oozed over the distance.

With a grunt that would have done Marsh proud, Abby hit delete.

Enough was enough.

Eight

MARSH DROVE ABBY into town to retrieve her car, taking care to drive down Bay instead of Central, not that she even noticed. Still, he felt wise and insightful that he'd thought to protect her from the accident scene for the second time today. Too bad you couldn't brag about a thoughtful action without its luster being thoroughly dimmed. Besides, he reminded himself like the seminary prof he was, it was the Lord Christ he served.

Abby had given him back his sweatshirt all toasty from the dryer in her apartment, and he had it on against the cool wind off the ocean. She had on black jeans, a red knit shirt, and a black blazer. She looked sleek, stylish, intriguing. Too bad she was pushy and independent to a fault. Slightly quirky, too, with all those historical ladies she kept referring to.

"How come you drive a Taurus?" She rubbed her hand over the gray fabric of the passenger seat.

He frowned. Now there was a question from left field. "What's wrong with a Taurus? It's sturdy, dependable, and reasonably priced."

She nodded. "But you own a house on the beach. Doesn't money like that mean owning a BMW or a Mercedes or something?"

"Why waste the money when a Taurus does fine?"

She looked at him, surprised. "A strange if practical statement for a man who just paid a fortune for a house you'll only live in part-time."

He shrugged. "The house is worth every penny."

"Why?"

"Why? Are you nuts?" The answer should be obvious, even to someone as trouble prone and flighty as she. "Peace. Quiet. Recreation and regeneration. Ambiance, beauty, the rhythms of nature at your very doorstep. Privacy." He said the last in tones of reverence.

She nodded her understanding until his last word. Then she shook her head. "Privacy? With neighbors mere feet away on both sides?"

"I don't know them, and they don't know me." He set his jaw. "That's the way I plan to keep it."

She looked aghast.

"Besides," he added, "they're vacationers. They're only here for a week or two tops."

"Walker and Jordan are here for the whole summer, like you and me."

He made a face. "Great." All he needed were two little boys peering over his shoulder trying to read as he wrote, assuming, of course, that they could read.

"Don't you like kids?" Abby looked at him with suspicion.

"Sure, as long as they're someone else's."

She studied him, her dark eyes trying to penetrate his skull to see how he ticked. At least that's what it felt like. He resisted the urge to squirm.

"No wonder you're not married. Who'd have you?"

He sniffed, stung in spite of her gentle, sorrowful tone of voice. "I could get married anytime I wanted." As long as she wasn't like Lane, but how could he ever know that? "I'm too busy to be bothered. And I happen to value my privacy."

"So you said. Just you and Fargo against the world."

"What's wrong with that? We like the arrangement."

"Uh-huh." She nodded, obviously finding him deficient. "I bet you two have very stimulating conversations." She turned to stare out her window.

He was more than a little miffed at her attitude. "I've got stuff to do, important stuff." He frowned as he heard himself. He sounded pompous and defensive even to his own ears. Defensive he could live with. But pompous? Pompous was his father's meat and potatoes, not his. *Oh, Lord, please don't let me become him.*

He flicked a glance across the car. What did he sound like to her?

And why did he care?

She turned briefly to him, then back to the window. "Yeah, important stuff."

He imagined he heard a slight tinge of disdain dripping from her soft voice like melted butter from a hot roll. Her tone reminded him too much of his father's manner, and in one instant miffed gave way to irate. All his worst qualities rushing to the fore, he became even more defensive and obnoxious.

"I'll have you know that I have a Ph.D. in philosophy."

"There's a marketable skill," she muttered.

He ignored her. "I also have a D.Min. in practical theology. That's Doctor of Ministry."

"I know." Her tone was patience exemplified.

"I teach at Tyndale Theological Seminary in Ohio. I've got classes to prepare, papers to write. Haven't you ever heard of the publish or perish principle?"

"A seminary professor, huh?"

Was that a touch of respect he heard in her voice?

"And of course I've heard of publish or perish. I may be a children's librarian, but I know about big people stuff too."

"Well, good for you."

"I'll have you know that it takes brains and staying power to keep up with all the little Sonduks I meet in the course of a day."

"What in the world are Sonduks?"

"Sonduk, singular. She was an ancient Korean queen whose genius was evident even as a child."

He stared at her. Quirky. "You know this because?"

"The story goes that the Chinese sent her father some peony seeds and paintings. She looked at the paintings and said it was too bad the flowers didn't smell. Her father wanted to know how she knew that fact. 'No butterflies and bees in the picture,' she said. They planted the seeds and sure enough, up came scentless flowers."

"But peonies have a strong fragrance," he said, thinking of the beauties his mother used to grow.

"Well, this variety must not have."

Right. "This story about little Princess What's-her-name proves what particular point?"

"It shows what a challenge being a children's librarian is because kids can be so smart."

"Of course."

"They are." She folded her arms and glared straight ahead. "And I have an advanced degree too."

"A Ph.D. in kiddie lit? Whoa, now there's a hard field."

"A master's in library science with a specialty in children's literature."

"Children's literature. Isn't that an oxymoron? Did you specialize in the reading of those great tomes or the writing of them?"

"The care and keeping of them, but I'll have you know that writing kid's books is no easy task!"

"Written any?" he asked as he pulled up beside her car. He wasn't sure why, but he relished teasing her. She rose to the bait every time, and she didn't fail him now.

"Not yet." Her black eyes flashed. "But I will. You just wait!"

"Until I'm old and gray."

She glared at him; he glared back. He knew he could look meaner than she could any day. Little girls with black-eyed Susan eyes and curly hair could never do mean. That was for big men who loomed. He turned toward her and leaned. She squared her shoulders and raised her chin.

Suddenly the ridiculousness of it all struck him. Here they were, two well-educated, mature adults, playing dare and double dare. He laughed. He couldn't help it. For a moment she stared at him in surprise. Then she began to laugh too.

"For two smart people we sound more than foolish about now." He held out his hand. "Truce?"

She slid her small hand into his and shook. "Truce," she agreed with appropriate solemnity. Then she grinned cheekily. "But my dad's still bigger than your dad."

As he laughed, he thought of his father and doubted it. No one was bigger than Senator Marcus Winslow, except maybe the president, and sometimes even that was debatable.

She reached for the door handle. "I want to thank you for bringing me to get my car." For once she sounded sincere. She batted her big, black eyes at him. "As landlords go, you're okay."

For some reason the compliment both irked and pleased him as he thought of some of the landlords he'd known. "Have you had dinner yet?"

She looked surprised. "No."

"Hungry?"

She thought for a second or two. "Yes."

"Follow me. I'll take you to the best seafood place in Seaside. It's a hole in the wall that most tourists miss."

She hesitated a minute before she said all right. It wasn't until after they were seated and given menus that she informed him she didn't like seafood.

"What?" He couldn't imagine anything sadder.

She placed her elbows on the table, her chin in her hands. "Except shrimp cocktail. I like shrimp cocktail, but only because the sauce drowns the taste of the shrimp. I think that's what I'll have."

"Sounds good." He turned back to the menu, which offered so many tantalizing choices that he couldn't make up his mind. "Do you see anything you want for the main course?"

"Shrimp cocktail."

He looked up. "But that's an appetizer."

She nodded. "But where does it say it can't be a main course too? Margery Russell and Dorothy Petty would have selected it as a main course if they wanted to." She turned to their waitress. "A Caesar salad and a shrimp cocktail. Please serve the shrimp and salad together as my main course."

"I know I'm going to regret this," Marsh said as their waitress hurried off with their order, "but who are Margery Russell and Dorothy Petty?"

Abby grinned. "Margery Russell was an Englishwoman who took over her husband's import/export business after he died around 1300. When some Spanish pirates robbed one of her ships, she robbed two of theirs."

"Ah, just the kind of woman you'd be proud to have as a mother."

Abby smiled. "Dorothy Petty was a preacher's daughter who

lived during the Renaissance and sold insurance. She was one of the most honest and successful insurance agents in London."

"I didn't know they had insurance that long ago."

"I didn't either until I found her story."

He stirred more sugar into his iced tea. "What do they have to do with you ordering shrimp cocktail?"

"Nothing. But they have a lot to do with coloring outside the lines. Ordering an appetizer as an entrée is my small scribble outside the lines."

Fascinating. "It's important to color outside the lines?"

She became very serious. "I must, Marsh, or I'll die. I've been confined to inside the lines my whole life. I've got to draw my own pictures!"

Marsh had heard that same intensity, even desperation, in her comments a couple of other times today. "How did you feel confined?"

She played with her silverware for a few minutes, and he thought she wasn't going to answer. He couldn't blame her. She didn't know him except in the most superficial way, and he'd asked a very pointed, personal question, one he wasn't certain he wanted anyone to ask him.

In that moment his secret life weighed on him like a millstone pulling him under. What did it say about you if you did color outside the lines but went to great lengths to conceal those bold strokes of color?

"I was always the good girl," Abby said in a rush. "I was obedient, compliant, and cooperative. Sometimes I think that if my parents had told me to jump off a cliff, I would have." She shuddered. "I was without a spine, and I didn't even know it. Then I married Sam right out of college and became his sweet little wife."

"That was a bad thing?"

"In that it meant I was a nonentity, yes."

"Maybe it was just that your goals for yourself and their goals for you agreed."

She looked up from the invisible design she'd been creating on the place mat with her fork. "Maybe." She stabbed the fork in his general direction. "But I don't think so. I think now that I was a girl, then a woman, with no mind of her own. The most criminal part of this whole situation is that I didn't even realize it until recently."

Marsh thought of the feisty woman who had been driving him crazy all day and had a hard time with the picture she was painting. "I hope you'll pardon me if I say I haven't seen anything of this sweet, compliant woman."

"You haven't?" She looked like he'd given her a great gift.

He shook his head and couldn't resist adding, "Though sweet women can be very restful."

She snorted. "Boring. That's what they can be. At least that's what I was."

"But no more?" He leaned back as the waitress set his flounder stuffed with crabmeat before him. He looked at her Caesar salad and puny shrimp cocktail. "Are you sure that's enough food?"

"It's just what I want." She tossed the salad with her fork.

Without thinking he bowed his head and said, "Thanks, Father God, for the food, the kind inside the lines and the kind outside. We appreciate your bounty."

Her amen was louder than his.

He was savoring the taste of his flounder and crab when she said, "Enough about boring me. Tell me about what you teach and why you teach it."

He enjoyed the academic life, so it wasn't hard telling her about Tyndale, his students, and their endless debates on the fine points of doctrine.

"But the ministry isn't all doctrine, I tell them. It's people, and people are messy. So are their problems."

"Practical theology," she said.

Pleased she remembered, he launched into some of his favorite people tales, and with little effort he soon had her laughing. She had a very nice laugh.

Dinner passed easily, quickly, and soon she was following him home. They parked side by side and walked to the staircase. He put a hand on her elbow and prepared to help her.

"No." She pulled her elbow free and stepped away from him. Her warm smile robbed the movement of any sting of rejection. "I've had a wonderful time for my one night of riotous, intoxicating freedom."

He shook his head. If dinner at Moe's was her idea of riotous, intoxicating freedom, she did lead a too-circumscribed life.

"I thank you for providing such a relaxing ending to what was a very stressful day. But now—do you remember the old ads on TV? Mother, I'd rather do it myself?"

He nodded.

She looked up the steps and took a deep breath. "Me too." Slowly she took herself upstairs. He waited to be certain she made it all right, then went inside. He had to agree with her; it had been an unexpectedly good evening.

He was floored when she came back down and drove away at eleven o'clock.

Nine

CÉLIA FITZMEYER looked at her sleeping daughter as she lay in her hospital bed, looked at the red brush burns and deep blue bruises, at the pink fiberglass cast on her right arm. A single tear breached the dam of her lower lid and slid down her face. She swiped at it and clenched her teeth to keep them from chattering. She couldn't stop the tremble in her lips no matter how hard she pressed them together.

So close!

Karlee lay relaxed, her arm in the cast resting on the white hospital blanket, her scraped face slightly turned in to her pillow.

So close!

Celia forced herself to take deep, quiet breaths and turned her face to the window. The last thing she wanted was to frighten eight-year-old Jessica again.

"Mommy, it's okay. She's going to be all right." A small arm slid over Celia's shoulders, and a gentle hand patted her back. "The doctor said so."

Celia nodded and turned to Jess who stood beside her chair. The girl's light brown hair hung straight to the center of her back and was riddled with enough knots to give both of them a headache tomorrow when it was time to brush them out. Celia kissed her older daughter's cheek.

"I know she'll be fine, sweetie. She's just so little, and every once in a while it hits me how close we came to losing her." She rested her head on Jess's fragile shoulder and drew comfort as Jess leaned her head to rest on Celia's hair.

"I love you, Jess," she whispered, her voice catching.

"I love you, Mommy. And I love Karlee."

Jess's voice broke on her sister's name, and she began to cry in great, gasping sobs that came from deep in her chest. Celia wrapped her arms around her older daughter and pulled her into her lap.

"Shush, baby. Shush. You mustn't cry. It's like you said. Karlee's going to be fine."

"I kn-kn-know," Jess hiccupped. She wrapped her arms around Celia's waist and burrowed her face in Celia's breast. Her slim shoulders were tense, and Celia could feel her distress.

She made little circles on Jess's back, remembering to be easy with the pressure. Jess wasn't a client at the spa looking for a deep massage. "Isn't it funny how we sometimes feel worse when the emergency is over? You'd think we'd feel better."

Jess took a deep, jagged breath. "I yelled at her last night, Mommy. I told her she was a baby, and I didn't want her around me ever again."

Celia smiled sadly. Poor Jess, awash in guilt. How Celia understood. "You didn't mean it, honey."

"I did then."

"You thought you did then, but you didn't really. You're too wonderful a girl to ever want anything bad to happen to a person, especially your sister."

Jess sighed. "She gets in my things all the time and messes up my Barbies. I hate it when she does that, but I know it's because she's little. She's only four."

"She loves your Barbies."

"She has her own."

Celia heard the proprietary steel in Jess's voice. Apparently guilt went only so far. "But she can't make her dolls as pretty as you make yours."

Jess nodded. "Of course she can't. I'm eight." And that said it all. "I had all my Barbies dressed up for a fashion show. I fixed their hair with barrettes and bows and flowers and everything, and they were wearing their best clothes." She turned in Celia's arms until she was looking at her sleeping sister. "*She* combed all their hair."

Celia bit back her grin. She'd seen Karlee's idea of combing a doll's hair many times. Halloween fright wigs looked good in comparison.

"She gets into your things and plays with them because they're yours, and she wants to be like you. She thinks you're wonderful."

"I'm terrible," Jess whispered, renewed tears in her voice.

"No, honey, not at all. People get mad at each other all the time. What makes us a loving family is that we don't stay mad. We forgive each other, and we love each other."

Jess was silent for a minute, thinking about her mother's words. "Is that why Daddy left?"

Celia blinked. "What?" Had this new catastrophe somehow brought the old one to Jess's mind? She hadn't talked about Eddie for months.

"Did Daddy leave because he stayed mad?" Jess's voice was small and desperate. "Did he stay mad at something I did?"

Celia hugged her daughter and kissed her on the top of her head. Had the girl been carrying this worry and guilt inside for years and only now had the courage to voice it? "Daddy stayed mad all right, sweetie, but not at anything you did."

"Are you sure?"

"I'm sure."

"Absolutely sure?"

"Absolutely sure."

"But he told me I was stupid and couldn't do anything right."

Celia wished Eddie were here right now so she could scorch him with her X-ray vision. Saying such a thing to a child, any child, but especially to your own daughter, was criminal. What had she ever seen in that thoughtless— She stopped and took a deep breath. She counted to ten, reminding herself that not only didn't she say words like that anymore; she didn't even think them.

"He was wrong about you, Jess." Celia put as much authority in her voice as she could. "You are very smart, and you did not do anything that made him leave." Except maybe be alive, Celia thought. But then, the same could be said of her.

"Then was he mad at something Karlee did?"

"No, not at all." Celia stared at the wall over Jess's head and forced out what was regrettably a lie. "He loved you girls both very much."

Jess was silent, and Celia knew she wasn't buying it. She couldn't blame the little girl. Eddie had made it clear that he resented his daughters. Of course he resented the whole world, but that didn't ease a daughter's pain when her daddy told her he didn't like her.

"Then was he mad at you?" Jess asked in a small voice.

Celia sighed. How much of Eddie's ranting and raving had Jess heard? "Mad at me?" If only it were that simple. "It's very sad, honey, but Daddy got mad at everything and everybody. Me. His boss. His parents. Life. Everything except you and Karlee."

Jess sat up and blinked at Celia. Her mouth was a little round O of astonishment. "Was he even mad at God?"

Celia looked at her daughter's huge, brown eyes, so like her father's down to the gold flecks that swam in the irises and the thick lashes that shadowed them. This older daughter of his had his wonderful facial features miniaturized and feminized, and Celia had no doubt that she would one day be a stunner, just like Eddie.

But please, God, not his deceitful heart. Not his duplicity and weaknesses.

Even thinking about Eddie saddened her, not as much because of the loss of her marriage as because without a backward look, he threw away the very best and didn't even realize it. "He's mad even at God," Celia agreed.

"That's sad, Mommy."

"Yes, it is."

"Because God loves him. And so does Jesus."

Celia and Jessica sat in silence for a few minutes. They had been in Karlee's hospital room for several hours now, watching, weeping, thanking God. There was no extended family to come see them, to surround them with love and concern. There were just the three of them, interrupted once in a while by the nurse who came in to check Karlee for potential concussion.

"I'd like to talk to the doctor who cared for Karlee," Celia had told the nurse several hours ago. There were questions to ask and answers to get.

"Of course you do," she had answered. "The orthopedist who

set Karlee's arm is gone for the weekend, but Dr. Schofield will be in later tonight. He'll have Karlee's complete file and will answer any questions you have."

Celia thought of the very handsome pediatrician they had visited soon after their move to Seaside to sign up the girls as his patients. Money might be tight, but the girls would never suffer medically if Celia had anything to say about it, and her boss had given Dr. Schofield high marks indeed. "He comes in on a Friday night?"

"He frequently comes in late at night." The nurse's voice was reverent. "He cares about his patients."

A knock at the door made Celia turn her head in surprise. "Come in." Maybe Dr. Schofield was here already.

No, it was Paul Trevelyan, the young pastor of Seaside Chapel. He was wearing jeans and a sweatshirt that read Seaside Beach Patrol across the chest.

"Pastor Paul." Celia knew her jaw must be hanging open. She set Jess down and scrambled to her feet to shake his hand. "How did you know we were here?"

"I have my sources," he said, smiling. He walked to the side of the bed and looked down at Karlee. "How is she?"

"She's a bit banged up and has a broken arm, but the angels must have been working overtime protecting her." Her voice broke, and she had to swallow the lump in her throat. "She'll be fine in no time."

He nodded. "I'm so glad." He reached out and ran a gentle hand over Karlee's hair.

Celia smiled. It felt good to have another adult concerned about Karlee, rejoicing that she would be all right. Sometimes, in spite of the girls, she felt so very lonely.

She and the girls had moved to Seaside almost two months ago, and they had gone to Seaside Chapel since the first Sunday. All three of them liked the warm atmosphere and the informality of a shore resort church combined with a sincere reverence for the God they were worshiping. As an added bonus, the girls loved their Bible school teachers too.

But that Pastor Paul had come to the hospital for them—well, it was almost more than she could take in. People didn't do nice things for her.

"She's four, isn't she?" Pastor Paul asked Jess.

"Last week," Jess answered. "Tuesday. When Mommy came home from work, we had a party with hats and streamers and a cake and all."

"Sounds like you had fun," the pastor said. "When's your birthday?"

Jess made a face. "Not until December."

He nodded with understanding. "It's not too close to Christmas, is it?"

"It's December 2. It's early enough that I get presents both times."

He winked. "Good." He turned his attention to Celia. "I wanted to let you know that you're not alone even though you're new in town. Karlee's name has been put on the church prayer list, and even now she's being prayed for."

Tears rose in Celia's eyes again, but these were tears of gratitude. She'd felt so alone for so long that it was almost beyond understanding that people cared. When Pastor Paul laid his hand on Karlee's forehead and prayed for her rapid recovery, Celia had to bite her lip to keep from sobbing aloud. *Thank You, God. Thank You, God.*

When the pastor left after a ten-minute visit, Jess climbed back onto Celia's lap. "He's nice."

"Mmm. Very nice."

"I'm glad we go to his church."

"Me too. Now why don't you close those beautiful brown eyes of yours and get some sleep? Tomorrow I imagine Karlee's going to hate lying in bed, and you're going to have to help me entertain her."

"I can entertain her alone when you go to work," Jess said. "There's adults here to watch over us."

"I'm not going to work, honey."

Jess straightened and looked into her mother's face. "Did Pinky give you the day off?"

"Not exactly." In fact Saturday was one of their busiest days at the spa. "But I can't leave Karlee. The doctor'll probably tell us she can go home, and we've got to be ready to pick her up when we get the word."

Jess nodded, but she looked apprehensive. Celia hated that their financial situation was so precarious that her children worried. She sighed. She couldn't afford to lose this job at Seaside Spa. It was literally a matter of the family's survival. But what could she do? Her baby needed her.

Celia kissed the tip of Jess's nose. "Don't worry, sweetie. We'll work it out. God will work it out."

Please, God, don't let that be a lie. I need You.

Jess looked unconvinced, but she settled back in Celia's arms. Celia felt her relax, and soon a gentle snuffling indicated the child slept. Celia laid her head against the back of the chair, no longer able to keep herself from the anxiety that had been pressing on her. Sometimes she felt like the soft half of a piece of Velcro, and worry was the prickly piece that glommed on and stuck tight. She wanted to trust the Lord, but worrying was so much easier!

What would Pinky say when she didn't come to work tomorrow? She was still in her three-month probationary period, though she knew her boss liked her work. And so she should. Celia was one of the best massage therapists going. She'd graduated from school at the top of her class in spite of all the chaos in her life. She had good hands and a sixth sense about her work. Clients requested her more than any other of Pinky's therapists.

But a boss didn't care how good you were if you didn't come to work.

Once again the guilt of being a working mother with long hours cut at her. If she'd been home, Karlee wouldn't have been going to the store. She wouldn't have been at that intersection, crossing that street, getting hit by that car.

But she hadn't been home. She's been at the spa working on a man who had wrenched his back trying to surf. That a man as out of shape as he was had expected to stand on a surfboard still stunned her. She didn't quite know why she was so surprised. Men did all kinds of foolish things in the name of sport. One of her jobs was to try to put them back together, or at the very least, relieve some of their pain.

So she'd been pummeling the sore muscles of an overweight, out of shape, middle-aged man while her baby got hit by a car.

She took a deep breath, a difficult thing to do with the heavy weight pressing on her conscience. It didn't matter how much she told herself she had no choice—and she didn't; she knew she didn't—she still hated leaving Jess and Karlee with a baby-sitter. This one had proven so undependable. The foolish woman had let a four-year-old go to the store alone.

"But she told me she wanted to, Ms. Fitzmeyer," the woman had said. "Karlee likes to help."

Help, schmelp. A four-year-old needed closer supervision. Celia needed to find another baby-sitter by Monday at the latest. Her headache intensified.

A knock roused her, and she blinked as a slim woman in black jeans, a red shirt, and a black blazer came hesitantly into the room.

"Ms. Fitzmeyer?"

Celia nodded. "Yes?"

"I'm Abby Patterson." The woman's eyes settled on the bed. Her face crumpled as she saw Karlee.

"It's not as bad as it looks," Celia hastened to say. "Brush burns. Bruises. They'll hurt for a while, but they aren't serious. She'll probably go home tomorrow."

"Really?" Abby turned a hopeful face to her. "I'm so glad! I couldn't sleep without seeing for myself that she was all right."

Abby Patterson. Why did that name sound familiar? "Ah. You're the eyewitness."

Abby looked pained. "So they tell me. I'm afraid I don't remember. It's like this curtain of gray gauze is strung across that part of my memory."

Celia stood, Jess a dead weight in her arms. "Come on, let's pull that other chair over here so you can sit down."

Abby looked uncertainly at Celia. "I don't want to impose. I—" She hesitated. "I was afraid I might upset you."

"Why?"

"Because I can't tell the police who the driver was."

Celia saw Abby's anguish. She made her smile gentle. "Neither can I."

Abby gave a little bark of laughter at the unexpected answer. "But you weren't there."

"But God was. When He wants you to remember, you will."

Abby visibly relaxed, her shoulders lowering, her mouth softening. "Thank you. That was a kind thing to say."

"But true."

Abby nodded. "I agree. But I have to tell you, this waiting for His time is terrible."

Celia decided that she liked this woman who had cared

enough to come see Karlee, even if it was—she checked the clock on the wall—eleven-thirty at night. Curiosity struck. "How did you get up here? Visiting hours are long over."

"I checked the hospital map in the lobby and came right to this floor. There was only one nurse at the nurses' station, and she was busy doing something on the computer. I just walked down the hall like I belonged here." Abby grinned. "It worked."

"Now that you're here, stay a while. Keep me company. It's going to be a long night."

Abby looked at Celia as if she was trying to decipher whether the words were merely polite or truly meant.

"Please. Stay. We have no family, and I've been alone all evening."

Abby gave a single nod and walked to the other padded chair in the room. She slid it across the floor, coming to a stop not far from Celia's own chair. Abby sat stiffly, slowly, like she was in pain, like she was the one who had been hit by the car.

Celia moved to Karlee's bed, lowering Jess over the bed rails until she was lying beside her little sister. She pulled at the covers to get them out from under Jess, but they wouldn't budge.

"Here," Abby came to the bed. "You lift her. I'll pull the blanket and sheet free."

Celia lifted Jess, straining under the combination of dead weight and odd angle. "She's getting too big for this."

Abby gave a hesitant smile and pulled the covers free. When Celia put Jess down, Abby tucked her in, turning the top of the sheet over the blanket and smoothing both until all the wrinkles were gone. Celia leaned over and kissed Jess on the forehead. She did the same to Karlee. When she turned from the bed, she was surprised to see tears in Abby's eyes. Uncertain what to say, she took her seat, and the two sat in silence in the dimly lit room.

"I had a daughter," Abby said suddenly.

Had? Celia felt her heart contract. She had come too close to *had* this very day. How did one stand it when *had* came true?

"Her name was Maddy, Madeleine. She would have been five."

"Karlee's four."

Abby looked at Celia, desperation in her face. "I had to see for myself that she was okay." She lowered her face into her hands. "Oh, Celia, why can't I remember?"

$\mathcal{T}$HE BACK ROADS worked well, just as he'd known they would. All those little black lines on a map were relatively empty even on a Friday night, and the traffic he did meet was headed south and east to the shore while he was headed north and west. Again he counted the one piece of good fortune he'd had: The damage to the car was on the right, away from oncoming traffic.

He bypassed Hammonton and turned onto 206 and followed it across Wharton State Park. The closer he got to Atsion, the more the memories crowded him. He drove past a ramshackle trailer and in his mind saw the filthy blue-and-white one he'd lived in for too many years. It was parked by itself well outside town, surrounded by pinelands. His mother had tried to keep it clean, but she was so obese that she was physically unable to do the work. It was all she could do to punch the cash register at the Food Fair.

He'd decided when he was five that he wasn't remaining in that poor excuse for a home a minute longer than necessary. He was going to have a house like the one that flashed on the screen at the beginning of *Dallas*. Big and white with lots of pillars. It took him longer to figure out how he'd get that house, but he'd always been a smart kid.

His present house didn't look like Southfork, but

only because it didn't sit in the middle of a ranch. Instead its pil-
lared porch and brick drive were surrounded by two acres of oaks
and pines, azaleas and rhododendrons, flowering cherries and
Bradford pears. Inside the place was worthy of *Architectural Digest*
with its Scalamandré fabrics and costly antiques.

He forced himself to concentrate on today's mansion instead of
yesterday's trailer. Gone also were the ratty pants and holey T-shirts
from Goodwill. He looked down at the well-tailored slacks and
hundred-dollar knit shirt he was wearing. He rubbed his hand over
the car's leather interior again and shuddered at the memory of
walking miles and miles because there was no other way to get
somewhere, not even a rusty old bike like McCoy had.

His temper soared. He couldn't lose what he'd worked so hard
for. He couldn't. Not because of a little girl in pink who was foolish
enough to stand in the middle of the street. It simply wasn't fair!

He turned off at the old iron forge and drove deep into the
Pines, back where even the Pineys didn't go. He took the dirt road
to Quaker Bridge, then on beyond that, following the barely pass-
able sand roads that snaked ever deeper into the heart of the Pines.
The forest pressed in on the car, rubbing against its shiny black
paint, and the scraping and scratching chilled his blood. Not that
it actually mattered. He was abandoning the car.

He drove off the sand track into a dense clump of scrub. He
leaned over and emptied the glove compartment of the maps, reg-
istration, insurance information, and miscellaneous papers, careful
not to leave even the smallest scrap that might provide a clue to
his identity. Pulling a handkerchief from his pocket, he wiped
down the interior, then climbed out. Immediately his trousers
caught on a broken branch. Swearing, he disentangled himself,
moved to the rear of the car, and popped the trunk. He pulled out
his gym bag. As he shrugged out of his good clothes, he studied
the snag in the slacks before he put them, neatly folded, into the
bag. A total loss.

He pushed his legs into his sweatpants, his arms into the
matching jacket. He pulled the zipper up all the way, bringing the
collar to his ears. He'd be too hot, but the mosquitoes would feast
on any skin he left uncovered. He already had a bite between his
shoulder blades. To keep the bloodsuckers out of his eyes, he put
his sunglasses on, making the already dim forest dimmer still. He

traded his high-gloss leather loafers with their tassels for his New Balance sneakers.

Taking his tire iron, he pried the license plates off the front and back of the car. It was hot, sweaty work, and what he really needed was a screwdriver. Finally they came free. Again using the tire iron, he dug a hole several inches deep in the sandy soil. He laid the plates in it and covered them.

He heard one of the countless streams that laced the Pines gurgling nearby. He forced his way through the underbrush to its edge. The water ran a clear brown. Cedar water, turned tea-colored by organic compounds leached from the soil. He knew that for all its strange color, it was some of the purest water to be found anywhere. He lowered himself and drank. He rinsed out an old Gatorade bottle he found in his gym bag and filled it.

The mosquitoes buzzed him in dark, undulating clouds. Grimacing, he reached into the water, drew out some mud, and plastered it all over his face and neck. Anything to keep the biting marauders at bay.

He collected some more mud and carefully coated all the chrome on his car. The last thing he needed was for some adventurous hiker to see a reflection and investigate.

He arranged the undergrowth carefully to camouflage the vehicle. Then he walked ten feet away and looked back. He could see nothing, and he knew it was there. For the first time since the accident, he felt a rush of genuine hope. No one would find the car for years, if ever.

Gym bag in hand, he began the long walk back to 206. He hadn't remembered how dark it got under the pines and oaks. And there were the noises of the night creatures. He found himself looking over his shoulder at each rustling of leaves, each crunch of ground cover. He knew there were timber rattlers in the Pines, slithering across the floor of pine needles and fallen oak leaves. Did they slither around at night? Some people said there were cougars too, though no one had seen any for years.

A blood-chilling scream ripped the air. He felt his heart drop to his shoes. The cougar? A woman being murdered? The Jersey Devil itself? He and McCoy and every other kid in the area had scared themselves silly with tales of midnight encounters with the famed Jersey Devil, meetings from which no one ever returned.

Reason told him it was only a screech owl, but still the hairs on his arms stood up straight and his heart, returned to his chest cavity, pounded wildly.

When he finally got to 206, he was hot, sweaty, and in a foul humor. He had several mosquito bites on the back of his neck, and one on his left calf in spite of the elastic on the leg of his pants. It was driving him nuts, but every time he bent to scratch, his jacket separated from his pants and the mosquitoes attacked him.

He began to thumb a ride. If he could get out to Route 30, he could get back to Seaside easily. He should be home in plenty of time to do all he needed to do tonight. He couldn't deviate from habit. It would raise too many questions.

He hadn't had to depend on the kindness of strangers for years. Now he remembered why: Lots of strangers weren't very kind. They zoomed by, kicking sand and cinders into his face. Finally a fat man in an old blue Ford pickup stopped.

"If you don't mind riding in the back, I'll take you."

If it weren't for the Doberman chained to the truck bed with a chain that reached to within four feet of where he was plastered against the tailgate, he might have enjoyed the ride in the soft night air. With relief he slid to the ground when they reached 30 and watched the dog and his fangs disappear.

It was Friday night, and everyone was heading down the shore. A carful of guys from South Philly picked him up within five minutes of sticking out his thumb. They shared their beer with him, and for once he didn't care that all of them, including the driver or maybe especially the driver, were crocked. He nursed one bottle and made believe he was looped. They were too far gone to recognize his playacting for what it was. The good thing was that they'd never remember him. In fact, with their fried brains they'd be lucky if they remembered their own names.

But he made it. Home, invincible, and still possessed of the finest reputation. He grinned as he showered quickly and slid into his classy clothes. He was beyond touching.

Eleven

CÉLIA REACHED OUT and grasped Abby's hand. "It's all right. Really. When God wants you to remember, you will."

Abby turned her hand over and gripped Celia's hard. "That's what I keep telling myself. But what if I never remember? What if he gets away?"

"I don't know." Celia looked at Karlee. "I've been so consumed with making certain that she's going to be all right and that Jess isn't too upset that I haven't given much thought to the driver. I guess I figured the police would catch him."

"But what if they don't? What if I could help and I can't?"

Celia didn't know how to answer the despair in Abby's voice. "It's not your fault, Abby. It's not. You had nothing to do with what happened."

"In theory I know that, but I still feel responsible."

"Yeah." Celia sighed. "Me too."

"You? But you were at work. I was there."

"Yeah, I was at work. A *good* mother would have been home taking care of her kids. A *good* mother would have known where they were at all times. A *good* mother would have seen to it that her little girl didn't try to cross a busy street like Central."

Abby sat up straight. "Are you saying that no

children of good mothers get hurt? That the only good mothers are ones who are at home all the time?"

Celia felt as if a basset hound with a sad, droopy face had turned pit bull and bitten her. The despairing woman of a minute ago had transmogrified into a forceful asker of hard questions.

"Well," Abby continued, "I was a mother who was home all the time, and my daughter died." She spoke like she dared Celia to challenge her mothering credentials.

Celia didn't. "How did she die?" she whispered.

Abby leaned her head back, staring at the ceiling. "Automobile accident." She must have heard Celia's exhalation of sympathy, but she kept her eyes on the crack that wandered aimlessly over Karlee's bed.

"No wonder today upset you so much." Celia knew that was stating the obvious, but she didn't know what else to say. "I mean, anyone would be upset, but you have all your own memories to deal with too."

Abby nodded. "I feel so foolish that I can't separate the two."

"Was it a hit-and-run like Karlee?"

"No, a man ran a stop sign because he was trying to dial on his cell phone and wasn't paying attention. He hit us going full speed."

Celia shivered at the image. "Were you driving?"

Abby shook her head. "My husband. He was killed too."

"Oh, Abby!" Celia couldn't imagine losing both husband and child at the same time. At least Eddie went years ago. She had only one tragedy to cope with today.

Abby shrugged. "It was three years ago. You'd think I'd be over it by now, wouldn't you?"

"No, I wouldn't." This was territory Celia was familiar with, and she could speak with authority here. "My husband left me three years ago. While I'm over it now, I know it takes a long, long time to come to terms with such deep hurts. Besides, I don't know that you ever get over the death of a child."

Celia watched Abby as tension sluiced away and her whole body relaxed. She turned to Celia with a grateful look. "Thank you. That's the second time you've said exactly the right thing."

Celia tucked a leg beneath her as she snuggled more deeply into her chair. "People have been giving you the old get-over-it line?"

"All the time. Especially my parents. It's not that they're insensitive. They just want me to get on with my life."

"Would that it were that easy."

The women looked at each other with perfect understanding.

Celia rested her head on the back of her chair. It was her turn to study the crack in the ceiling. "When Eddie left us, he looked right at me. 'Let me be honest here, Celia,' he said. 'I don't love you. I don't think I ever did. I don't even like you, and I don't care what happens to you. If you can find me, you can try to make them make me pay child support, but I don't think you'll find me.' And he walked out the door." She glanced at Abby to deliver the kicker. "It was Christmas Eve."

Abby looked properly, satisfyingly aghast. "So what did you do?"

"Cried all night."

"Just one night?"

"Well, the next day being Christmas, I had to act excited for Jess. Karlee was too little to know what was going on. After Christmas, then I cried a bunch more. Not over Eddie, you understand. It was almost a relief that he had gone, even though his farewell speech devastated me. I would have stayed in our marriage because I believe that's what the Bible asks of us, but it would have been strictly obedience to God that kept me there, not love for my husband. He had long ago killed any affection I felt. I cried because I was terrified."

"I don't blame you, alone with two little girls to support. When Sam died, at least I had insurance money."

Insurance money. The luxury of it made Celia's mouth water. "I married right out of high school with hormones calling the shots. I thought Eddie was wonderful." She snorted. "I had the brains of a nit."

"Come on. Don't be so hard on yourself."

Celia smiled. This Abby was a nice person. She was a good listener too. Celia found herself saying things she'd never said to anyone. It must be a combination of late night, the darkened room, and relief that today hadn't ended in tragedy.

"Once we were married, Eddie decided he didn't want the responsibility or the constraint of a wife."

"A little late to come to that conclusion," Abby said dryly.

"Tell me about it. Jess came along within the first year, and he hated having a kid. He went out every night with the guys, partying, drinking, living it up like he was single. When Karlee was born, it was too much for him. By then he'd disappear for weeks at a time, and I knew it wasn't the guys keeping him company anymore. Then he disappeared period." .

"You don't know where he is?"

"I have no idea." *And I don't want to.*

Abby looked at the sleeping girls, then back at Celia. "How have you managed?"

"The year after he left, I waitressed nights. The lady next door baby-sat. By that I mean she let the girls sleep in her spare room, charging me an exorbitant amount for the convenience." She shrugged. "At least I was home when they were awake."

"When did you sleep?"

"I didn't. That's why I came to the conclusion that something had to give."

"I had a point like that, too."

"When you couldn't sleep?"

"When I knew something had to give."

Celia waited for clarification, but none came. "What'd you do?"

"Nothing, at least not right away." Abby looked uncomfortable, embarrassed. "I used to be a terrible wimp."

Celia laughed. She couldn't help it. That this classy looking lady with the slim crossed legs and elegantly expensive boiled wool jacket had ever been anything but aware and in charge was hard to imagine.

Abby gave a sad smile. "It's true. I allowed myself to be manipulated for years, and I didn't even realize it."

So, Celia conceded, maybe looks could be deceiving. Hadn't she once thought Eddie the handsomest thing on earth? "So what happened?"

Abby took a deep breath, almost like she was getting the courage to confess to something horrendous. "I'm an only child, and I was the good girl, the kind all parents want. I enjoyed being good, pleasing my parents. I loved them. I still do."

"But?" Celia prompted.

Abby grimaced. "It's embarrassing."

"And my story's not? Hormones calling life's most important choice except Jesus? Wandering husband? Brains seriously lacking?"

Abby shifted, rubbing her right thigh. "I commuted to college, never leaving my pink-and-white bedroom. I worked for my father's firm in the summers. I rode to work with him. At college I met Sam, a handsome, very assured guy who seemed to be fascinated with me. I learned too late that it wasn't *me*; it was my pliable nature. He loved to control me. When I started to develop a mind of my own at about twenty-four, he didn't like it one bit." She looked disgusted at herself. "Twenty-four. Talk about a late bloomer."

"What in the world did you do that upset him?" Somehow Celia couldn't see this sweet woman doing anything rebellious.

"I decided I wanted to go back to college for a master's in library science."

Celia waited for more, but Abby seemed finished. "That's it?"

Abby nodded. "That's it. That's the whole dirty truth. I wanted to go back to school."

Celia couldn't help it. She laughed again. "Oh, you rebel, you."

"After sweet little Abby for all those years, it must have seemed that way to Sam. He was undoubtedly waiting for me to come out dressed all in black with piercings all over my body and hair a different color every day."

"Why didn't he want you to get your degree?"

"He wouldn't be there on campus this time, guiding my every step, my every thought. I'd be all by myself, thinking by myself."

"Dangerous, dangerous."

"Apparently he thought so. I, on the other hand, found it painful. When you realize your husband loves you conditionally, it hurts."

Celia snorted. "Try when he doesn't love you at all."

Abby shifted again, tucking her left leg under her. "So what did you do? If you didn't feel you could keep on waitressing, what?"

"I saw an ad on TV for a school for massage therapy."

Abby sat up straight, all attention. "You're a massage therapist?"

"Yeah. Why?" *Don't tell me you're one of those who think we all work in seedy massage parlors with clients who come in with bags over their heads to prevent recognition.*

"I need to find one."

Relief rolled through Celia. Abby wasn't like Aunt Bernice.

"I'm new in town, so I need to locate a massage therapist to keep my hip and leg from getting too tight. If they cramp, then my back acts up, then my neck. You know the drill, I'm sure." Abby rubbed her hand up and down her right hip and thigh.

"I'd love to help you. What's wrong with your hip? Congenital problem?"

"From the accident. Our car was pushed into the tractor-trailer waiting at the stop sign on the other side of the street. I was sitting in the passenger side and got pinned against the truck. My hip was crushed."

Now that she thought about it, Celia realized that Abby had limped when she walked across the room. "Call Pinky at Seaside Spa tomorrow, and we'll set you up with an appointment."

Abby nodded. "I'll ask for you."

Celia grinned. "What if I'm no good?"

"Somehow I doubt that."

"I am good. I graduated at the top of my class." She couldn't keep the pride out of her voice.

"How did you manage to keep working, care for the girls, and go to school all at once?"

Celia rubbed her forehead. Even thinking about the past year could give her a migraine. "We moved in with Great-aunt Bernice."

"From your reaction, I take it we're talking last resort?"

"Aunt Bernice is—difficult, to put it kindly. She didn't want us with her, though Poor Uncle Walter didn't seem to mind."

"*Poor* Uncle Walter?"

Celia brushed a piece of blanket fluff off her shirt. "Everyone puts the *poor* in front of his name. It's Poor Walter like it's Mary Lou or Billy Bob. After all, he's lived with Aunt Bernice for almost forty years." Celia sighed. "They're just about the only relatives I have and are definitely the only ones with money. I didn't know where else to turn. I was scared to death when I asked if we could live there for a year while I went to school. 'Well, girl,' Aunt Bernice said to me, 'I don't know about helping a woman who chased away her husband.'"

Abby looked horrified. "She didn't actually say that!"

"Oh, yes she did. 'I'm a good, God-fearing Christian, and I'm not sure I want you and those little girls in my house.'" Celia raised an eyebrow. "It was always *my* house, never *ours,* though Poor Uncle Walter paid all the bills."

"What did he do for a living?"

"He was a mailman, the kind who walks his territory every day with a huge pack of mail hanging from his shoulder. But at night he played the stocks and securities markets on the Internet. He might be a Milquetoast, but he's a whiz at investing."

"So Poor Uncle Walter isn't so poor after all."

Celia gave a puff of frustrated laughter. "Big house. Beautiful furniture and clothes, but it wasn't until I said that I'd work weekends and give her all I earned that she said we could stay. All I wanted to do was learn a way to care for my girls without hovering at poverty level for the rest of my life." She mimicked Aunt Bernice right down to the toss of her head. "'And massaging people's naked bodies is the way to do that?'"

Abby appeared fascinated with her story, so Celia continued. "I told her I didn't want handouts. I wanted to be responsible the way God wants me to be. Responsible. That was the word that did the trick. Or maybe it was mentioning God. For nine interminable months, the girls and I lived in Aunt Bernice and Poor Uncle Walter's museum, taking care not to touch anything or to express an independent idea. Aunt Bernice never ceased complaining about the great 'upsetment' they were to her. Leaving Aunt Bernice's forever was almost as sweet as graduating at the top of my class and proving to Eddie in absentia that I was smart and capable."

Celia giggled suddenly. "Poor Uncle Walter took advantage of graduation to prove he wasn't quite the Milquetoast I thought he was. He slipped me an envelope graduation night. 'Hardship pay,' he called it. The envelope contained a cashier's check for five thousand dollars."

Abby laughed. "I think I like Poor Uncle Walter."

"Everybody does, though they pity him more."

Both women fell silent for a minute, a comfortable silence that signified an ease with each other. Celia was filled with hope. Maybe Abby would be the friend she was longing for.

Abby rose and limped to the bed. She straightened the already straight sheet and blanket covering the girls. Celia had to smile at her care of the girls, almost like they were hers.

"So," Abby asked as she took her seat, "do you like massage therapy? Was it worth the terrible year?"

"I can't believe how much I love it. I'm helping people, making them feel better. Pinky—that's my boss at Seaside Spa—she's great too."

"How long have you been there?"

"Two months. I just hope she understands about tomorrow."

"What happens tomorrow?"

"I can't let the girls go back to the same baby-sitter, not after today. So I'll have to stay with them." She smiled at her daughters' sleeping forms. "Besides, I'll probably have to take Karlee home."

"Is there any reason why I can't watch the girls?" Abby asked.

"What?" Celia looked at the woman she'd met less than an hour ago.

"I'd like to watch them. I like kids. I'm a children's librarian."

Lord, is she an answer to my prayer, or would I be foolish to trust her? I know I like her, and I appreciate her coming to check on Karlee. But let her have the girls for the day? "I don't know."

"You'd be doing me a favor." Abby pressed her argument. "It would help relieve my guilt, and it would be like having Maddie back for a day."

A knock on the door saved Celia from having to give an answer before she had time to think. "Come in." She jumped to her feet as a man in a white jacket with a stethoscope sticking out of one pocket walked in. The doctor had arrived.

"Hello, Ms. Fitzmeyer. How are you this evening—or should I say tonight?"

Celia stepped forward, hand extended. "Dr. Schofield. I'm so glad to see you." When had doctors gotten to be so handsome? Her pediatrician when she was a kid was a wizened old man who looked like the trolls in the books at school and who had hair growing out of his nose and ears. He was nice enough, a very good doctor, but handsome? Never. Sean Schofield belonged on the cover of *GQ*.

"I'm sorry I've been so late in getting to speak with you." His smile was charming. "It's been a long day."

"Tell me about it." Celia smiled back.

Dr. Schofield moved to the bed and looked at the sleeping girls. He glanced up, flashing his killer grin at Celia again. "You have beautiful daughters."

He couldn't have said anything to please her more, and she was certain he knew it. Still it was wonderful to hear. She watched as he quickly and efficiently checked Karlee without waking her, though the little girl made a terrible face when he checked her eyes with his little flashlight.

"She looks fine." He straightened, sticking his flashlight back in his pocket. "Chest's clear and pupils are equal and reactive. The brush burns and bruises look terrible and will hurt her for a while, but they aren't serious. I checked the films of her arm. The break isn't complicated and should heal quickly." He looked at the sleeping child again. "She's a lucky pup. If nothing unforeseen happens, she can go home tomorrow morning. The paperwork should be finished about nine."

Celia let out the breath she'd been holding. "I was certain you were going to tell me some terrible medical something that everyone else had been keeping from me."

Dr. Schofield laughed, flashing beautiful white teeth. He made certain he included Abby in the smile as he started toward the door. "No such thing. Karlee's in very good shape."

Thank You, God. "Do we come to your office about her arm, or do we go to the orthopedist?"

"The instructions will be with her release papers. You just sign on the dotted line tomorrow, and Karlee's all yours."

Decision time. Celia's stomach churned. She glanced at Abby, who looked solid and trustworthy. She was kind and compassionate and understanding. Celia knew that from their conversation. She was gentle with the girls. She had been a mom, and she was a children's librarian. The woman knew kids.

But the fact remained that she didn't know Abby. Not really.

Then she thought of Pinky's reaction to her missing the busiest day of the week with no forewarning. She'd missed a half day three weeks ago when the baby-sitter had a doctor's appointment. Pinky hadn't been very happy, and she knew in advance then.

Celia had ten clients scheduled—three half hours and seven hour-long massages. How would Pinky ever find someone to cover for her? Where would she find someone? It would all be lost income. Celia could deal with it even if it meant taking some of Poor Uncle Walter's nest egg, tucked safely away in a money market that he had recommended. But what about Pinky? The spa was a relatively new business venture, and Celia knew her boss was nowhere near being financially secure. Pinky was a single mom, but her kids were teenagers, able to fend for themselves when necessary. Would she remember what it was like to have babies? To have nowhere to turn? Celia caught her breath at the thought of losing this job she so desperately needed. And if she lost her medical coverage, how would she ever pay for Karlee's medical expenses?

Oh, God! She took a deep breath. *I'm trusting You, Father, to make this be all right. Besides, I don't know what else to do.*

"I won't be picking her up tomorrow," Celia said. "My friend Abby will be getting her because I have to work."

Dr. Schofield smiled at Abby but spoke to Celia. "It's a good thing you mentioned that. Without your prior written approval, we wouldn't release Karlee to anyone but you."

"Then let's sign those papers," Abby said, suddenly looking very tired. "It's been a hard day."

Dr. Schofield nodded, his expression full of understanding. "I know what you mean."

"Abby saw Karlee's accident," Celia explained.

Dr. Schofield stopped in his tracks. "What?"

"Now if I could only remember what I saw." Abby gave a wry smile.

Dr. Schofield looked confused.

"Hysterical amnesia," Abby explained. "That's what they called it."

The doctor cleared his throat. "Are you feeling well enough to watch little Karlee tomorrow?"

"Oh, I feel fine. No injuries or anything. Just a blank spot in my memory that I pray fills in quickly."

At the nurses' station, Celia was given the proper papers to sign to authorize Abby's getting Karlee. She signed with a flourish.

"If there is any trouble with Karlee tomorrow, don't hesitate to call me," Dr. Schofield told Abby. "I don't want you having any problems, especially if I can fix them for you."

Celia watched with interest as he turned the full power of his personality on to Abby, who flushed under the blaze of his smile. He nodded good night and disappeared into another room. Celia turned to Abby.

"I can't thank you enough for what you're doing."

"It's my pleasure, believe me. Now I think I need to go home and get some sleep if I'm to have two beautiful girls for guests tomorrow."

Celia walked slowly back to Karlee's room. Once again God had provided. Hadn't He?

Twelve

$\mathcal{M}$ARSH THREW HIS arm across his eyes and groaned. Where was she, for heaven's sake? Where did a woman new to town drive off to in the middle of the night? Had the day been so traumatic that she'd given up? Had she driven all the way back to Scranton? Somehow he doubted that.

He punched his pillow and rotated his shoulders, trying to find a comfortable position. He groaned again. Not only had the blinking colon of the readout on his bedside clock radio kept him awake for hours, but concern about Abby had given him a king-sized headache. It couldn't have hurt more if a pair of pileated woodpeckers had been thonk-thonking against his skull. His pupils were dry and gritty, and it felt like little gremlins with pitchforks were poking them. His stomach gurgled in displeasure at all the aspirin he'd already taken. Another and he'd overdose, he was certain, but at least he'd stop worrying about her.

No. She hadn't gone home to Scranton. No matter how many other things she might be, she wasn't—he sputtered as he tried to come up with the right words; that's what came of being a writer: you edited even your own thoughts—she wasn't lacking in courage. Feisty, determined, spunky little creatures like her didn't run home to Mama and Papa, not when the whole point of being here was to get away from them.

So where had she gone? He tossed and turned and worried, then tossed and turned and lectured himself about the foolishness of worrying. She was an adult. She was allowed to go wherever she wanted. She could take care of herself.

Right. If he believed that, he'd be sound asleep.

It was two o'clock in the morning when she finally pulled into the driveway. 2:03 to be exact, if the fluorescent digital readout on his radio was correct. 2:03! He rolled to a sitting position on the edge of the bed, then staggered upright. He glared at Fargo, sprawled over two-thirds of the bed, snoring softly.

"How can you sleep, you big idiot?" He reached over, thwacking him gently on his rump. "We've got trouble on our hands."

Fargo lifted his head and turned sad eyes on Marsh, his disappointment in his master for awakening him most obvious.

"Give me a break, you mutt. That was just a love tap. Now come on. We've got to make sure she's okay."

Fargo looked at him a minute longer, blinked, yawned, and collapsed back on the bed. He stretched his huge body another couple of feet, now occupying three-quarters of the mattress. In nanoseconds his soft snore competed with the hum of Abby's motor. Marsh knew that when he returned, the entire bed would be filled with somnolent rottweiler.

With a final disgusted look at Fargo, Marsh stumbled across the room and grabbed his jeans. As he stuffed his legs in them, he muttered several uncomplimentary things about *her* under his breath. How had he ever gotten stuck with such a renter?

A children's librarian. He pushed his feet into his Top-Siders. What could be safer than a children's librarian? He pulled a T-shirt over his head. He remembered how pleased he'd been when he saw her occupation on the rental agreement. After all, everyone knew that children's librarians were quiet, timid women who spoke in whispers, baked lots of brownies, smiled a lot, and left their landlords in peace.

Instead, he had gotten stuck with a skinny, quirky, opinionated cat lover who cited obscure women in history to justify her every move and who in one day had destroyed his tranquility.

Surely, Lord, I haven't been wicked enough to deserve her!

Her car's motor died. He pictured her pulling her key from the ignition. Now she would need him. As he stomped outside to play her knight in shining armor, he could think of only one reason for a single woman to be coming home at two in the morning. He knew too that if she had been partying at the clubs on the mainland and had had too much to drink, she'd never make it up those steps unassisted.

Why he felt uncomfortable about letting her fall down said stairs, breaking her pretty little neck in the process, he wasn't sure. He just knew he didn't want her blood on his hands. Nor did he want a lawsuit if all she did was break her legs.

But he knew one thing for certain: He wasn't going to carry her up those stairs all summer. Not by a long shot. He'd install one of those little seats that ran along the railing like a miniature ski lift first. Rather that expense than the ruination of his back, not that she weighed enough to ruin his back. It was the principle of the thing.

He rubbed his stomach as he stood in the shadows of his porch. The flounder stuffed with crabmeat he'd had for dinner was still swimming vigorously around in his belly. What he wouldn't give for a giant roll of Tums. He sighed, rubbing a temple with one hand and his midriff with the other. He didn't think that even his father had ever peeved him as much in so short a time as she did, and that was saying something.

She was such a contradictory package. On one hand she had needed his help big-time after the hit-and-run, when she'd understandably fallen apart. On the other she was determined to be independent at almost any cost, taking after all those historical ladies who did whatever it was that they did. If she could remember all those crazy women, keep their dates and activities straight, he bet she'd even memorized all the millions of little categories in the Dewey decimal system.

He sighed and watched her climb out of her car. Those first couple of steps when she didn't know he was watching would tell him a lot. Of course with her bad hip she looked tipsy even when she was as sober as the proverbial judge.

When she stood, the line of her back and the slump in her shoulders, silhouetted by the streetlight, screamed fatigue. She took a couple of steps, her limp more pronounced than he'd seen all day, even after the rescue of the kid next door. He squelched the unexpected burst of sympathy. It was her own fault for staying out half the night.

He stepped out of the shadows and stood, hands on his hips.

She gave a little scream and grabbed her chest.

"It's me," he said, irritated at himself for scaring her and at her for being scared. He dropped his hands to his side so he wouldn't loom.

She sagged against her car. "Marsh, you idiot. You scared me to death! My heart will never be the same."

He sniffed the air. He couldn't smell any alcohol. He studied her eyes. She had beautiful eyes, black-eyed Susan eyes that a man could get lost in. Not that he was likely to, but he bet other guys did. Probably her dead husband did, or if he didn't, he should have. Of course her eyes probably hadn't shot sparks like little yellow petals at the husband. Marsh sighed. Those angry flashes were just for him.

Whoopee. How fortunate he was.

Forget black-eyed Susans, man. Think bloodshot.

He blinked to clear his head, studying her carefully. Her eyes looked fine, what he could see of them in the limited glow of the light above the doorway. Still, you never knew. "Are you all right?"

"Of course I'm not all right! You scared me to death."

"You already said that," he complained.

"Don't ever do that to me again! Do you hear me?" Full of outrage, she swung at him, catching him in the chest with the flat of her hand. "What if I had a weak heart? You could kill a person that way."

He rubbed at the spot where her hand had connected. It stung. "I heard you go out at eleven. It's now after two. I thought maybe you ran into a problem."

She narrowed her eyes at him just like that malevolent cat of hers might. "Because you thought me incompetent, you waited up for me?"

"I don't think you incompetent."

"You're as bad as my parents!"

"I am not." He was insulted. "I was just worried."

That stopped her for all of ten seconds. "Do you worry like this about all your renters?"

"I never had a renter before."

"Oh." She studied him long enough to make him twitch. "I know. A girlfriend you didn't trust."

"What?" He bristled. "You are not my girlfriend."

Her chin came up. "A fact for which we both are grateful, I'm sure. Now what was her name?"

He compressed his lips, feeling like a child who refused to open up for his spinach.

"Come on. Who was the sweetheart who got away? Or did you give her the boot?"

When he said nothing, she began guessing, each name more outlandish than the last. "Imogene? Eugenia? Edwina? Ermentrude? Oh, dear, I'm stuck on e-names. How about Lorelei? Pollyanna? Jadwiga? Lantana?"

"Almost," he muttered and wanted to kick himself.

"Lantana?" She peered at him. "That's a flower."

"Lane. Her name was Lane." He bit out each word.

"Old money," she guessed. "That's an old money name."

"Lane is not a topic open for discussion." He thought his voice was the epitome of cool, but she heard something anyway. He could see it in the way she stilled, then studied him without the irritation she'd had earlier. Then her mouth gave a slight hitch upward. Somehow he knew he was in for it.

"Well, whatever your motivation, I think you should know that I spent the evening with a friend." She put special emphasis on *friend*.

A friend? What friend? Where had the friend come from? He didn't like the sound of this at all. "You don't have any friends."

Her head jerked.

"In Seaside, I mean. None but me."

She yawned, covering her mouth gracefully and ostentatiously with her hand. "That's what you think."

That's what he knew. Otherwise, he wouldn't have had to abandon Craig and Marguerite and run to the hospital to bail her out earlier in the day. No, make that earlier yesterday.

She gave a little hoity-toity sniff. "You'd better go back to bed, Dr. Winslow." She moved past him and grabbed the banister. "My company arrives very early in the morning."

"Company?" Company meant noise, people, lack of privacy. He'd wanted to get another chapter done before Rick showed on

Sunday. He couldn't wait for Craig to give Marguerite her comeuppance. Craig had to bring Snelling down too, but it was Marguerite's chastisement that captured Marsh's imagination. He was practically salivating in anticipation of Craig's wit and superiority. "You can't have company, especially early company."

She glanced at him over her shoulder. "Why? Because I don't have friends?" She took the first step, then turned to smile at him like a princess condescending to acknowledge a commoner. "Tomorrow I shall be Katie Luther and seat vast numbers around my table. The fact that feisty old Martin is missing may slow us down a bit, but I shall encourage loud conversation on issues of great theological import and the boisterous exchange of opinion, political and otherwise. Of course, we shall do our best not to disturb you or your beauty rest," she said insincerely, "but I make no promises."

She gave a little royal wave, then turned away.

He watched her ascend the steps, uncertain whether he wanted to strangle her for complicating what was supposed to be a calm, restful, and productive summer or applaud her for her spunk. He'd never met anyone like her. When he heard her door shut, he dragged himself back to his bed, shoved Fargo onto the floor where he belonged, and collapsed into his pillow.

It seemed he'd just fallen asleep when he heard a little voice right outside his bedroom window yell, "Mrs. Patterson! I'm Jess. I'm here, and we can get Karlee anytime after nine-thirty."

Thirteen

Abby STOOD WITH her arm about Jess's shoulders as they waved good-bye to Celia.

"I'm glad you've come to spend the day with me," she told the girl.

Jess looked uncertain. Abby knew it must be hard for her to be left with a stranger. What had seemed fine when her mother was telling her about it must seem much less exciting now that her mother was gone.

Abby turned from the landing, drawing the girl with her. "You'll get to meet my parents. They're coming later this morning."

Jess blinked. Abby could almost hear her thinking, "You have parents? But you're old."

"You can think of them as grandparents for a day." Abby smiled. "They like little girls. After all, I was a little girl once myself, and they liked me."

Jess giggled at that absurd picture.

Abby nodded. "Hard to believe, isn't it? But if you ask my father what I used to look like, he'll show you the picture of me as a chubby little girl that he still carries in his wallet."

"He still has a picture of you as a little girl?"

"A very little girl with a potbelly out to here." Abby held her hand as far from her body as she could. "Silly of him, isn't it?" It also indicated how he still perceived her today. "Want a doughnut and some hot chocolate?" Abby turned toward the kitchen.

"My dad doesn't carry my picture. He doesn't even have one."

The soft words pierced Abby. She knew for a fact that being smothered was bad, but there was no question: being deserted was worse. She turned and wrapped her arms about Jess. "Oh, baby, if he doesn't carry your picture, he's not too smart. Anybody'd be proud to carry your picture. Lots of your pictures. You're smart and pretty and nice." She kissed Jess's forehead.

Jess gave a tentative smile. "Do you really have hot chocolate?"

Abby nodded. "The kind with little marshmallows. I also have doughnuts with chocolate glaze and sprinkles so we can drip all over ourselves or powdered sugar so we can blow tiny clouds."

They had just seated themselves at the glass-topped table on the porch when doors slammed in the driveway.

"Oh, Len," a soft voice cried. "Look at those stairs!"

Abby grimaced. The parents. Already. They must have left home at the crack of dawn. Before the crack of dawn. It was only—she glanced into the kitchen—eight-thirty now. She'd hoped for a couple more hours of freedom.

"Maybe she's on the first floor," her father said. Abby heard him rap on the door below. She took a bite of her chocolate iced doughnut. She knew she should go to the top of the stairs and greet her parents, but she couldn't resist enjoying her last few breaths of liberty. Besides, she wanted to see what would happen when Marsh answered. Maybe he'd chase Mom and Dad away. She smiled to herself, then felt a wash of shame. What a terrible thought.

"How sharper than a serpent's tooth it is to have a thankless child! Away, away!" she muttered as she quoted Shakespeare's *King Lear*.

"What?" said Jess around a bite of powdered sugar doughnut. A little cloud puffed out, making her giggle.

"Nothing, sweetie. I was just muttering under my breath in a very unladylike, impolite manner."

She heard Dad rap on Marsh's door again, more heavy-handed this time.

The door opened. "Yeah?" a sleepy and slightly querulous Marsh asked. Well, she'd warned him company was coming early.

Abby still couldn't believe he had been waiting for her when she came home last night. After she got over the scare he gave her when he stepped out of the shadows like some giant assailant, she was touched that he had worried. Not that she let him know, of course.

When she tried to assess why she appreciated his worry and squirmed under that of her parents, she decided it was his acerbic attitude. He got her dander up just as her folks did, but instead of making her feel guilty like they did, his ire gave her the freedom to fight back. Every time she sassed him or challenged him, she felt her spirit unfurling a bit more, like a tightly wound spool of multi-hued ribbon freed from its constraint. Curls of vibrantly colored grosgrain and satin exploded, filling her with golden-and-ruby rushes of wonder and sapphire-and-emerald vistas of hope.

She'd never tell him, but he was her slightly grumpy, very handsome liberator. In his own special, ever so querulous way, he was God's gift.

"Abby Patterson?" her father asked the sleepy Marsh, his clipped voice sharp.

"Upstairs," Marsh growled.

"Thanks," Dad answered.

"The stairs," Mom gasped again. "They are hers."

"She does quite well with them." Marsh's sleep-deepened voice floated up to her, defending her. She felt like hugging herself. He had listened to what she'd told him last night at dinner. He had even understood! "She's a female Sir Edmund Hillary, climbing her own private Mount Everest."

She heard her father's surprised, "What?"

"Of course I realize that the sex is wrong and the example too contemporary for her encyclopedia of women eccentrics, but it works for me. And speaking of her," he continued, his you-woke-me-out-of-a-sound-sleep grouchiness in full flower, "I think she's cantankerous, opinionated, and too independent for her own good. She's also beautiful, quirky, and gives me a headache. But then I'm sure you've been experiencing that tightness above the left eye for many years." With that pronouncement, he shut his door.

She grinned. He might be a grousing wretch, but he knew how to mete out a compliment. He thought she was beautiful! And independent!

It appeared that he'd robbed her parents of their powers of speech. The silence from below was absolute. Never had anyone told them such outlandish things about their sweet, oh-so-cooperative darling. Maybe, just maybe, they'd see her through his eyes and give her credit for being a grown-up. Maybe the weekend wouldn't be one long how-could-you-Abby-have-you-lost-your-mind session.

Oh, Lord, please. She looked at the wide-eyed Jess and winked.

She'd hoped too soon.

"Cantankerous? Our sweet Abby?" Dad's voice reflected his outrage at the attack on his baby.

"Well, I never!" sputtered Mom. "Opinionated? Quirky? Independent?"

"Beautiful," Dad said. It sounded like he'd been told she was dying, not that she was attractive.

She sighed and got to her feet. She walked ever so quietly over to the landing and peeked down. Mom and Dad stood, faces red with anger, midway between Marsh's door and the stairs.

"She must move at once," Mom said. "She simply cannot stay in a house with an uncouth man like that."

"She needs to come home," Dad said. "He's dangerous."

Abby closed her eyes in a combination of frustration and prayer. *Lord, what am I to do with them?*

Her father glanced up the stairs and saw her. Immediately his frown gave way to a wide smile. "There she is! Hello, baby." He rushed up the steps to gather her into a bear hug.

Mom followed more sedately, but her pleasure in seeing Abby was every bit as real. "I missed you," she whispered as she hugged Abby. "I felt so empty without you around."

Oh, Lord, help! Abby pulled away as soon as she could and turned, all business, toward the sliding glass doors.

"Let me show you my home." She used the word *home* on purpose. "But first let me introduce my new friend Jess." She walked to Jess, stood behind her, and placed a hand on each shoulder. Jess smiled hesitantly.

"Why, what a lovely new friend," Dad said. "How do you do, Jess?" He held out his hand for her to shake. Awkwardly Jess offered hers back.

"Hello, Jess." Mom smiled with genuine warmth. "I see Abby is sharing her favorite breakfast with you."

Jess looked at the half-eaten doughnuts and empty cups. "I love it too."

"What's not to like?" Dad turned to Abby. "Have any more?"

Assuming he meant doughnuts, not kids, Abby nodded.

"Oh, let me get them," Mom said. "Just point me to the kitchen. I'll make a carafe of coffee while I'm at it. You know how your father loves his coffee."

Was there censure in that comment about the lack of coffee ready at the moment? One of the more irritating things about Mom was her ability to say something that could be construed as critical. Abby never knew whether she was being chastised or merely hearing a meaningless comment. The uncertainty drove her crazy.

"Have a seat, Mom." Abby took Jess's hand. "We'll serve you. You're our company."

"Pshaw," said Dad with a great warm smile. He was the only man Abby knew who actually said pshaw. "We're family. Let Mom be Mom, just to keep her happy."

"No," Abby said, voice clear and a shade too loud. "I will serve you. You are my guests. Sit. Watch the ocean."

As she turned to walk into the apartment, she saw her parents exchange one of their patented looks. She squared her shoulders. "Jess, bring our cups so we can refill them, okay?"

When her mother reached for the cups, Abby stopped. "Jess?"

She watched her mother pull back her hands. Then she turned and marched into the kitchen, followed by Jess. Already the weekend was too long, and they'd been here all of five minutes. How would she survive until late Sunday afternoon?

Instant guilt grabbed her by the throat. An ungrateful child. That's what she was. They had loved her back to life after the accident. They had put their personal lives on hold for her. Her mother had quit her job as an administrative assistant at the hospital to stay home with her.

But, Lord, that was then. This is now!

She and Jess were just returning to the porch, fresh mugs of hot chocolate and the box of doughnuts in hand, when there was a noisome clatter on the steps. Walker and Jordan exploded from the stairwell onto the porch.

"Hey, Mrs. Patterson," Jordan yelled. She could have been

down at the ocean's edge with the waves roaring in her ears, and she'd have heard him. She smiled to herself as she thought of Marsh. She hoped he had given up the idea of sleeping in.

"I beat you!" Jordan turned to Walker and stuck out his tongue, then danced out of reach. "We saw you from our house." He pointed to the numberless windows making up the perimeter of his home. "So we decided to come for a visit."

"You only beat me 'cause I let you!" Walker shoved his little brother in the back.

Jordan staggered but kept moving, arriving at the glass-topped table at the same time as the doughnuts. "Wow!"

Abby grinned. "Want one?"

"And some hot chocolate like you got?" He peered into Jess's mug. "Look, Walker. Little marshmallows."

"Do you want some too, Walker?"

He nodded, then sidled up to Abby. "Who's she?" He was staring at Jess who was taking doughnuts from the box and putting them on the serving dish. Her concentration was intense, her forehead furrowed, but her long brown hair shone in the sunshine and her red shirt put blooms in her cheeks.

"That's Jess. She's here for the day."

Walker nodded. "She's pretty." He followed Jess into the house as she went to get more napkins at Abby's request.

"I think the boy is smitten," Abby said.

"What's smitten?" Jordan asked. No one answered.

"Who are all these children, and how do you know them?" Mom asked. "You've only been here one day."

"There's another coming in an hour or two," Abby announced, smiling.

"We live next door." A snowfall of powdered sugar erupted from Jordan's mouth. He pointed at Abby. "She saved Walker's life."

"What?" Mom and Dad turned to Abby, horror on both their faces.

"He would have drowned." Jordan sipped his hot chocolate. "I told him not to go in."

"Napkins." Abby rushed inside. "Where are the napkins, Jess? Is the coffee ready yet?" The last thing she wanted was to discuss her plunge into the sea. In the kitchen she found Jess looking warily at Walker.

"Who's he?" she whispered, moving close to Abby. "He stares."

Abby leaned down. "He's Walker, and he lives next door. He likes you, I think."

Jess made a face. "He's a boy."

Abby nodded. "Too true."

Jess leaned in. "Girls rule; boys drool."

Walker stiffened. "I heard that."

Jess grinned. "Good." Napkins in hand, she sailed past him out to the porch.

"Here, Walker." Abby handed him two clean mugs. "Carry these to the table please. Give one to my mom and one to my dad."

Walker nodded, eyes still on Jess. In a daze he walked to the porch, Abby following with the carafe of coffee.

A shrill voice cut the air. "Walker! Jordan! Where are you two? Get your little selves back in here this moment!"

Jordan raced to the side of the porch and waved his doughnut. "Hey, Mom, we're up here. Mrs. Patterson's giving us breakfast."

"What? Were you begging again? You think we don't have cereal?"

"Doughnuts and hot chocolate's better."

"Like she wants you two bothering her. Get down here!"

Abby winced at the strident tone. She walked to Jordan and smiled down at his mother. She had the Sophia Loren look with lots of black hair, a creamy complexion, and a figure to die for. She'd be a very pretty woman if she didn't look so unhappy. "Come join us. We're just having doughnuts and coffee or hot chocolate. There's plenty to go around."

Her anger undercut by Abby's invitation, the boys' mother seemed unsure how to act. "Oh. Okay, I guess." She looked over her shoulder at the upstairs windows of her spectacular house. Abby looked too. The vague outline of a man could be seen through the darkened glass of one of the oversized windows. He appeared to be watching the boys' mother.

"Bring your husband," Abby invited before she remembered that Walker had said his mother and father were separated.

"Are you kidding? I don't go nowhere with him." She flounced over to Abby's. Flounced. Abby watched, fascinated. She'd never seen anyone flounce before. Shoulders and hips undulated at an alarming rate. Whiplash seemed imminent. Then, as she reached the bottom of the steps, she glanced at the upper windows again. When she was certain she was being watched, she tossed her head with disdain.

Like Mary Tudor haughtily sending Lady Jane Grey to the Tower and the ax, Abby thought. *Whoever he is, he's dead.*

"I'm Vivienne deMarco," she announced when she reached the porch, holding out a hand with nails long enough to poke out an eye.

"Well, Vivian, I'm pleased—"

"No. Not Vivian. Vivienne."

Abby listened to the heavy accent on the last syllable and nodded. "Have a doughnut."

Vivienne shuddered, her hands moving to caress her hips. "Thank you, no. Cooked in fat."

Abby nodded, thinking of the one she'd already eaten and the one she intended to eat. "A cup of coffee then?"

"No sugar or cream. You got any Equal?"

Abby shook her head. "Sorry."

"I have some," Mom said, diving into her huge purse. In a few moments she resurfaced, triumphant, a blue packet in her hand. Vivienne smiled her thanks as she ripped the package open and tipped it into her mug, her fuchsia fingernails flashing in the sunshine.

Breakfast went well in spite of the disparate collection of participants. Still, Abby was relieved when the clock showed nine-thirty. "Jess and I have to go to the hospital to get Karlee."

"What hospital?" Mom looked alarmed, though Abby wasn't certain whether at the idea that Abby knew about the local hospital after only one day in town, or that Vivienne was eyeing Dad with a predatory hunger. Dad, to his credit, seemed oblivious.

Jess jumped up to go with Abby. "He's still staring," she whispered, glancing over her shoulder at Walker to be certain she was reporting accurately. She was.

"He still likes you," Abby whispered back.

"Yuk. Maybe he'll be gone by the time we get back."

"Maybe."

The two walked to the car. As they climbed in, Abby glanced

next door. The deMarcos' new house was built so that the first floor of living area was where a second floor would normally be. The ground floor was nonexistent. Instead the space held several pilings driven deep into the sand to support the house. The idea was to give room for a storm surge to wash right through without damaging or destroying the house. In the great storm of 1962, this end of the island had been hard hit by such a surge with scores of houses washed off their foundations. In some areas the ocean actually met the bay. Damages had been in the millions. New building codes hoped to stave off another such catastrophe.

In the open area between the many pilings were parked the deMarco cars: a BMW convertible and a rich-looking navy blue Lexus convertible with a dented gold grill.

A shiver went up Abby's spine. She climbed out of her car and slowly circled the Lexus. Her breath caught when she reached the far side. There the damage was much more extensive than it had first appeared. The entire length of the car was scratched and smashed.

It looked just like it might if the car had careened around a corner and scraped along the sides of several cars as it tried to avoid a little girl crossing the street.

Fourteen

"NEVER SEEN A car that needs body work?"

Abby jumped at the unfriendly voice and spun. She lost her balance with the quick motion and put out her hand to the car to steady herself, feeling the rough gouges in the metal under her palm. A big man with dark angry eyes and dark hair swept straight back from his forehead stared at her from the other side of the convertible, placing him between her and her own car.

"Such a shame, this damage." She hoped she didn't sound as unnerved as she felt. "It was a lovely car."

"You're an authority on cars, are you?"

His sarcasm was so sharp she flinched. What had she ever done to earn his ire? "I'm sorry. I didn't mean to bother you. I just couldn't resist looking." She hurried to her own car, giving him a wide berth, not caring how badly she limped. Speed and distance were all that mattered. She was aware of him watching her. She shivered in spite of the warm day.

"Is that Walker's father?" Jess asked in a small voice as Abby slid behind the wheel.

"I don't know." Abby grappled with her keys, which didn't want to slip in the ignition. "Maybe someone besides Mr. deMarco rents the top floor, like I rent above Dr. Winslow."

"He's mad, isn't he?" Jess stared at him with wide

eyes. "Daddies get mad. Then they leave."

"Oh, no, Jess." Abby's hand stilled on the keys as she turned to the girl. "Lots of times men get upset about something, but they don't leave. They work it out, especially Christian men who love Jesus."

Jess looked skeptical, and why not? In her limited experience, men left.

Abby tried again. "My dad would never leave my mom no matter how angry he got at her. He made a deal when he got married, and he'll keep it. Lots of men are like that." Marsh would be like that, she thought. She didn't know how she knew, but she did.

Abby glanced next door, catching the dark-haired man, eyes closed, shoulders slumped, running his hand through his hair. She started in surprise. He looked absolutely miserable and anything but threatening. Pity began to replace her fear. Something was upsetting him, and he was dealing with it by lashing out.

He must have felt her watching him because he straightened his shoulders, opened his eyes, and glared. Abby, overwhelmed at the animosity she saw, felt the blood drain from her face. She quickly averted her eyes. Her fledgling pity disappeared from one heartbeat to the next. There was no doubt; the man was not a nice man. But was he dangerous? Abby wasn't taking any chances, especially with Jess in the car. Slowly she extended her index finger to the door lock, and pushed. All four locks snapped down.

The man heard the click. He took a step toward her. She stabbed at the ignition again. This time the keys slid home. She backed out of the drive with more speed than caution. She wouldn't feel safe until she and Jess were several blocks away.

"Jess, would you reach into my purse and grab my cell phone for me?" Abby was pleased her voice sounded steady. "I also need the business card in the zipper pouch."

Jess rummaged around for a minute before she pulled out the phone and the card. She held it to Abby who took it, pulled to the curb, and dialed the number Greg Barnes had penciled on the back.

"Mr. Barnes, this is Abby Patterson calling."

He didn't sound surprised to hear her voice. "Mrs. Patterson, how are you today?"

"I'm fine, but I just saw something you might want to check."

Greg listened as she recounted finding the damaged Lexus. "I know it's probably nothing, but I felt I had to call. Besides, the guy was scary." *Like a hit-and-run driver would be.*

"You did the right thing," Greg said. "We'll check it out."

Abby felt the tension leave her shoulders. "Thank you."

"I take it that seeing the car didn't jog any memories loose?" Greg's voice was curious but not hopeful.

The undefined feeling of failure that had been sitting passively on her shoulder much of the time since the accident reached out and grabbed her by the throat. She actually coughed. "I'm sorry. I wish it did." With a sigh, she disconnected.

A small hand reached out and patted her leg. "Don't feel bad, Mrs. Patterson. You'll remember when God wants you to." Jess took the phone, putting it back in Abby's purse. "That's what Mommy says."

Abby wished she felt as certain as Celia.

At the hospital it didn't take long to spring Karlee. Abby signed the necessary papers at the nurses' station. When she and Jess got to Karlee's room, the little girl was waiting in a wheelchair. She looked fragile and weary, but she giggled like any little girl as the orderly who wheeled her to the front door called, "Make way for Princess Karlee and her royal steed." Abby doubted that Karlee knew what a royal steed was, but she certainly liked being a princess and having people wave to her as she rolled past. Soon she was settled in the backseat of the car, reclining on the pillow Abby had brought for just that purpose.

As they drove down Central, they passed a police car coming toward them. Abby tried to see if Greg Barnes was in it, but she couldn't. Tinted glass. Still she didn't doubt that it was coming from the deMarcos'. She started to sweat at the idea of seeing the man next door again. If he'd been angry before, what was he now that she had sent the police to his house?

It was with great relief that she saw no one as she pulled into the drive beside her father's car. The damaged Lexus was where it had been when she left, but the irate man was gone. She'd half expected him to be lying in wait for her, yelling and screaming and furious.

She climbed quickly from her car, her goal to get Karlee and Jess upstairs before he reappeared. He had already frightened Jess once, and poor bruised Karlee had had more than enough trauma.

"Put your good arm around my neck, sweetie," she instructed Karlee as she reached into the backseat for the little girl. "Jess, will you carry the pillow for me?"

Abby was straightening with her armful of child when a large palm slapped the roof of the car, making her jerk and smack her head on the top of the doorjamb. Jess and Karlee gave little screams at the abrupt sound.

"Just who do you think you are to sic the police on me?" His roar made Abby's stomach drop. "What did I ever do to you to deserve that?" His scowl drew his eyebrows together in one fearsome line from temple to temple.

Abby straightened, Karlee in her arms. Her head throbbed where she'd smacked it, and fear made her mouth dry, but she looked at the man as calmly as she could manage. She had to for the sake of the children. She'd never forgive herself if somehow she added to their fear. "You're frightening Jess and Karlee."

The man blinked, seeming to see for the first time the little girls who stared white-faced at him. Karlee had Abby's neck in a vise grip, and Jess pressed against the back of Abby's legs as she tried to make herself invisible.

A look of bewilderment raced across his face, followed by what appeared to be genuine concern. "She's hurt." He pointed to Karlee.

"Yes, she is. Automobile. Hit-and-run." Abby watched him for a reaction.

"Hit-and-run? That's terrible!" Then his face turned red as he fit pieces together. He pointed to his car, so upset his hand was shaking. Then he pointed to Karlee. "You think I did that to her?" He looked stunned. "That's why you called the cops? You actually think that if I hit anyone, especially a kid, I'd keep on going?"

"How do I know?" Abby wanted to yell at him, but she couldn't get the words to come out.

"What kind of man do you think I am?" He was back to angry again. "I've got kids of my own!"

"What's the trouble here, Abby?" Marsh strolled off his porch, coming to stand beside her. Without thinking she leaned toward him for protection, for comfort.

"She called the police on me," the man said before Abby could figure out how to explain everything. This time there was more disbelief than belligerence in his comment.

Marsh extended his hand. "I'm Marsh Winslow, by the way, and this is Abby Patterson. These lovely ladies are Karlee and Jess Fitzmeyer. And you are?"

"Rocco deMarco." He shook hands, then rubbed his hand along his jaw. His heavy beard rasped even though he'd obviously shaved that morning. His black eyes were stormy as he looked at Abby. "She called the cops on me!"

Abby lifted her chin and leaned closer to Marsh. She would not apologize. It had been a logical thing to do, the right thing to do, given the situation. She winced as her hip began to complain, shooting sharp pain darts across her lower back. With a start she realized she was placing unwise weight on her vulnerable side. Hoping Marsh hadn't noticed her leaning into him, she straightened, cheeks flushed. Immediately her hip felt better but she felt vulnerable.

"I'm sure she had a good reason for making the call, didn't you, Abby?" As he spoke, Marsh moved until his shoulder lightly brushed hers.

Thank you, she thought. *Thank you for somehow knowing.*

"His car," she said, nodding toward the vehicle. With disgust she heard the quiver in her voice. Still, she was doing better than the old Abby would have done. The old Abby would have gone to pieces with someone screaming at her. The new Abby was like Catherine of Aragon standing up to Henry VIII when he wanted a divorce. Catherine fought Henry, Cardinal Wolsey, and the Pope for eight long years and never did yield. All Abby needed was strength for a few more minutes. Of course, Catherine ended up in prison for years for her efforts.

Marsh ran a gentle hand over Karlee's head. "Hey, Karlee, sweetheart. Remember me?"

She peered up at him without loosening her grip on Abby's neck and nodded. "Church," she whispered.

"Good for you. And don't you worry. Everything's going to be all right."

Karlee's grip on Abby's neck eased.

Marsh smiled as he patted Jess on the shoulder. "Do you remember me, Jess?"

She studied him from behind Abby, then nodded. "I don't remember your name."

"I'm Dr. Winslow. I live right here." He pointed to the house.

"Mrs. Patterson lives here, too," Jess said.

Marsh nodded. "She lives upstairs, and I live downstairs."

"Where does he live?" Jess whispered, looking toward Rocco deMarco.

"He lives next door."

"Is he Walker's father?"

Marsh looked at the man, who nodded. "Yes, he's Walker's father."

"He's very mad." Jess looked at Abby.

"Yes," Abby said softly, "but he isn't leaving. We're going to work it out."

Marsh gave Abby a glance and a little smile. "I'll be right back." He walked to the battered Lexus, Rocco following on his heels. A blond fallen angel-cum-hero and a black-haired villain-cum-father. What a pair.

Marsh raised an eyebrow as he examined the damage. "What happened?" he asked Rocco in an easy, interested voice.

"A guy driving one of those rented vans and pulling his car behind ran me off the road. He pulled in too soon after passing me. I had to swerve or get creamed." He turned from Marsh to Abby to Marsh as he talked. "If there hadn't been a guardrail, I'd have gone down an embankment."

Abby wanted to believe him for Walker and Jordan's sakes, even for Vivienne's, but she was uncertain what to think.

Marsh nodded as he rubbed a finger along a particularly deep gouge. "Where did this near accident happen?"

In spite of Marsh's neutral tone, Rocco erupted again. "Who do you think you are, questioning me? You got no right! I'll get a lawyer after you. I'll sue for defamation of character!"

Marsh waited until Rocco took a breath, then jumped in, his voice firm but uncompromising. "We'll talk again sometime when you can talk, Mr. deMarco, not scream. Until then—" Marsh turned and walked back to Abby and the girls, leaving the astonished Rocco to stare after him, mouth hanging open.

Marsh winked at Abby, then turned to Karlee. "Hey, sweetheart. Let me carry you upstairs, okay? Abby's arms must be wearing out by now, holding a big girl like you."

Karlee lifted her head; her eyes were dark with fright and fatigue. Abby's heart broke. She bent to place a kiss on the little girl's cheek. She transferred Karlee to Marsh and watched as she snuggled against his chest, her cast resting in her lap.

"Comfy?" Marsh asked.

Karlee nodded, her little face too serious.

"Relax, honey," Abby said, resting a finger against her little nose. "We're all fine. The trouble is over." At least for the moment. "Dr. Winslow has you, and he'll keep you safe."

Marsh looked at Abby, his expression somber. Then his eyes glinted, and Abby held her breath.

"She's right. I've got you all right and tight. I *know* you'll be easier to manage than Abby was. She was an armful when I carried her up the stairs, let me tell you. She kicked and squirmed the whole way. I almost dropped her on her head."

Jess looked from Abby to Marsh in disbelief. "Did you really carry her upstairs?"

Marsh grinned at Abby. "I did. And she weighs a ton, Jess. A ton!"

Abby scowled with exaggeration. "Don't you believe him. I'm light as a butterfly."

Jess giggled and followed Marsh and Karlee up the steps, dragging the pillow behind her. Shaking her head at Marsh's nonsense and flexing her arms to get the circulation going again, Abby started toward the steps and froze. Standing where the cement and sand met was her father. One look at his face told Abby that he heard everything Marsh told Jess.

"Did you have a good walk?" she asked brightly.

"Abby!"

"There's nothing like an invigorating morning walk on the beach, is there?"

"Abby, what's he talking about?"

She just shook her head and grasped the banister. She was still quaking inside from the confrontation with Rocco deMarco, and her arms ached almost as much as her hip. *Not now, Dad.*

"What did he mean, he carried you up the stairs?"

Abby didn't know what to say, so she said nothing.

"Was he being forward? Inappropriate?"

"Marsh was fine, Dad. He's never been anything but fine."

"But why would you let him carry you? Oh, Abby, what would Sam say?"

Thinking that for obvious reasons, Sam's opinion was the least important thing to consider at the moment, Abby began pulling herself up step by step. "Marsh was just teasing Karlee, Dad. He likes to joke." She knew she'd be more convincing if her cheeks weren't so red.

Her father reached out a hand and held her still. "Are you saying he didn't carry you?"

She couldn't meet his eyes. How had such a silly episode taken on all the trappings of a major seduction?

"Abby, I don't like that man touching you. You can't stay here."

"Dad." She swallowed her frustration. "Marsh is fine. He really is. I—I like him." What would Dad say if he knew Marsh had waited up for her last night? That didn't bear thinking about.

A slammed car door drew her attention. Rocco deMarco had climbed into his battered Lexus. She watched him careen into the street and bolt down Central. She hoped no one was between him and his destination, given his present ugly mood.

"I say the man is unsavory."

Abby glanced at the empty parking spot. "It's okay. I can stay out of his way."

Dad stabbed his finger toward the deMarco house. "Not him." He jabbed at Marsh's place. "Him."

Marsh was unsavory? She almost laughed. Infuriating, yes. Aggravating, yes. Kind to children even when they invaded his privacy, yes. But unsavory? "Dad, he's a tease. He's also a seminary professor."

Dad blinked, nonplussed, though he recovered quickly. "That doesn't mean you can trust him."

"Trust him with what?" Abby asked. "My jewels? My virtue? My life? He's just the guy who lives downstairs, nothing more. Don't go making mountains out of molehills."

Dad looked at her. "Now I know you're hiding something."

Abby stared at him. "What do you mean?"

"Mountains out of molehills. A cliché. You always talk in clichés when you're hiding something."

Abby resisted the urge to scream. She took a deep, calming breath. "Dad, give it a rest. Even if I were hiding something, I'm allowed. I'm twenty-nine years old. I can have secrets if I want, even from my parents."

Dad stared at her, eyes heavy with sorrow. "Abby, you've changed."

I hope so, but she knew to say it would just hurt him.

"Come home with us, baby, before it's too late." His eyes pleaded, repeating the entreaty in his voice.

She turned back to the stairs and continued up. "No, Dad. This is my home now." She passed Marsh midway as he returned to his place. "Troublemaker," she hissed without looking at him.

"My pleasure," he hissed back, laughter in his voice. As he passed Dad, he nodded his head and said in a most civil tone, "Sir."

"Uh," Dad managed, and it was all she could do not to giggle at his disgruntled tone.

When she reached the porch, she found Karlee lying on the chaise lounge with Mom arranging pillows behind her.

"This dear child was hit by a car," Mom said, appalled.

"Yes, I know." Abby put her purse on the now cleared table. Mom had been at work, and this time Abby appreciated the help.

"She saw it." Jess pointed at Abby.

Fortunately Mom was too busy cooing over Karlee and Dad was too busy staring suspiciously down the steps after Marsh to have heard. Abby breathed a sigh of relief. She caught Jess's eye, put her finger to her lips, and shook her head. Jess looked surprised, but she nodded and put her hand over her mouth. Abby relaxed. At least there was one topic she wouldn't have to explain to Mom and Dad.

Or so she thought.

Fifteen

HE CRUMPLED THE newspaper and tossed it in the trash on his way outside. *There was an eyewitness*. It was confirmed right there on the front page just below her picture.

The very thought of it made him break out in a cold sweat. She could ruin it all, bring him down with just a word. All she needed to do was remember something, anything, and it was all over. The appointment would be out the window.

Of course she might never remember. Frequently, people never fully recalled moments of great trauma. Still, he couldn't depend on her faulty brain chemistry. It would be putting himself too much at risk. He had to find a way to destroy her before she destroyed him.

It was too bad in a way. She was a very attractive woman in spite of the limp. Under other circumstances he would have enjoyed getting to know her. She had a lovely smile, and those black eyes of hers were memerizing. He grinned as he raced along the off-island roads of Ventnor on his cycle. How he could have enjoyed himself as he made those eyes sparkle with extra life. He had a marvelous and much deserved reputation with the women, a reputation he took care to nurture with his ready charm. They all loved him, even when he broke up with them. She would have been no different.

The fact that she was his enemy rather than his potential lover was but one more sign of the unfairness of life.

Of course, the ultimate way to rid himself of the danger she represented was to kill her. He blinked. Kill her? He frowned. Where had that thought come from? It was common knowledge that McCoy had killed and gotten away with it. In fact, the streams deep in the Pines were probably slowly devouring more than one victim of McCoy's fierce hatred. He made it a general rule to avoid McCoy these days. He had put all his energy into legitimately escaping the Pines and his beginnings. McCoy had turned to the dark side, to the doing of horrendous deeds and the getting away with them.

Both of them had succeeded beyond anyone's wildest dreams.

But kill her? Become like McCoy? Never! Besides, how would he do it? Shoot her? Run her over? Poison her? One thing he knew for an absolute certainty: He could never, never ask McCoy for help. A shudder rippled through him at the thought of what would happen if McCoy ever had such a hold over him. Blackmail would be the least of it.

Then there was that oath he'd taken: *First, do no harm.* No, deliberate murder was a whole different ball game, one he was not going to play.

He drove down the night-quiet road, flashing past the darkened houses on his street. Another thought gripped him as he pushed the remote to raise his garage door. He drove in and parked, revving the motor a couple of times before he turned the key.

Physical violence would just involve the cops more. That was the last thing he wanted. Even now he cringed at the risks he'd been forced to take to dispose of the car, risks taken for nothing if her memory returned.

His stomach growled, and he laid a hand over it. He'd missed dinner, something that hadn't happened in years. Fine food was one of the great pleasures of his carefully constructed life. A sudden vision of macaroni and cheese shimmered before him. He shuddered. Growing up he'd eaten too many dishes on too many nights. Macaroni and cheese with hot dogs. Macaroni and cheese with tuna fish. Macaroni and cheese with bologna. For a break it would be macaroni with canned spaghetti sauce poured over it.

And white bread. Mom brought home a loaf of Wonder Bread every day. He and his father—when he wasn't sleeping—filled in their hunger holes with the squishy stuff. He liked to crush it into hard pellets and see how long it took a pellet to melt in his mouth. Sometimes he and McCoy took the bread pellets and went fishing in the Mullica River or one of the streams lacing the Pines. Then dinner had been something worth eating.

He'd been twelve when he became the family cook. His mother announced that she wouldn't be making meals anymore. Her legs hurt too much after her shift at the Food Fair. She couldn't understand why they were so painful when she was only thirty years old. She'd look down at them with a puzzled expression, though he doubted she could see them over the lump of her stomach.

"I'm too young for arthritis," she'd say. "Old people get that."

He'd stare at her and her close to four hundred pounds. Did she honestly not understand the link between excess weight and bad knees?

She drove an old red Chevette as rusty as the old bike he'd found at the dump. The car listed to the left so much it was a wonder the tires on the right didn't leave the road. Kids sniggered every time they saw her drive by, especially McCoy.

"The left side's gonna scrape the ground any day now," he'd say.

He wasn't the only one who made comments.

"I saw your mom in the store yesterday," a kid at school would say. "Man, how does she ever fit in that small space beside the cash register?"

Or "Where does she find enough material for those tents she wears?"

One day the prettiest girl in class looked at him. "You're built just like your mother, aren't you? You look a lot like her."

The comment hadn't been particularly barbed. Now he recognized it as the comment of a junior high girl who didn't realize the power of words to curdle the spirit. Or galvanize it. On that very day he established an exercise regimen and had kept it up to this very day. Then he'd run and lifted old cans he filled with sand. Today it was the sophisticated routines developed for him by his personal trainer. He had kept the promise he made to himself that long-ago day: He would never, never look like his mother.

He lowered the kickstand on his cycle and set his helmet on the seat. Once inside he went directly to the liquor cabinet. He poured himself a tumbler full of Scotch neat and collapsed on the sofa.

He forced himself to stop thinking of life in the Pines. He'd successfully escaped that prison. It was today's problem that he needed to concentrate on. No matter how he looked at things, he was stuck with the problem of how to defuse a live time bomb before it exploded all over him.

Sixteen

*M*ARSH WATCHED WITH disbelief as person after person ran up and down Abby's stairs all day. He'd never seen anything like it. If it wasn't a little person with a high-pitched voice that curdled his eardrums, it was an adult with a tread like a gorilla.

Didn't she have at least one friend with a light step and a pleasant voice? Just yesterday he was the only person in Seaside that she knew. Where did they all come from anyway?

Well, he wasn't going to let her or her friends drive him indoors. It was his house, and he'd work outside on his own porch if he wanted to! That was part of the dream, and he'd paid enough money for the privilege.

He opened his laptop and stared over his rail at the dunes and the ocean beyond, waiting for his thoughts to gel. Instead, he heard a high giggle that he fervently hoped didn't belong to Abby. Then the two boys clambered down the steps with enough noise to wake the proverbial dead, ran next door, reappeared with arms full of toys, and climbed noisily back up.

"We got it, Jess," Walker called.

"We got some other stuff too," yelled Jordan. That kid had the lungs of a carnival midway barker.

The high-pitched giggle floated down, and Marsh sighed in relief. It wasn't Abby.

Abby. He'd been more impressed than he wanted to admit by the way she'd stood up to the madman next door. Not many people could handle a large, irate man screaming in their face, but she had. He felt a strange pride that she'd done so well.

If only she wasn't such a gregarious person, he'd appreciate her even more.

He turned back to his laptop, gritting his teeth, applying all his formidable concentration to Craig and Marguerite. Once Rick arrived, Marsh's present book would be temporarily shelved while they concentrated on *Shadows at Noon,* last year's release, and last year's characters—Nathan, Dixie, and the dastardly Valdez.

Rick was going to be a great Nathan if the script was anywhere as good as Rick had indicated. Marsh knew it had been good when he finished writing it, but so many fingers got stuck in this particular type of pie before a shooting script emerged that Marsh always worried until the final version of the screenplay was in his hands. His contract called for him to have final approval, but exercising that final approval was one of life's great challenges, especially when he was on the East Coast and the movie entertainment people, at least the creative community, were on the West Coast. Then there were the on-site changes made during shooting.

"Mrs. Patterson, watch!" a shrill little voice commanded.

There followed a few seconds of silence during which the little demon who belonged to the demanding voice presumably performed. Jordan, he thought. Marsh held his fingers above his keyboard and waited.

"Wonderful, honey!" Abby applauded loudly, whistling between her teeth while her parents could be heard giving more moderate approbation.

Someone ought to tell her that a lady didn't whistle like a jock. He thought about the tantalizing idea of telling her himself, but only for a couple of minutes. He was smart enough to know a lost cause when he saw one. She'd just tell him about some crazy woman in ancient history who had invented that particularly offensive sound.

"Lunch," Abby's mother called.

Amid more thumps and bumps, the herd went inside. Silence

ensued; his ears actually rang with it. Marsh grinned and started typing.

Craig looked at the horse with growing concern. It was Magdalene—Maggie—Marguerite's mare, as proud in her own way as the woman herself was.

"Magdalene?" he'd scoffed when he first heard the animal's name. "What kind of a name is that for a horse?"

Marguerite looked at his dappled gray and, just short of sneering, said, "And Smokey is a better name?"

"He's gray." Craig had always thought Smokey the perfect name for his noble steed and was dismayed to hear how defensive he sounded.

"I didn't mean to denigrate the vast expanse of your imagination," she said, barely concealing a yawn. She eyed him with condescension. "You do know what *denigrate* means, don't you?"

Only by sheer will did he manage to keep his jaw from dropping to his chest in appalled surprise. Of all the gall! How had a gentleman like Abner Frost produced a snob like her?

She then turned and patted her horse's neck. When she spoke, her voice was warm with affection. "Magdalene's name is to remind me that if God can make her namesake into a woman of faith, He can make me into what He wants me to be too."

If it hadn't been for the haughty toss of her head, he might have been impressed. As it was, he thought she needed a few lessons from God—or His emissary—on the evils of pride. Craig itched to volunteer for the job, but he had too much respect for God and too little for her to take on a task of that proportion. Thinking he didn't know what *denigrate* meant. Mocking Smokey's name. Looking down her beautiful nose every time she saw him.

It was one beautiful nose, he had to admit. In fact, she was enough to make any man's mouth water, her dark hair catching the sunlight and shining brightly enough to blind anyone foolish enough to glance her way, her movements a symphony of grace and elegance, her glorious eyes casting spells that entangled all who looked. Too bad she wasn't as beautiful in character.

As he neared the solitary horse standing just off the road, he realized the mare's reins were still draped over her neck, neither tied nor trailing. Something was definitely wrong. Marguerite would never leave her horse improperly tethered.

He stopped beside Maggie. She stood unconcerned, nibbling at a patch of scrub grass.

"Marguerite!" Craig stood in his stirrups, scanning the area. "Marguerite! Where are you?"

He saw and heard nothing to disturb him. The silence made his skin prickle.

"Marguerite, you fool woman, where are you?"

Like she'd deign to answer that question. He sniffed. *Deign*, he thought. *I came up with that all by myself.* Too bad she'd never know. As he scanned the area for a third time, he wondered how he could let it drop oh-so-casually that he had a degree in animal husbandry and land management.

Good night! I want to impress her, he thought, scandalized by his own lack of character.

God, save me from myself. He meant every word of the prayer with the fervency usually reserved for the care of the beautiful, spare land that surrounded him. A roadrunner streaked by, neck stretched forward like he could arrive at his destination faster if he reached for it. It was debatable who was more startled at the sight of the other, the bird or Smokey, who shied.

"Easy, boy." As he calmed the horse, he studied the row of cottonwoods off to the south. They lined the creek that was the center of the water dispute between Mr. Frost and Otis Snelling. At least it was the stated cause of the dispute. Craig thought that the War between the States was the greater cause.

Otis Snelling, a Confederate veteran, hated Abner Frost, a former Union army colonel. To Snelling it mattered not that the war was over more than thirty years ago. He had come west after the war, settling in this obscure corner of New Mexico, only to find his neighbor had stood near Grant when Lee surrendered at Appomattox. Snelling would never forget the shame of that day as he stood in the ranks of defeated Rebels. His hate for his Yankee neighbor festered.

Add to that Frost's success with his property in contrast to Snelling's inept and unwise use of his, and the bitterness grew. With Frost's declining health, Snelling saw his opportunity. He just hadn't counted on Randall Craig.

Marsh was vaguely aware of a car pulling into the parking area beside the house. He glanced up to see an attractive blond woman walk toward the steps leading up to Abby's.

Now who?

The woman felt his gaze and looked over. She smiled shyly. "Hi, Marsh."

Jess and Karlee's mother. What was her name? He'd met her in church a couple of times. He scrambled mentally. "Hi, Cecelia." Yes, that was it. He sketched a little wave.

"Celia," she said and disappeared upstairs. He heard a cry of, "Mom!" as the sliding door opened, then closed. Silence again descended.

Well, he'd been close.

Most of the precious Anasazi Creek flowed through Frost land, but there was a short section where it coursed across Snelling land as it made its way down from the mountains. What gave Snelling an advantage in the water dispute was that the water flowed from his land onto Mr. Frost's. Snelling's threat was to dam up the water, to divert it so none flowed onto Frost Spring Ranch—unless an exorbitant fee was paid. The law, such as it was in this rugged area northeast of Albuquerque, spoke clearly about water rights. If you bought them with your land, they were yours. If you failed to, tough.

Abner Frost had bought water rights, but Snelling conveniently overlooked this fact as he saw a way not only to make money but also to control everyone downstream.

"You do as I say, old man," Snelling threatened Abner

Frost, "or you'll have no water." In this dry, barren, eerily beautiful land, water was as essential as oxygen, treasured more than gold.

It was because of these threats that Mr. Frost contacted Randall Craig, son of an old army buddy.

"I need someone young and strong," the old man said.

Craig, bored with his father's well-run Pennsylvania farm, took the next train to New Mexico, looking for challenge and adventure. He just hadn't expected anything like Marguerite to be part of the bargain.

Surely the fool woman knew enough to stay away from the boundary between the properties. Surely she understood the dangers. Snelling's men were all one step from jail, either coming or going. Craig shivered at the thought of what they might do to someone like her.

Thumps, thuds, and excited voices interrupted him and announced the departure of the upstairs retinue for the beach. They descended from above with arms laden with chairs, towels, and coolers—coolers? They would be less than a hundred steps from their house! They couldn't walk home for a drink?—and all the other trappings people seemed to think were necessary to sit in the sun. There was even a beach umbrella tucked under Abby's father's arm to keep the sun they were going to sit in from shining on them.

Marsh couldn't help noticing that Abby's hands were completely empty. Her mother and father, by contrast, looked like pack animals. Even the little girl carried an armful of towels.

I guess you can't color outside the lines with full arms.

Abby was wearing her bathing suit with a shirt thrown over it. He couldn't help but notice the scars that slashed across the top of her right leg. Even looking at them three years after the injury, he cringed. He couldn't imagine what she had suffered, and he knew physical pain was the least of it.

"Go get your suits on, boys," Abby said to Walker and Jordan. "That is, if your mom says it's okay. You'll see us right down there on the beach." She pointed to the sand.

She was standing with her back to Marsh, but the two boys

faced him. Not that they noticed him. Their little faces were fixed on Abby, and they nodded earnestly at her instructions. Marsh knew infatuation when he saw it. Somehow those two little boys had become Abby's slaves.

At least she hadn't turned them into beasts of burden.

As he watched, Celia came down the stairs. She kissed Jess. "You be good for everyone."

"I will, Mom."

"Remember, we expect you to stay for dinner," Abby said as Celia climbed into her car. "Don't worry about Karlee. Mom and I'll take turns watching her. She'll probably sleep the afternoon away."

"I'm going to take a turn too, Celia," said Abby's father. "Little girls are my specialty." He slung an arm around Abby's shoulders and squeezed. Marsh thought he saw Abby stiffen, but it might have been his imagination.

Celia looked close to tears. "I can't thank you all enough."

"Then don't try," Abby said as she stepped away from her father. "Get yourself back to work before you miss your next appointment."

Everyone waved good-bye like Celia was leaving for an around-the-world tour and wouldn't be returning for five years instead of five hours.

"Here, Jess." Abby's mom handed a totebag to the girl, whose arms were already full of towels. "My books and cross-word puzzles."

Books plural? How fast could the woman read?

"Call me around two-thirty," she called over her shoulder to Abby as the entourage, burdened with more paraphernalia than a rock group, moved to the beach.

"I will," Abby called as she climbed the steps.

Whoops. Apologies, Abby, for thinking you weren't carrying your share of the load.

Once again quiet descended. He felt his shoulders relax, and the mists of frustration blew away. He breathed deeply and put the confusion of today's meeting of the 4311 Central Avenue chapter of the Abby Association from his mind. Except for one loud, "Here we come!" from Jordan, for the rest of the afternoon Marsh lived at Frost Spring Ranch, kept company with Marguerite and Craig, and plotted to hog-tie Snelling. He picked up his plot where Craig was riding the range searching for Marguerite, who, like the troublesome woman she was, had disappeared.

Craig dismounted and walked to Magdalene. She looked up at him and blew softly out her nostrils. He put his hand on her neck and patted her. She wasn't the least bit skittish. *Better controlled than your mistress, eh, girl?* He walked around her, looking for some indication of trouble—a loose stirrup, a broken bit—but Maggie and her equipment were fine.

He felt down her legs. Maybe she'd pulled something, and Marguerite had decided it would be damaging even to walk her. Had the woman started back to Frost Spring on foot? No, even she wasn't that foolish. Not in country laced with wild animals, snakes, and two-legged varmints.

On Maggie's right leg Craig saw a scratch, not serious but undoubtedly painful when received.

"Did you react to the pain and throw her, girl?" He lifted her leg to look for other injuries. To his surprise, her hoof was covered with dried mud.

The fool woman had gone to Anasazi Creek. Muttering under his breath, he gathered Maggie's reins and remounted Smokey. He set off for the cottonwoods, Maggie loping behind.

As he rode, he tried to control his imagination, but it was hard. As he neared the cottonwoods, a storm of seed fluffs sailed through the air like late spring/early summer snow. He batted away one that chose his nose as its landing place.

"Marguerite," he called. "Where are you?"

There was no answer.

He rode up to the edge of the stream, uncertain what he'd find, and stared in disbelief. The water was not flowing. The muddy bed lay revealed, marbled with small fissures where the hot sun beat down and dried the mud, sort of like an elderly woman whose varicose veins were exposed to the world by an unexpected wind.

Snelling! He had diverted Anasazi Creek just as he threatened.

Craig kneed Smokey forward and followed the drying bed upstream. Somewhere he was certain to come across Snelling's men and the actual diversion of the water. He didn't even pause when he came to the boundary spike demarcating the end of Frost land and the beginning of Snelling's property.

Had Marguerite done what he was doing? Had she met and challenged Snelling and his men? Did they have her, hoping to use her as a hostage, a bargaining chip to get control of Frost Spring Ranch?

The phone resting on the table beside Marsh rang. He grabbed it. "What?"

A low laugh traveled across the line. "I can see you're in a good mood. Won't the heroine cooperate? Or is it the hero's horse that's giving you trouble?"

Marsh felt his shoulders relax. "Rick! Are you in Philadelphia already?"

"I'm at LAX, trying to escape from Billie."

"Who's Billy?"

"Just call me Billie," Rick said in a falsetto voice.

"Ah, Billie with an *ie*, not a *y*."

"You can always tell a guy with a Ph.D." Rick's deep voice rumbled through the wires. He had the richest timbre of any actor Marsh had ever heard. "They figure things out right quick."

"And you can tell the cowboys because they say things like 'right quick.'"

There was a moment's silence as the men grinned at each other across the miles.

"Does Billie have a last name?" Marsh was always embarrassed by how fascinated he was with the people Rick knew. He felt like a groupie. "Would I know who she is?"

"No and I hope not."

"What?"

"Just call me Billie. I'm sort of like Cher and Madonna, you know? Or Lucy." Again he spoke in a falsetto.

"Lucy had a last name," Marsh noted for the record. "Is she like Cher and Madonna?"

"Only in her own mind."

"So what are you doing with her?"

"I don't know. I can't get her to go away."

Marsh heard the frustration in Rick's voice. "It's your curse to attract beautiful women. Sounds like you need a wife to protect you."

"Yeah, I do."

Marsh pulled the phone from his ear and stared at it for a beat. "Isn't that a rather dramatic change of mind?"

"It is. But I'm lonely, Marsh." His sigh echoed down the line. "I've found balance and stability in the Lord. I don't need or want to run around anymore, hiding my emptiness in activity and carousing. I feel like Adam must have when the Lord said that it wasn't good for a man to be alone."

"Sounds like you need this vacation, old buddy."

"I need to go back to being Rick Yakabuski. Life made sense back then."

"You'd be bored inside a week."

"I don't know, Marsh. I tell you, I don't know."

"You need time on the beach with no Billies in sight. When will you arrive?"

"11:35 P.M. I'm going to crash at the hotel at the airport. I'll be down tomorrow morning in time for church."

"I'll look for you."

"I can't wait to hear what you think of the script." The bounce was back in Rick's voice. "I think it's great."

Marsh grinned. "Well, you just—"

"Wait a minute," Rick said. "Someone's trying to get my attention."

"When isn't someone?"

"Not usually in the men's room."

"You're calling from the men's room?"

"Billie can't follow me in here."

Marsh thought he'd choke on that line. There was the muffled sound of voices, a minor roar of "What?" from Rick. Then he was back on the line.

"She sent some poor schlep in here to see if I was all right." Rick sighed. "If the men's room isn't safe, what is?"

"Will she follow you here?"

"No."

"You're sure?"

"She doesn't have any money, and I won't tell her where I'm going."

Marsh was laughing when he hung up, and it felt good. He knew he'd been a grump all day, but Rick had cheered him up. He was still smiling when he heard a noise and looked over at the woman starting up the steps. It was Abby's mother coming to relieve Abby. She was staring at him, and if looks could harm a body, Marsh knew he'd be twisting in agony.

His smile fled. He frowned and went back to his novel. What had he ever done to her to make her so hostile? He blocked her out and let Craig take over his thoughts, Craig and the missing Marguerite.

Craig's neck started to prickle again, and he slowed. Cautiously his eyes moved from side to side, missing nothing. He was much more savvy about the unscrupulous character of some men than she, and if there was an ambush waiting, he wasn't falling into it. He scanned the high desert that rose off to the north. He studied the line of cottonwoods behind and beside him. He looked across the creek bed to the south where there was nothing to see but mile upon mile of sand and scrub.

The moan was so faint he almost missed it. If the water had been flowing, its currents still strong from the melt off in the high mountains, he would have. But he heard it, a whisper of sound, a mere breath. His blood turned to ice.

He spun Smokey and there she was, dirty, blouse torn, her right arm held close to her body. She half lay, half leaned against a cottonwood and had been there for some time, if the halo of fluff on her hair was any indication.

He dismounted, grabbed his canteen, and strode to her.

"Don't say it," Marguerite managed to whisper between dry lips.

"Don't say what?" He was appalled at the size of the bruise spreading across her right temple.

"Whatever nasty thing you're thinking."

"Huh." He knelt and held the canteen to her mouth.

"More," she said when he pulled it back.

"In a minute." He ran gentle fingers up the arm she cradled against herself.

"Broken." She flinched when he hit a particularly painful place, but she didn't allow any noise to escape. "A snake scared Maggie. Rattled right under her feet. She shied. I was so busy watching the dry streambed that I was taken by surprise and thrown. I've never been thrown before in my life." She sounded scandalized.

Craig took the scarf from around his neck and wet it with water from his canteen. He wiped the dirt from her face, moving gently around the bruised area. He saw only a small break in the skin just above her hairline, but infection was still too real a possibility.

She sat with her eyes closed. "Feels good."

He wished the creek were flowing, that he had a source of water to soak his scarf and thoroughly wash the area of the bruise, but it would have to wait until they were home. He wasn't willing to use their drinking water in such a manner.

He turned his attention to her arm. He shook out his scarf again, fashioned a sling, and tied her arm to her body. She closed her eyes against the agony and her already ashen face paled further.

"This is going to hurt," he said as he bent to lift her. He slid an arm around her waist and another under her knees.

"Like tying on the sling didn't," she managed. Her eyes were huge with pain.

He lifted her. She gasped, wrapping her good arm around his neck. She buried her face in the curve of his neck as she tried not to cry. As he carried her to the horses, he marveled at how light she was. And how unexpectedly brave.

He was unprepared for the gravelly voice that shouted, "Stop right there! You're trespassing!"

End of chapter.

Nodding in satisfaction, Marsh hit save. The screen cleared and he put the machine on standby. He got out of his chair and moved his creaking body toward the house, Fargo at his heels. Marsh had been sitting without moving anything but his fingers for three solid hours. He desperately needed sustenance and relief.

"Excuse me," a male voice said just as Marsh reached for his sliding door. The speaker sounded much too vibrant and eager.

Marsh turned, sighing with the ragged patience of a man who had had a very long and trying day. "Yes?"

A handsome man with hair just silvering at the temples smiled. "I'm looking for Abby Patterson."

Who wasn't?

Seventeen

ARSH JERKED HIS thumb upward. He wasn't certain which of the baby-sitters was up there at the moment, but he was confident someone was. The man smiled and started up the steps. Disgruntled, Marsh watched him until his feet, shod in brown loafers and no socks, disappeared from view. Who was he? The "friend" of last night? Someone from Scranton who had driven down to visit Abby?

Whoever he was, Marsh thought sourly, he was too handsome for his own good.

He let himself and Fargo into the house and wandered to the kitchen. He went to the refrigerator, pulling out a cold bottle of water. He forced his mind from the visitor in the bright blue knit shirt with the pony over the heart back to the book.

What did Snelling plan to do with Craig and Marguerite now that he had them?

Where was he going to take them?

How would they escape, especially with Marguerite injured? Should she develop a fever and hallucinate, or were the broken arm and the sore head enough?

As he made his way back to the porch, he considered possible answers to his questions and found none that satisfied him. What he did find was the whole tribe from upstairs in the drive beside his porch, rinsing off sand, laughing, talking, and completely destroying his illusion of being in New Mexico territory in the 1890s. He picked up his laptop, turned it on, and looked at Fargo, who looked woefully back.

"At least Puppy's still upstairs," Marsh said. "Probably hiding under a bed." Fargo licked his lips.

"Don't even think about it."

Fargo slumped to the floor, pouting.

Marsh laughed, then settled back in his chair to watch and listen. What else could he do?

"Can we come back after we change?" Walker asked Abby as he stuck a foot under the spigot that protruded from the side of the house. Abby, who had her hands full rinsing a wriggling Jordan under the open air shower located three feet from the spigot, didn't answer.

"It's almost dinner, dear." Abby's mother answered for her. "Your mother will be waiting for you."

"No, she won't." Jordan shook his head, spraying Abby in a remarkably good imitation of Fargo shaking himself after being caught in a rainstorm. "Will she, Walker?"

Walker, who was mesmerized as he watched Jess blow spit bubbles while she rinsed the ocean from her hair, said, "She won't care what we do. Ever since Dad left, she doesn't care."

"But your father's here," Abby's mother said, gently pushing the thoroughly rinsed Jordan next door. "Abby met him earlier today." She took Walker by the shoulder and turned him from Jess toward his house.

Jordan nodded. "She called the cops on him. Mommy's mad about that."

"All the more reason for you to be there with your parents. Good-bye, boys." Abby's mother waved for good measure. Then she turned her back and began hanging up wet beach towels.

Jordan grabbed Walker's hand as they walked among the pilings under their house. "We'll be back after we change," he called over his shoulder. "Mom may hate you, Mrs. Patterson, but we don't. We like you lots."

"Oh, dear," said Abby, looking after the boys as she picked up a pair of beach chairs with one hand and reached for the banister with the other. "Nothing like getting along with your neighbor."

Jordan suddenly turned all the way around and yelled, "We

like you too, Mrs. MacDonald, even if you do want us to go home."

Marsh couldn't help smiling. *That kid belongs in politics. He's got the volume and the people skills, playing up to Abby's mother like that. I must introduce him to my father.*

His father. He was coming on Tuesday. Marsh shuddered, then stilled. What in the world was he going to do with Rick while Dad was here? All the good senator needed was to meet a TV star houseguest, and Marsh's goose was cooked.

Mrs. MacDonald frowned at the boys' backs. "You are going to have to be strong with those two, Abby, or mark my words, they will live here all summer."

Abby shrugged and grinned at Jess as she ran past her up the stairs, sand bucket and flip-flops in her hand. "Worse things could happen."

"I'm just trying to protect you, dear. You are still fragile."

Marsh saw Abby freeze, her hands closing into fists. "I am not fragile," she said. "I am fine." Each word was clipped, full of indignation.

"Of course you are, dear," Mrs. MacDonald hastened to say as she put the last clothespin on the last towel. "I didn't mean to indicate you weren't. It's just that two boisterous children climbing all over you all the time, whether literally or metaphorically—well, I don't like to think of you dealing with something like that. Think of your nerves, if not your hip."

"There is nothing wrong with my nerves, and my hip is doing fine." Abby spoke with remarkable calm for someone whose knuckles, where they were wrapped around the chairs she was carrying, were as white as a puffy summer cloud. Her voice only shook a little. Marsh couldn't help but nod his approval.

Mrs. MacDonald waved Abby's comment away as if it wasn't worth acknowledging. She seemed to miss Abby's distress completely, but then from the little Marsh had observed, she always knew she was right even when he knew she wasn't. Maybe she was the one who should meet his father. They'd deserve each other.

He must have made some sort of noise because Mrs. MacDonald spun and glared at him. "Enjoying our conversation?"

Quickly he turned to his laptop and began typing. *Swrtyhinpo dgleighut hensim tehoheddtm.* He tried not to feel the brand of Mrs. MacDonald's eyes.

"Mother, who are you talking to?" Abby turned halfway up the stairs.

"Him." Mrs. MacDonald jerked her thumb as she started up the steps after Abby. "He's so rude."

Marsh raised his eyebrows. *Me? I'm just sitting here on my own porch, minding my own business.* He stopped. *Well, maybe I am a little too curious, but how am I supposed to not hear you when you're yelling loud enough for the world to listen?*

"Mom!" Abby was clearly embarrassed as she came down a couple of steps to silence her mother.

Mrs. MacDonald lowered her voice to a whisper, but it was the kind actors used to project to the farthest corners of a theater. "He's not only rude; he's dangerous."

"Marsh?" Abby squeaked.

Me? Dangerous? I'm willing to admit a touch of rudeness, but that's it.

"Why, I wouldn't be surprised if he were the one driving that car."

What? Marsh's eyes went wide with disbelief and affronted pride. Like he'd ever leave the scene of an accident! What kind of a person did she think he was?

"Mom! Please!" Abby bent and glanced his way. To spare her, he made believe he hadn't heard. He typed *thimnderfulinthebes tyellowrjoud.* She straightened and tightened her grip on the beach chairs. "Get up here, Mom," she hissed, "before I lose my apartment!"

"Stop right where you are, Abby," Mr. MacDonald commanded from above.

Ah, Marsh thought, *he's been the most recent baby-sitter.*

"You shouldn't be carrying those chairs by yourself."

"Dad, please. I'm fine. They're not that heavy. They're only aluminum beach chairs."

Mr. MacDonald made little tsking noises, but he didn't rush to help her. In less than a moment Marsh saw why.

"And look, baby. You've got company."

Marsh saw the long legs of the silver-templed man move down the steps.

"I'll take those for you, Mrs. Patterson."

Marsh caught Abby's flash of surprise as she looked at the man.

"Dr. Schofield?" She pushed her dark curls off her forehead.

Marsh noted that her nose was red. She probably got so caught up playing with the kids that she forgot her sunscreen. He shook his head. She needed a keeper, but he had to admit she looked cute.

"You stopped to see Karlee." Abby sounded impressed. "How thoughtful of you. I didn't know doctors still paid house calls."

"Only for very special people." It was obvious he didn't mean Karlee.

Abby blushed.

The MacDonalds preened.

Marsh rolled his eyes.

In no time everyone was upstairs and a semiquiet reigned once again. Marsh knew he should get back to Craig and Marguerite, but all he could think about when he wasn't thinking about pushy doctors was being considered dangerous. He couldn't decide whether to laugh at the absurdity or take offense at the slur. Just because he'd been a bit grumpy when the MacDonalds had wakened him this morning. If their daughter had come home at a decent hour, he'd have had a good night's sleep and been his usual charming self.

He grinned. Dangerous. Errol Flynn swinging from the rigging. Luke Skywalker dueling with Darth Vader. John Wayne taking on the bad guys. Keanu Reeves on the speeding bus.

Then his grin slipped away as he thought about Mrs. MacDonald's accusation: He was the driver of that car. That meant she thought he was too much of a coward to stop and help an injured child, someone too frightened, too concerned about himself to help a little girl who needed help desperately.

His already grouchy mood descended further into the dumps. It didn't help that soon the aroma of wonderful things cooking wafted into the air, torture for a man who lived on frozen entrees much of the time. When Marsh caught Fargo sniffing and looking toward the stairs, he scowled at the animal.

"We are hibernating for the summer, remember?" he growled. "We are pulling in the drawbridge, shutting out the world. The idea is to create a masterpiece here. We are not going to be seduced from our purpose by the mouth-watering scent of what smells like real, made-from-scratch spaghetti sauce."

Fargo gave him a disgusted look.

Marsh swallowed the saliva that pooled in the back of his throat as he sniffed again the tangy bouquet of tomatoes, garlic, and the mysterious combination of herbs that made spaghetti one of his favorite dinners in the whole world. He forced himself back to his laptop. He backspaced over his last two unintelligible entries and then reread what he'd written today.

He frowned. It sounded heavy on the romance, for Pete's sake. Of course he had romance in his books. It was a big asset in attracting women readers. The movie versions of his tales would have added romance if he hadn't already put it in, and all for the courting of women viewers.

But romance per se? He didn't care if it made up the largest segment of the popular fiction market. He didn't care if the readers were as dedicated as any Penn State alumnus was to the Nittany Lions. He didn't care if the writers of romance garnered sales figures and incomes in stratospheric numbers. He was not writing romance.

He respected his heroines, wrote for them all the politically correct though historically inaccurate things that today's women readers expected. But moonlight and roses? Lavender and lace? Never! If he could get away with it, his heroes would ride into the sunset kissing their horses, not the girls.

What was it about women and romance anyway? He had never felt the stars fall or the earth tilt, and neither did his heroes. They were men of honor and ethics, not fire and passion, men like him, except they were smart enough to avoid women like Lane and the resultant first-degree burns.

Even now it hurt to remember Lane, she of the beautiful face and flawed character. Not that he missed her; he didn't. He thanked God with a fervent heart that he'd escaped before the vows were said. What hurt was the knowledge that though he'd basically groveled at her feet, mistaking his infatuation with her beauty for love, she'd never really cared for him. She had loved the prestige of being engaged to Senator Winslow's son, the excitement of campaigning, of being treated with special deference, of getting to sit on the platform. She had positively panted at the idea of developing a political dynasty like the Kennedys and Bushes with Marsh himself as the second lead. She, of course, had the starring role. His father had shared her dream.

The only difficulty had been that Marsh didn't like politics.

"But you're out there campaigning every day," Lane had said five years ago when it finally dawned on her that he wasn't going to cooperate. "You've put your graduate program on hold for a year to help your father. You must love it."

"I love my father and want for him what he wants," Marsh said. "This past year has been difficult for him since Mom's death. I want to be there for him, and helping in the campaign is one way I can do that. Because he wants the senate seat so much, because he's very good at being a senator, and because the election only happens once every six years, I'm willing to help. But hear me, Lane. Help is the operative word."

"But I love politics." Her face had that stubborn cast he'd seen before when she was thwarted. As before, he ignored the warning.

He smiled and took her hand. "I'm going to seminary as soon as the election's over."

"Seminary! But you've already got a Ph.D. in philosophy. If you've got to get more education, though I don't know why you do, go to law school."

"Why would I go to law school? I don't want to be a lawyer."

"But think how many politicians are lawyers. The two go together."

"Lane, I'm not going into politics. I'm going to seminary."

She stared, appalled. She jerked her hand from his. "You want to be a minister?"

"I told you my plans when we started to date." He remembered with clarity how he'd told her his heart dreams six months ago when they met at a party fund-raiser. She'd smiled and nodded, looking so beautiful he couldn't believe he was lucky enough to capture her attention. Apparently she hadn't listened after all.

She shook her head, her platinum hair swaying. "I didn't think you meant it, not really, not with the chance to work in Washington with your father and prepare for your own career in government."

He'd taken her hand in his again, aware that she was looking at him like he was daft. "I don't want a career in government. I'm too private a person to want to be scrutinized like that."

"What about me?" She stared at him with angry eyes. "What about what I want?"

"I thought you wanted to be my wife." *Ask not for whom the bell tolls,* he thought. *It tolls for you.* With a sinking heart he looked at her lovely face. "You don't, do you? Want to be my wife, I mean. You want to be Senator Winslow's daughter-in-law."

"Well, I certainly don't want to be a seminarian's wife! Or a minister's." She shuddered. "What's it to be, Marsh? Me or seminary?"

His father had gotten into the argument too, after Lane went to him with crocodile tears. "Marsh, Marsh," he said in his most political, sorrowful voice. You'd have thought he was orating at the funeral of a powerful political ally or grieving over the misuse of campaign funds by someone in the other party or dealing with a recalcitrant foreign dignitary over grave human rights issues. "You have become too religious. Show moderation, Son. You don't want to become a fanatic."

Marsh knew his conversion had distressed his father. It was good to go to church, to be photographed there, even to be pictured carrying a Bible. But to read that Bible? To believe it? To build your life around it and the Christ it taught about? Extremism.

"God has called me, Dad." Even as he said it, Marsh knew his father didn't understand. "I have to obey."

"What about law school instead?"

Marsh shook his head.

"You're going to lose Lane with this hardheaded attitude of yours, and you don't want that." The senator spread his hands wide and smiled with great warmth. "Think how she'll look, standing at your side when you announce for your first political contest."

"No, Dad."

He had lost Lane. He'd also lost his close relationship with his father. Marcus Winslow was proud of Marsh's Ph.D. and D.Min., but he never told anyone they were in philosophy and theology. He was proud that Marsh taught on a postgraduate level, but he never told anyone that he taught at a seminary. Rather it was my-son-the-college-professor. Any visits were brief, any conversations surface.

What would the good senator think if he knew about Craig and Marguerite? The thought made Marsh shudder.

At six-thirty Celia again climbed the stairs to Abby's and was greeted with a chorus of "Mommy, Mommy!" The running thuds across the porch above sounded more like Jack and the Beanstalk's ogre than the steps of a little girl.

"Jess, my love," drifted down, followed by, "Karlee, sweetheart, how are you, my little pumpkin?"

Marsh rose and walked into the house. Now seemed a good time to take another break. Five minutes later, his frozen pizza nuking in the microwave, he walked back to the porch, prepared to grind Marguerite into the dust as Craig nobly brought her home.

As he positioned his laptop, he watched with disfavor as the two little boys from next door pushed and shoved each other up the stairs. In less than a minute, the littler one was at the railing. "Hey, Mom! Mrs. Patterson invited us for spaghetti! We're going to eat with Jess and Karlee! Okay?"

When Marsh heard the word *spaghetti,* he lost all interest in his frozen pizza. He put his feet on the railing and attacked his laptop. The only trouble was that when he stopped to read what he'd written, it was terrible. Dull. Lifeless. Worst of all, it was pro-Marguerite.

He was preparing to hit delete when a little purse dropped out of the sky and bounced off his ankle. It landed on the porch next to Fargo's nose, startling him into a loud whoof! Marsh set his laptop aside and leaned forward over his railing. He looked up.

No one was looking down, though obviously the bag had fallen from upstairs. A fluffy black-and-white tail flicked and dropped over the edge of the upstairs rail. Marsh knew what had happened. Puppy the cat—it caught in his throat every time he said it—Puppy had knocked the purse over.

Sighing, he bent and picked it up. It must belong to one of the little girls, who didn't realize what the cat had done. He decided to return it before she was worried. First, though, he had to find something he wanted to take along.

When he stepped onto the upstairs porch, he found Abby and three youngsters pulling chairs up to the glass-topped table. Karlee lay on the chaise, and her little bruised face pulled at his heart.

"How are you feeling, sweetie?" he asked as he sank to his knees beside her.

"I'm fine," she said, but she looked very tired in spite of having napped most of the afternoon. Her pink cast lay in her lap.

Marsh pulled the felt-tipped pen he'd brought from his pocket. "May I sign your cast?"

Karlee looked at Abby for guidance. Clearly she didn't know about signing casts. Abby nodded. "That's a very nice idea."

Uncapping his pen with a flourish, Marsh said, "When someone has a cast on, she's supposed to collect everyone's names on it."

"Why?"

"Because it's fun. People write things like 'Get Well Soon' and 'Hi, Karlee.'"

He balanced her cast on his knee and started to write. She leaned forward to watch. "What are you saying?"

Running his finger under each word, he said, "Hey, hey, Good Looking."

Karlee giggled. "But I got bruises."

He put the cap back on the pen while they examined his work. "You're beautiful all the time, sweetie, bruised or not." He bent, kissing the top of her head. He held the pen out to her. "This is for you. Get lots of others to sign too."

Karlee's eyes shone with excitement.

Marsh rose, turning to the others on the porch. Abby was watching him with a half smile curving her lips. He smiled back. "Well, if it isn't Katie Luther and the Luther League."

"Who's Katie Luther?" asked Jordan.

"What's the Luther League?" Walker wanted to know.

"Lutherans is a kind of church," Jess said.

"There's no church up here," Jordan said. "Churches got steeples and pews and priests." He giggled. "We got spaghetti."

Abby patted the boy on the head. "Dr. Winslow's making a joke, obscure as it is." She smiled at him again, very sweetly, impressed, Marsh hoped, that he'd remembered her threat of last night.

"Are you Lutherans?" Jordan asked. No one answered. "I guess that means no."

Marsh nodded to Jess. "Does this belong to one of you?" He held out the purse.

"Oh! Where did you find it? I put it over there—" She pointed.

Everyone looked at Puppy who was seated on the railing at the exact spot Jess indicated, ignoring them all for the joy of washing her face.

Jess walked to Marsh who handed the purse over. "Here you are. It's a very pretty purse."

The sliding glass door opened, and Mrs. MacDonald looked out. The aroma of spaghetti sauce grew stronger and made Marsh's mouth water.

"It's ready, everyone," she said with enthusiasm. Then she saw Marsh. "Oh."

Marsh smiled his most charming smile. "Good evening. So nice to see you this lovely evening."

"Mom, I'd like you to meet Marsh Winslow." Abby looked at him with warning in her eyes. No more stories about carrying her upstairs. "He lives downstairs and is my landlord. He's a professor. My mom, Hannah MacDonald."

A tall man stepped out behind the woman.

"This is my father, Len MacDonald," Abby said.

Celia emerged next with two plates of steaming spaghetti. "Hi, Marsh."

He nodded. "How are you, Celia?" This time he was sure he got it right. "I'm glad to see Karlee's doing so well."

The man with the silver temples emerged with two more plates of spaghetti.

"This is Dr. Schofield, Karlee's doctor," Celia said. "He stopped to check on how she's doing. Wasn't that considerate of him?"

Dr. Schofield smiled in a charmingly deprecating way. Both Celia and Abby looked at him with that look women give someone they think has done something wonderful. Marsh wanted to grind his teeth. Like it was such a big thing for a doctor to make a house call, especially at dinnertime. What about a writer who tried to write with the whole world talking and laughing right over his head? Who gave someone like that any praise?

Marsh nodded at the doctor, smiled again at the kids, winked at Abby, and met the glare of Len MacDonald without flinching.

"Don't let us keep you from your dinner," Hannah MacDonald

said, her smile a poor disguise for the true meaning of her words.
Get lost.

"Right." Marsh said as he started downstairs. "Enjoy."

It was amazing how tasteless a frozen pepperoni pizza could be.

Eighteen

ABBY WOKE ON Sunday morning to a room filled with sunshine. She lay for a moment, enjoying the fact that she was in her own home, her very own place, starting her new life. She smiled at the picture she had hung on the wall facing her bed, a glorious English garden done in watercolors. It wasn't very seashoreish, but the hollyhocks, roses, lavender, and some other flowers she couldn't identify filled the frame with color and a misty, summer morning feel. Every time she looked at it, she smiled, sort of like she did every time she looked at the ocean from her porch.

Who said you couldn't begin all over again?

A knock at the door broke her reverie.

"Come on, sleepyhead." It was her mother, a lilt in her voice. "Breakfast is ready."

Abby's smile faded. Breakfast was ready? How could breakfast be ready? She hadn't made it yet.

Logically she should be glad that Mom wanted to cook. Everyone, including Abby herself, would eat better. One of Sam's great disappointments had been that Abby had never developed culinary skills of her mother's caliber. Even when she followed her mother's directions explicitly, the dishes never tasted the same.

"It's all right, dear," Sam always said with a sad little

smile. "I don't mind." After Maddie came, it was, "We don't mind."

But it was obvious he did, and meal after meal tasted like dust in Abby's mouth.

But Mom being better wasn't the point. Abby knew she was being petty, but it felt like Mom had taken over. As usual. Last night she hadn't said anything when Mom had commandeered the kitchen to make dinner. There had been too many people around to make a scene.

But this morning it was just the three of them, and she was the one who should be fixing breakfast for her parents, not the other way around.

She glanced at the bedside clock. It was only 7:45. It wasn't like she had slept the morning away. Feeling grouchy and out of sorts, she pushed back the sheet and summer blanket and climbed out of bed. She pulled on a pair of shorts and a knit top, then crossed the hall to the bathroom. Seeing her scowl in the mirror over the sink just made her scowl harder.

Time warped and she could hear her mother saying to her as a child, "Oh, Abby, dear. You mustn't frown like that." Gentle hands smoothed away the grooves on her little girl's forehead and placed a soft kiss there. "You'll get premature wrinkles."

Well, who cared! Maybe a few wrinkles would give her character. As she washed her face in the freestanding sink with more vigor than necessary, her elbow collided with her mother's travel bag of toiletries and cosmetics, resting on one edge of the sink. The flowered bag flew across the little room, struck the far wall, and tumbled to the floor, spilling vials of prescription medications and over-the-counter sinus capsules, little tubes of hand and body cream, tiny squirt bottles of hair spray and sunscreen, a disposable razor, a nail file and a bottle of soft pink polish, a tube of mascara and an eyelash curler, foundation, blusher, and two lipsticks that promptly rolled under the clawfoot tub. The pill vials preferred to hide behind the commode and under the radiator.

"Rejoice in the Lord always and again I say rejoice," Abby muttered as she got down on her hands and knees. She rescued her mother's Premarin and Synthroid from behind the toilet and the lipsticks from under the clawfoot tub. The hair spray and mascara had rolled under the radiator with the Tylenol. She had to lie on her stomach, sticking her hand into the darkness between the radiator and floor. She kept expecting some small but diabolical creature, probably one with eight legs, to grab her fingers, but the only life-form she found was a family of small dust bunnies.

As she pulled herself painfully to her feet, using the tub as a support, she muttered, "'I will rejoice in the Lord; I will be joyful in God my Savior. This is the day that the Lord has made; let us rejoice and be glad in it.'" She stuffed everything willy-nilly into the bag, zipped it shut, and stuck it behind the faucets until she finished rinsing her face. Why in the world had the woman left the bag open and on the edge of the sink anyway?

Abby looked for a better place to put the thing but saw quickly that there wasn't any. The mirror over the sink was just that, a mirror, not a medicine cabinet. The toilet tank was lined with her own things—her hair dryer and curling wand, her giant bottle of sunscreen, her skin cream, her shampoo, and her collection of pill vials. Her father's shaving kit was on top of the little radiator.

Wall shelves. That's what she needed. Wall shelves hung behind the toilet where the awful picture of sparkly, smiling seashells shimmered. She studied the room as she brushed her teeth. Dark green wicker shelves, she decided, to go with the dark ivy of the wide border at the top of the wall and the green tiles that marched single file around the otherwise white room. Maybe she could find white curtains printed with ivy to replace the dark green ones now on the window. They were too heavy, too dark.

As she left the bathroom, Abby wasn't smiling, but much of the grouchiness was gone. The next time Mom and Dad came to visit, she'd have a nice bright bathroom with plenty of space for their things. That was the joy of having her own place. She could fix it up, make improvements and changes as she liked. Living the last three years in her mother's house had been difficult after years in her own home. No matter how often Mom said, "This is your home, too," Abby knew it wasn't.

But this wonderful, shabby apartment on the beach was hers. She hugged herself. Freedom. She was actually smiling when she reached the table and found her father sitting there reading the Sunday *Philadelphia Inquirer.* Orange juice sat at three places and she could smell bacon.

"Pancakes," Dad said, answering her unasked question.

Abby made a face. She'd never liked pancakes. In fact, she had told her mother innumerable times, but Mom regularly made them anyway. The only explanation Abby could come up with was that for some reason, pancakes meant love to Mom. Like the dutiful daughter she'd always been, Abby usually forced herself to eat one. At least Dad seemed to genuinely enjoy them. He certainly ate enough.

"Hey, sweetie." Mom walked into the dining area with a huge platter of pancakes in one hand and a plate of crispy bacon in the other.

Abby stared at the mountains of food. "Mom, there are just three of us. You shouldn't have made so much."

"Why not, I'd like to know?" Mom set the pancakes in front of Abby. "Besides, pancakes freeze well. They'll be a quick breakfast before you rush off to work."

Resigned, Abby helped herself to a pancake and two strips of bacon. Maybe when Mom wasn't looking, she could pop a piece of bread in the toaster.

"Oh, honey, no wonder you're so thin!" Mom reached over, putting two more pancakes on Abby's plate.

Abby stared malevolently at the pancakes. She didn't want three pancakes. She didn't even want one. Always before she'd eaten however many of the wretched things Mom had given her. Always before she'd been the good, cooperative daughter. But not today. She sat up straight, girded for battle. She skewered the top two pancakes and lifted them from her plate.

"Thank you, but no." Her voice was flinty. With an exaggerated flourish, she returned the offending food to the serving platter while her mother watched with open mouth.

"I do not like pancakes." Abby enunciated each word as she slathered butter on her single remaining cake.

"But Abby," Mom began.

"I repeat: I do not like pancakes. I am twenty-nine years old. If I do not like pancakes, I do not have to eat them." She grabbed the maple syrup and doused her pancake.

"I never knew—"

"Because you didn't listen," Abby interrupted in what she knew was a deplorable tone of voice. She just couldn't seem to help herself. "I have told you for years that I don't like pancakes." She took a bite of her cake, forcing herself to swallow. "For years!

Just like I've told you and told you that walnuts make me feel ill. But did that stop you from putting them in the brownies and chocolate chip cookies? Uh-uh. I also don't like seafood. I don't like spinach except raw in salads with lots of bacon dressing. I don't like jelly or jam on my toast. I can't abide mushrooms. And I hate being told what I should eat!" She slapped her hand on the table for emphasis.

Abby shoved another bite of her one pancake into her mouth and chewed in the utter silence that followed her outburst. She shuddered with revulsion as she swallowed.

"Abby," her father said mildly, "don't you think you owe your mother an apol—?"

Abby put her hand up to silence him. She took a big bite of bacon and the only sound was its crunch-crunch as she chewed. "What I do like are things that crunch, things like toast and crackers and pretzels and potato chips. And crispy bacon!" She waved her bacon strip in the air. "I thank you for the bacon."

At that, she got up, walked outside, down the stairs, and onto the beach. Tears poured down her cheeks. Walking on the sand with her blurred vision was difficult and she stumbled. She swayed but stayed upright.

Oh, Lord, I'm a horrid person! A horrid person!

"Hey, you'd better watch where you're going." A warm hand grasped her elbow. "You're going to fall on your lovely face."

Marsh! Abby ducked her head, embarrassed. Here she was crying again, and she hadn't brushed her hair or her teeth. "Go away."

"Can't. You'll kill yourself if I do, lurching along like that."

"What do you do?" she asked, sniffing. "Sit there on your porch and wait for me to make a fool of myself so you can gloat?"

"Am I gloating? Here I thought I was being nice."

Abby looked at him, then looked away. She sighed with self-loathing. "I'm sorry. Really I am. I'm usually very nice. It's just—"

Marsh glanced back at the house when she didn't continue. Abby looked too and then wished she hadn't. Mom and Dad stood at the rail, watching her. Dad had his arm around Mom's shoulders and even from this distance Abby could tell Mom was crying.

"Ah," Marsh said, his voice suffused with great understanding. "The parents."

"I'm such a terrible person," Abby mumbled as new tears fell.

Marsh pulled his T-shirt out of his shorts, took the hem, and reached up to wipe Abby's tears. "You may be a little nuts, but you aren't terrible."

Abby sniffed. "Yes, I am. If you only knew how terrible, you wouldn't be so nice to me."

Marsh took her elbow again and began walking toward the water. "Watch your footing, sunshine."

She didn't and staggered again. She grabbed at him, catching a handful of T-shirt to steady herself.

"It's okay." His voice and his hands were gentle. "I've got you."

"They leave tonight." She took a long breath, letting it out on a sigh that came all the way from her toes. "I can make it until then."

"Of course you can," Marsh agreed, unclenching her fist finger by finger to reclaim his T-shirt.

When they reached the firm sand revealed by the receding tide, Marsh dropped her elbow. He turned them north, and they walked for a while in silence "My father comes on Tuesday."

Abby nodded. "Is he as nice as you?"

Marsh blinked. "You think I'm nice?"

Abby smiled through her tears at his surprise. "At least some of the time. Like now. Like when you gave Karlee the marker. Like when you let me cry all over you at the hospital."

"Huh." Marsh studied the horizon intently, and Abby could have sworn she had just embarrassed him. He cleared his throat. "Well, what I was going to say was that if you think your parents are controlling, you haven't seen anything until you've seen the good senator."

"The good senator?" Abby's mind whirled. Winslow. Senator. "You mean that Senator Marcus Winslow is your father?" Her voice ended on a high screech of disbelief.

Marsh shrugged. "Well, someone's got to be his kid."

"But you live in Ohio."

"Not as an adult. It's not a requirement that a senator's adult children live in their parent's state, you know."

Slightly embarrassed at her foolish remark, Abby said, "Boy, would my father flip if he knew."

"Good flip or bad flip?"

"Oh, good. He thinks your father walks on water."

"Yeah." Marsh stuck his hands in his pockets and started walking back the way they'd come. "Most people do. Even those who don't like his politics like him."

Abby turned to him, surprised by the sorrow in his voice. "You don't like him?"

"Oh, I love him. No question. It's just…"

Abby waited, but he said nothing more. Whatever the difficulties between Marsh and his father, apparently he wasn't talking about them today.

"Your mother died several years ago, didn't she?"

Marsh nodded. "I still miss her. She was a great lady." He grinned. "She knew how to manage my father better than anyone I've ever seen, including all his political advisors. 'Now, Marcus,' she'd say, 'you just listen to me.' And she'd tell him how it ought to be done. She was usually right on the money."

"How about your dad's new wife? Is she as adept politically?

Marsh looked vague. "She's not Mom."

"Will she be coming with him on Tuesday?"

Marsh took her elbow to lead her over the soft sand to the house. "I hope not. It'll be easier on all of us."

Abby wondered what that comment was supposed to mean.

An hour later with her hair combed, teeth brushed, lipstick on, and red pantsuit ironed, Abby entered Seaside Chapel with her parents. The chapel was a building of weathered cedar topped with a white steeple. It looked very seashoreish, pleasing Abby's sense of place.

Abby didn't know about her parents, but she wasn't in a very worshipful mood. Neither Mom nor Dad had mentioned her temper tantrum and unprecedented flight, so she hadn't broached the subject either. Instead, it hung in the air between them like a drunk's giant pink elephant, unseen by everyone else but very present to them.

Oh, God, I'm afraid to talk about it with them! I'll say things I'll regret forever with my emotions as raw as they are right now. Please, Lord, show me how to be both independent and loving. Please! I'm so afraid that for us they are mutually exclusive.

They were barely inside the front door of the chapel when Jess ran to Abby and grabbed her hand.

"We saved you places," she said as she pulled Abby toward the door to the sanctuary. "Mommy didn't want to wait in the lobby with Karlee."

Smiling, Abby let herself be pulled along. Her parents followed. It wasn't until they were seated that she saw Marsh and a friend seated in the row ahead. After their meeting Friday morning, she had been so disappointed that her landlord was such a bear. Then she'd learned that he wasn't. He was funny and kind and—be honest, girl—sometimes grouchy. But she liked him. He was going to make a wonderful friend to enjoy in her new life.

Everyone stood to sing a worship chorus, which was followed by a time of greeting one another. Abby watched Marsh turn to her parents.

"Mr. MacDonald." He grinned a wide welcome as he stuck out his hand. "Mrs. MacDonald. So nice to have you visiting with us this morning."

Her father tried to smile back. Her mother didn't even make the attempt.

"Thank you," she said abruptly, turning to Marsh's friend.

With a shrug Marsh turned to Jess and Karlee. "I see a pair of princesses right here in my church," he said with mock astonishment. "Beautiful princesses."

"Oh, Dr. Winslow, we're not princesses," Karlee said earnestly. "We're just Jess and Karlee."

Marsh blinked and rubbed his eyes. "Why so you are." He leaned forward. "But the beautiful part is true."

The little girls giggled, happy with the compliment.

When Marsh reached for Abby's hand, she saw his eyes were twinkling. "Just who are you this morning, if I may ask? Not a princess, I don't think. Lydia, the seller of purple cloth who hosted a church in her house? Or maybe Phoebe, the deaconess who cared for those in need? You seem to be feeding the whole world up in your apartment. I'm sure you're not Sapphira, the liar."

Abby folded her arms, trying to look threatening. "How about Jael who put a tent peg through her enemy's head?"

Marsh laughed in appreciation as he took his seat, and Abby felt pleased with herself. She made believe she didn't see her parents' horrified looks. It was amazing, but in two days, she was more at ease with Marsh the Grump, who wasn't all that grumpy most of the time, than she'd ever been with Sam.

A shaft of sorrow pierced her heart, not because she missed Sam but because she and Sam had had so little. She never would have bantered with him about Jael. He'd have been horrified.

"I love your quiet and gentle spirit," Sam had said over and over.

She used to think he was complimenting her, but now she wondered if he hadn't been programming her. She missed the first part of Pastor Paul Trevelyan's message as she thought about this new idea. It seemed that the longer she was a widow, the more she realized how unequal their partnership had been. Sam had dominated completely, and she had let him.

But she was breaking free!

"Come home with us," Abby pressed Celia after the service. She needed a buffer to get her through the afternoon with the parents. "Karlee can sleep at my house as well as yours, and Jess can play with Walker and Jordan."

Jess wrinkled her nose. "Not those two!" But she was barely out of the car before the boys ran over, and she went running onto the sand with them.

"Stay away from the water," Celia called after her.

Jess nodded and waved.

When the adults and Karlee reached Abby's porch, they could see Jess and the two boys digging in the wet sand, building a castle. There weren't many people on the beach, June not being a month in which Seaside bulged with tourists and guests. It would be easy to keep an eye on the kids.

"I thought I'd send Dad for some fresh flounder and make us flounder stuffed with crabmeat," Mom said as she turned from waving to Jess.

Abby's hands were fists before she even realized it. "No, Mom. You are my guest." She forced her hands open. "I'm in charge of the meal."

"Nonsense, dear." Mom pulled the sliding door open. "Feeding people is what I do best. Len, go to the seafood place over on Bay. Get me some flounder and crabmeat."

Dad nodded, pulling his car keys back out of his pocket.

"No, Mom." Abby's voice was part steel, part desperation. She couldn't let them take over her home. She couldn't. She'd never be free if she did. "I am making dinner. You may sit on the porch and read the paper or take a walk on the beach—whatever you want—but you are not making dinner. I am."

Mom looked poleaxed. Dad looked angry. "Abby, that's no way to speak to your mother."

Quaking inside, Abby looked him in the eye. "I'm making dinner, Dad."

"I'll just help then," Mom said, heading for the kitchen.

"No." Abby stepped in front of her mother. "Celia will help me. You go find something to do until dinner's ready."

There was a moment of awkward silence, but Abby stood tall and unyielding. Dad broke first.

"Come on, Hannah. Let's go take a walk."

"Len." Entreaty laced Mom's voice.

He gave a little shake of his head and led the way to the stairs.

I feel like Alvild, the Swedish princess who defied her parents and ran away to become a successful pirate. Abby rubbed her forehead as she walked into her kitchen. *At least I didn't get even by becoming a pirate. Just a children's librarian. And all I want to do is cook my own dinner in my own house!*

Nineteen

H ANNAH MACDONALD walked to the car with Len. It was time to go home, back to Scranton, but she had a plan, a plan that Len had agreed to. Her heart beat against her ribs like a wild bird against the bars of a cage as she thought of carrying it out, but she was certain she was doing the right thing.

Help it work, Lord. Help it work.

Len turned to her. "You're sure?"

Hannah nodded. "We have to do something before it's too late."

"She's not going to appreciate it."

"Maybe not today, but she will later." Hannah spoke with confidence. "If there's one thing I know, it's Abby's heart."

"You're a good woman, Hannah MacDonald," Len said as he leaned in and kissed her. "I think I'll keep you."

Hannah wrapped her arms around his middle, resting her head on his chest. "Like you could get rid of me."

They stood quietly, holding each other, until a red sports car pulled into the parking area, surprising them as it screeched to a stop inches from Len's bumper, blocking his car in the drive. Marsh climbed out of the driver's seat, a huge smile creasing his face.

A boy and his toy, Hannah thought. *A rude, crude*

boy and a flashy, trashy toy. Oh, dear Father, protect Abby from him!

The passenger side opened, and a very handsome man climbed out, his hand over his heart. "Remind me never to let *you* drive again," he called to Marsh.

Hannah stared at the newcomer in astonishment. "He looks just like Rick Mathis," she whispered to Len. Same tousled dark hair, same wonderful brown eyes, same shoulders stretching from here to there and back, same aura of power and masculinity.

"Who?" Len whispered.

"Duke Beldon. *A Man against the West.* Can't you just see him sitting in the saddle or waving his gun at the bad guys?"

Len nodded. "Oh, yeah. Loved that show. But what would someone like that be doing with someone like Marsh Winslow?" Len said Marsh's name with a distaste that matched Hannah's own.

"I love it, Rick." Marsh bounced on his toes with pleasure. "There's no way I'm not driving that baby again."

Rick looked resigned. "I was afraid you'd say that."

The men gave one last fond look at the little car and started for the house. Marsh seemed to suddenly see Hannah and Len. He stopped beside them. "Rick, meet Mr. and Mrs. MacDonald. Their daughter Abby is my upstairs tenant."

"Pleased to meet you," said Rick with a charming smile. "I'm Rick Yakabuski. Let me know when you're leaving. I'll move my car for you."

"I think you'll need to move it right away." Hannah smiled in apology at the young man as she pointed to the duffel Len carried.

Rick nodded, held out his hand, and caught the car keys when Marsh lobbed them to him. He folded himself into the little car, gunned the engine, and backed onto Central. With a wave he disappeared around the corner.

Len looked at Marsh. "We didn't mean for him to leave."

"He's not leaving. He just couldn't resist driving around the block. Or two. Or ten. Rick has a thing for that car."

"I take it it's new."

Marsh shook his head, paused, then nodded.

Well, is it new or not? Yes or no? Seems a simple question with a simple answer to me.

"It's a rental," he explained. "So it's new because he never drove it before, but it's not like it's his personal new car."

A rental? Hannah stared after Rick. You could rent cars like that? For how many million dollars? She eyed Marsh as he stood relaxed in his drive, gray T-shirt stretched across shoulders that rivaled Rick's, jeans riding low on his hips, feet stuffed sockless into Top-Siders, and golden hair gleaming in the setting sun. Too attractive by half. Put him and Rick together, and women of all ages and sensibilities would experience heart palpitations. Add little red cars and houses on the beach, and women would topple like sand castles before the encroaching tide.

Just where did they get the money for such outlandish and wasteful perks? Drugs? Industrial espionage? Computer fraud? Mob connections? Surely there was no way to earn that much by legal means.

She squared her shoulders, more confident than ever that her plan was wise.

The little red car roared up to the curb and Rick climbed out. As he walked past, Len couldn't resist. "Did anyone ever tell you—?"

Rick nodded, all but rolling his eyes. "All the time, especially since we have the same first name." He followed Marsh to his porch. "Nice to have met you," he called over his shoulder. Marsh threw a negligent wave.

Len flung his duffel into his trunk. "Well, hon, it's time."

"Hey, you two," Abby called from the top of her stairs. "Trying to sneak off without saying good-bye?"

"Drat," said Hannah as she smiled and waved. "Let's go. Quick."

As Abby made her slow way down the stairs, Len climbed behind the wheel. Hannah leaned in and kissed him.

"Same time next week," she said. "I'll miss you."

Len kissed her again and put the car in reverse. He waved and called, "See you next Friday evening, Abby." Then he was gone.

Abby halted on the bottom step, disbelief written all over her face. "Dad left without you."

This, Hannah knew, was the crucial time. She nodded and smiled. "He'll be back."

"Next Friday." Abby stared at her mother. "He left and you stayed."

Hannah shrugged as she walked toward Abby. "Dad and I talked, and we decided you shouldn't be left alone."

"You decided what?"

Hannah didn't like that tone of voice. "You're not used to being alone, dear. You've never been alone in your life."

"What if I want to be alone? What if I *yearn* to be alone?"

"Shush, baby." Hannah put her finger to her daughter's lips to quiet Abby's rising voice. The last thing she wanted was for Marsh and his friend to be privy to their family business. Or the strange deMarcos next door, for that matter. "We know you're having trouble adjusting. We want to be here for you."

"I'm not having trouble adjusting," Abby snapped. "I'm doing just fine."

Hannah ignored her and kept talking. Abby had always been easy to talk over, easy to wear down. The girl's innate politeness and malleable spirit would take over. Abby ended up listening and agreeing. Hannah gave an encouraging smile. "You don't know anybody here, and I worry about you, you know."

"I do too know people. I know Marsh and Celia and the deMarcos and Sean Schofield. I'll know my coworkers after tomorrow and will work in a public place where I can meet people all the time. What do you mean, I don't know anybody? I think that for two days in town, I've done very well."

Once again Hannah made believe she hadn't been interrupted. "I don't want to lose any beauty sleep fretting over you. At my age I can't afford to, you know." She smiled at her own little joke.

Abby seemed to find nothing funny in what she said. She just stood, staring belligerently. One day knowing Marsh Winslow hadn't made the girl that rude, had it? "Dad has to go to work this week or he would have stayed too. When he comes back on Friday, he'll be here with us for two weeks. Won't that be fun?"

"You never asked me what I thought." Abby's voice started to rise again. "You never asked! This is my house. I'm supposed to give the invitations, not you."

Hannah looked at Abby. Her daughter's face was white, her eyes wide, and Hannah realized that her plan was going to be a harder sell than she'd thought. This new independent streak of Abby's was rearing its ugly head much too often. It had to be squashed. "We love you, sweetheart."

Abby opened her mouth, then closed it. She pressed her lips together like she was trying to hold words back. Or like she was furious. But why should she be mad? She should be thankful that her mother and father loved her enough to put themselves out for her.

Did Abby think that Hannah would rather sleep alone in that tacky guest room than with her much loved husband in their cozy bedroom at home? Did she think that Hannah would like reaching out in the night to touch Len and finding nothing? Who was she to share her heart with? One look at Abby's closed stance, and it was obvious that she wouldn't be listening anytime soon.

What about Len, at home by himself, cooking his own dinners, washing his own clothes, sleeping alone. Didn't Abby realize that they were paying a price for loving their only child so very much, a steep price of self-sacrifice, and that they'd been doing it all her life, especially the last three years? But, Hannah thought with a touch of pride, they were paying it willingly.

"Once you've had time to get used to the idea, I know you'll be delighted that I could stay and help you out. We can spend the days on the beach, and in the evening we can go out for dinner and then to the boardwalk to shop. We can have a just-us-girls week." She put her hand over Abby's where it still rested on the banister and squeezed. "We'll have such fun."

Abby turned without responding, pulling herself along by the banister. She didn't look at Hannah, nor did she say a word. It was like Hannah wasn't there.

A spurt of anger flashed through her. Ungrateful child. Still, her mother's heart hated to see the girl work so hard to do something as simple as climb stairs. She hurried forward, taking Abby's arm to help her.

To Hannah's great surprise and consternation, Abby wrenched herself free, her movement so fast that she almost overbalanced and went tumbling. Only her grip on the banister kept her from falling.

Hannah put a hand on Abby's back to steady her. "Careful, dear, careful. We don't want you to fall."

Abby's response was to pull herself up two more steps.

"Come on, Abby. Don't be stubborn. It'll be much easier if you just let me help."

Abby shook her head and climbed. Sighing, Hannah followed. She had to figure out a way to break through Abby's foolish and uncharacteristic resentment. Hannah brightened as an idea struck.

"How about if I fix us some popcorn?" Abby loved popcorn. "We can sit on the porch and talk, just you and me. There were so many people around this weekend that I didn't get a chance to talk with you, just you."

Her daughter continued silent and resentful.

"Abby, I'm talking to you."

Abby acted as if she hadn't heard. She crossed the porch, opened the door, crossed the living room, and disappeared down the bedroom hall. There she stopped, looked at her mother, and said, "Alvild." She then turned on her heel and very firmly shut her door, just a fraction this side of a slam.

Miffed, Hannah stood in the living room, staring after her daughter. What was the matter with her? And who or what was Alvild? Another of those weird women who had given Abby so many of her bad ideas?

Hannah turned on her heel and strode back to the porch. There she paced, waiting for Abby to emerge and apologize. As she did, vignettes of Abby through the years flashed across her mind like so many movie outtakes and trailers.

Abby as a baby—happy, gurgling her joy with life, rarely crying.

Abby as a toddler—curious, active, but never a terrible two.

Abby as a precocious preschooler—reciting the alphabet at three, learning to read all by herself as a five-year-old, negotiating peace whenever the neighborhood kids got into fights. When she began school, her teachers loved her for her keen mind and her obedience, and the children loved her because she was kind.

Abby as a teen—more a friend than a daughter, cooperative, pleasant, popular, respected, never rebellious.

Abby as a college student—meeting Sam, falling for him, graduating magna cum laude with a degree in elementary ed, marrying the weekend after graduation.

Abby as a young married—decorating their apartment and then their house, learning to be a good wife to Sam, the perfect husband for her with his solicitous attitude and protectiveness.

Abby as an elementary teacher—charming the students, impressing the administration, and grading papers, always grading papers.

Abby as a loving young mother—doting on Maddie, bathing

her, feeding her, playing with her, enjoying her.

Abby as a patient—terribly injured, her survival uncertain for weeks, then her sorrow, her depression, her tears, her incredible pain, her long recuperation.

Now at twenty-nine, Abby rebellious and uncooperative.

What have I done to deserve this treatment, Lord? What have I done but pour my life into her, especially these last three years.

The low rumble of men's voices rose from the porch below. Hannah couldn't understand the words, but she didn't need to. She didn't want to. In fact, she'd be glad if she never saw or heard from either of those men again, and doubly glad if Abby never saw them again.

A different series of pictures played across Hannah's mind screen.

Abby smiling at Marsh last night on the porch.

Abby letting Marsh hold her elbow and help her across the sand.

Abby letting Marsh dry her tears—with his T-shirt no less!

Abby flirting with Marsh at church this morning.

And that was just what she'd seen. How much more was there? Len told her Marsh had carried Abby up the stairs. Carried! It was more than enough to make a concerned mother go gray in spite of her hair treatments.

The back of Hannah's neck itched as she heard the men downstairs laugh. She squared her shoulders. The accident had changed Abby, and not for the better, but Hannah would protect her from the wolves, especially those within the fold.

That's what mothers were for.

Twenty

HE KNEW WHAT he was going to do. The idea had come to him as he stood in his marble shower stall, enjoying the blasts of water from six jets. His workout this morning had been rigorous, and the hot water loosened and eased his muscles. It also stirred the idea marinating in his subconscious. He fine-tuned the plan as he toweled himself dry with a cream-colored, over-sized towel. He dropped the towel on the floor for Carmen to clean up and moved to the sink. He grinned at his reflection as he lathered for his shave.

Since it would be imprudent to harm Abby Patterson physically, he would undermine her reputation. He would destroy her credibility. That way if she ever remembered anything, her word would be suspect. If she accused him, who would believe someone like *her*?

She looked like such a gullible, trusting woman. It was obvious that there was no place like the Pines in her background to toughen her up. He had no doubt that she'd fold under the slightest pressure. Without a hardscrabble background, she hadn't the experiences necessary to put the steel in her spine she'd need to escape him.

It would be easy to ruin her, easier than it had been

sinking Joe Rothman. Rothman's once shining halo lay on the floor, tarnished beyond recovery. He would never be a threat again, never a force, never a possibility for the appointment they had both sought. All it had taken was a word or two in the right place, a whisper of corruption, of incompetency, of philandering. Such things still mattered around here in spite of the influence of Atlantic City and the casino crowd.

The first time he'd killed a reputation, he had chosen his father as scapegoat. It was part of his plan for escaping. As far as he was concerned, anything was fair game if it would get him out of the Pines. Let those sympathetic, foolish teachers think he was being harassed by his father, harshly punished, and mocked for trying to succeed. A couple of times when he'd hurt himself roughhousing with McCoy, he'd let them think his father had inflicted the bruises.

Mrs. LaDow, tenth grade biology, had been especially gullible. Funny he should think of her. He stretched his neck taut to pull the razor over his Adam's apple. What would she think if she could see him now?

"The Pine Barrens are the eighth wonder of the world, students," she always told her classes. "Appreciate them! You are so fortunate to live where you do."

Not that any of them believed her. It was hard to put much confidence in a lady who admitted to sleeping with baby opossums to keep them warm. But she'd believed everything he told her, his face full of sorrow, his voice halting.

He'd played her and some of the others for three years. When it came time to be recommended for scholarships, he'd received more than his share of both recommendations and awards. He'd have been grateful to her and the others except he felt he'd earned the money himself.

This time he didn't have the luxury of a long campaign. Her memory could kick in any time. He splashed aftershave on as he considered the steps he would take.

Twenty-one

CELIA LOOKED AT Karlee as she lay sleeping in the shabby blue bedroom the girls shared. She could hear the TV playing softly in the living room as Jess watched the Disney movie on ABC. It was Sunday night, two days after the accident, but still Celia's heart contracted and her stomach pitched every time she looked at Karlee and thought of what might have happened if the driver hadn't swerved at the last minute.

What kind of an idiot feels grateful to a hit-and-run driver because he didn't hurt her child as badly as he might have? She frowned. *He* didn't hurt her child? Maybe it was a she. He. She. Either way, she reminded herself grimly, the person hadn't stopped. How could he not stop? How could she just drive on, leaving a child lying in the street?

Lord, I don't know who the driver was and I know I'm nuts, but I do feel thankful to whoever it was that he or she was willing to swerve. Work in the heart of that person. Help whoever it is to come forward and admit guilt. The law deals more easily with those who confess, doesn't it? And there is such a thing as responsibility. I'll never believe that any driver would hit a child on purpose, but every driver should be a big enough person to admit responsibility, to stop and help or at least call for help.

Celia reached out, pushing Karlee's hair back from

her forehead. She made her touch butterfly light so as not to hurt her baby. Tears stung her eyes as she looked at the bruises and the scrapes.

Celia let her head fall back, looking beyond the cracked ceiling of the shabby bedroom with the twin beds wearing limp, washed-out blue chenille bedspreads and no headboards. Her eyes squeezed shut. *Oh, God, thank You for keeping her safe!*

She lowered her head, and her eyes fell on the pink cast that enveloped Karlee's right arm. It was now covered with the signatures of everyone who had been at Abby's house yesterday and this afternoon, even a rocky J-o-r-backwards d-a-backwards n from Jordan.

Abby. Celia smiled. Another gift from the Lord. It amazed Celia how her new friend had stepped in with her offer to watch the girls yesterday. People just didn't do things like that for her. There was the invitation to be part of the fun at Abby's place today, like she belonged. Celia couldn't remember the last time she had felt so accepted, so wanted. She hugged the warm feeling to her like Karlee used to hug her security blanket. It was true that God did bring good things out of bad. If not for the accident, she'd never have met Abby.

But Abby started her new job tomorrow and couldn't help with the girls again. So what was she to do with Karlee and Jess all day? It was a given that the woman who had been in charge of Karlee on Friday wasn't getting near her ever again.

Celia scowled. If she felt a weird gratitude to the driver, she felt nothing but resentment and bitterness toward the woman to whom she'd entrusted Karlee and not a little anger at herself for choosing so poorly. All she could say in her own defense was that she had been desperate for help, and the woman had seemed nice. In fact, she probably was nice. She just shouldn't be responsible for small children.

Celia shut her eyes and swallowed. Letting herself get angry with the woman wasn't helping anything. It was creating its own nasty wrinkle in her spirit, a wrinkle that would grow, expanding until she was so rumpled spiritually and emotionally that she'd be fit for only the rag pile.

Whatever happens, Lord, don't let me become like Aunt Bernice, all nastiness, suspicion, and bitterness. But, Lord, I do have to go to work tomorrow. What am I to do? I can't not go to work. I need the job. I need the income. I need the insurance coverage.

Tears stung her eyes. Sometimes she got so tired of fighting to survive.

She looked again at her sleeping daughter. What would they have done if there had been no health coverage? She knew how rare it was that fledgling massage therapists were employed full-time with all the perks that entailed. Pinky, that brilliant and flamboyant owner of the Seaside Spa, was one in a million. She was also a single mom who understood what it was like to be squeezed in the ever-present, ever-tightening vise of no relief. No relief from the financial problems of paying the rent or buying new shoes for little growing feet. Crank it tighter. No relief from the laundry, the shopping, the cleaning. Crank it tighter. No relief from the presence of kids, the disciplining of kids, the energy of kids, the needs of kids. Crank it several turns tighter.

"Oh, Lord, what should I do?" she whispered into the darkened room. "Help me, please!"

"Mom." Jess stood in the doorway. She held out the cell phone. "It's for you."

Celia looked beyond the ceiling once again. "You use cell phones today instead of still small voices?"

Smiling at her joke, she took the phone from Jess, who raced back to the living room and her movie. "Hello?" The tiny cell phone was the only phone she had. She couldn't afford both a traditional phone and a cell phone, so she had never activated the line into her small apartment. With the cell, she would always be within reach, should the girls ever need her. Not that being available had done anything to save Karlee on Friday.

"Celia? This is Pastor Paul."

Celia blinked. Not God's still small voice, but that of one of his emissaries. Maybe God did answer through cell phones.

"I'm calling to ask if you need help with your girls tomorrow."

Astonishment kept Celia tongue-tied.

"Celia? Are you there?"

"Yes, yes, I'm here. In fact, I was here praying for an answer to that very problem."

"Tell me what you need, and we'll see what we can do. I've

already had a couple of ladies call me to volunteer. They didn't want to call you without my calling first since you haven't been part of Seaside Chapel long enough to know them. I'm calling to vouch for them and their characters."

"They know me?" Celia couldn't believe it.

"They know Karlee. The prayer chain, remember? They saw her in church this morning. That little bruised and battered face is enough to break anyone's heart."

Celia's throat choked with emotion. That these wonderful people in Seaside cared enough to come through for her was another miracle of the first order. She had to swallow several times before she could answer. "Both Jess and Karlee need care all day. I work from nine till six, six days a week."

Celia was sure that the long hours and six-day involvement would kill the desire of anyone to help. It was just too much. Well, she understood that because it was too much for her many times, and it was her survival she was fighting for, her girls whom she loved more than life itself.

"Okay, no problem," Pastor Paul said. "There are a couple of grandmoms who would love to help. Their own grandkids live quite a distance away, and they want a kid fix. I'll have them call you to finalize the plans rather than stay in the middle and confuse things. Expect to hear from Doris Winsky and Mona LaFever. I think Mrs. Winsky will be the main baby-sitter."

Grateful beyond words but ever cautious, Celia asked, "How much do these women charge?"

"Oh." She could hear the surprise in Pastor Paul's voice. "There's no charge."

"What?" Celia's voice was a squeak.

"No charge," Pastor Paul repeated. "They're doing this as a service to the Lord."

Celia hung up in a daze. Responsible day care and no charge! How could this be?

The phone chirped again, making Celia jump. It couldn't be Doris Winsky or Mona LaFever already.

"Celia, it's me, Abby."

"Why are you whispering?" Giddy with relief over the resolution of the baby-sitting problem, Celia wanted nothing more than to giggle at her friend's bizarre behavior. "Are you hiding from the bad guys and need rescuing? Or is Fargo after you, and you've escaped up a tree and don't want him to know which one? Or did you somehow get a sore throat in the last couple of hours?"

"I don't want my mother to hear," Abby hissed.

"Your mom? I thought she and your father were going home early this evening."

"I thought so too."

"They didn't leave yet?"

"He left. She's staying."

Celia heard the anger and distress in Abby's voice. "That's not a good thing, I take it."

"It's a terrible thing!" Abby all but wailed, forgetting to keep her voice down. "I don't want my mother to be my keeper."

"But she loves you," Celia said, thinking how wonderful it would be to have a mother who was so interested in her daughter that she stayed with her to help her get settled.

"Does she?" Abby gave a sad little hiccup of a laugh. "Then why can't she let me live my own life?"

Celia didn't have an answer. "What can I do for you?"

"Come to dinner tomorrow night."

"I was just there yesterday and today. Aren't you getting a bit tired of me and the girls?"

"Celia, you've got to come! I'm afraid of what I'll say to Mom if you're not here. Please come. Please."

Although Celia thought Abby was overreacting, the woman was clearly desperate. She thought of Abby sitting with her in the hospital Friday night and baby-sitting yesterday, and she knew she had to help no matter what she thought. "I can be there by about six-thirty."

"Wonderful!" Relief flowed out of the receiver in waves, washing Celia in its rosy glow. "You are my new best friend."

Celia hung up feeling bemused. Abby's new best friend, huh? She could deal with that very well, though she had to admit that she didn't understand what was so terrible about having your mother for a houseguest, especially when she was as nice as Mrs. MacDonald. Now if the houseguest were her own mother, whom she hadn't seen since she married Eddie, then there'd be a problem.

Awful as Eddie had been, he'd been better than her embittered, hate-filled mother. Anything was better than her mother, even living with Aunt Bernice and Poor Uncle Walter, even struggling alone and constantly hitting your head against the proverbial brick wall.

But Mrs. MacDonald was fun and helpful and loving. She was also a mean cook. Still, Abby knew her mother much better than Celia. Maybe the warm public persona wasn't evident in the intimacy of family. Lots of people thought Aunt Bernice was the soul of Christian love, but they'd never bothered to check their opinions against the experience of Celia or Poor Uncle Walter or even the girls.

Celia was tired to the bone when she fell into her narrow bed in the smaller of the two bedrooms in their third-floor apartment. She always had to remind herself to duck when she got into or out of bed because of the steep pitch of the roofline. The first time she'd made up the bed, she cracked her head hard enough to bring tears. The headache lasted for two days. But it was her apartment, her bedroom, her faded pink walls and ugly pink floral curtains.

And she had Doris Winsky to watch the girls. Even over the telephone she had sounded warm and grandmotherly. God was good.

When morning came, Karlee was in an ugly mood. She sat on the sagging sofa, aching all over, lower lip stuck out in a pout to end all pouts. She tried to cross her arms, but the cast kept foiling her attempts, which only made her grumpier. She proclaimed in a loud voice that she didn't like any of the four kinds of cereal in the house, she wasn't about to let Celia leave her with a lady she'd never seen, and she didn't want to have anything to do with any lady named Doris Winsky.

For her part, Celia was delighted with Mrs. Winsky. She was in her late fifties, had been a widow for "way too long," which translated to seven years, and had three kids who lived all over the country.

"California, Indiana, and South Carolina," she said, looking not at all like a Norman Rockwell grandmom. Instead of gray hair, Mrs. Winsky's was a warm brown. Instead of old lady curls or a bun, she had a sophisticated wedge cut. While Celia couldn't call her slim, she was trim, dressed in jeans and a T-shirt.

I hope I look half as good when I'm her age.

"I'm glad my kids are all doing so well, but the loneliness gets to me every so often." Mrs. Winsky picked up the dirty breakfast dishes and carried them to the sink. "I always ask God to give me projects to serve Him and keep the loneliness at bay. Your sweet girls are just the thing. I have one little granddaughter, but she belongs to the son who lives in California, so I don't get to see her much. I don't know when the other two will ever get married, let alone give me some more little ones."

Doris Winsky sighed at the unfairness of it all, then shook herself for all the world like a retriever emerging from the water. "So don't you worry about Karlee. We'll be fine. I need her, and she needs me."

"Mrs. Winsky, I can't begin to tell—"

"It's Doris, dear, and don't bother. Go. Have a good day. After we clean up here, we'll go to my house. I've got lots of kid stuff including a swing set."

To her surprise, Celia did have a good day. There was only one open hour in her appointment schedule, and the surfboarding gentleman of last week called to fill that. Abby also called, scheduling an appointment for Wednesday evening at five o'clock. As she had promised, she asked for Celia.

"I am so pleased at the way your schedule is staying filled up," Pinky said as she looked over the calendar for the next day. Her pink T-shirt, pink capris, and pink tennies should have looked ridiculous on her, but they didn't. Instead they looked like Pinky. "I've never hired anyone full time before, and I wasn't certain if it was a good idea or not. I just thought it was worth a try because I was getting so tired of balancing all the part-time schedules."

"I'm glad you took the risk, what with Karlee's accident and all."

"What accident?" Pinky was all concern. "Is she all right?"

Celia had to laugh at herself. Since Karlee's accident was the main item in her life at the moment, she had assumed it was of equal importance to all others too. Here was proof that the majority of the world not only didn't care about Karlee, they didn't even know!

"A hit-and-run?" Pinky shrieked when Celia told her what happened. "Some lowlife hit your little Karlee and ran?"

Celia nodded, thinking about Mrs. Ebsen, lying on her back in the next room, wearing nothing but a pink sheet. In theory the woman was relaxing to the soothing music piped into the room, but with Pinky shrieking at full volume, the desired tranquility might prove unattainable.

"What are the police doing?" Pinky demanded, her bottle-blond hair with just the hint of pink to it quivering with indignant energy. "Have they arrested anyone yet? Were there any witnesses? Any physical evidence? You did say that Karlee's all right? Is she in the hospital? What in the world are you doing here? You should be with her!"

Pinky's face was fuchsia with emotion and distress, a fine match to the multiple shades of pink in which the spa was decorated. Celia had never quite figured out how the place managed to avoid looking like Dame Barbara Cartland's boudoir.

Calming Pinky took ten minutes of earnest talking, gave Mrs. Ebsen time for a nice little power nap, and threw Celia's schedule off by that amount for the rest of the day. Still, before she knew it, the day was over and she found herself on Mrs. Winsky's doorstep, nervous about how Karlee had fared. Jess let her in with a smile on her face, and Karlee looked up at her from her seat on the sofa with all the hauteur of a young Queen Bess surveying her subjects.

"Mrs. Winsky told me this is my sofa," she announced as soon as Celia kissed her hello. "No one, not even Jess, can sit here unless I say so. That's because I'm sick, and it's important I get treated good."

Doris laughed. "That's a close approximation to what I said, although I don't remember having my nose quite so high in the air."

"It is what you said," Karlee assured her.

"Did you have a good time?" Celia asked as soon as she and the girls were buckled into the car.

"I did," Karlee said. "She made me hot dogs."

Jess smiled. "She's very nice, Mommy. Much nicer than the other lady."

"Well, you don't have to see that other lady ever again," Celia promised as they pulled up to Abby's house and parked behind a big, powerful motorcycle. They weren't even out of the car before a little red sports car squealed to a stop in the drive. To Celia's surprise, Marsh Winslow was driving it. Somehow she hadn't thought him the little red car type.

"Is this your car, Dr. Winslow?" Jess, impressed, asked when he climbed out.

"You like it?"

Jess nodded, glancing at their car and trying to hide a sigh. Poor baby, Celia thought. Embarrassed by our car. But at least it runs.

"I like it too, but it's not mine." He sighed deeply, theatrically, and let his shoulders slump. The kids giggled. "It belongs to my friend Rick over here."

Celia had been watching Jess, but now she turned her attention to Rick and blinked. As he walked around the car and stopped beside Marsh, she said, "Did anyone ever tell you—"

"Yeah," he said, putting his hand up to stop her. "But my last name is Yakabuski."

She nodded, thinking he was every bit as handsome as the famous movie and TV star he so resembled. She had watched Rick Mathis as Duke Beldon on *A Man against the West* every week for five years, wondering if there were any men on the planet like Duke—considerate, clever, and principled—or if he was just the figment of some writer's imagination. Duke had ridden into the sunset three years ago, and now Rick Mathis played cowboys both on TV and in the movies, but she still missed Duke.

Even Eddie had watched *A Man against the West*. "Now there's a man's man," he'd say. "He don't let no woman or screaming kids tie him down."

Now that she thought about it, it was the nights Duke Beldon rode into their home that Eddie was the nastiest. Was it the contrast he saw between himself and the fictional cowboy, or was it Duke's freedom that he desperately wanted? The latter without doubt, considering how he finally scarpered.

Celia became aware that Rick was staring at her. She tried not to squirm, but she knew what she looked like, all weary and dirty from a tiring day, makeup long gone, shirt wrinkled and spotted with oil, and her hair all wild from the open car windows. Maybe now she'd get up the courage to touch enough of Poor Uncle Walter's five thousand dollars to get the air-conditioning fixed. But then again, why should she? The damage was already done.

When Rick turned and looked at the little girls, she sighed in relief.

"And who are you angels?"

Her oldest grinned, as susceptible as any woman to the smile of a handsome man. "I'm Jess and she's Karlee."

"Are you related to the beautiful blond angel standing beside Dr. Winslow?"

Beautiful blond angel? Celia felt like turning to see who was standing behind her.

Jess had to look too. "You mean our mom?"

She need not sound quite so surprised, Celia thought.

"She's too pretty to be a wife and a mom," Rick said, looking at Celia. She felt her cheeks flame.

Jess shrugged. "Well, she is. At least she's a mom."

Rick shot a glance in Celia's direction. As clearly as if he'd spoken, she could see him thinking *but not a wife?*

Rick turned back to Jess. He raised his hand to his mouth and used it as a shield, like his question was a secret no one was to hear. "What's her name?" he stage-whispered.

"Mommy," Karlee answered before Jess could say anything.

Celia couldn't help it; she laughed.

"No," Rick said with commendable kindness. "I mean the one big people call her."

"Celia," Jess said. "Celia Fitzmeyer."

Rick stepped close and stuck out his hand. "Hello, Celia Fitzmeyer."

Feeling foolish and special at the same time, Celia shook his hand. When was the last time anyone had flirted with her, even as harmlessly and aimlessly as this? "Nice to meet you, Rick."

"Believe me, the pleasure is all mine."

The low rumble of his voice slid across her weary nerves like salve over a scrape. His eyes locked on hers, and she stared back like an idiot. Her tongue stuck to the roof of her mouth. Her mind went blank.

Karlee shifted, and her cast struck Celia's knee.

Celia winced, but whether from pain or embarrassment, she didn't know. Either way, the spell was broken.

"That's a very little car." Karlee pointed to the sports car. She looked at the two tall men. "How do you fit into it?"

Rick grinned at Celia before answering. "We fold ourselves up again and again like you fold a secret note to a friend."

Karlee bit for just a minute; then she shook her head. "You do not!"

Rick placed a finger on her nose. "You're right. We do not."

"I think red is pretty," Karlee said. "My car was black."

"No, sweetie," Celia said, pointing to their battle-scarred Yugo. "It's white."

"Not our car. Mine. My car what hit me."

Twenty-two

$\mathcal{K}$ARLEE LOOKED AT the astonished faces staring at her. "But it was bigger than that," she added, pointing to Rick's car.

Celia knelt beside Karlee. She searched the child's eyes, wishing she could see into her mind. "Are you certain, honey? It was a scary time for you, and I don't expect you to remember."

"I'm certain," Karlee said, nodding for emphasis. "It zipped around the corner and boom! It got me." She stared at her cast for a minute. "He got lots of other cars too. It was so loud!"

Celia nodded. Her mind flew in a thousand directions all at once. One thought, a ridiculous one no doubt, was that black was very close to navy blue. Could it have been Rocco deMarco after all?

As if thinking of their father brought Walker and Jordan into existence, they raced from next door.

"Hey," Jordan said, peering at Karlee with bright eyes. "Your bruises are worse than yesterday. How come?" Clearly he was a match for his mother in diplomacy.

"Mrs. Winsky said my face has to get a glorious purple before it begins to get grotesque green and yukky yellow." Karlee giggled. "She said I'm a living rainbow, and most people don't get to be so lucky."

"Who's Mrs. Winsky?" Walker asked, staring at Jess.

"I never got to be that lucky." Jordan pulled a long face, looking up in surprise when the adults laughed.

Walker looked too, and his eyes widened until they filled his whole face. "Jordan." His voice was an awed whisper. "It's Duke Beldon. Look. It's Duke Beldon!" His voice rose in volume as he spoke, the last words shouted.

Celia watched as Rick and Marsh exchanged a look.

"Sorry, guys." Marsh stepped between Rick and Walker. "This is Rick Yakabuski, a friend of mine. He's come for a visit, so we don't want to bother him with all that you-look-like stuff."

"But he's Duke Beldon," Walker persisted. "I see him on TV all the time."

Jordan nodded. "Reruns. Every day. Three-thirty. Fox Family."

"I guess I'll have to watch sometime to see if he looks as much like me as people say," Rick said lightly.

"He does." Jordan was emphatic. "A lot." He turned to Karlee and Jess. "You eating at Abby's again?"

"Not Abby, Jordan." Jess looked horrified. "Mrs. Patterson. You have to call her Mrs. Patterson. Only rude children call adults by their first names."

Well, Celia thought, *maybe Aunt Bernice was good for something after all.* She'd harped on that point often enough over the year they were with her. It had been another of her pointless harangues, pointless because Jess and Karlee always called adults Mr. and Mrs.

Jordan thought for a full second, then nodded agreement with Jess's statement. "Okay. Mrs. Patterson. Can we eat with her too? Dr. Schofield's here to see her again."

Celia caught Marsh's jerk of surprise and displeasure. Hmm. Interesting. She wasn't foolish enough to think Karlee was the attraction again—if she had been that first time he'd come. Apparently neither was Marsh.

"He talked with Mom for a while," Walker said. "Then he went upstairs." He pointed his chin toward Abby's steps.

"Jordan! Walker! Get over here!"

Celia's head swung with the children's to see Vivienne deMarco, resplendent in tight white pants and a soft rose top that made her look pretty in spite of the petulant set to her mouth.

She stalked down her front stairs. "Get over here, you two! Right now!"

Walker and Jordan turned back to Celia, ignoring their mother. "Can we eat here?" Jordan repeated. "Please?"

"Get over here," Vivienne screamed again, "or I'll get your father after you."

Both boys turned to her. "Is Dad still here?" Walker asked, hope filling his voice.

Celia flinched in her heart. She'd heard that same note of longing in Jess's voice when she asked about Eddie. "Go on, guys. When your mother calls you, you are always to go to her."

"What if you don't want to?" Walker asked quietly. "It's so much more fun over here."

"Yeah," Jordan agreed. "I don't even remember when our house was fun."

"Oh, guys," Celia said, her voice tight with tears. "I'm sorry, but kids have to obey their moms. That's the way it has to be."

"Why?" Jordan asked. "Because they're bigger?"

"Because we're supposed to be smarter."

If Celia had ever seen skepticism, she saw it in the faces of the two boys.

"Come on, Jordan." Resigned, Walker took his little brother's hand and started to pull him toward home, only to find that Vivienne had stalked over to join them at the curb. The woman opened her mouth, ready to explode. Celia braced herself.

Then Vivienne noticed Marsh and Rick.

The pout disappeared, replaced by a silky smile. "Hello," she purred. "I'm Vivienne." She rested a hand on Rick's arm. "I've met Marsh, but I haven't met you, handsome."

Celia almost gagged. "Vivienne." There must be something she could do to prevent the woman from drooling all over Rick. "Didn't you want to take the boys home?"

Vivienne smiled sweetly at her sons. "I think they want to stay." She turned her smile on Rick. "Why don't we all stay?"

"What about your husband?" Marsh didn't look all that happy at the thought of Vivienne staying.

She waved her hand like she was shooing away a fly. She moved to within an inch of Rick, then cast a glance over her shoulder. Celia glanced over at the deMarcos' too, and sure enough, there was Rocco standing in an upstairs window, staring down at them.

Whatever game Vivienne was playing, it was cruel and uncalled-for.

Rick ignored Vivienne, no easy task since he could barely breathe without bumping into her. "Celia, I think you need to place a call about Karlee's information, don't you?"

"I do." She reached into her bag for her cell phone. "Kids, why don't you go play on the beach? We'll call you."

Walker nodded like an old sage. "They're going to do adult stuff, and they don't want us around. Come on, guys. Let's go."

Jordan and Walker were on the sand before Karlee and Jess took three steps. Celia had to admit that a pair of firecrackers like those two boys could reduce any mother to screaming after a while, let alone someone as high-strung as Vivienne seemed to be. She pulled Greg Barnes's card from her bag.

"The cops again?" Vivienne's voice reverted to shrill. "Rocco didn't have anything to do with that accident. You're nuts if you think he did."

Celia nodded but said nothing. She punched in the number as everyone, including Vivienne, followed Marsh onto his porch. Vivienne made certain she was next to Rick, and Celia smiled to herself at his less-than-delighted look.

"She told you it was black?" Greg asked.

"Black and bigger than a sports car, or at least the one parked at the curb out here at Abby's."

"Well, the black is right, so maybe the size is too."

"The black is right?"

"There was paint residue on the cars that were hit."

"Oh." She felt somewhat deflated, having imagined her information would break the case wide open. She thought for a minute. "Can you tell the make of the car from the paint?"

"Yes," Greg Barnes said.

Celia waited but he said nothing further. "Right. Roger wilco, over and out."

He laughed. "Call if you learn anything else."

She hung up. "They're making progress, but they're not sharing the details." She nodded to Marsh, told Rick it was nice to meet him, and smiled without enthusiasm at Vivienne. After she called the girls back from the beach, she reached for Karlee to carry her upstairs.

"I can walk up by myself."

"Sure you can," Celia assured her, "but I missed you today and want to hug you. I promise my hug will last only as long as it takes to get you up the stairs. Once we're up there, I'll be hugged out, and you can walk by yourself."

Karlee grunted, but she let Celia pick her up. As she squirmed to get comfortable, her cast thumped Celia on the vulnerable spot on her elbow.

"Ow. Watch it, sweetie."

"Here. Let me." Before Celia even realized his intent, Rick Yakabuski gathered Karlee in his arms. He smiled at the little girl in his easy, natural manner. "You're going upstairs?"

Karlee smiled back. "To Mrs. Patterson's house. She's having us for dinner."

Celia watched her daughter and the large handsome man. *Oh, to have someone so drop-dead gorgeous hold you and give you that amazing grin.* He said he wasn't Rick Mathis. Could have fooled her.

Rick strode to the steps. Celia watched a frustrated Vivienne grab both her boys by their wrists and stomp home. It must rankle when a man preferred a four-year-old to you. Celia smiled broadly as she followed Rick upstairs. She watched with interest as Rick and Sean met, each cautiously sizing the other up. It wasn't quite the territorial posturing of Sean and Marsh, but it was a close second. Did Sean give off a scent that only men picked up, one that automatically raised their hackles?

Mrs. MacDonald had made stuffed pork chops that melted in your mouth. Celia couldn't remember the last time she'd eaten anything so tasty and so classy. She never cooked anything like this, and it was a cinch that Aunt Bernice hadn't. She cleaned her plate, wishing she could lick it to get all the wonderful flavors.

Even as she delighted in the food, Celia was conscious of the discord between Abby and her mother. Oh, they were scrupulously polite to each other. No yelling or name-calling here. But they also weren't talking to each other beyond, "May I have the salt, please?" At least Abby wasn't. All her comments were directed at Celia or Sean. The tension made Celia nervous. Even the girls sensed something was wrong and darted looks between Abby and her mother. Sean seemed oblivious. How typically male.

Dessert, a homemade chocolate cream pie, was almost finished when Sean jumped slightly. He grinned, reaching for his belt. "My beeper vibrated. It always surprises me, though you'd think I'd be used to it by now." He pushed back from the table as he read the number. "Excuse me a minute while I make a call." He stepped out onto the deck, dialing his cell phone as he went.

When he left the room, the women ate in silence. Celia wracked her brain for some way to help defuse the friction that fairly danced around the room. No ideas came. She never had been good at dealing with controversy.

Sean hurried into the room. "I've got to go. An emergency." He looked at Abby and smiled that heart-stopping smile. "I'll call."

Abby managed a small smile back.

"Oh, Abby," Mrs. MacDonald sighed as the sound of Sean's footsteps trailed off. "He's wonderful! Handsome, rich, established. You are so fortunate to have him interested in you."

"Too bad I'm not interested in him." Abby rose, taking her dirty dishes to the kitchen.

"But Abby," Mrs. MacDonald began.

"I will not talk about it." Her clipped voice left no room for arguing or discussion. Mrs. MacDonald sat with her lips pursed, expression stony.

As she rinsed the dishes for Abby to place in the dishwasher, Celia couldn't decide which woman made her more uncomfortable—Abby with her refusal to talk or her mother who chattered like nothing was wrong. Either way, she wouldn't be sorry when it was time to go home. She'd had her fill of living with tension at Aunt Bernice and Poor Uncle Walter's.

Immediately she felt small-minded. After all Abby had done for her, the least she could do was manage an evening of polite, veiled hostility. After all, she had had a lot of practice, and none of it was directed at her, a most pleasant change. So she smiled and talked about Pinky and the spa, ignoring the fact that all she got from Abby were occasional *uh-huhs* and *yeahs*.

As soon as the dishes were finished, Celia turned to her daughters. "Want to go for a quick walk on the beach before we have to go home?"

"I'll come with you," Abby said, almost running out the door. As the women walked across the sand at a pace Abby could manage, the girls scampered ahead. In less time than it takes to think about it, Walker and Jordan came tearing over the sand to join them.

Celia eyed Abby. "Is it my company that you want, or your mother's that you are avoiding?"

Abby was silent for a minute, staring at the little wavelets kissing the beach. "I know I'm wrong, Celia, but I'm so upset I could scream."

"She loves you."

Abby nodded. "I know. She just doesn't love wisely. I feel like she's ripping my life from me. At this rate, I'm going to end up hating her."

"Whoa, Abby." Celia glanced back at the house. "It can't be that bad." Bad was your mother lying around watching old movies and eating candy all day while you did all her work.

"Do you hafta vacuum right now?" Mom would ask from the sofa where she reclined like Cleopatra, surrounded by true confession magazines and beer. "No. No, you don't got to do it now."

When she was thinking instead of feeling desperate and ill-used, Celia used to imagine slaves fanning Mom with palm fronds while others fed her figs and honeyed candies, à la the famous queen of the Nile. Of course Cleopatra was probably more gracious than Mom, but then everyone was more gracious than Mom.

"This is the best part of the movie," she'd gripe. "The vacuum noise will be too loud for me to hear. Get out of my way! I can't see. Go do the laundry or something. And don't forget to change the beds and clean the bathrooms. They ain't been done for a long time. Oh, and I don't think there's any more bread. You got any money?"

Like she had some way to get money.

Bad as being the household drudge was, her mother's suspicions were worse. She could never figure out a way to fight them.

"I know you're sleeping with that no-good-for-nothing Eddie," Mom had screamed after Celia's third date with him.

Celia felt something shrivel inside. "Not me, Mom. I'm only fifteen. I don't want to have sex. I'm trying to be a good Christian. We just went to a movie."

"Christian, my foot. You just want people to think you're a good girl. That's why you go to church. Well, I could tell them a thing or two. Don't think I couldn't. You're just as phony as the rest of them."

"I'm not, Mom." Why she always tried to convince her mother, she didn't know. A psychologist would say it must be some deep desire for approval, something she knew she wouldn't ever get, but something she desperately wanted. She tried to tell herself that it was enough that God loved her. While she didn't know what she'd do without God's love, it was so hard to be emotionally orphaned.

"You think I don't know what the kids of today are like?" Mom stared at her with contempt. "I watch TV. You're not as pretty as those girls. If they have to put out for a date, you do too."

"Well, I don't."

"Who'd have thought I'da raised a tramp?" And she was gone, back to the Fred and Ginger movie, swaying to "I Won't Dance."

By the time Celia was seventeen, running away with Eddie seemed the natural, logical thing to do. Anything was better than staying under her mother's roof.

Talk about out of the frying pan.

Twenty-three

CELIA WATCHED THE man with the gray ponytail sticking out the back of his baseball cap. He wore a ratty T-shirt and baggy shorts with a fanny pack about his waist. He was walking slowly down the beach, swinging something back and forth in front of him. "What's he doing?"

Abby smiled. "Oh, he's looking for treasure in the sand. That's a metal detector he's swinging."

The children spotted the man too.

"Look, Walker," yelled Jordan. "Let's go find out what he's doing." He took off at a dead run. "Come on, everybody," he called back over his shoulder.

Jessica looked at Celia, pleading without words for permission to race after Jordan and Walker.

"Clooney's okay," Abby said. "I met him last week when he found a beautiful bracelet in the sand."

Celia was uncertain. Strange men. Little girls.

"Put your imagination away," Abby said with a smile. "Besides, we can see everything that goes on."

"Hold you sister's hand," Celia called.

Jess nodded, and she and Karlee followed the boys as fast as Karlee could move.

"Maybe he'll find them some money," a deep voice said from behind them, sending that soothing honey feeling flowing along Celia's nerve endings again.

Celia made a face. She still hadn't combed her hair or put on makeup, and when she glanced down at herself, the oil spots on her shirt seemed to grow as she looked, covering her whole front.

Ah, well, Lord, I wouldn't want to impress a beautiful man now, would I?

She looked over her shoulder at Rick. "With my luck, he'll find them each a penny."

"You never know," Abby said. "He wears a diamond stud earring that I'd love to own. He said he found it with his detector."

"Really?" Rick looked interested. "Maybe I should take up metal detection instead of my current job. Walking on the beach all day sounds pretty good about now."

Celia heard the wistfulness in his voice. "Don't you like your job?"

He shrugged. "It's okay. There are just times when the people are more than I want to deal with."

She nodded as Aunt Bernice flashed across her mind. And Eddie. And Mom. She knew all about people who were hard to deal with. "What do you do for a living?"

Rick was quiet for a minute, and she realized that he and she were walking slowly down the beach toward the metal detector and the kids without Abby.

She glanced back and saw Abby staring out to sea. Marsh was walking toward her. Celia smiled. Abby'd be all right with him to watch out for her. The sparks those two shot off in the presence of each other were like nothing she'd ever seen. Lethal. Lovely. Too bad neither of them seemed to realize what was happening.

She glanced up at the house. Mrs. MacDonald stood at the rail, watching her daughter. Celia had a flash of insight. The woman didn't like Marsh. That was why she stayed. Or maybe it was a matter of liking Sean better.

Celia had no doubts which man Abby liked better.

"Public relations," Rick said.

"What?" Celia looked at him blankly.

"Public relations," he repeated. "It's what I do for a living."

"Oh. You don't like it very much?" An adventurous wave surged up the beach and broke over Celia's feet. She laughed and jumped away, bumping into Rick. He put his hand to the small of her back to steady her. When he dropped his hand, she felt its absence as strongly as she'd felt its momentary presence.

He shrugged. "On certain days I don't like it. Other times I do. How about you? Do you like what you do?"

"I do, in spite of the oil stains, the long hours, and the baby-sitting worries. I feel like I'm helping people."

"Marsh says you're a massage therapist."

She nodded. "At Seaside Spa."

He grinned that devastating grin. "And are you?"

"Am I what?"

"Helping people?"

Celia kicked at a clump of sand. It exploded and thousands of tiny sand granules floated in the air. "There's this guy who's fifty-seven and hasn't done a lick of exercise in years except maybe push his self-propelled lawn mower. He used to vacation here in Seaside with his parents when he was a teenager. He's back with his own family for the first time in thirty-something years. He remembers surfing at seventeen and decided it was like riding a bike: You never forgot how. So he bought himself a board and went."

"Got creamed by a wave, did he?"

"Most of the time the waves around here aren't the creaming sort, but he still got worked over pretty well. After two days of climbing on and falling off the board, he could hardly move. Add to that the waves twisting him all around." She turned to frown at Rick. "What is it with men and sports?"

"You mean Sports Syndrome, the disease that makes us all see ourselves as NFL or NBA caliber no matter our age?"

"That's the one."

"Strange. I've always thought of it as an unparalleled opportunity for women to develop their particular illness, what I call the Callous Condition."

"The one that makes us say, 'It's all your fault, you idiot'?"

"That's the one."

Celia nodded. "There's definitely a correlation between the two conditions with my would-be surfer. His wife kept growling that he was ruining everyone's vacation with his moaning about his aches and pains. When he couldn't stand her griping any-more—or maybe it was his pain he couldn't stand—he came to see me."

Rick grinned at her. "And your healing hands cured him."

She looked at her hands. "It's not quite that simple. He needs several more weeks before he's back to anywhere near normal, but at least he's walking enough to make it to the beach and the board-walk—if he doesn't feel compelled to go on the roller coaster or one of those rides that whips you around."

"Does the boardwalk have many rides?"

She nodded. "It's a nice boardwalk."

"What's your favorite?"

She looked wistfully out at the ocean. "We haven't gone on any of the rides yet."

Rick raised his eyebrows. "How long have you lived here?"

"Two months."

"In all that time you haven't taken the girls to the boardwalk? Scandalous."

There spoke someone who didn't have to worry about how expensive such an evening would be. "We've gone to the board-walk, but it was a while ago, and the rides weren't open for the season yet." As she'd known they wouldn't be.

"Then you need to take them back now that they're open."

"Yeah, well, sometime." She promised herself that she'd take Jess and Karlee when Karlee was better, no matter how much it cost. The girls deserved it.

They walked for a few minutes, watching Clooney and the children. Even Jordan grew still and stared when Clooney pulled out a red beach spade and dug a hole. When he reached down and pulled out something, the children clustered around. One by one they reached out a forefinger, touching whatever it was. Then Clooney straightened, putting the treasure in the pack around his waist.

"Go to the boardwalk with me tomorrow night."

Celia stopped dead and stared at Rick. A sudden gust of ocean breeze blew her hair across her mouth. She spit it out, pushing it behind her ear. "What?"

He stood with his hands in his pockets and his feet spread. "You heard me."

She swallowed against the sudden rapid beat of her heart. "I guess I did, but it's been so long since a man asked me to go any-where that I thought I heard wrong."

"They should be standing in line to take you out."

She blinked. Feeling shy all of a sudden, she dropped her eyes and stared at a piece of broken clamshell beside her foot. "Um."

"It'll be fun," he said. "Come on."

She frowned at the clamshell and the clump of seaweed lying next to it. "I'd have to bring the girls." She knew she'd just rung the death knell to her first date possibility in longer than she could remember. No man wanted two little girls he didn't know tagging along, but a baby-sitter was unacceptable for several reasons, most of them green with denominations noted in the corners. "They're at a baby-sitter's all day. I can't leave them all evening too, especially Karlee."

"Of course you can't," he said without missing a beat. "I expected them to come with us."

Celia forced her gaze upward, studying his face. If he was unhappy about the presence of the two little chaperones, he was a very good actor. She saw no signs of distress or unhappiness. "Thank you." She flushed. "We'd like to go."

She cleared her throat. She'd just agreed to her first date in over seven years. Panic made her pulse pound. Did she even remember how to act? "It'll be fun," she managed. It'll be nerve wracking. "The girls will be delighted." At least that was true.

Rick looked at her thoughtfully. "He was an idiot, you know."

"Who?"

This time it was Rick who reached out to pull the hair from her mouth and put it behind her ear. "Whoever he was who left you. An absolute idiot."

Twenty-four

THE PAGE THAT called him from Abby's dinner table had been for a patient who had a severe reaction to some medication. The boy was fine now, his hives gone, his breathing normal, and the prescription changed. Doubtless he was back in his own narrow bed with its *Monsters, Inc.* sheets, already in dreamland. The only ones to lose sleep over the crisis would be the parents.

He turned the key in his cycle, then revved the engine. He flipped back the kickstand and pulled out of the hospital lot. All his emergencies should be as easy to deal with.

Of course he loved the challenge of even such a straightforward puzzle—which was one reason he liked medicine so. The dilemmas, the dramas, shifted daily, hourly, teasing and testing his abilities, his intellect. He always had liked to tackle tough issues, no matter what they were. That characteristic was one of the reasons he was able to get out of the Pines. Once he looked at his escape as a maze he must traverse, a quest that he as the hero must win, he was able to formulate plans. McCoy had struck out blindly at anyone in his way, fueled by hate and despair instead of cool reason. Sean shook his head. That way lay emotional disintegration.

The challenge of Abby Patterson was one he savored, like a chef delighting in the fine tastes he created. He brought his fingers to his lips and kissed them like an Italian chef might.

Thus far he had won every battle life presented him. He would win this one too. He ran his plan through his mind once again, then grinned. Its simplicity didn't take away from the satisfaction it gave him. Any other person would struggle for days, weeks, to come up with such a clever idea. McCoy could have thought for the rest of his life and never imagined anything of such subtlety.

He almost felt bad that he had to ruin her. She was, in her own Goody Two-shoes way, an interesting person. Despite her fragile physical appearance, she had steel in her spine, though he wasn't certain whether it was tempered enough to withstand the hurricane that was her mother. At dinner he had gotten an intense charge over the animosity between the two women even as he made believe he was unaware. He wasn't certain of the cause for the friction. In spite of his considerable and well-developed ego, he didn't think he was what they were arguing over. Then again, the mother was pushing him down Abby's pretty throat, and he didn't think she wanted to swallow.

All he was certain of was that Abby didn't suspect him, and that was what mattered in the long run.

As he pulled into his garage, he wished there were some way he could be present to see her face at his preemptive strike. It probably said terrible things about his character—or lack of character—but he wanted to know that she was suffering at least as much as he was.

Tomorrow the destruction of Abigail Patterson would begin.

Twenty-five

ABBY ROSE FROM her desk in the back corner of the library where the children's collection was housed, absently rubbing the ache in her hip. She'd been sitting too long. There was just time, late in the afternoon of her second full day at her new job, to check out her little kingdom before she left for home.

The children's section of the library had been the recipient of a large grant last year, and not only had the book collection been expanded significantly but also wonderful peripherals had been added—extra computers, educational software and games, books on tape, and a small but fine collection of children's art, all reproductions of course. New furniture in bold primary colors made the area attractive and inviting.

She wandered around her domain, reveling in the fact that she was the one in charge. She had achieved this goal against the odds even if she hadn't yet gained her larger goal of independence. Not that she'd given up that struggle. No, sirree, Bob. In fact, she had just begun to fight.

She came to a computer screen stalled halfway through a learning game. Undoubtedly some mother's patience had run out at this point. Abby hit choice *B* with a touch of the mouse, and the computer said, "You are so smart! Congratulations." Applause rang behind the words. She grinned and set the game back at the beginning for the next little user. She stopped to straighten a top-pling pile of videos sitting on the floor beside a little girl with her nose in *Ramona the Brave*. The child never noticed her, a fact that delighted Abby.

I want to turn little girls like her into modern day Megg Ropers, well-educated women who, though they might not learn Greek, Latin, and philosophy as Megg did, love books and learning.

Tomorrow would be her first opportunity in a group setting with StoryTime at ten. She had her book picked out, her props ready. She couldn't wait for all the little eager faces to grow fasci-nated by the story, to watch the children edge closer and closer to her as they forgot the real world and lived the adventure.

With the summer season about to explode, next week StoryTime would move to twice weekly on Tuesdays and Fridays. She sighed happily.

She stopped by the children's audio collection to straighten and re-alphabetize it. She was working on the third shelf when she felt a tap on her shoulder. She turned to find her boss, head librar-ian Nan Fulsom.

"Have you got a minute, Abby?"

Nan looked so serious that she made Abby nervous. She nod-ded. "Of course."

"Come to my office, will you please?" Though phrased as a question, it was an order.

Nan turned and walked toward the front of the building with-out waiting to see if Abby followed. With a frown of concern, she did. When they entered the office and Nan closed the door behind her, Abby's mouth went dry.

She was in trouble; she knew it. She just didn't know why. She ran through the last two days in her mind. As far as she could tell, nothing had happened to precipitate Nan's abrupt attitude.

Nan took her seat behind her desk, indicating a red faux leather chair for Abby. She sat and watched Nan lean forward to finger a piece of notebook paper that sat in the middle of her amazingly neat desktop. Nan's computer sat on a lower desk that formed an *L* with the main desk. A screen saver picture of Nan with some people Abby assumed were her family flashed, only to slowly diminish in size and bounce around the screen before pop-ping back to full size again.

"I received an unsettling letter today," Nan announced, draw-ing Abby's eyes back to her. "I'm not certain what to make of it."

Abby nodded even as she wondered what this could possibly have to do with her.

Nan was silent for a minute, studying the paper in front of her. Then she held it out to Abby. "I think you need to read this."

With a strong feeling of premonition making her stomach flip, Abby took the proffered paper and began to read. She was mindful of Nan's eyes on her. Watching for her reaction?

> Mrs. Fulsom,
>   Are you aware that the woman who is your children's librarian has spent several years under psychiatric care? Do you think it's wise to have someone so unstable look-ing out for our children? I know it makes me uncomfort-able, and I do not plan to bring my family to the library until she is removed. I would appreciate you addressing this matter immediately.

Abby felt like a fist had been thrust into her gut. She stared at the accusatory words. Someone thought she was a danger to the children? She, Abby Patterson? But that was ridiculous! She loved children, absolutely loved them.

"Who?" she managed to get out between her dry lips. She scanned the letter. "There's no signature." She looked at Nan.

"I know." Nan reached for the paper. "That fact makes me very uncomfortable. Something isn't right here, but I still feel that I must ask about the contents." She held her hands out, palms up. "I'm accountable for this library and all who work and visit here. I have to check."

Abby swallowed hard. "You mean you want to know whether I was under a psychiatrist's care?"

Nan nodded.

"Is that legal?" Abby asked. "Your asking, I mean. Certainly there's nothing illegal or wrong in someone seeing a psychiatrist."

Nan again nodded. "I just need to know, Abby. I don't want to know what you saw one about, if you did, and I don't plan to tell anyone. I just want to know."

"Are you aware that I'm a widow?"

"I didn't know." Nan glanced at her screen saver and the tall, thin man with glasses who stood with his arm about her shoulders. "I'm sorry."

Abby shrugged. "It was three years ago. You'd think I'd be used to it by now." She shivered. *Maddie. Sam.* "An automobile accident killed my husband and our two-year-old daughter Madeleine." This time it was Abby who glanced at the screen saver and the three daughters ranged around Nan and her husband. Three living, vibrant daughters.

Nan studied her daughters too. "How did you stand it?"

"I didn't have a choice." They were both silent for a moment. "Yes, I did see a psychologist for a time for grief counseling. I saw him weekly for six months, then once a month for six months. He was a very wise man, a Christian. He helped me a lot. Time has helped too." Abby smiled without humor. "Though I have to admit, seeing your three daughters still stabs me in the heart."

Nan looked away, staring out her window at the parking lot half full of cars.

"Please don't misunderstand me," Abby said quickly. "I'm not going to fall apart because your girls are alive and mine isn't. I would never wish for you that pain. It's that I'll never know what Maddie might have been at the ages of your girls."

Nan turned back to her computer picture, nodding. "I understand."

She didn't, Abby knew. No one did unless she'd been there, but Abby appreciated Nan's attempt at empathy.

Her boss studied the letter lying on her desk, her lip curled in distaste. "Do you have any idea why someone would write something like this? Do you have any enemies? Any personal troubles that would cause someone to attack you?"

"No one, at least no one I know of. Certainly no one from home. I only moved here on Friday. I haven't had time to develop enemies yet. Not that I'm planning to." A thought struck her. "But I did witness a hit-and-run Friday. Maybe this note is related to that, though I don't see how."

Nan considered the possibility for a moment. "I don't see how either, but even if it were, how would someone know such personal information?"

Abby shivered. It was creepy to think of someone delving into the most private parts of her life. "That's a very good question. To my knowledge, no one in Seaside is privy to that part of my life. It's not the kind of thing you tell people. Hello, I'm Abby and I was in counseling for a year."

Nan gave a small laugh at the comment.

Abby continued, "It's the Internet, I imagine. Someone who knows how to get around can find out almost anything he wants about anyone."

"What I really don't like," Nan said, "is the fact that the letter's anonymous. Someone's a coward, willing to throw dirt but unwilling to face the accused."

Abby felt sick at the thought of someone purposely writing a nasty letter about her. What possible motive was there to attack her? She was such a Goody Two-shoes that no one had ever accused her of doing anything wrong in her whole life. Except Marsh, of course. She smiled. He thought she was an idiot whose sole purpose in life was to make him miserable.

For some reason, thinking of him made her feel better. It also made her want to discuss the letter with him. He had such a practical mind. "May I have a copy of the letter?"

Nan nodded. "I'm sorry about this, Abby. I don't know what's going on here, but I don't want you to worry. I've had at least three people seek me out today to tell me how much they like the new children's librarian."

Abby left Nan's office feeling somewhat better, but there was a definite prickling of unease every time she glanced at her copy of the hateful letter.

Who?

And why?

Lord, what's going on here? I feel like Anne Boleyn, accused over something that was way beyond her control. She had the audacity to birth a girl to Henry VIII and I to mourn over my family and seek help coping with the soul-deep pain. She gave a wry smile. *At least I'm not about to be beheaded.*

When she reached her desk, she unlocked the bottom drawer,

pulling out her purse. She folded the letter carefully and slid it into the inside zipper pouch. She glanced at her watch. 5:20. Time to start for home.

Home. Her stomach cramped again. She knew her attitude was silly, maybe even sinful. Still, she felt that her mother had taken over her home. The apartment was such an overwhelming symbol to her of her need to stand by herself, to establish her own life based on her own desires and the leading of the Lord, not on her parents' wishes, not on Sam's. Homeless, that's what she was, figuratively if not literally.

At this moment Abby didn't much like her mother.

Marching side by side with the resentment was guilt. Abby knew better than anyone—except maybe her father—all that her mother had done for her since the accident. She had held her when Abby cried, had cried with her, had sat with her hour after hour both in the hospital and at home, reading to her, talking to her, encouraging her, had transported her to appointment after appointment week after week, month after month. That Abby should feel so angry at that person revealed the true nastiness of her heart.

How was it possible to love and resent the same person with equal intensity? If things kept going like this, maybe she'd end up at that psychiatrist's office yet!

Stop stalling, girl. Go home.

The trouble was that tonight she wouldn't have Celia and the girls as buffers. It'd be just her and Mom, who would undoubtedly want to talk "girl talk" for hours. It was more than she could deal with, especially with that letter burning a hole in her purse. With her nose for trouble both real and imagined, Mom would ferret out the letter in no time. The last thing Abby wanted was for her to have additional ammunition in the fight against Seaside.

With a sigh, Abby left the library and climbed into her car. Instead of turning toward home, however, she drove downtown. The new Kmart was just what she needed to distance herself for another hour or so. It could also give her a project to fill the night.

In the bath department Abby found exactly what she wanted, a wicker wall unit of two shelves. The only trouble was that it came only in white, and she wanted forest green. So she'd paint it. She smiled. Something else to fill the evening.

As she climbed back into her car with the wicker shelves, the green paint, and all the accompanying paraphernalia, guilt again seized her. She sat for a minute with her eyes closed, praying.

Lord, I don't know how to handle this. Most people rebel in their teens, and their outlook at that time is so self-centered that they think little of the parents they may be hurting. Leave it to me to wait until almost thirty. She sighed at her own folly. *All I keep thinking is how I'd feel if Maddie had grown up and turned against me. Not that I've actually turned against Mom.*

Oh, no? seemed to thunder from on high. *"Be kind and compassionate to one another, forgiving each other, just as in Christ God forgave you."*

She sighed again. All those verses memorized as a kid to earn free weeks at camp leaped to her mind at the most inopportune moments. How pointed they often were. How they could pierce her heart.

Okay, Lord, I get it. She reached in her purse for her cell phone. *She may be wrong, but that's no reason for me to be nasty in return.* Abby punched in the apartment number. *I just don't know a nice way to separate myself from her interference.* She listened to the ringing at the other end. *I mean, if I'm kind, won't she think that's an invitation to be more controlling? Won't she think I'm giving in again?*

"Mom, it's me," she said when the receiver was picked up. "I had to run an errand. I'll be home in a few minutes."

"Where are you, Abby? Did something happen? Did you fall? I've been so worried! You're late."

Abby closed her eyes as she listened to the concern and the reprimands. The unhealthy combination made her skin crawl. She glanced at her watch. "It's not that late, Mom. It isn't even six-fifteen yet."

"You finish work at five. Your drive takes less than five minutes. You're late."

Abby leaned her head against the rest, aware that her back hurt, her hip ached, and she had a killer headache. "Is there anything I can pick up at the grocery store for us?" She forced her voice to sound neutral.

"Not now, thank you. I plan for us to go to the store tonight to stock up big-time. You have hardly anything here."

Abby bit her lip. She felt like she was five and Mom had just said, "Leave your dolls, dear. We have to go to the grocery store." In a voice as calm as she could make it, Abby said, "I can't go to the store tonight, Mom. I have a project planned."

There was a short silence. "You never told me."

You never told me either. "Sorry."

"Well, just get home before dinner's ruined."

Abby hung up, picturing Mom's compressed lips and stony expression. The only thing that Mom hated more than having her plans messed up was having her carefully cooked meals ruined.

Maybe she'll be mad enough for the silent treatment! Hope bubbled. Just as quickly, remorse kicked in. *Oh, Lord, how awful of me. Help me. I'm going nuts here.*

When Abby pulled into the drive, there was barely enough room for her, given the presence of a stretch limo with U.S. government plates.

Marsh's father! How had she forgotten?

Oh, Marsh, how's it going? Are you surviving?

She climbed out of the car, reaching into the backseat to gather her purchases. With the wall shelving unit tucked under one arm, the paint can and bag with the brushes and solvent in the other, she walked to the steps. She could hear voices coming from Marsh's living room through the open sliding door.

She couldn't help looking over. She'd never seen a real live senator before, and she'd love a little glimpse of Senator Winslow. No luck. The black screen in the door effectively blocked even the most cursory glimpse.

She turned to the steps and realized that she wouldn't be able to carry everything up in one trip. She still needed the banister for stability, though she felt she was getting better at this climbing bit every day. By Labor Day she should be running up, hands waving over her head in victory à la Rocky on the steps of the Philadelphia Museum of Art.

She bent to put the paint and bag on the ground when a hand reached out, taking them from her.

"Let me."

She jumped. "Marsh!" She smiled. "Where did you come from so quickly?"

He took her elbow in the now familiar grip. "I saw you through the open door. You're my chance to escape for a minute."

The first sentence was spoken at a normal level, but the second was *sotto voce*.

She glanced at the door herself. "That bad?"

"Worse."

She studied him. His shoulders were tense, his eyes desperate. "It's only for a day," she offered as comfort.

"Yeah, but he brought his wife with him."

"Your stepmom? I take it you don't like her?"

He rolled his eyes. "She makes your mom look like Mother Teresa."

Abby grinned. "Well, come on up and say hi to the sainted woman."

"That'll make her evening." His voice was dry.

"I could use the protection, and you could make believe you're Sir Galahad."

He looked a question and she confided, "I'm late." He was appropriately scandalized.

"Marshall," a voice purred from behind them. "Who do we have here?"

"Uh-oh," Marsh breathed. He turned, a false smile plastered on his face. "This is Abby Patterson. She lives upstairs."

Abby turned and found herself staring at a beautiful young woman standing at the edge of Marsh's porch. Her hair, a sleek, sophisticated pageboy of a lovely ash-blond shade, was perfect even after a day in the high humidity of the Jersey shore. Abby looked in vain for a freckle, a mole, a sunburned nose, anything to mar the perfection of her face. She looked like she had just slipped into her blue silk shirt and white linen slacks.

How has she worn linen all day and not gotten wrinkled, Abby wondered, feeling every one of the wrinkles she knew creased her poplin slacks. Then there was the spot of baby vomit on her shoulder from when she'd held an infant so its young mom could help the three-year-old brother pick out some books. As for makeup, perfect or otherwise, Abby knew hers had long ago worn off, and her red nose undoubtedly shone like a beacon on a dark night.

"Abby," Marsh continued. "This is Lane Winslow, my father's wife."

"Hello, Lane, it's nice to meet you." Because her first response to Lane had been so catty, Abby put extra graciousness into her greeting. Then her brain clicked.

Lane? As in Marsh's ex-fiancée? Had she heard correctly? Certainly there weren't many women with that name, and to have two connected to the same family seemed too much. But married to his father? Only by supreme effort did she keep her jaw from dropping all the way to her knees.

"Lane? Marshall? Where are you?" A commanding voice boomed from the living room.

"Out here, darling," Lane purred over her shoulder. "Meeting Marshall's neighbor."

How did she do it, Abby wondered, putting such an ugly, suggestive spin on her ordinary comment? Marsh stiffened beside her, the hand he still had on her elbow tightening painfully. She poked him discreetly in the ribs, and while he loosened his hold, he didn't let go.

The sliding door flew open and out stepped Senator Winslow. He looked just like all the pictures Abby had seen of him: confident, charismatic, and handsome. He carried his authority with ease and his age with distinction. He joined them, sliding an arm around his wife. Lane glanced at him over her shoulder, giving him a lovely smile.

What was it like for the senator to know that his wife had first chosen his son and he was second choice?

What was it like for Lane to be married to a man nearly twice her age? Of course power was a strong aphrodisiac, and the senator possessed that attribute in spades.

Marsh introduced Abby. "I'm just going to help her upstairs with her packages."

"How sweet," Lane purred.

Marsh started up the steps, paint can and bag in hand, towing Abby behind him. She flashed a brief smile over her shoulder at the senator, then at Lane.

"Nice to meet you," she called as, shelves held awkwardly under her free arm, she grasped the banister. Feeling Lane's eyes on her, it was all she could do not to twitch her shoulders. She gritted her teeth and tried not to let her limp show. Not that Marsh was any help in that department. He practically dragged her up the stairs, accenting rather than disguising her disability.

"Oh, Marsh," she whispered as they neared the landing and she thought it safe to speak without being overheard. "Lane? *The* Lane?"

He nodded, lips compressed.

"Your poor father!"

Marsh halted, one foot on the top step, one foot on the landing, a look of utter disbelief on his face. "Poor Dad?"

Abby nodded. "And lucky you!"

He looked at her, shaking his head. Then he grinned. "You never cease to amaze me. You're right, of course. Poor Dad." He set the paint and bag on the nearest chair. "I've got to go."

Abby nodded. She wished she could ask him to stay for a few minutes to look at the nasty letter. She'd love his opinion, but she knew now wasn't the time. Besides, Mom would undoubtedly walk out as she showed it, demanding to see it too.

She balanced the shelves on the edge of the porch rail. "Just remember," she said softly. "Lucky you."

He was grinning as he loped down the stairs, and she felt pleased to have relieved a bit of his tension even if only for a minute or two.

She had just turned to go inside when Lane spoke.

"How kind of you to help the cripple, Marshall. But aren't you slumming a bit?"

Twenty-six

ABBY FELL BACK as if she'd been slapped, coming to rest when she bumped into the apartment wall. Mortification washed over her, burning her cheeks, chilling her spirit. Never in the three years since the accident had anyone called her a cripple.

Oh, she'd seen plenty of looks of pity, especially when she was first learning to walk again. She'd been asked plenty of questions from the politely curious to the downright nosey. But cripple, especially used in so pejorative a manner? Never.

And slumming! How thoroughly demeaning.

She heard Senator Winslow's horrified, "Lane!" and Marsh's low, fierce, "Shut up, Lane."

Then she heard Lane's merry, if slightly strained laugh. "Easy, gentlemen. Can't you take a joke?"

Some joke.

Honesty forced Abby to admit that much of the hurt came because Lane was the source. Beautiful Lane. Elegant Lane. She was probably the toast of Washington, the glamorous, savvy young wife of a powerful political force. Invitations to her parties were doubtless A-list treasures in the status-conscious city. No one wrote notes about her being a bad influence on children.

Hardest to think about was that Marsh had loved her.

Pushing away from the wall and walking to the rail to look out at the vast, calming sea, Abby admitted that last thought was the one that bothered her most. Marsh had loved Lane.

With a sigh she acknowledged that she'd never stand a chance with him. After beauty like that, why would he settle for someone like her? After the sleekness of blond Lane, how could he like her unruly mass of black curls that went every which way in the humid shore air no matter how much extra-extra-extra ultrahold hair spray she used? How could he be attracted to her skinny face with its sun-reddened nose and dark, strong brows after Lane's movie star perfection. She glanced down at herself and shuddered. Body shape didn't even bear thinking of.

"Well, you're here. Finally."

Mom. Abby scrunched her face at the acerbic tone, pasting on a smile as she turned. "Hello, Mom."

"You should have told me you were home."

"I just got here." Abby tried to keep her voice devoid of emotion, but she wasn't certain she succeeded.

"Yes, well, come on. Dinner gets more rubbery by the moment."

The meal was an exercise in exquisite torture for Abby and, she suspected, her mother. Conversation was awkward and sporadic with Mom giving rundowns on people from home as if Abby had been away for a year instead of less than a week. Finally Mom asked the question Abby had been dreading.

"What's wrong, Abby? Tell me what's wrong." She leaned back in her chair, planning to settle in until she had her answer.

In the past, Abby would have poured out her heart, sharing what bothered her with relief. Even when she was married, she and her mother had talked about her problems, analyzing them, dissecting them, finding solutions for them. Always she had been proud of the relationship she had with Mom, the openness.

A sudden thought hit Abby. Had they ever talked about any of Mom's problems, looked for alternatives for her, wondered about what were her best steps to take, her wisest course to follow? Not that she expected Mom to tell her about problems with Dad, though she herself had blurted out enough about Sam. But what about work? Church? Neighbors?

With a grim smile, Abby realized Mom had never once asked

for her input, her advice. Mom willingly gave, but she didn't take, not even after Abby was a woman grown.

Therein lay the problem. Abby was a woman, yet Mom still expected their relationship to be like it was when she was growing up. When they conversed, they weren't two women friends, peers. They had never made that adjustment. They were still mother and daughter, authority and wisdom facing need and ignorance.

In a strange way, the accident was responsible for bringing all that inequity to a head. For a time Mom had been needed, desperately needed. She had met that need with love and a willing spirit. She had given above and beyond what could be expected of her, and Abby had accepted the help without question out of both habit and necessity.

Now Abby was healed. She was no longer needy. In fact, she was no longer anything like the woman she'd been the day she had ridden into that intersection with Sam. How could she be, going through what she had? She had passed through the fire, been tempered, been matured. She'd pushed through far more than her physical therapy, emerging a woman who wanted— what? What did she want?

She'd thought she wanted independence, the freedom and space to stand alone. That was why she came to Seaside. After a lifetime of people telling her what to do, she wanted to be responsible to no one but God, to be on her own. Not that she wanted to be like Amalsuntha, who back in the 500s ruled the Roman Empire for years all by herself, ending up banished and strangled for all her fine work. A craving for power wasn't in Abby's makeup.

Nor, she was beginning to think, was autonomy. That way lay loneliness. But she didn't want the cosseting her parents offered either. That way lay suffocation.

She thought of Lavinia Fontana, a talented Italian artist of the late sixteenth century. She found a husband who acknowledged her talent to be greater than his and who agreed to be the house husband while she conquered the artistic world of her day. Lavinia painted for the Spanish royal family as well as being appointed court painter to Pope Clement VIII.

Was that the kind of marriage partnership Abby wanted? Well, yes and no. She knew from her brief friendship with Marsh that she found comfort and encouragement in having someone to talk to, someone who respected and accepted her as she was, a gift Lavinia's husband appeared to have given her. However, she had no ambitions to take the world by storm, so the comparison to Lavinia broke down here. Children's librarians weren't the stuff of international fame.

Could she find a man who was willing to meet her on level ground? One who would let her be herself, even encourage her in that way? Could she find someone to accept her as his sweet Eve, created just for him, bone of his bone and flesh of his flesh, yet also that other Eve who ate the apple, who made less-than-sterling choices, and was sometimes cranky and demanding, greedy and foolish? Who could acknowledge and honor her as both personas? Such a man would be worth yielding her independence for.

When a vision of Marsh wiping away her tears with his T-shirt sprang to her mind, she pushed it away. Better to let this paragon of male maturity remain faceless. It was easier on a heart that had already been bruised so badly by life.

Abby jumped when Mom leaned across the table and touched her hand.

"Come on, Abby." Mom smiled her wise, slightly superior smile. "Tell me what's troubling you. Is it that man downstairs? Don't you like your job? What?"

It took all Abby's forbearance not to blurt, "It's you, Mom!" Instead she said, "Nothing's wrong. I'm fine. Are you going to the grocery store? If you are, I'll do the dishes so you don't lose any more time." She smiled and looked over her shoulder into the living room. "My car keys are in the dish on the end table by the door."

Without meeting her mother's eyes, she stood and carried dishes to the sink. She rinsed everything, placing it in the dishwasher. When she returned to the table for the rest of the dishes, Mom was just rising.

"Abby," she said, her expression troubled.

"Don't forget to get pulpless orange juice," Abby cut her off. "Pulpless. No pulp. I hate pulp."

Mom looked bewildered. "But we always get pulp. You've always liked it and it's good for you."

"It may be good for me, but I've always hated it." *As I've been telling you for years and years.* "Dad's the one who likes it. Since this is my house, please get no pulp. Here, let me give you the money."

She walked to the end table where the keys were and picked up her purse. She pulled out what she thought would be a sufficient amount of money and held it out to her mother.

"Abby!" Mom looked shocked. "I can't take your money."

"I beg your pardon?"

"I can't take your money. I'll buy the food."

"Mom, it's my house and my food. Take the money."

"Abby, you're my daughter. How can I let my child buy my food?"

First the letter, then Lane, and then that nerve-wracking dinner. Now money. Abby felt her temper rising, her control slipping. "Mom, you're the guest. The host buys the food." She grabbed her mother's hand and stuffed the money in it, closing her fingers over it. "If you weren't here," she paused, reminding her mother that she should not be here, "I'd be going to the store, shopping with my own money, not yours. I am far from destitute. Use my money." She gritted the last out slowly, word by word, through her clenched teeth.

Then she stalked out of the room. As she closed her bedroom door and leaned back on it, her anger still churned in her gut. She wasn't used to being so full of ire, so undisciplined in her speech. Flopping onto her bed, she stared without seeing at the ceiling.

She was amazed at how draining it was to be a powder keg.

She replayed the conversation about the money, planning to warm herself with righteous indignation. Trouble was, in the replay she heard her tone of voice. *I'm a harpy!* In no time, she was flushed with embarrassment at her bad behavior.

"And you want to be treated as an adult," she scoffed. "You have to act like one first."

She heard Mom leave, heard her walk down the stairs, heard the car pull out. Maybe when she came back, they could talk about sharing the expenses. That way Mom would feel included, and Abby wouldn't feel like the child. She rubbed her hand wearily over her forehead. Why hadn't she thought of that simple yet practical compromise before she blew up?

I'm as bad as Locusta, the professional poisoner, she thought. *She used poisoned mushrooms to kill the Emperor Claudius to make way for*

Nero to ascend the throne. At Nero's orders, she then poisoned Brittanicus, the new emperor's half brother and potential rival. I, on the other hand, might not annihilate Mom with a literal poison, but I am in the process of killing our relationship with venomous words.

It was a very sobering thought.

"Be kind and compassionate to one another."

The padding of little cat feet on the door reminded Abby that Puppy liked to be in the bedroom with her. She opened the door and found Puppy sitting, staring up at her.

"Hello, baby." Falling to her knees, she picked up the huge furry beast. Puppy promptly went noodle-limp in her arms, purring with abandon. Abby sank all the way to the floor, sitting with her back against the doorjamb. She raised Puppy to her face, rubbing her cheek in the soft fur. There was something so soothing in the silky feel, the tactile sensation.

"We'll make it somehow, won't we, baby? If we've come this far, we'll figure out how to go farther, right?"

The night Sam had brought Puppy home was one of the good memories Abby had of that far-distant place called her marriage. Not that the other memories were bad; they weren't. They were just fuzzy, insubstantial, fading. But recall of the night Puppy came was as clear and sharp as the sky in crisp midwinter.

Maddie had just turned two, and she was thrilled with the rambunctious black-and-white kitten tumbling about her floor. Her little face was alight with joy, her big dark eyes, so much like her mother's, dancing with delight.

"Puppy!" she screamed as she launched herself at the kitten, grabbed it about the neck, and squeezed.

Sam and Abby dove to save the cat, only to find the animal purring, eyes at half-mast, as the little girl hugged it.

"Kitty," Abby said as she stroked a finger down the kitten's back.

"Puppy," Maddie said.

"Kitty," Sam said, a bemused smile on his face as he watched his daughter.

"Puppy," pronounced Maddie, face set, voice uncompromising. She climbed to her feet, picked the animal up around its middle, and walked across the room with it draped over her arms like a furry throw. She turned to stare at her parents, totally unimpressed by their size and supposed authority, her little feet planted as far apart as she could manage, her chubby toddler's jaw set at a very firm angle. "Puppy."

Thus Puppy the kitty had become.

Abby picked herself up from the floor, not an easy feat with Puppy still draped over one arm, and walked to the kitchen. She set Puppy on the counter where the cat collapsed, promptly falling asleep.

"Don't tell Mom I let you get up here," she instructed. "Somehow I don't think she'd approve."

In answer Puppy sighed out a huge puff of air.

"Yeah, I can see you're scared of her," Abby said. "Me too."

When the dishes were finished, Abby went to the porch. Puppy jumped from the counter and followed. There Abby laid newspapers all over the top of the glass table as well as the floor surrounding and under it, while Puppy jumped into her favorite chair and curled in a ball, falling back to sleep.

Abby set her white wicker wall shelf on the table on its back with her paint can beside it. She pried the lid off, stirring the paint like the man at Kmart had told her. She picked up her brush and dipped it into the can. With quick brush strokes, she turned the top of the unit deep green. She grinned. Next came one side, then the bottom.

When she began the second side, she kept bumping her elbow against the paint can. There wasn't enough room on the table to paint this side with the can staying where she had originally placed it. She picked it up, then set it on the wide porch rail. She adjusted some of the newspapers so that they covered the small stretch of floor between the rail and the table. The last thing she wanted was to get green paint on Marsh's soft gray floor.

Finishing the side, she went on to the inside of the shelf, moving around the table for best access to all the corners. Getting the green between all those intertwined strips of whatever—she very much doubted it was real rattan—was no easy chore, and the wicker drank the paint like a thirsty man in the desert drank water.

The can was almost empty, but she was almost finished. She should have enough and a bit to spare. She hummed as she worked, happy to be doing something that was working out so well. She straightened from her position on the side of the table farthest from the rail and froze.

Puppy was on the railing, walking purposefully toward the paint can. When had she awakened and left her comfy bed in the chair across the porch?

"No, Puppy!" Abby called, hurrying around the table, but she was too late. The cat butted her black-and-white head against the can of forest green paint, lifting to rub her cheek against the smooth surface. She came up under the handle as it lay against the can's side, and the almost empty can lifted, tilted.

Abby squeezed her eyes shut and heard the dull thud as it tipped over, smacking the rail. She cracked open her eyes and saw green paint spreading like an oil slick on a pond. Why hadn't she put newspaper on the rail? She'd never even thought to. Now forest green would discolor the pristine white of the railing. She stared at the spreading green blob and sighed. It was a fitting end to a terrible day.

It got worse quickly. Puppy butted the bottom of the leaking can. Abby gave a tiny scream as it clattered over the rail and crashed to the porch below.

She rushed to the rail and peered over. She moaned. A green stain was spreading across the seat of Marsh's red Adirondack chair, the one he pulled up to the railing so he could rest his feet as he pecked at his laptop and took periodic glances at the ocean. The can itself lay in the deep V of the seat, and more paint was dripping through the slats of the chair onto the gray floor.

She slapped her hand over her mouth in horror though she wasn't certain whether it was a fit of hysterical giggles or sobs that threatened to escape. How had an almost empty can produced so much paint? She knew she had to clean it up before he saw what she'd done.

Maybe he's out to dinner with his father and Lane. Lord, let him be out so I can clean up the mess before he gets home.

She was ready to grab her rags and rush downstairs when she heard Fargo begin to bark in that obnoxious whoof of his. She peered over the rail again, and there sat the beast, front feet planted in the green pool where it had leaked through the chair. He was looking back over his shoulder, calling, "Come here, Marsh. See what she's done now," as clearly as if he could speak.

Marsh came, peering up at her, his face a mask of I-don't-believe-it! She smiled wanly and waved. He didn't snort with disgust or yell at her. He said with quiet resignation, "Abby. Why am I not surprised?"

"It was Puppy."

He spread his hands to the sky and nodded. "Of course. The cat." He turned his face to his dog. "Fargo, are you hungry? Furry takeout is being served upstairs." The rottweiler's hind end began to vibrate.

"Hey!" Abby called, belatedly grabbing Puppy and dumping her on the floor. "There's no need to get hostile."

Marsh looked at her once again. "Right." He looked down at his chair, and Abby saw his shoulders slump.

"Try and think of it this way," she offered. "Your laptop wasn't hurt."

"That's a real comfort." Again he wasn't sarcastic or unkind. In fact, it would have helped if he had been. Then she could have gotten defensive.

"I'm sorry, Marsh," she whispered, blinking against sudden tears. "I'm so sorry."

He looked back at her with a wry smile. "It's only a chair. And a floor." He studied her. "You're not going to cry, are you? Don't cry. My tenants aren't allowed to cry. Don't you know? There's no crying in Seaside."

She couldn't help it; she smiled. "Tom Hanks. *A League of Their Own.*"

"Marshall, what's wrong?" The senator's voice boomed from the house. Abby flinched.

"Nothing, Dad," Marsh called over his shoulder. "I'll be right there."

But of course the senator couldn't stand not knowing all that was happening. Abby heard the door open and his intake of breath. "What happened here?"

The next thing she knew, she was staring down not only at Marsh but his father.

"Senator," she said in a shaky voice. "How nice to see you again."

Then she was looking into the mocking eyes of the beauteous Lane. "Well, had a little accident, did we, ah, Mandy, isn't it?"

"Abby," Marsh and Abby said at the same time.

Lane smirked. "How sweet. A duet."

Marsh grabbed the handle of the paint can and picked it up. "Lane." There was warning in his voice.

"Whatever." Lane raised her eyes to Abby again, mockery more than evident. "Whoever."

As she looked up, a pool of paint that had gathered at the slightly downward outer edge of Abby's railing lost its surface tension. A deep green stream dropped with a precision worthy of a smart bomb right onto Lane's head, mingling the viscous green with her oh-so-carefully and professionally spun silver-gold.

Lane's look of outrage as she jumped back was wonderful. Abby gave a bark of laughter. She couldn't help it. Lane's snarl as the paint ran down her face onto her blue silk shirt and white linen trousers sent Abby into more nervous laughter.

Horrified at herself, she backed away from the rail, hand clasped over her mouth, until she was pressed against the wall of the house under the shade of the great awning. She fought to control the laughter, gulping, gasping, trying to get enough air to calm her pounding heart, to ease her throbbing head.

She sank to the floor, overwhelmed. *It's just too much, Lord. Too much.*

She began sobbing with exhaustion, embarrassment, and distress.

Lord, this was supposed to be a summer of sunlight and new beginnings. How did it become one of so many summer shadows?

Twenty-seven

Sniffing back her tears, Abby cleaned the paint off the railing as well as she could. It would have to be repainted. She would visit the paint man at Kmart again for the needed supplies. She thought that at this rate, he and she were going to become fast friends.

As she cleaned, she looked over the railing once and saw Marsh mopping up the mess she'd made in his chair. She felt guilty about him doing what was her responsibility, but there was no way on earth that she could bring herself to go downstairs while Lane and Senator Winslow were still present. She simply didn't have the courage to face them. She'd never have the courage to face them.

She heard their driver say, "It's nine o'clock, Senator. Are you ready to leave?"

"Thank you, Morris. Let me get my wife."

"Uh, Mrs. Winslow! What happened?" Abby could hear the surprise in Morris's voice.

"Shut up, Morris," spit the ever-pleasant Lane. "Just get me home."

Abby couldn't resist rushing inside to peer out her bedroom window. She watched Lane climb into the rear of the limo wearing what could only be one of Marsh's T-shirts and her own paint-splotched slacks. Her hair hung like limp blond snakes with occasional green streaks where her quick shampoo had failed.

Marsh came into view walking beside his father. The senator would have kept walking to the car with no farewell at all if Marsh hadn't stuck out his hand. His worried eyes on the car, the senator absentmindedly shook Marsh's hand. Then he climbed in after Lane, and they were gone.

Marsh stood alone in the drive long after the car had disappeared, his face a picture of sadness. Abby felt tears once again rise. Why did parent-child relationships have to be so complex, so complicated, so fraught with pain? Would she and Maddie have been reduced to the tense interactions she shared with Mom? Or worse, to the stiff, polite nonrelationship of Marsh and his father?

Oh, God, it's not supposed to be this way! Help me. Please help me.

Mom pulled into the drive just as Marsh disappeared onto his porch. Abby went to help bring up the bags of groceries.

I will be nice. I will be kind. I will be forgiving. I will not lose my temper. I will not speak hastily.

"Abby, what do you think you're doing?" Mom asked when Abby appeared beside the car.

Abby's brows rose at the tone of Mom's voice, but she answered mildly enough. "I'm helping carry the food upstairs."

"You are not." Mom looked horrified. "You cannot do things like this. You'll give yourself back spasms."

"Mom, don't."

"Don't what? Remind you of your limitations? Save you from pain?"

Abby leaned over, grabbing a bag. "Don't try to prevent me from being a normal person." She started for the stairs.

"But you're not a normal person. That's my point." Mom reached for the bag in Abby's arms. "You are crippled."

Twice in one day! Abby shut her eyes against the anger that flared white-hot. She kept a firm grip on the bag full of cold food, biting her lip to keep from saying something she'd regret.

"Come on. Give it to me." Mom wrapped her arms around the bag.

"No." Abby twisted to pull the bag free, and a spasm of pain shot across her lower back. It was enough to steal her breath and make her leg buckle. She leaned against the car for a minute, eyes pinned on her mother, daring her to try and take the bag. She blinked back the tears and told herself pain was all in the mind. She forced herself to walk to the steps, put a hand on the banister, and started pulling.

She pictured Helene the physical therapist standing at the top of the stairs calling, "Push through, Abby. You can do it. Just push through the pain! You did it before. You can do it again."

After forever she reached the kitchen, put the food in the refrigerator or freezer, and folded the bag. She slid it neatly into the opening by the refrigerator where she'd decided to store such items. She said not a word to her mother who was unloading the two bags she'd carried. Abby knew there were more bags in the car's trunk. She also knew she couldn't handle the steps again, not when it was all she could do to simply stand.

She walked down the hall to the bathroom and rummaged through her bottles and vials for the strongest pain medication she had. She dropped two tablets into her hand, downed them with a glass of water, and went to her room without saying good night. The medication soothed the pain, but it was still a restless night.

It was barely past sunrise when she dressed in jeans and a T-shirt and slipped out of her room, taking care not to waken her mother. Picking up her Bible, she went out to the porch. She'd planned to sit at the table reading and praying, but the water called her name.

When she reached the edge of the dry sand, she sank down in the beach chair she had brought along. It was one of the low chairs, just a few inches off the sand. It was the best she could manage with her Bible in one hand, the chair in the other, and no hands left for her cane. She'd just have to struggle when it was time to rise, hoping and praying she didn't twist her back again. It was either manage to get up or crawl back to the house.

Wouldn't Mom like that.

Abby stared at the waves, soothed by their movement and sound, marveling at the contradiction they were: constant yet always changing. Sort of like life. Even when someone died, life went on for all those left behind. A different life certainly, but still the constant of breath in, breath out, the ceaseless churning of the mind absorbing information and spitting out conclusions, the inevitable complications of people touching your emotions, your heart.

Oh, God, what do I do about Mom? I love her. I do. But she's wrong about my frailty. I admit I've got problems, dear Lord, lots of them, but I'm not weak. I'm ignorant, confused, uncertain, hurting, but I am not fragile. I refuse to be fragile. Knowing You makes me strong. You can even make me wise. Oh, Lord, please do!

She opened her Bible to Psalm 102 and read the comforting words. "Hear my prayer, O LORD; let my cry for help come to you. Do not hide your face from me when I am in distress. Turn your ear to me; when I call, answer me quickly."

Turn Your ear and answer, Father. There's the matter of that note. Why does someone dislike me enough to write something ugly like that? I don't understand it.

She flipped back several chapters to Psalm 54. "Hear my prayer, O God; listen to the words of my mouth. Strangers are attacking me; ruthless men seek my life—men without regard for God.... Surely God is my help; the Lord is the one who sustains me."

Strangers are attacking, Lord. Protect and sustain me. Restore my memory. Let me be able to help by remembering Karlee's accident. And when I get all upset about not remembering, calm me down.

She turned to Psalm 94, a favorite during her long recuperation. She needed the assurance of its promises again. "When I said, 'My foot is slipping,' your love, O LORD, supported me. When anxiety was great within me, your consolation brought joy to my soul."

Abby leaned forward in her chair, resting her chin on her drawn-up knees as she wrapped her arms about her legs. Her struggle with her mother felt like the stuff of epics. The hit-and-run and the note felt like acts in the eternal drama of good versus evil.

In contrast, last night's debacle had been pure farce. There was nothing noble about it. Just thinking about it made her flush scarlet even as she had to giggle yet again at Lane's expression when the paint hit. She knew she could never face the married Winslows again. She even wondered how she could look Marsh in the eye after her performance.

"Hey, Abby." As if thinking of him had conjured him up, Marsh appeared at her side with two mugs of coffee. He held one out to her.

"Hi." She took the mug, studying the scene of Seaside's boardwalk printed on it rather than look at him. It amazed her how important this man's opinion of her had become in such a short time. It actually scared her that he might think her an idiot.

Marsh sank to the sand beside her low-slung chair. He too studied his mug. Then he looked out to sea. "I must apologize to you."

Startled, Abby turned to him. "You? I was the one—"

"For Lane." He took a sip. "I'm sure you heard her nasty remarks."

"You mean cripple?"

He nodded.

"And slumming?"

He sighed. "I thought so."

"I also heard how shocked your father was, and I heard you tell her to be quiet."

Marsh's mouth quirked sardonically. "As I recall, *be quiet* is too polite for what I said."

She found she could smile too.

"Of course you more than got back at her." Marsh looked at her over the rim of his cup, eyes twinkling.

Abby squeezed her eyes shut as if she could block her mind-reel from replaying the scene. "I didn't do it on purpose. You do know that?"

"Of course you didn't. You couldn't. First off, you're too nice, and secondly, no one is clever enough to time something like that to the precise second."

"I shouldn't have laughed."

"Probably not." Then his mouth started to twitch. He fought it a minute, gave up, and smiled broadly. Then he started to laugh, great gusts of hilarity escaping him. "She ran into the bathroom, threw her clothes in the wastebasket, and climbed into the shower. She was there so long I thought she'd scrub her skin off."

"Oh, dear."

"Then she wrapped herself in a huge beach towel and ordered my father to find her some clothes."

Abby could imagine Lane, eaten with anger, stalking about the apartment, her hair wet and dripping, her makeup gone. "What did he do?"

"He didn't know what to do. I gave her a pair of my shorts

and a T-shirt to wear home. She took the shirt but refused the shorts. She pulled her slacks out of the trash."

"Were they wrinkled?"

"Very. Now why does that make you smile?"

Abby slapped her hand over her mouth, shaking her head. "It's too catty of me. I hope it wasn't a favorite shirt."

"Nope. I knew I'd never see it again." Marsh sifted sand through his fingers. "You were right, you know. Poor Dad. Lucky me."

Abby looked at him closely. "You don't mind that you lost her?"

"It's a bit awkward that she's married to my father—"

"I would think that's an understatement."

He nodded. "But I thank God every day that she's not my wife." He looked at her and gave a shy half-grin. "Especially recent days."

Abby flushed and ducked her head, pleased beyond reason at the comment. She looked out to sea and drank her coffee.

"What about you, Abby? Do you still miss Sam?"

It was Abby's turn to hide her nervousness by playing in the sand. "It's sad, but I don't miss him anymore. I feel bad about that. He was a nice man, and he deserves to be missed. Now Maddie." Her throat closed; she had to clear it before she could go on. "I'll miss her until the day I die."

Marsh reached out and took her hand, and at once she felt comforted. They sat in silence for a minute, neither making any move to unlink their hands. Then he asked, "Can you tell me about Sam?"

Abby took a deep breath. "He was a strong personality. He was also very good looking, very charming. I was eighteen when I met him, and I was bowled over. I found it amazing that he was taken with me and comforting that he always knew what was right for me, for himself, for the world. Life didn't look so frightening with him there to solve all the puzzles and answer all the questions."

"Your parents liked him?" Marsh asked.

"They did. They felt he would take good care of their baby girl. We married the day after I graduated. The first couple of years I was very happy. Cozy. Sam was attentive and kind. Then as I slowly began to think for myself, he felt threatened. As my relationship with the Lord deepened and matured, he felt uncomfortable. It upset him that I thought things or wanted to do things he didn't. I'm not certain why. I wasn't trying to undermine him or his position."

"Maybe he wasn't as confident as he seemed. Maybe he needed you as his acolyte, not his equal."

She thought about Marsh's comment for a few minutes but couldn't decide whether she agreed or not. "Maybe. Who knows? I do know that we would have stayed married in spite of the tensions. We wouldn't have been joyously pleased with each other, but we wouldn't have been seriously displeased either. There never would have been cause for divorce." She waved her hand in a vague circle. "And who knows—he might have changed, loosened up."

"I'm sort of surprised your mother liked him." He made the comment warily, like he wasn't sure what her reaction would be.

Abby grinned. "You're thinking of how fond she is of you."

"Yes, though I don't think fond is quite the right word."

"She liked Sam a lot. It hurt her terribly when he died." Abby stared at their clasped hands. "I think what she liked most was that he would keep me the pliant, pleasant daughter I'd always been."

"Who wants pliant?" Marsh gave her hand a squeeze. "Though pleasant can be very nice."

She screwed up her face, contrite. "Pleasant seems to have gone missing lately. I lost my temper at Mom again last night." It felt like a confession.

He studied her face. "Why?"

"Aren't you going to tell me how terrible I was and quote, 'Honor your father and your mother' at me?"

He shrugged. "Maybe sometime later when I find out what happened, but right now I'd like to know why." He took her empty cup from her hand, setting it in the sand. "I figure you feel guilty enough without my help."

She studied his profile as he twisted the mug back and forth in the sand, drilling it deeper with each twist. "You're a very nice man, Marsh Winslow." It was as close as she could come to articulating how much she appreciated his assumption that she had a good reason or at least some reason for her behavior.

He just smiled and waited.

"She was taking over again. She wanted to pay for all the food."

"And you didn't want her to?"

"It's my house. I'm the hostess. I buy the food." Her voice was dogmatic and more than a little defensive. She waited for his rebuttal.

"Sounds reasonable to me," he said, completely disarming her.

But there was more to confess. "Then she didn't want me to carry any of the grocery bags upstairs."

He raised a finger. "Let me guess. You insisted."

"I grabbed the bag away from her when she reached for it." Abby grimaced. "Sort of like a mad little kid yelling, 'It's mine!'"

He tilted his head, eyeing her. "But you very much regret behaving like that."

"I do. I really do." She was so thankful he understood. Here she'd told him she'd been a rude idiot, and he still held her hand. No doubt about it, he was one in a million.

He smiled at her with a special warmth that made her chest tighten. "In fact," he said, "I admire you greatly for standing up for yourself."

She loved him; she knew it. Anyone who thought her a reasonable, thinking woman capable of wise choices was without doubt the man for her.

"Believe me," he said. "I know how hard it is to go up against a strong parent."

Abby nodded. Senator Winslow was like a steamroller flattening anyone who got in his way or who disagreed with him. Except Marsh, who had stepped onto his own path and made his own choices.

"When I told Dad I wasn't going into politics, he was very unhappy. He had always wanted me to follow in the family business. When Lane came along, obsessed with the same idea, he became even pushier. I took a year off from graduate school to campaign for him in the last election, and I did very well. I even enjoyed it. He thought he had me. So did Lane. When I said I still planned to go to seminary and hoped to teach there as a career, Dad was furious. Not only had I defied him, I had also become too religious, an embarrassment."

"But you stood firm," Abby said, proud of him for his courage. "You held your ground."

"Because I knew what God wanted of me, and I was committed to follow Him wherever He led."

Abby heard the pain in his voice. "Following the Lord cost you your relationship with your dad, didn't it?"

"To a large degree. I disappointed him terribly. Then he married Lane, and that strained things to the breaking point."

"So he lost you by his own choice and gained Lane."

"That's about it. She's added a whole layer of difficulty to an already complicated situation." He looked lost. "I hate it. I miss him."

Abby reached out, laying her free hand on his cheek. "I wonder if he has any idea what a genuine treasure he threw away when he settled for that counterfeit brass ring."

"Excuse me." The voice intruding was cool to the point of chilling.

Abby jumped, dropped her hand from Marsh's cheek, and spun to see her mother standing behind her. "Mom, you startled me!" She tried to slip her other hand from Marsh's, but he tightened his grip until she could escape only by making a scene.

"Good morning, Mrs. MacDonald," he said pleasantly.

"You might think about getting ready for work rather than wasting time sitting on the beach," Mom said without looking at Marsh. "I have your breakfast on the table."

Abby looked at her watch and blinked. "I had no idea it had gotten so late."

Marsh stood, reaching out for Abby's other hand. She offered it, and he pulled her effortlessly to her feet. He stepped close, smiling. "Go ahead, Abby. I'm going to sit here for a few minutes. I'll bring your chair up when I come."

With a nod Abby turned to her mother and found her watching Marsh with a cool, almost antagonistic stare. Abby sighed. She and her mother started across the sand together, walking slowly so Abby wouldn't slip. Halfway across the beach Mom spoke.

"You've got to stop meeting that man. He's all wrong for you."

Twenty-eight

I UNDERSTAND THERE's a beautiful new children's librarian around here somewhere, Miss. Could you help me find her? I think I'd like to check her out."

Abby spun. "Sean!" She laughed up at the handsome doctor. "What are you doing here?"

Standing next to the small tables and chairs made Sean Schofield look even taller than he was. His navy slacks and navy plaid shirt made the gray at his temples stand out against his tan face. No doubt about it; he was an impressive man.

He looked around, clearly interested in her little kingdom. "I figured you saw me at work. It's time for me to see you in your milieu."

Milieu, Abby thought as she waved her hand toward her work area. *He actually said milieu. I don't think I've ever heard anyone say that word in a regular conversation before.* And he had been impressive before.

"Well, this is it." She gave him the VIP tour, which took about three minutes.

"I like these best," he said, sitting down in front of one of the computers. He clicked the mouse to begin a new game. His concentration was intense, and he smiled every time the computer said, "You're so smart."

"Not too hard for you, was it?" Abby asked with a laugh when he finished.

"Nah. I went to kindergarten on a scholarship."

With no warning a little redheaded boy sitting at a nearby table with another boy jumped to his feet. "You stink!" he yelled at his friend and grabbed his blue chair. "Youstinkyoustink-youstinkyoustink!" He lifted the chair over his head, clearly planning to bring it down on his friend's head.

Abby threw herself across the table, grabbing the boy about the waist with one arm and the chair with the other hand. She spun him away from the table and felt his body vibrating with intense emotion. His breathing was harsh, fierce. She held his back to her front and talked softly into his ear.

"Put the chair down slowly, okay? That's a boy. Slowly. Slowly. We don't want anyone to get hurt."

"Yes, we do!" he cried even as he lowered the chair. "I want to hit him!"

The chair's chrome legs touched the floor, and Abby put her hand over one of the boy's where it held the chair. "Let go of the chair, okay? Just open those strong fingers and let go. That's right. Let go. That's the way. Good."

She could feel the boy still shaking, but it wasn't the wild, uncontrolled vibrating of a couple of minutes ago. She thought it safe to release him around the waist, but she wasn't willing to let him go completely. He still felt like a ticking bomb.

She slid her arm from about him, and when he tried to bolt, she grabbed his hand. "Come on. Let's sit over here and talk."

She led him to a pair of little chairs in front of an aquarium and gently pushed him down into one. She took the other, still holding his hand. "I'm Mrs. Patterson. Who are you?"

The boy mumbled a name as he stared at his feet. He tried to break her hold on his hand but couldn't no matter how hard he pulled and twisted. She hadn't taught elementary school all those years without learning a trick or two about restraining recalcitrant children.

Abby reached to him with her free hand and brushed his red bangs aside. He didn't quite flinch, but it was close enough that her heart constricted. Did people raise their hands to him only in anger? "Can you tell me your name again but louder?"

"Monty," he all but screamed.

Abby smiled, ignoring all the curious people, drawn either by the original incident or the boy's yell. "Hello, Monty." She made her voice as warm as she could.

He looked at her hand holding his and tried to pull free again. "Let go of me!"

Abby maintained her grip. *Lord, please no bruises on this little wrist. All I need is for some lady to go to Nan with the story that I purposely bruised her son.* "Do you like the library, Monty?"

He shrugged. "It's okay."

"Did anyone ever tell you that you have to be quiet in the library?"

"My mom."

So where was the woman while her son committed mayhem? "Is she looking for a book of her own to read?"

"She's shopping."

Abby frowned. Using the library as a free baby-sitter was not kosher, to put it mildly. "Is that little boy over there your brother?"

Monty shook his head. "I don't have any brothers."

Abby waited for more information, but none came.

"Have you known him long?"

"I don't know him at all."

Interesting. Abby pointed to the book still sitting on the table. "What were you reading?"

"A book about Elmo," he said, shoulders hunched like there was something wrong in reading a Muppets book.

Abby laughed. "I like Elmo too, but I like Cookie best."

Monty looked at her in surprise. "He said it was a baby book." He looked toward the boy whom he'd wanted to brain. Not surprisingly, the boy was gone. Abby looked toward the front door and saw him being pulled outside by his mother. She wondered if she'd ever see them in the library again.

"Who cares what he said. We don't think it's for babies." Abby waved her hand at the nearby bookshelves. "Do you know why we have so many books? Because people like all kinds of books. I bet I like some you don't."

Monty looked at her like she was crazy. "Of course you do. You're a big people. You don't have pictures."

Abby nodded. "Very true. Now I've got to tell you something, Monty. You're not allowed to hit people in the library. Not with your hands and not with a chair. You said you know about the rule here that says you need to be really quiet so that other people can read and work without being bothered. Hitting people isn't being very quiet."

"He made me mad." Monty's jaw was set.

"But that doesn't mean you can hit him with a chair. It would have hurt him a lot."

He nodded. "Yep."

Abby looked at him, her expression stern. "Nope." She stood. "Come on. Let's get Elmo. Then you can wait for your mom by the front door." Where someone would see her and grab her when she returned, telling her a few of the facts of life.

Abby walked across the library to the checkout desk, Monty in tow. She smiled at the perky old lady with blue-tinted hair who was manning the desk. "Mae, this is Monty. He needs to sit with you for a minute while I speak to Nan."

Mae looked over the desk at the little boy. "Okay, kiddo, come on back here and take that seat. But you got to be quiet, you know. This is the library."

Monty dragged himself around the desk with the enthusiasm of a toddler going to the doctor's office for an injection. He climbed into the chair Mae indicated and opened his Elmo book. He put out a finger, touched the picture of the red creature, a slight smile tugging his lips.

Abby's heart bled a bit as she watched him, a boy who dealt better with a red puppet than with people. She turned to go to Nan's office only to find her standing not five feet away.

"Well done," Nan said.

"Thanks." The two walked away from the checkout station to Nan's office where they could talk unimpeded. Abby told the story while Nan listened intently. She concluded, "The poor kid's a little volcano just waiting to erupt."

Nan grimaced. "Just so he doesn't erupt here.

Abby nodded, aware now that the crisis was past that she had wrenched her hip, doubtless in that dive across the table. The pain was fierce. She was seeing Celia at five for a massage, but five seemed days away.

"Go get lunch," Nan said. "Mae and I'll keep an eye out for the mother and try to talk to her."

Abby limped back to her desk, wincing with every step. Tylenol. She needed some Tylenol. She couldn't take one of her strong pain meds because they made her too fuzzy.

"That was a most interesting situation." Sean sat in her chair, looking at her over her own desk.

"Sean!" She'd forgotten he was here, but he didn't need to know that. Besides, a handsome man was always good for what ailed you.

"I hope you don't mind my sitting here." He rose and stood with his hands in his pockets. "The other chairs all looked a bit too small, to say nothing of a bit weak for my weight."

"And I'd hate to see you sent crashing to the floor." She walked around the desk and reached into the top drawer. "You'd probably sue us just for the fun of it." Her smile told him she wasn't serious. She pulled out a bottle of Tylenol, tipping three into her hand.

"Three?" Sean looked at her in question.

"Wrenched my hip grabbing Monty. If I don't do something, I'll be crippled by evening."

Sean took her arm. "Here. You sit. I'll get you some water."

"No, don't bother. I have some here." She reached into her bottom drawer this time, pulling out a bottle of water. She broke the seal and swallowed the Tylenol.

"Let's go somewhere for lunch, okay?" he said. "That's why I came in the first place."

"To have lunch with me?"

He laughed at her expression. "You needn't look so surprised. I like to get to know a pretty girl when I meet one."

"Checking her out, huh?" Abby picked up her purse. "Okay, let's go."

He drove downtown to Bitsi's. "They have great food and are one of the places open this early. This weekend will bring the town alive until after Labor Day, but today Bitsi's is still the best bet."

They took a booth and placed their order.

Sean put his elbow on the table, leaning his chin into his palm. "I've got to tell you that I never knew a job like yours could be so exciting. I thought all you did was put numbers on the spines of books and yell at kids who returned stuff late."

"We are a full-service facility. Numbers on spines, yell for silence, read stories, prevent homicides." Abby opened her napkin and spread it across her lap. It wouldn't do to have the tomato in her BLT drip onto her gauze skirt, though if it did, it'd get lost in the pattern. "Fortunately I don't often see trouble like this morning's."

"What did the other kid do to set the redhead off?"

"He told Monty his Muppets book was for babies."

"And Monty thought this was an offense worth decapitation."

"You know, most of us work up to it before we lose our tempers. One thing happens, then another. We slowly get more and more angry. We start at one, working our way up to ten over time. If we're wise, somewhere in the early build-up of the negative emotions, we confront the problem and solve it."

She thought briefly of her anger at her mother. She feared she was past the early build-up stage, and no solution was in sight. What a mess. At least beaning her mother was an option she wouldn't consider.

She pushed her potato chips around her plate and continued. "Not only do kids like Monty have no problem-solving skills— that's largely because of their age—they're at eight on the anger scale all the time. There's no building of emotion; it's everything on high boil, waiting to scald. Brain the kid because he says you're reading a baby book."

Sean considered that idea. "I've met a few people like Monty, always angry. Makes me think of a guy I know named McCoy. The least provocation, and it's Mount St. Helens all over again."

"Don't you wonder why?" Abby sipped her iced tea. "What's happened in Monty's life to make him so angry? Is it his mother going off and leaving him? When I pushed his hair back, he jumped like he expected me to hurt him. Is he being physically abused?"

Abby thought of Vivienne deMarco. She seemed furious always, even when she was purring over Sean or Rick or Marsh. Whatever Rocco deMarco had done, she was livid, and she wasn't giving an inch.

"Do you think Monty can't help it?" Sean asked. He had a large order of french fries that he bathed in vast quantities of ketchup. Abby shuddered. He saw her reaction and smiled. "I can't help my ketchup fetish. Eggs. Steak. Meat loaf. Hamburgers. Hot dogs. Cheese steaks. Toast."

"Toast?" She watched a glob of ketchup fall from the fries as he brought some to his mouth. "Poor man. I'm sure there's a twelve-step program for you somewhere."

"Hello, I'm Sean and I'm a ketchupaholic."

It was a relief to leave problems like Monty for a time and listen to Sean's funny stories of his miniature patients. No wonder he was such a successful doctor. It was obvious he enjoyed all the children he treated.

"I'm delighted Karlee is doing so well," Abby said. "I still feel that somehow this is all my fault."

"Come on, Abby. You know better than that."

"I do. It's just that I see this little girl in pink overalls and a ponytail with a pink scrunchie skipping along, singing, happy with life and herself. Then—" She spread her hands. "Nothing."

"Just relax. If it's going to come, it will. If not—and with hysterical amnesia often memory doesn't return—there's nothing you can do about it."

"How about hypnosis?"

He looked thoughtful. "Have the police suggested it?"

She shook her head, pulling the last of the iced tea through her straw.

"Then I wouldn't worry about it." Sean put the tip on the table. "Time to get you back."

It was five minutes before one when they pulled into the library parking lot. Abby watched a young mom with three young children parade past with arms full of books. "I wonder if Monty's mother has come for him yet."

"If she hasn't, you've got part of the reason for his anger."

"How does he learn to control himself if there's no one to teach him?"

"I'm guessing he doesn't."

"That's too terrible to think about. He has to learn to control himself. Part of becoming a responsible adult is learning to act appropriately."

"You think all adults act appropriately?"

"Your cynicism is showing." Abby pushed the car door open. "And no, I don't. I know better. Just look at the person who hit Karlee."

Sean nodded. "May I call you or stop by the house?" he asked as she made to shut the door. "Maybe we could go somewhere together."

"You surprise me," she said. The last thing she ever expected was for Sean Schofield to take an interest in her. "But certainly you can call." Whether she'd actually go out with him she could decide later. She shut the door and headed up the walk.

"That's an example of appropriate guy behavior when he sees a pretty girl," he called through the window he lowered. "Like we were just talking, you know."

Laughing, she walked into the library. She was relieved to see that Monty wasn't behind Mae's desk. Of course, neither was Mae. She'd been replaced by another volunteer, a white-haired gentleman with a bushy mustache and a cravat.

A cravat, Abby thought. *A real cravat. That's sort of the sartorial equivalent of milieu.*

Abby sat at her desk, realizing as she did so that her hip wasn't hurting too much at the moment. Five o'clock and Celia no longer looked quite so far off.

She saw that someone had put the Elmo book on her desk. There was a slip sticking out of the top, marking a page. The message read: *I'm sorry. He did it when I wasn't looking. Mae.* Abby opened the book and found a page torn from top to bottom, most of it gone. All that was left of what must have been a large picture of Elmo was one part of his foot. Monty had decided to take his friend home with him.

Abby felt a black veil of sadness descend as she thought of Monty. Poor kid.

What about me? Have I become an adult version of Monty? Am I bubbling at an eight, a nine, a ten? Granted it's taken me a long, long time to get this mad, but the irate feelings don't go away.

She heard her own words. *"Part of becoming a responsible adult is learning to act appropriately."*

She stuffed her purse in her bottom drawer and pulled a manila folder toward her. She opened it and began studying the material.

"Abby, excuse me."

Abby looked up at Nan Fulsom. Standing just behind her was a Jimmy Stewart look-alike. The expressions on both their faces were serious.

"There's been another note," Nan said.

Twenty-nine

ABBY LAY ON her stomach with her face resting on the padded doughnut that stuck out from the end of the massage table. She knew that when she turned over, she'd have crease marks on her face and the front of her hair would be an absolute ruin from the pressure. Who cared? Time and a curling wand would correct the problems.

She was so glad to be there, to anticipate the relief that Celia's magic fingers would bring. Her whole right side felt as taut as a violin string and as twisted as a pretzel.

It was that one sentence: There's been another note.

When Nan had spoken those words, all the relaxed feelings she'd experienced over the course of her lunch with Sean had vanished, dissipating like steam rising from a boiling pot. Instead, the talons of tension sank deep. As a result, she'd had back spasms off and on all afternoon.

"Whoa, Abby." Celia gently ran her hands down Abby's back and side. "You're in spasm from L5 to S1."

"Tell me something I don't know." Abby sounded cranky even to her own ears.

"Okay. Your erector spinae are contracted and tight, and your pelvic crest is contracted into the gluts," Celia offered. "How's that?"

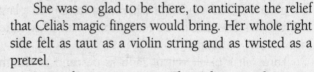

"I'm sorry if I sound grumpy, Celia. It's been a hard day."

Celia moved to Abby's feet and began massaging. "After Aunt Bernice and Poor Uncle Walter, I'm immune to grumpy. What happened?"

Abby sighed as Celia's fingers dug into her muscles. "It started with one little boy trying to brain another with a chair. To prevent it, I had to dive across a table. Not a good move for someone like me."

"Did you save kid two from kid one?"

"I did, but it was a close call. If I hadn't been looking or if I hadn't been near, kid two would be in the hospital as we speak." Abby winced as a tight spot in her calf reacted to the pressure of Celia's thumb.

"Am I pushing too hard?" Celia asked, lightening her touch.

"No. Keep up the pressure. I need some major kinks released."

Abby heard Celia pour some more oil and rub it into her hands. Then the soothing strokes began again. As casually as she could manage, Abby said, "Sean took me to lunch."

"Sean Schofield?" Celia laughed her surprise. "He actually did something social in the middle of the day? I sort of got the impression that he lived and breathed his practice. I mean, anyone who stops to see patients after midnight on a Friday night has to have a limited social calendar."

"Well, he did come out to the house Saturday evening and Monday."

"Yeah, he did. In time to get fed both times."

"Celia Fitzmeyer, you are a cynic."

"I'm a realist. You'll notice there was food involved with Sean's visit this time too. Makes you wonder if it's true about the way to a man's heart. Where did he take you?"

"Bitsi's."

"He disappoints me. I thought, being a doctor and all, that he'd take you someplace ritzy."

"Not for lunch on a workday. There's not enough time."

"Excuses, excuses."

They fell silent as Celia finished working on Abby's left leg. Since this part of her didn't hurt much at all, the massage felt wonderful.

"So," Celia said as she chopped the edges of her hands up and down Abby's leg, "you've got both Marsh and Sean chasing you, eh?"

Now it was Abby's turn to laugh. "Sean just wanted to see where I worked. He said I'd seen him in the hospital, so he wanted to see me in my—" she couldn't bring herself to say *milieu*—"setting."

"I've seen him at the hospital too," Celia said as her fingers attacked a recalcitrant knot in Abby's right thigh. "But he's never come to the spa to see me in my setting."

"Do you want him to?" Abby asked after she caught her breath at the unexpected jolt she felt to her toes as Celia's thumb dug deep. "Or is Rick enough?"

"He is a sweetie."

"I take it that means you had fun last night on the board-walk?"

"I had a wonderful time. So did the girls. I don't think we've laughed so much in a long time. We certainly didn't last year at Aunt Bernice's."

"Did people think he was Rick Mathis or call him Duke?"

"A couple of people kept staring, and one kid asked for his autograph. Poor guy. He'd worn a baseball cap that he kept pulled down over his forehead and a pair of mirrored sunglasses. Still people thought they recognized him."

"You don't think he really is Rick Mathis traveling incognito, do you?" Abby asked.

"Come on," Celia scoffed. "What would a big star like that be doing bunking with a friend here in Seaside?"

"Well, even movie and TV stars have friends and go on vacation. I imagine they don't like to go alone any more than the rest of the population. Marsh is a senator's son. Maybe Rick's one of those stars who gives to political causes, and they met each other that way."

"Yeah, but…"

"Yeah, but what?" Abby asked.

"Well, the guy's dating me. What movie or TV star is ever going to do that?"

"Any man with half a brain would love to date you. You're a wonderful person, and you're cute as can be. You're even a natural blonde."

Celia made a small self-deprecating noise. "And I have two little girls who come as part of the package. What guy wants that?"

"So you don't think you'll see him again?"

Celia giggled as her sensitive fingers worked the tight muscles around Abby's lower back. "He asked himself over for dinner tonight."

"And you are going to feed him what?"

"Maybe I told him not to come," Celia said.

Abby hooted. She couldn't help it.

Celia sighed. "I tell you, Abby. All this interest from a guy like Rick scares me to death."

"Celia! Why do you say that?"

"The last man interested in me was Eddie."

"So?"

"I jump from a loser like Eddie to a winner like Rick just like that?"

"So you told him not to come tonight?" Abby couldn't believe it.

Celia's smile sounded in her voice. "I may be scared, but I'm not an idiot. He's coming tonight, and Karlee asked him if he wanted to go to MacDonald's with us tomorrow night."

"And he said?"

"Yes." She sounded amazed. "He said it would be fun. And," her voice grew soft, "he asked me to dinner, just me and no girls, on Saturday."

"Wow!"

"My thought exactly." Celia moved up to Abby's shoulders and began to work on them, following the muscles down the edge of her shoulder blades, probing, working, and applying pressure. Abby shut her eyes and relaxed when she wasn't wincing. She let her mind shut down, but she fought sleep. When you slept, you didn't feel all the wonderful untying of knots.

When Abby left Seaside Spa, not only did she move a bit more easily, she'd also avoided thinking about the letters for an hour. A major if temporary lessening of tension.

"Friday," Celia said as Abby walked out the door. "You need to keep those muscles supple."

"I'll be here." She climbed into her car and started home. At least Mom knew she was going to be late tonight, so she couldn't complain. Still the idea of a tense evening after the lovely looseness of the massage was distressing.

Abby reached for her purse after she parked in her spot in the drive. As she did, her eyes fell on the folder that contained her copies of the two letters about her that had come to the library. The fear she had managed to contain at the spa rushed back, chilling her to her marrow. She picked up the folder and opened it. On top lay the letter that had arrived today.

When Nan had come to her, she hadn't felt any prickle of forewarning, any anticipation of danger. Hadn't Nan complimented her on the handling of Monty just a little over an hour prior?

"This is George Martindale," Nan had said indicating the young Jimmy Stewart look-alike. "He's the editor of the *Seaside Journal.*"

Abby smiled and felt like she should look over Mr. Martindale's shoulder for Harvey, the invisible rabbit, so strong was his resemblance to Stewart.

"Do you have a minute?" Nan asked abruptly. "Come to my office."

Abby went cold all over. Not again! She followed Nan and Mr. Martindale. In Nan's office she took the same seat she'd taken yesterday. Mr. Martindale sat in another red faux leather chair a few feet from her.

"Mr. Martindale is chairman of the library board," Nan explained.

Abby nodded and looked at Mr. Martindale, who studied her as if he were trying to read her mind.

"I received a very distressing letter in the mail today," he said.

Abby felt the blood drain from her face. Without any more discussion, Nan handed her the letter.

> Mr. Martindale:
>   As chairman of the library board you need to know that you have an unfit person working as children's librarian. When we were at your library, she touched my child inappropriately. I cannot tell you how appalled I am. I do not want any other child to suffer as mine has. She is unstable. If she is fired, I will not press charges.

Abby had stared at the letter in disbelief, then at Nan. "No," she whispered. "Never!"

"Why would someone send a letter like this if it wasn't true?"

Mr. Martindale asked. He didn't sound at all like Jimmy Stewart used to, all warm and understanding. His voice was cold and brusque.

"I don't know." Abby blinked against the tears rising. She felt helpless. How did one prove one's innocence of a charge like that? "I don't know."

They all sat in silence while Abby stared at the letter. She sat up straight. "There's no signature."

"That's the reason we aren't asking for your resignation," Mr. Martindale said. "We cannot prove anything." Even without the words being spoken, he couldn't have been any clearer about wishing he could fire her outright.

"Please check with my former employers," she begged. "I taught elementary school for several years before our daughter was born. They can tell you I'd never do something like this letter implies."

"Thank you for the suggestion, Abby." Nan kept her face neutral, wiped of any emotion that Abby might take comfort from or grow upset over. "We'll talk to you later."

Now sitting in the car in her drive, Abby let fall the tears that she refused to cry earlier. She cried until her head ached, her nose was stopped up, and her reflection in the rearview mirror showed red puffy eyes. Clutching her purse and the folder to her chest like they could offer her protection, she climbed from the car. She leaned on the fender, looked at the steps to her apartment, and winced, not at the stairs themselves but at the thought of facing her mother, who waited above. Mom would take one look at her eyes, all red and swollen, and rush to her, arms open wide.

"Oh, Abby, baby! What happened?" she'd say. "No, don't tell me. I don't want to know. Not yet. Just come lie down. Let me get you a cold compress and a cool drink." She'd shake her head. "I knew this job was a bad idea. I knew you were still too fragile."

She'd tuck a summer blanket around Abby and smile softly as she did so, openly cheerful that she'd been proven right. She'd pat Abby's cheek, a gesture Abby hated. It made her feel like a pet dog. "A couple of Tylenol and some chamomile iced tea. Then a long nap. We'll just wait on dinner. Sleep, sweetheart, sleep." She'd pat Abby's cheek again and kiss her forehead.

Abby shuddered at the all-too-probable scenario. She saw

herself looking just like Snow White, lying comatose on her bed, only with short, curly hair, a red nose, and swollen eyes instead of Snow's fairy-tale peaceful beauty. She pictured Thumper and all the forest animals standing around looking sad. No. Wait. That was the wrong movie. It was seven little guys who should stand around and look sad.

She took a long steadying breath and longed for Marsh to appear. He could be her Prince Charming, and he didn't even need to give her a kiss to revive her. He just needed to listen. Granted, he wasn't always the smoothest operator, but more times than not he'd gotten her through a tough situation.

His parking place was empty. So was Rick's. Well, the latter was to be expected. He was eating at Celia's, which was fine. It wasn't Rick she wanted. It was Marsh. She knew it should concern her how much she wanted him, but it didn't. She could be concerned about the depth of her feelings when the crisis was over. Right now comfort was her most overriding need, and he was the one who could give it. If he had any wisdom, she'd take that too.

She turned sad eyes to the first-floor deck. Where was her hero when a woman truly needed him? With a sigh she walked slow step by slow step up the driveway, knowing there was no escape. Mom waited.

But Mom wasn't the evil queen foisting a poisoned apple on her. Her agenda wasn't to kill or maim Abby, though that might well be the outcome anyway, at least emotionally. She was just an overprotective, highly opinionated mother who didn't realize that parenting of such intensity should have ceased years ago. Life hurt at times, and Mom didn't understand that Abby needed to deal with her personal hurts her own way in her own personal space and at her own pace.

"Mrs. Patterson! Mrs. Patterson!" Jordan rushed up to her, Walker hard on his heels. "Where's Karlee and Jess?"

She looked down into Jordan's upturned face. So open and trusting. So normal, even if he was more than slightly hyperkinetic. "They aren't coming tonight. I'm sorry."

"Rats!" This from Walker.

"What are you two doing?" demanded a cutting voice. "Get over here."

Abby looked over at the irritated Vivienne, making believe she didn't hear the low groan from Jordan. "Hello." She made herself smile in a neighborly fashion.

Lovely as usual, Vivienne wore a sundress in shades of blue ranging from aqua to teal, looking like the ocean in the Caribbean, not New Jersey. Her hair was tied back with a ribbon that matched the mid shades of her dress. Teal sandals finished off her outfit. If the woman ever smiled, she'd be one of the most gorgeous women Abby'd ever seen.

"The boys don't bother me, Vivienne. They're good guys. I don't mind them coming over."

"Well, I do." As she talked, she moved down the drive so she could look onto Marsh's porch. Checking for the men?

The street door to the deMarco house opened, and Rocco stepped out. He looked as bad as Vivienne looked good. He wore several days' worth of beard, his T-shirt was wrinkled, his jeans shredded at the knee, his white-stockinged feet dirty, but it was his eyes that stopped Abby. Hers might be red and swollen, but Rocco's were full of pain.

The boys scampered toward him, and he walked forward to meet them.

"Hello," Abby said again. "How's your car?" She gestured to the navy Lexus.

"It goes into the shop tomorrow. It's going to cost big bucks to fix it, but at least I don't have to pay. The insurance has okayed the repairs."

"Good," Abby started to say when Vivienne's voice cut in.

"Like you couldn't afford it." She looked at him in challenge. "You can afford anything you want—almost." And with a toss of her head, she stalked off, leaving no doubt about what he couldn't afford.

As she watched Vivienne disappear around the house, Abby remembered one of the boys telling her that their father was now rich. She glanced at Rocco and felt a stab of pity at the longing in his eyes as they followed his wife until she was out of sight. She noticed that the boys each held one of his hands. They, too, watched their mother's retreating figure.

The very intensity of the sorrow of the three deMarco males made Abby think that the unhappiness they were facing was a relatively new thing, that there must have been a happy time for them.

What had happened? Had Rocco been unfaithful?

"What's your business, Mr. deMarco?" Abby asked, instinctively trying to find a topic that wasn't hurtful for him.

He looked blank for a minute while he forced his attention from Vivienne and tried to process her question. "I'm not working right now," he finally said.

"Oh." It wasn't the answer she expected. If ever she'd seen a man who needed his mind occupied with work, it was Rocco deMarco. Anything had to be better than mooning over Vivienne like he was.

"He was in dot-coms," Jordan volunteered. His little chest swelled with pride. "He made a killing."

Abby couldn't help grinning. Did the boy even understand what he was saying?

Walker nodded, anxious to support his father too. "He sold out just before the bottom fell out of that market and made millions." He took a step closer to his father.

Rocco grinned halfheartedly. "My fan club."

Abby noted that he didn't refute their claims. "You're fortunate to have such loving sons."

He looked over to where Vivienne had disappeared from view. "I am." Still holding his sons' hands, Rocco walked slowly back to his house, rich, loved at least by his sons, and miserable.

Abby sighed, starting toward the steps again. She put one foot on the first tread, stopped, and stared out across the beach to the horizon. Maybe Mom was right. Maybe she was still too fragile. Here she was, a grown woman whose mother felt it absolutely fine to move in without an invitation. *And I let it happen without a single word! And I can't even make myself tell her to go home.*

Mom was like a plastic bag wrapped about her, cutting off her oxygen, smothering her independence, stifling the real Abby or who she hoped was the real Abby. The sad part was that she herself was the one who allowed the suffocating bag to remain in place. She should be clawing her way free, tearing the constricting encumbrance to shreds, proclaiming her freedom. Granted she'd tried to break free when she moved to Seaside, but her great adventure into independence had stalled after exactly one day and remained at a standstill ever since.

Oh, Lord, what do I do? About Mom? About the note? About the amnesia? And where's Marsh?

She glanced up the stairs, swerved left, and walked onto Marsh's porch.

Thirty

THE LETTERS SHOULD have arrived by now. The very thought of it made him grin. He wished he had been a fly on the wall so he could have seen that librarian's face when she read that first letter.

What were the exact words again? Oh, yes. *Are you aware that the woman who is your children's librarian has spent several years under psychiatric care?* Nothing like the term *psychiatric care* to get people nervous, especially if the people who needed psychiatric help worked around children. Pretty clever choice of words, if he did say so.

He frowned as he eyed the confusion of folders and papers on his desk, a sign of the heavy caseload he'd seen today. His shoulders tensed at the clutter. Each morning Molly, his faithful girl Friday, put a list of appointments on his clean desk and the files of each patient to be seen on her desk. Somehow by evening, every file ended up on his desk.

It wasn't Molly's fault. He liked to keep each file with him through the parental consult that ended each visit. He'd also noticed that the parent, worried over her child's illness, seemed to take comfort in the evidence of his busyness. It confirmed her decision to make him her child's physician.

Then too, Molly wasn't allowed in his office except

by invitation. She'd broken that rule only once, and he knew she'd never do it again. Still, he should not have to live with such disorder. He clicked his intercom. "Molly, come get these files, please."

His voice was a bit too abrupt, but he needed to see the desk all ordered, immaculate. Stress sometimes made him compulsive, and now was definitely one of those times as he dealt with that oh-so-charming thorn in his side, Abby.

Five minutes later he ran a hand over the surface of his desk. Its beauty and size pleased him immensely after all the years in med school when he worked on an old door set on two little towers of cinder blocks he'd stolen from a building site. The gleaming cherry, the vast expanse, the gold-plated triangular sign reading "Sean M. Schofield, M.D." sitting on the far left side, even the high-backed executive chair done in soft black leather—all made him feel the power of his position, the sweetness of escape. He sank back into the enveloping comfort of his black leather, enjoying the sensation of his shoulders relaxing. Order. Control. They were the secrets of life. Exerting them over others was life's great pleasure.

He'd been disappointed that Abby was so cheerful at lunch today. He thought she'd be reeling from all the nasty things written about her, whispered about her, squirming like a worm on a hook as she drowned in a stream of accusations.

But no, she had smiled, been attentive to him, encouraged his interest in her. It must be that the librarian chose not to mention the first letter. Well, she couldn't ignore the second one. Allegations of impropriety toward a child were a death knell to anyone's reputation, doubly so to one who dealt with children.

Too bad McCoy hadn't been around to add his evil touch to this whole process. No one could do bad as well as he. Sean remembered how McCoy had faced down Win Johnson in sixth grade.

Win had complained to the teacher that McCoy was trying to copy math off him. Mrs. Patton had then read McCoy the riot act, threatening him with failure. Like McCoy cared about his grades.

He did, however, care about Win carrying tales. Honor dictated that adults not be brought into kid problems, and Win had violated that code. For the rest of the year, McCoy stole Win's homework as often as he could, copied all the answers onto his own homework, changed all of Win's solutions by one or two digits, then sat back, laughing as Win failed paper after paper. On tests, he switched answers too, several times making the changes on Mrs. Patton's own desk when she was busy in another part of the room or had stepped into the hall.

"McCoy is after me," Win sobbed to Mrs. Patton, thereby earning everyone's double scorn.

"Not me," McCoy said. "Why should I bother with him when he's getting so many wrong, and I'm getting them all right?"

Of course McCoy went on to major in violence and hate, but Sean always admired his early cleverness. In fact, he remembered it many years later as a college sophomore. By that time he had decided med school was his ticket out of the Pines.

Early on it became obvious that the competition for grades high enough to get into med school was intense. When Dr. Hager, four months from retirement at the ripe age of seventy, set up an old-fashioned lab test where everyone walked from station to station viewing slides through a light microscope, Sean made certain he was one of the first to go through the exam. As he left several stations, he carefully brushed his thumb on the edge of the slide, shifting it enough that the students following were looking at something Dr. Hager hadn't planned on. Under the guise of reviewing before he handed his work in, he returned to several stations, correcting ones he'd corrupted, misaligning some he'd not touched previously.

He got the highest grade on the test, and old Dr. Hager never understood what happened to the work of so many of his brightest students. From that day on, Sean was the fair-haired student of the biology department.

Now, instead of shifting something as concrete as slides, Sean was altering that nebulous, most precious of personal attributes: reputation.

Abby Patterson's word was now in doubt. Her squeaky clean character was suspect. Maybe she'd even lose her job. How sad. Then she'd have to go home to wherever she came from.

It was enough to make him rub his hands together in glee.

Thirty-one

ABBY WALKED TO Marsh's bright red Adirondack chair. She ran a hand over its back and was glad to see that the dark green paint hadn't left too great a stain. She glanced at the floor. On the lighter gray, the stain was more obvious. At least the chair blocked it somewhat, and an art nouveau collage of typed papers just about covered the rest.

She studied the things sitting on the small table beside the chair: a mug filled with pens and pencils, a couple of lined tablets with various things scribbled in sloppy handwriting, an empty bottle of water, a couple of computer disks, some more typed pages. He'd left his laptop on the table too, so he wasn't going to be gone long. That was a small comfort.

She sank into his chair and placed her feet on the railing like he did when he wrote. The only problem was that his legs were a lot longer than hers, and the position wasn't nearly as comfortable as it looked when he assumed it. Sighing, she dropped her feet to the floor, leaning her head against the chair back.

She rested her hands on the folder containing her letters. It took all her self-control to let the missives rest quietly in her lap. She wasn't going to read them again. Why inflict more pain? Besides, she knew them by heart.

She longed to tear them to shreds, run across the beach, and throw the confetti of hatred into the water. It would swirl away, deteriorating, disintegrating, disappearing into the vastness of the sea. She would be safe once again, an ordinary woman, a common woman, not the subject of a campaign of invective.

She sighed. If only it were that easy.

She opened the folder, feeling like someone with a hangnail that she couldn't stop fiddling with, even though each time she pulled on it, there was more pain.

Oh, Lord, what am I going to do?

In her mind's eye she saw Nan's expression as she handed over the second letter. Nan might have dealt well with the first letter, but two? What if there were more? Abby shivered. Who could hate her so much? Who would make such grave and specious accusations?

There was also Mr. Martindale to worry about. He seemed unable to imagine that someone was lying. Not that Abby blamed him. She would no doubt question anyone who was the object of such allegations too, especially if she didn't know that person as Mr. Martindale didn't know her. He was chairman of the library board. He had a responsibility to the library, to Seaside, to every child who came there. He should be concerned if an unfit person might be working for him.

But I'm not unfit! I'm not! I'm Yours, washed clean in the blood of the Lamb. I've never done anything like those letters suggest. Oh, Lord, I've only got one reputation. What happens when it's ruined?

Unstable. Questionable influence. Those accusations were bad enough, but "touched my child inappropriately"? It defied the imagination that someone would write that about her. She was the good girl, the obedient one, the conscientious one, Miss Goody Two-shoes.

Oh, Lord, You know I've never been anything but appropriate around the kids. You know I love them. You know I'm not a danger to them in any way. You know—

Tears came again, and again she let them fall unchecked. She sniffed, gasped, all the while trying to be quiet so her mother upstairs couldn't hear if she happened to come outside onto the porch.

Oh, God! I don't deserve this! Haven't I gone through enough?

She lowered her face to her hands, letting self-pity run riot in her heart.

For all of two seconds. Then the face of her PT, Helene the Horrible, appeared.

"Come on, Patterson. Push through. You can do it. Remember, it's either pain or failure. What's your choice?"

But, Lord, do I have to be so intimately acquainted with so many different kinds of pain?

She grabbed the hem of her full gauze skirt and scrubbed at her face, drying the tears. Any mascara that remained after this last crying spell got lost in the material's colorful pattern. She sniffed a time or two, studying the skirt, then shook her head. She might use it as a towel, but she couldn't bring herself to use it as a hand-kerchief. She settled for sniffing and swallowing.

To stop herself from becoming more maudlin and falling headfirst into the Slough of Despond, she picked up some of the typed pages on the floor. She'd tidy up Marsh's workspace for him. At the same time, her eyes would have a chance to lose some of their red before she dealt with her mother. She straightened the papers into a neat pile, then began to arrange them by page numbers. Without thought she began to read.

Marguerite quivered with rage. Even the sling that held her arm immobile fluttered. She was furious because he had disagreed with her. Then Mr. Darlington and Mr. Murray disagreed with her too.

"Sorry, Miss Frost," Mr. Murray said.

She sniffed, raising her chin. In the end even Mr. Frost agreed with Craig on his dream about containing Snelling.

"Margie, we can't go to war with him," Mr. Frost said. "You will have to bow to our decision."

"Don't talk down to me, Father," she snapped. "I'm not sixteen anymore."

"Nor are you the authority at this ranch," Craig said in what he thought was a reasonable tone of voice. "That is your father, and when he's not available, me."

You'd have thought he slapped her to judge by the flush that washed over her cheeks. He just wished she didn't look so lovely all rosy with fury, her glorious dark eyes flashing sparks. Craig knew she would explode as soon as Darlington and Murray left the room.

Mr. Frost walked to the front hall with the two men to bid them good-bye. As soon as they left the room, Marguerite turned to Craig.

"You are despicable," she hissed. "Manipulating Father and those men to your own plans. Ingratiating yourself with a sick man, grasping power behind his back." She fairly spit the words, she was so incensed.

Just to aggravate her further, he smiled. "Why, Miss Frost, what terrible things to say about your father."

"You deserve—" The surprise on her face as his words penetrated stopped her cold. "My father?"

"Sick, incapable to make judgments, weak enough to be manipulated. *Tsk-tsk.* He'd be most unhappy to know that's how you see him."

"That's not how I see him!" She vibrated with outrage. He was glad she didn't have her sidepiece strapped on, or he'd surely have a hole through his heart. "He's the most wonderful man in the world!"

"Then why not trust him?" Craig asked with such logic that she blinked and went speechless.

Abby grinned. She liked it when a hero and heroine stood toe-to-toe. It made a book fun, seeing how their original antipathy was resolved. But what modern heroine wore a sidepiece?

She glanced at the top of the page. It read: Winslow/West, *Showdown at Frost Spring*, p. 77.

Showdown at Frost Spring? It sounded like a Louis L'Amour title or something from Colton West. Her father'd be happy to read this. He loved Westerns. He never failed to ask her if a new Colton West title had appeared yet.

"I'm the children's librarian, Dad. I don't know about Colton West."

"Ah, baby, he's the best. The very best."

She had seen a couple of TV movies made from Colton West books, but that was because Dad had practically forced her and Mom to watch with him. She had to admit she enjoyed the shows, but that was as much because of Rick Mathis as the story itself.

Wait a minute. Abby's eyes darted back to the header. Winslow/West was noted as the author. Not just Winslow. Not just West. Winslow/West. Marshall Winslow and Colton West? A Colton West heroine could wear a sidepiece.

Did Marsh read West's novels for him before publication? Critique them?

Or—astonishing idea—was Marshall Winslow actually Colton West? Eyes narrowed, Abby nodded. If Marsh were Colton West, it would explain a seminary professor having a house on the beach. Didn't movie companies pay big bucks to option a book? It would also explain the hours at the computer.

But why the secrecy? Because seminary professors didn't write Westerns? But why didn't they? Especially ones as complex and theocentric as West's novels were.

A car door slammed out on the street. Abby jumped. Marsh was home. She straightened the papers again, setting them in a neat pile on the little table. She folded her hands and tried to look innocent. Another car door slammed.

A voice called from upstairs, "Is that you, Abby, dear?"

Abby grimaced. She wasn't up to seeing her mother yet. Her eyes still felt hot from the crying, and she could tell they were still swollen. Mom would pounce the minute she saw the evidence of tears. Then she'd begin that relentless, persistent questioning that made Abby crazy. In no time she'd find herself tucked into bed, pouring her troubles into Mom's oh-so-patient listening ear.

No! She'd run away from home to avoid just such scenarios. She would not walk into the fiery furnace if she didn't need to. She'd stay here cowering in Marsh's Adirondack chair until he returned or until she felt more able to cope, whichever came first.

"Abby, dear?" Mom called again, louder this time, as she walked across the porch above. Abby stared upward, following her mother's progress with her eyes. Mom walked to the landing. "Abby?"

Then to Abby's horror she began descending the steps. Panicking, wishing herself as invisible as the emperor's new clothes, Abby glanced wildly around.

A wooden bin about four feet high and two feet deep stood by Marsh's sliding doors. Presumably it held beach supplies. In a mad dash, Abby threw herself into the L formed by the bin and the wall it rested against. Mom couldn't see her there. She sat, back against the bin, knees drawn up under her chin, purse and folder clutched in her arms.

Mom's steps continued down the stairs. Abby closed her eyes like a good little ostrich, burying her face in her lap. If she couldn't see Mom, then Mom couldn't see her.

"Abby?" Mom walked down the drive to Abby's car. "Where are you, dear?" Abby could hear the bewilderment in her mother's voice. Grimacing at her own foolishness and cowardice, Abby leaned her head back against the storage bin and opened her eyes. She looked up directly into Marsh's curious face as he watched her from the other side of his sliding door.

And she had thought her eyes hot from crying. The flame that scorched her at the embarrassment of being caught hiding like a three-year-old put the mere flush of crying to shame.

"Abby?" Mom, her voice sharp with concern, was now approaching Marsh's porch. Her footsteps sounded like the footfalls of the guards come to take the condemned man to the gallows, and Abby was that man. Disaster was imminent. All that was missing was someone calling, "Dead man walking."

Marsh must have heard Mom too because he opened his sliding door, stepping out. What he would do or say, Abby had no idea. She leaned her head against the wall and prepared to die of embarrassment and shame.

"Mrs. MacDonald, hello." Marsh stopped beside Abby. He didn't look down or acknowledge her in any way. He just stood, leaning a hip against the bin. When she turned her head toward him in surprise, she had an up-close, unimpeded view of his hairy legs below his tan shorts. And hairy they were too.

"I'm looking for Abby," Mom said, walking onto the porch but stopping at the edge. For once Abby was glad Mom didn't like Marsh. She wasn't likely to get too close to him. "Have you seen her?"

"What time was she due home?" he asked, avoiding the lie.

"After an appointment with Celia," Mom said, her voice perplexed. "Her car's in the drive, so she must be around here somewhere."

"She likes to take walks on the beach, doesn't she?"

"Well, yes, but—"

"Don't worry yourself, Mrs. MacDonald. She'll come home when she's ready."

"But this isn't like her at all."

"Admittedly I haven't known her as long as you have, but it sounds just like her to me."

Mom sniffed. So much for Marsh's opinion. "Abby has always been the most cooperative of people. She's never caused me trouble before." She stressed the *before*.

Abby shook her head. The clear implication was that if she was causing trouble now, it was all Marsh's fault.

"I think she moved here with the idea of being her own woman, didn't she?" Marsh asked politely. "Doing spontaneous things might well be part of her new game plan, sort of like Celia Fiennes."

Abby blinked. He was dropping names now too? And Celia, no less. Abby had always liked her, though even thinking about her thirteen thousand miles on horseback, rating travel opportunities in Renaissance England, tended to make her bottom sore.

"Who?" Mom asked as she walked farther onto the porch. Abby's heart tripped, and she tried to squeeze closer to the wall.

Marsh took a step forward, his right foot kicking out as he moved, sending Abby's gauze skirt flying into her face even as his bare foot connected with her shin. Abby grabbed the skirt, realizing with horror that it had draped itself out onto the floor when she hid. What a nit she was! Had Mom seen the material puddled there?

In her distress she lost part of the conversation. When she picked up the thread again, she realized Marsh was defending her.

"Celia began her travels in Olde England as a lark. She was spontaneous, like Abby longs to be. Don't you worry about her, Mrs. MacDonald. She'll show when she's ready. In the meantime, I suggest you eat now rather than wait. It'd serve her right if she missed your wonderful cooking while it's fresh."

"You don't understand." Mom's voice was strained. "I worry about her."

"Why? She's an adult."

Mom sniffed, unhappy with Marsh's challenge. "You don't understand what it's like to be a mother and see your only child almost die."

"True enough," Marsh agreed. "But that was three years ago. She's fine now."

"It's like yesterday," Mom said. "And she's not fine."

Abby sighed. That was the trouble. Mom did think it was yesterday, and she did still see her as unwell.

"Um," Marsh said. "I hope you don't mind too much, but I must disagree with you. I think she's quite well. In fact, I think she's very strong, stronger than many."

Abby's heart warmed. To have someone believe in her as she was, especially with her cowering here like a quivering rabbit hiding from a marauding fox, was so wonderful!

Mom didn't quite harrumph, but she came close. Abby didn't move as she listened to the tap-tap-tap of Mom's steps as she stalked away. She must have been miffed because she stomped up the steps in what was for her a fit of temper. Abby followed her footsteps overhead and heard the swish of the sliding door opening and closing. Then silence from above.

Silence on this porch too.

Abby sighed, then sighed again. Her mother was upset, and Marsh must think she was an idiot, all scrunched up behind the bin, even if he did stand up for her so eloquently.

She tucked her legs under her, preparatory to standing. She gasped as a spasm grabbed her lower back. She'd sat too long in an awkward position, tense with worry the whole time. Her muscles had knotted, and the nerves were protesting with a vengeance. She bit back a scream, grabbing her back.

Marsh dropped to the floor beside her, concern on his face. "A cramp, I presume?" he said softly. "Serves you right, hiding from your mother like that."

"Oh, shut up." She rubbed and massaged and made believe tears of self-pity weren't pricking her eyes again.

"Hey, I'm teasing." He reached out, wiping the tear that had broken free to roll down her cheek. "Or are these because of the pain?"

She gave a weak grin. "I know you are." She gasped as the vise of cramp tightened.

"Turn." He swirled his finger to show what he meant. "Give me your back."

She nodded and turned, clamping her teeth to keep from crying out.

"Show me where."

"Here." She placed her hand on her spine just below the waist and to the right. He placed his large hand where she indicated and began to knead.

"Relax, Abby. Just relax. Whatever's the problem, we'll fix it in a bit. For now, just relax." His soft, soothing voice was a balm to her stretched emotions. Abby felt her shoulders sag, her hands unclench, her breathing deepen. In a minute or two the cramp released its vicious hold and in another minute receded completely.

She looked over her shoulder at him. He was so close she could see the flecks of gold in his irises. They matched his hair. "Thanks."

"Better?" He smiled, his hands moving to rest on her shoulders. He turned her slowly until her back was to the wall. She pushed herself back until her spine was fully supported. He slid to sit beside her, back against the wall too, shoulder just touching hers.

"Thanks for not giving me away." She found it hard to look at him, so great was her embarrassment.

His smile broadened, and he took her hand. "Rule number one when playing hide-and-seek: Make certain nothing is sticking out."

She nodded as she looked at their feet stretched out beyond the bin. Her black flats, resting primly side by side, looked so little next to his crossed bare feet. "Believe me, I'll never forget."

"Do you hide from your mother often?" There was no censure in his voice, only curiosity.

"First and last time. I'm not dealing well with the resultant embarrassment."

"Why are you embarrassed?"

She looked at him in disbelief. "Do you need to ask?"

"Because I found you?"

She felt herself flush again. She stared at her lap, nodding. "When I got to the house after work, I wasn't ready to talk to her yet, so I came over here and sat in your chair. Not to hide, you know. Just to give myself more time. I didn't think you'd mind."

"I don't. In fact, you can sit in my chair anytime you want, even when I'm in it."

"Right." Abby noticed his shoulder was now pressed against hers. Who had done the leaning into the other, he or she?

"I mean it," Marsh said, swinging his free hand out with a flourish. "My chair is your chair."

"Well, *su casa* seems to be *mi casa* for the time being, so I guess that follows. Still, thanks for the generous offer."

He nodded. "Now finish your story."

Abby took a deep breath. "When Mom came downstairs, I panicked and hid behind the bin. I thought you weren't home. Your car's gone."

"It's at the shop. I get it back tomorrow."

She nodded. "So I'm caught red-handed."

He grinned at her. "That you are."

The sliding door opened and Rick stepped out. His hair was still damp from the shower, and his jaw had the baby-soft look of the newly shaved. He blinked down at them as he stepped over their feet.

"May I remind you two that we do have chairs." He pointed to them.

"In a minute," Marsh said. "The floor's a lot more comfortable than you'd think."

Rick looked skeptical. "If you say so. I shouldn't be too late. Celia has to work tomorrow."

"You don't have a car," Abby said.

"Sure I do." He pointed across the street, and Abby saw his car parked just around the corner. "I parked over there so I wouldn't get blocked in when you came home." With a flick of his hand he was gone. "Enjoy eating alone," drifted back on the breeze.

"But I'm not eating alone." Marsh grinned at Abby as he rose and held out his hand. "Am I?"

Thirty-two

HANNAH MACDONALD stood on the porch staring at nothing long after Abby and Marsh went inside.

God, I don't know what to do!

She had gotten such a shock seeing Abby's car in the drive but no Abby. Immediately she'd imagined the worst. Abby had fallen somewhere. She was lying in pain. She'd already been taken to the hospital, unconscious so no one knew to tell Hannah.

Then Marsh walked out, and she went to his deck to check. Again no Abby, at least not that she was supposed to know about.

But she saw that wisp of skirt trailing on the floor, a skirt that she herself had bought for her daughter. She also saw Marsh kick it aside, and she heard him cover for Abby.

"Don't worry yourself, Mrs. MacDonald. She'll come home when she's ready."

It made her furious that he presumed to understand Abby so well. Who did he think he was? She was the one who knew Abby better than anyone on earth, she who had given the girl life and then nursed her back to life. She had earned her bone-deep knowledge about her daughter with tears and prayers and a will that refused to let Abby yield to her grief and pain.

How dare he challenge her! How dare Abby hide!

When Hannah rushed up the steps, fury like a red haze peppered with zigzags of heat lightning clouded her vision. She marched to the screen door, opened it, closed it, but didn't go through it. Instead, she tiptoed to the rail to listen. She had to know what they were plotting now.

She couldn't remember the last time she was so furious. Well, yes, she could. She'd been furious at the driver of the car who was stupid enough to cause the accident. Not for one minute did she think he intended to hurt her family, but he did. Because he was stupid!

She'd been angry with God too, furious that He would require all of them to go through such an ordeal. He'd let her down. How, she wondered for several months and sometimes even to this day, could she ever trust Him again? He'd taken her precious grandbaby, her wonderful son-in-law, and He'd left a maimed Abby.

She didn't talk to anyone about how she felt for a long time. She kept the lid clamped tight on the rolling boil of her rage, and only in the dark of midnight would she let loose the scalding emotions. She'd lie in bed railing at God in the nocturnal silence, telling Him exactly what she thought of Him while in the daylight she pleaded with proper circumspection for Him to heal Abby, to restore her to what she had once been.

This spiritual schizophrenia might have kept on indefinitely if Len hadn't confronted her.

"He's God, Hannah. You've got to let Him be God."

"But it's not fair!" she cried as tears streamed down her face. "It's not fair! I loved them."

He gathered her in his arms, kissing the top of her head. "So did He; so does He."

She frowned at him, her body rigid. "Simplistic, Len. Not fair."

"Sweetheart, where'd you ever get the idea that life should be fair? Games are supposed to be fair, not life. You either believe God is God—omniscient, omnipresent, loving, holy, and in total control—or all you've got is a flawed Superman who can't control anything or anyone. But know this: If you decide He is God, you've got to give up being mad at Him."

She'd been livid at Len for two days after that lecture, not speaking to him, barely looking at him. He was right, she knew it, a fact that made her fury burn all the brighter until it threatened to consume her.

Then Abby had a minor relapse. Of course Len was out of town on business again, just as he'd been the day of the accident. She was once more alone to face this latest tragedy. She sat in the waiting room, her heart gripped by her anger, the corrosive fury burning away her normal control.

When the doctors came looking for her to tell her it was just a matter of adjusting Abby's medication, Hannah didn't give them a chance to explain. She attacked, accusing them of everything from stupidity to willful malpractice. She ranted and raged, pacing, screaming, throwing her hands into the air. The doctors stood, faces impassive, looking over her head at some distant point like they were bored. Bored! The flames of her ire flashed through the room, using their passivity like oxygen to fuel her.

But even anger with a head of steam like hers eventually burned itself out.

"Are you finished, Mrs. MacDonald?" one of the doctors asked when she paused for a breath.

"Because if you aren't or even if you are, I'd suggest an immediate visit to a psychiatrist," said the other. "Immediate."

They turned and walked away.

Hannah became aware that everyone in the waiting room as well as several people in the hall were staring at her, mouths agape. She felt their condemnation, their icy disdain. She heard her own voice in memory, all the terrible words she had hurled. She turned hot, then cold all over.

She literally ran to the hospital chapel. There she fell to her knees, confessing the great sin of her anger against God and against everyone else for making her suffer. Her! Not Abby. Her!

She never thought she'd feel such anger again. Tonight was putting her to the test. Deceived by her own daughter! And that— that *man*. She heard them talking down there, softly, intimately. Then that Rick character came out, driving off into the night, and Abby went inside with Marsh.

Hannah shivered. *Oh, God!*

The phone rang. For a minute she thought she wouldn't answer. Then she thought it might be Len. She hurried inside.

"Mom, it's me," Abby said.

Hannah said nothing.

"Mom, are you there?"

"I'm here."

"Good." There was a silence. "I'm sorry I didn't call earlier."

Did she actually think a weak apology like that would undo the hurt she'd inflicted?

"I'm at Marsh's. He's giving me dinner. Then I'll be up for a few minutes."

"A few minutes?"

Abby cleared her throat. "Yes, then he and I are going for a walk on the beach."

Hannah closed her eyes against the pain. She was to get a few minutes. Marsh was to get dinner and a walk on the beach. Her anger blazed afresh.

"I love you, Mom," Abby whispered. The line went dead.

Hannah stood clutching the buzzing phone for some time. *"I love you, Mom."* She closed her eyes. *I love you, too, Abby. That's why I want to save you.*

Hannah went to the kitchen and looked at the rosemary baked chicken, the potato wedges coated with Parmesan cheese, the green beans with almonds and Italian dressing. She shook her head. Not tonight. She was too upset to eat. She set about storing everything away. When she was finished, she went out onto the deck and sat.

She had been sitting for about thirty minutes when she heard Abby on the steps. She listened, but she couldn't detect a second set of footfalls. At least Marsh wasn't with her.

Abby walked over, taking the chair next to Hannah. Her skirt foamed about her legs. "He fed me Lean Cuisine. Your reputation is safe."

Hannah looked at Abby with sorrow. "You've changed."

"Yes. I'm glad you see it."

"You're glad?" Hannah stared. "I'm not complimenting you, Abby. I think the changes are wrong, detrimental to you as a Christian and a woman."

"I know you do." Abby began to rub her lower back. "What changes do you see, and why are they wrong?"

Just remember you asked me. "You have become rebellious. You have developed a spirit that pits itself against your father and me. You only pay attention to Marsh who's so bad for you."

Abby's chin went up when Hannah mentioned Marsh. However, to Hannah's surprise she didn't respond to the comments about him.

Abby began to pleat her skirt, not looking at Hannah. "Why do you think I 'pit' myself against you and Dad?"

"Because you have developed a rebellious spirit."

Abby shook her head. "That's not what I mean. Why have I become rebellious at this late date in my life? Why don't I take your advice? Why don't I agree with you about what's best for me?"

"Marsh." One word said it all.

"No, Mom. It's not Marsh." Abby stopped playing with her skirt and leaned forward to give Hannah her full attention. "I was already rebelling before I even met him. What did you think this move to Seaside was?"

Hannah frowned. *A mistake.* "You know what I thought and think. It's a huge mistake, taking you away from your support system and all who love you. You're not strong enough to handle the physical ramifications of being on your own, let alone the emotional ones."

Abby studied Hannah thoughtfully. "Is it that you don't think I'm strong enough, or you don't *want* me to be strong enough?"

Hannah was appalled. "What a terrible thing to suggest. Of course I want you to become stronger and stronger."

"Do you? Or do you want me to remain dependent, sweet Abby, the obedient daughter?"

Hannah stared at Abby as if she'd never seen her before. "I have always wanted the very best for you, Abby. Always."

Abby nodded. "I know you have. The problem is that it's according to your definition of best, not mine."

Hannah bristled, the too-familiar anger beating a steady tattoo in her blood. "Since you were a baby, I have prayed over you and for you. I have taught you and watched you. Do you think I don't know you? That I can't see what's best for you?"

"Yes, that's what I think."

It took a minute for Hannah to find her voice. "Abby, how dare you!"

Abby continued, her voice controlled. "I think you believe you know me and my heart, but I know you don't. Maybe you did before the accident. I don't know. But I know you don't know me now. You haven't allowed for how the accident has changed me for the better. You look at the transformations just as rebelliousness or a temporary madness. Maybe they even represent a threat."

Hannah blocked the hurt, holding out her hands, imploring Abby to listen, to agree. "You have always been such a loving, compliant child, such a delight. You still are at heart. You're just off track at the moment."

"No, Mom. It's much more than that. I am permanently, positively changed. I am still loving, but I am no longer a compliant child."

"No!"

"Yes. I will never be who I used to be. If I met Sam for the first time now, I would not fall in love with him."

Hannah felt her mouth drop open. "How can you say such a thing?"

"Sam was a controlling man, Mom. As long as I agreed with him, he was warm and kind and loving. When I disagreed, he was cold, withdrawn."

"No, not Sam."

"Oh, yes. We were already having issues, especially over my going back to school."

"He wanted you to be his wife and Maddie's mother."

"Couldn't I have gone to school and still loved them, still cared for them? Did one have to preclude the other?"

"Abby, Sam knew what was best—"

"Sam was not omniscient. He didn't always know what was best. But that's not what we need to talk about. That part of my life is over. Sam is with the Lord. We would have stayed married, I'm sure. I would have felt stifled, I would have felt unfulfilled, but life would have gone on. However, the accident happened, and the whole world changed. The problem is that you haven't realized that."

"How dare you say that to me." Hannah's voice trembled with emotion. "How dare you! Who do you think sat by you, praying and crying and hurting so badly that I thought I couldn't breathe? Who stood at the graveside of beautiful, precious Maddie, weeping as they lowered that little coffin? Who stood in the receiving line at the memorial service for Sam and held his mother's hand while you lay in ICU suspended between life and death?"

"I'm not denying your sorrow or your pain, but you're speaking of circumstances, Mom. Circumstances. Incidents that happened. I'm speaking of heart and soul. I am different inside, very different from the woman who existed before that intersection. I am still a caring woman. I know that because I still love you and Dad. But I have learned to have steel in my spine. I had to if I were to recover both physically and emotionally."

"Abby, don't do this. Don't make me look the heavy while you're right about everything."

"I'm not saying I'm right about everything. I'm saying that I will never again be who I was. Never. I can't go back to being that dutiful daughter. I don't want to. Where I might have readily accepted your suggestions before, I can't and won't now. Where I might have automatically gone along with your wishes before, I can't and won't now. In short, I am learning to think for myself, albeit a bit late."

"You're disobeying Scripture, you know. Children, obey your parents. Honor your father and your mother."

"I'm not a child, Mom. I'm an adult answerable to God, not you."

"Abby!" Though Abby's voice was not angry, her words ripped Hannah's heart like a mighty wrenching would cleave a piece of material in two.

"My heart's desire is to honor you," Abby continued. "I acknowledge that if I don't do so, I am disobeying God's injunction. I love you, even though I'm sure you doubt it at the moment. All I'm asking is that you let me be an adult who makes my own choices. Meet me on a level playing field. Let me disagree with you without assuming it means bad things. Let me live my life as I think God wants me to without assuming you have to play Holy Spirit and interpret His leading for me. If I fall into sin, confront me, but if the best for me is just a matter of differing opinions, let me make my own decisions, even if I fall on my face."

Hannah opened her mouth to respond, but Abby leaned over, putting a finger across her lips. "No more right now, Mom. I have to go. Marsh is waiting. Just think about what I've said. Pray about it. That's all I ask for the moment."

And she was gone, hurrying down the steps to Marsh, leaving her mother alone. A phone rang again. Hannah realized it was her cell phone ringing. Len. Oh, how she needed him. She hurried inside, grabbed the phone from her purse, and sank onto the sofa.

"Hi, sweetheart," he said. "How's it going? Any better than yesterday?"

"Worse." She told Len about Abby's hiding, about Marsh's protecting her, about Abby's cruel words. Her voice caught on tears several times.

"Ah, Han, I'm sorry you're there to go through this alone."

She sniffed. "Thanks." Just hearing his words of empathy made her feel better.

"But she's got a point, you know."

Hannah stiffened. "Not you too!" She was unwilling to admit any such thing.

"Han." Len's voice was strong and certain. "We made a mistake. You should not have stayed. That's her house, not ours. We were incredibly insensitive."

"I just don't like him!" It all came down to Marsh; it was all his fault.

"I find it interesting that he wouldn't give her away. I think that's a good sign."

"What are you saying? His helping her lie is good?"

"Han, I've done a lot of thinking and a lot of praying while I've been home alone." He paused for a minute. "Do you remember how your mother felt about me?"

Hannah made a face. He was going to use their personal history as an argument for Marsh and Abby. But their story was different. Len was different.

"Do you?"

"Of course. She didn't like you."

"That's putting it mildly. She despised me."

"You weren't what she'd imagined for me."

"Why did you stand up to her on my behalf?"

"Because I loved you. Because I knew you were right for me. Because the Lord gave me peace about you."

"Was there any concrete reason for her to dislike me?"

"Of course not. You were a man of godly character. You had a good job. You were kind. She had just closed her mind to the possibility of you because she didn't like the way you wore your hair. Too long and unkempt. Long hair meant hippie, communes, godless."

"Have we closed our minds to Marsh for reasons just as foolish?"

"But he's so different from Sam!"

"Of course he is. And she's so different from Sam's wife."

Hannah scowled at the phone. Abby had said the same thing not so long ago.

"I think that she may have finally grown up."

"Len, she's not grown up! She's become like a defiant teenager, only worse."

"No, I don't think so. I think she's finally become her own woman. We should be thanking God, not trying to impede the process."

"You think that's what I'm doing? Holding her back?" Hannah's temper flared again. "Who still calls her baby all the time? Not me."

There was silence from the other end of the phone. As it stretched out longer and longer, Hannah sighed. "I'm sorry, Len. That was nasty of me."

"Maybe, Han, but you're right. I'm every bit as guilty as you are."

Hannah twitched and walked to the sliding door. She opened it, stepping outside. "I don't know if guilty is the right word, Len. If we're guilty of anything, it's of loving her so much, of wanting her to be happy."

He was quiet for another long minute. "What if the hopes and dreams we have for Abby aren't God's?"

"Len! We'd never want anything for her that wasn't honoring to the Lord."

"I know that in the general sense. But what about the specifics? Do we know what the Lord has planned for her in the jots and tittles of life?"

"If we don't have at least some sense of that, who does?" Hannah leaned against the railing and inhaled the salty air, hoping it would ease the horrific headache that had hatched at the base of her skull.

"Maybe Abby does?"

"But we're her parents!"

"We're not infallible. Maybe we've been wrong to try and hold her at home. Just because we thought it would be good for her doesn't mean that God thinks it would be good for her. I mean, did we ever ask Him if she should stay or go out on her own?"

Hannah knew she hadn't. Granted, she hadn't thought of it, but now that the idea had been presented, she recoiled from it. She watched as Abby and Marsh, hands clasped, walked onto the beach. They were tight in a world of their own as they talked intently about something. Probably about how horrible she was. "But Seaside, Len? It's so far away."

"Lots of kids live farther than that from their parents."

There was no arguing with that fact. "What if in her desire to get married again, she chooses unwisely? What if she thinks Marsh is more than a passing fancy?"

"What if he isn't? Are we willing to risk losing Abby by taking a stand against him?"

"She needs someone like Sam! He was so perfect for her."

"*Then* he was perfect for her. I don't know about now."

"You know what she told me? She said that if she met Sam today, she wouldn't fall in love with him. Can you believe that?"

"Yeah, I can."

Hannah felt like her world had shifted on its axis. "But they were blissfully happy." *Please, tell me I'm right here.*

His sigh slid down the line. "I don't think so, Han. I don't think they were anywhere near separating or anything, but I don't think they were all that happy."

No! I couldn't have been that blind. "You don't know what you're talking about."

"I do know what I'm talking about. Sam didn't understand that a wife who meets you halfway, who challenges you when you need it and even when you don't, who isn't afraid to express herself when she disagrees with you is the stuff of a lively and living marriage."

She thought of her gentle Abby. He was wrong. He had to be. "Where did you ever get that ridiculous idea?"

"Han," he said with a soft laugh, "I'm married to you."

That stopped her for a long moment. "Is that supposed to be a compliment?"

"The biggest and best. Am I ever bored? Never! I think you're the most interesting woman I've ever met. I thought it when I met you, and I think it now. But are you compliant?"

"I should hope not."

He laughed. "Think about this, Han. Here Abby is, the product of you and me, neither of whom is afraid to express an opinion. How could she not develop that quality herself? Genes will tell."

Hannah felt like she had to keep fighting. "But she was always such a good girl."

"Because we never gave her the chance to be otherwise. We dominated her from her first breath, and we're still trying to do it."

"But she needs us!" *God, she's got to need me. What do I do if she doesn't?*

"She needed us once upon a time. She doesn't now, at least not in the same way. She's almost thirty, Han. She's been through the most grievous tragedy and come out of it a strong and wonderful woman with a heart for God. We're going to lose her if we don't acknowledge that she doesn't need us. The fact is that we need her a lot more than she needs us."

With tears in her eyes, Hannah watched Abby turn to Marsh and say something that made him laugh. Her skirt whipped in the wind like the sea grasses that grew in the dunes.

"Han, it's about control to some degree. We want to control her."

"We do not," Hannah protested. How ugly that sounded. "I do not!"

"Don't we? Think back to preaccident. We orchestrated Abby's life. Who encouraged her to date Sam? Who encouraged her to be an elementary school teacher? Who encouraged them to settle two blocks over? Those are only some of the most blatant examples. Control."

Abby lurched as some sand gave way under her bad leg, and Hannah gasped. Marsh grabbed Abby around the waist to steady her, keeping his arm there as they continued to walk. After a few steps, she wrapped her arm about his waist too. For a brief second she dropped her head to his shoulder.

Unbidden came the thought that Hannah had never seen Sam and Abby walking arm in arm. It was almost like she had been

Prince Philip to Sam's Queen Elizabeth, always walking two steps behind. Hannah banished the thought as unworthy, too judgmental of Sam.

"Think about the time of the accident, Han. We lost all control. We didn't know what was going to happen from one day to the next. The lack of order and the absence of control were as difficult for us as watching Abby in such pain."

"Stop it, Len! Stop it. I can't deal with any more." Hannah felt like her heart was being torn loose.

"You've got to, sweetheart. We don't have much time to correct our mistakes."

"But he's so wrong for her!"

"Honey, our opinion isn't the one that counts."

"She barely knows him."

"Something clicks between them, Han. I could see that even in the short time I was there over the weekend. At first I was very distressed about it. But as I've thought about it more, I've come to think that it clicks on a much deeper level between her and Marsh than it ever clicked with her and Sam." He paused. "I think it clicks more like it clicks between you and me."

"Oh, Len." Hannah started to cry. "I wish you were here so badly I can taste it."

"Give me about two hours, and I'll tuck you in."

"What?"

"I've already taken the rest of the week off. I'm getting on the Blue Route in Philadelphia as we speak, heading for the Schuylkill Expressway, the Walt Whitman Bridge, and the Atlantic City Expressway. Destination: Seaside. Pack your bags, Han. I'm not tucking you in at Abby's. I've made reservations for us at a motel downtown."

Thirty-three

MARSH GRINNED AS he and Abby walked along the beach arm in arm. Who'd have thought a week ago that he'd even be walking with a woman, let alone holding her close beside him? And such a delightfully unpredictable one at that.

Fargo pulled hard on his leash, one of those that you could lengthen or shorten as desired by pushing a button. Marsh thought of a carpenter's measuring tape every time he clipped the lead to Fargo's collar. Thankfully Fargo didn't retract lickety-split like the metal ruler, though the image of the dog flying through the air at the flick of Marsh's thumb was wonderful. Too bad he didn't write cartoons.

Fargo didn't like being restrained, but he couldn't be allowed to run free. Aside from the leash laws, more and more people were on the beach. If the huge animal came bounding up to the wrong people, he'd send them screaming for help. The thought of the potential fines made Marsh shudder, to say nothing of the forwarded bills from the psychological counselors Fargo's victims would need to see.

Besides, he was a seminary professor. Seminary professors were supposed to obey the law.

"Have we talked the issue of your mother to death?" he asked Abby.

She nodded. "I think so, and I'm grateful for your help. I feel like we're Queen Louise of Savoy and Margaret of Austria hammering out *Le Paix des Dames.*"

"I beg your pardon?"

"You know. The Treaty of Cambria that created peace between France and the Holy Roman Emperor back in 1529."

"Where do you pull all these obscure women from, for Pete's sake?" She amazed him with her grasp of truly arcane trivia. "And am I Louise or Margaret?"

She grinned at him. "Take your pick. I just hope my peace attempts with Mom are more successful and long lasting than Margaret and Louise's."

"So your original conversation didn't go well? Even though you told her all that we discussed during dinner?"

"She was not impressed."

"The first confrontation is always the hardest."

"Says who?"

"Says me. Just remember, from now on, no more temper tantrums. No more running and hiding."

Abby rolled her eyes.

"What?" he demanded.

"I feel like one of your students."

He thought back over his comments. "So I was a bit didactic."

She blew a raspberry.

He dug his fingers into her ribs, delighted when she jumped. "I'm a teacher. I'm used to telling people things. Besides, I'm right, aren't I?"

"Yeah, but at the moment being *told* stuff doesn't go down well, even when the stuff is right."

He noticed that even though she was complaining, she wasn't stepping away from him. "We can't just chalk this up to telling the truth in love?"

She dug her fingers into his side, and he winced. "What do you think?"

"I guess not." He pushed the leash button to give Fargo lots of lead to chase a seagull.

"You treat me with great respect, Marsh, even when I don't deserve it." She smiled up at him, and those sparkling black eyes did funny things to his stomach. "I cannot begin to tell you how much that means to me. When we talked at dinner, we talked. Give and take. My thought, your thought."

He nodded. "So it's the imperative sentence that gives you heartburn?"

"Acid reflux of the emotions."

He thought about all the times his father gave him orders. He hated it. Then he thought of the times he'd been witness to his dad using the same authoritative manner on his mother. Or trying to.

"Marcus, you will not address me in that tone," Mom always said, her eyes stormy but her voice noncombative. "I am not one of your lackeys. Rephrase, please."

If his brash, pompous father had learned to rephrase, so could he. "Since the first conversation didn't go as well as you'd have liked, what are your next steps?"

From the look on her face, he could tell he'd just scored big points, all thanks to his father. Paradigm shift!

"Well, I won't lose my temper anymore. I won't run and hide." She ticked her points off by extending a finger for each. "I will address all issues with honesty and love, showing respect for her and Dad. I will pray that the Lord works in their hearts as in mine so that we don't wound each other but reach a Christ-honoring conclusion."

"You've got it." He studied her in the amber light of evening. Even these few days had made a difference in her appearance. Her pallor was gone, replaced by a rich reddish gold that washed across her cheekbones and nose. Her black curls defied her best efforts to contain them, the wind and humidity restyling to their specifications. Her eyes had lost some of the haunting shadows that sat in their depths. She was still too thin, but he had all summer to fatten her up.

Then there was her smile! It never failed to make him catch his breath. She was smiling now, pleased by his approval. He hoped her good spirits were up to his next question, the one he'd refrained from asking at dinner, the one that was gnawing at him. "Now tell me: What got you so upset today that you couldn't face your mother?"

She hesitated, the sparkle dimming, then disappearing.

"Come on, Abby. You can trust me."

"It's not that." She stared at their feet for a few seconds. "I'm almost afraid to tell you what upset me."

"Afraid? Of me?" He was surprised. "It's worse than hiding from your mom?"

She glanced up, then away as though unable to meet his eyes. "Yes, it's worse. Much worse."

He stopped, turning her to face him. "Abby."

"But I'm innocent!"

He had no doubts about this tenderhearted woman. "Of course you are." She hadn't the conscience to do awful things and survive. Look how the problem with her parents had tied her in knots.

She appeared grateful for his words of support, took a deep, fortifying breath, and blurted, "Someone's accused me of everything from mental instability to child molestation."

He was so floored he couldn't think of one thing to say.

"Two anonymous letters were sent, one to the head librarian and one to the chairman of the library board." Her expression was one of bewilderment as she told him about the letters and the reactions of Nan Fulsom and Mr. Martindale. "Why would anyone do something like that, Marsh? How can I ever prove myself innocent of such despicable charges?"

The worry and sorrow in her eyes tore at his heart. "You've worked at the library how long? Three days?"

She nodded.

He was silent for a minute, thinking, while she watched him uncertainly. Fargo, impatient with standing around, pulled his leash as taut as he could, running into the water and trying to bite the waves. Then he ran back, circled them, and headed for the water again. In the nick of time, Marsh saw the danger as the leash tightened around their legs. He dropped the lead.

"The letters don't make sense to me, Abby." Absently Marsh watched Fargo race into deeper water, then out again. "You would never do anything inappropriate to a child. All someone has to do is watch you with Jess and Karlee to know that, or listen to you talk about Maddie. You love kids."

Her eyes filled with tears. "Thank you," she whispered. "You have no idea how much that comment means to me."

Fargo went whipping around them again, preparing for another assault on the sea. Marsh put out a foot, stepping on the leash as it slithered by. Fargo jerked to a halt.

"Come here, you big oaf." Marsh pushed the button to retract the lead. Soaking wet and very disgruntled, Fargo sidled up to Marsh and Abby. He began to shake. Water flew.

Hands up to protect her face, Abby stared at the dog. "You did that on purpose."

Fargo stilled, tilted his head to one side, and raised his brown eyebrows. "Me? Never," he seemed to say.

"Probably," Marsh agreed, unperturbed. He raised his arm and brushed water from his cheek with the sleeve of his shirt. "Do you have a copy of the letters?"

Abby nodded. "Back at the house."

"How about the envelopes?"

"No." She bent and wiped her face on her skirt. Marsh liked it better when she used his T-shirt. "I never gave them a thought."

"But you have seen them?"

She nodded.

"Were they sent through the mail or hand delivered?"

Abby thought for a moment. "Mailed, I think. At least the one to Mr. Martindale was. I remember seeing a stamp on the envelope."

"He received it early today?"

She nodded.

"So the letter was mailed Monday or Tuesday at the latest." He looked at her, very pleased with himself.

She looked back, confused. "I'm not following you."

"The first letter, the one about you going to a psychiatrist, is just a nasty mistelling of a truth, right? The grain of truth hidden in the lie kind of thing?"

She nodded. "The second one is an outright lie."

"An outright lie mailed before you'd even worked two days at the library."

Abby's eyes widened as she saw Marsh's point. "I spent most of Monday with Nan as she showed me around, introducing me to people, telling me about library policies, having me sign insurance papers, stuff like that."

"There's no way you could have done what the letter accuses you of. Even discounting your heart for God and your high personal standards, there simply wasn't time. Such activity requires a modicum of trust on the part of the victim as well as a lot of privacy. You haven't been at the library long enough to know the kids."

"My desk is right out in the open. I don't even know where the hidey-holes are. Oh, Marsh!" She threw her arms around him, giving him a hug. "Why didn't I think of that? All I have to do is talk to Nan about the postmarks, and I prove my innocence. Thank you!"

He happily held her until she pulled back. There were still the questions of who wrote those letters and why, but they could discuss those issues later. For the moment he'd let her enjoy her vindication.

"My hero," she said, smiling at him in a way that made his heart turn over.

Eat your heart out, Randall Craig. I'll have to make certain you're a hero to Marguerite too.

"I've got a question for you," he said, thinking how strange it was that for a writer everything was story fodder. "Remember when we met, and you told me about some woman who was the first European woman in North America?"

"Sure. Marguerite de la Roque."

"Marguerite." He nodded. "I thought that was the name. Thanks." When he didn't say more, she looked at him in question. He made believe he didn't see.

You idiot, Winslow! You should not have asked that question. It had just popped out, the next logical step in his thoughts, but it led to a forbidden topic. To explain would mean to explain Colton West, something he knew he'd eventually have to do if his feelings for her continued to escalate. But not yet. He wasn't certain when, but not today.

"It's all right," she finally said, her voice bright, encouraging. "I know about your Marguerite."

He froze for a minute, then stepped back from her so he could see her face. She was smiling at him with that wonderful verve of hers, that joy that sprang from her heart in spite of her troubles. He enjoyed her, admired her, loved to spar with her, and couldn't remember a woman he'd ever felt so at ease with.

But talk to her about Colton West?

How did she know about Marguerite, and how much did she know? He had protected his secret for so long, refusing interviews, using his reclusiveness à la J. D. Salinger and Harper Lee as a PR ploy. His anonymity had worked like a charm on sales. He knew that if he acknowledged Colton West to her, she'd want to tell the world. She was a no-pretenses woman, allergic, he was certain, to secrets.

She waited, eyes bright, for him to tell her about Colton West, but as time stretched and he said nothing, her face shuttered.

"Oh." She closed her eyes briefly. When she opened them, tears glittered. "I see how it is. I open up. You don't. Foolish me. I thought we were friends who trusted each other." She gave him a sad little smile, turning back toward the house without saying another word.

He was beside her in two long strides, catching her arm. "Abby!" He didn't know what else to say, but he knew he couldn't let her walk away.

"Let go, Marsh," she said in a small voice. She wouldn't look at him.

"Abby, don't be like this."

"Abby, don't be like this?" She tried to pull her arm free.

He tightened his grip. "I–I can explain." But the words caught in his throat.

"I thought—" she began, then brought a hand to her mouth like she was holding words back.

He could imagine the words. *I thought we had something special developing. I thought we were honest with each other. I thought you liked me.*

Liked her? If he was honest with himself, he was probably falling in love with her, which scared the stuffings out of him. She wasn't Lane; he knew that. Still, no matter how many times he told himself she was different....

"I need to go, Marsh." She pulled her arm free. "I need to be alone."

He couldn't let her go. He couldn't let her walk away thinking he didn't care. He grasped her elbow to steady her on the sand, pacing himself to her.

"I don't want my father to know," he blurted.

"I already figured that out." She stopped and looked at him, her eyes serious and sad. "I think you're being foolish. I think he'd be proud of you."

Marsh made an indecipherable noise deep in his throat. Like she knew.

She saw his skepticism and turned away again. "Right. What do I know? I can't even figure out how to get along with my own parents. How could I ever know about you and yours?"

Marsh knew with unnerving certainty that the next few minutes would greatly affect the rest of his life. Even Fargo knew something was wrong. He sat beside them looking from one to the other with a worried expression. Perceptive animal. Too bad he couldn't give advice.

"How did you find out?" Marsh managed to ask around the lump in his throat.

"When I was on your porch, I started picking up the papers scattered all over the floor. I read part of a chapter."

"Ah." *Brilliant riposte, Winslow.*

Her lips pressed together, but he wasn't certain whether in anger or distress. "I'm sorry. I read what was intended to be private."

He watched her, marveling that he had so hurt her by his simple hesitation. He felt uncomfortable yet strangely pleased that he affected her so. He knew he didn't mean to wound her. To the contrary. He wanted to protect her, to care for her, to be with her.

"Nobody knows but Rick and my agent. And you." He paused, lifting her chin so she would look at him. She stared off into the distance beyond his left shoulder. Not quite what he wanted, but at least he could see her face. "I want you to know that I trust you with the information. I know you will protect it."

She became very still beneath his hand. Slowly her eyes focused on his face, and he could see the faint glow of hope in them. "I'm not used to sharing myself, Abby. The last time I did..."

"Lane?"

He nodded. "I decided after that fiasco that it was safer to keep my own counsel. Then she married Dad and, well, you know how things are."

"But don't you see?" She laid her hand on his arm in her earnestness. "Your writing is an area that is not controversial. Lane is touchy ground between you and your father, quite understandably. Your teaching is something he should be proud of, but because it smacks of too much religion to him, he isn't. But Colton West?"

He rested his hand over hers as it lay on his arm. He couldn't believe how much he liked to touch her. Almost as much as he liked to talk with her, debate with her, laugh with her. "I write hack Westerns, Abby. Why should that impress him?"

"You do not!" The light was back in her eyes as she defended his work to him. "You write good books, and they're made into first-rate TV movies staring quality actors like Rick Mathis. How many people can say that about their son's work? Marsh, Colton West is your bridge to your father."

He studied her, eyes narrowed. Was she right? "I never saw it that way."

"I want you to know something." She spoke so seriously it made him nervous. "Though I don't think you need to keep your authorship hush-hush, I will not reveal your secret. You have my word."

He looked into her beautiful face. *Dear Lord, what have I done to deserve the friendship of a wonderful woman like her?* "Thank you, Abby." He bent, kissing her cheek.

She gave him a hard stare. "Do you have other secrets I should be aware of? Because if you do, I'd appreciate it if you'd tell me now. After all, you know all mine."

"That's it." He hooked his arm about her shoulders. "I'm really an uncomplicated guy."

"Yeah, right." She laid her hand on Fargo's head, as he leaned against her. Marsh stared at the animal who had apparently given her his sympathy in the recent discussion.

Traitor, Marsh thought. *But I don't blame you. I like leaning against her too.*

She scratched behind Fargo's ear and he leaned harder. She in turn had to lean against Marsh to remain upright.

Thanks, old man. You're a good dog. I apologize for calling you a name.

"What about Rick?"

"Rick?" He was confused for a moment. "Ah, Rick."

She nodded. "He really is Rick Mathis, isn't he?"

"His name is Rick Yakabuski."

"Okay, maybe he was born that, but he's Rick Mathis, right?"

"It's not my secret to share, Abby. You can't tell anyone either, not even Celia. Especially not Celia."

"That's not fair. She needs to know."

He shrugged. "Probably, but it's Rick's choice. All he wants is to be treated as a real person. If Celia knew who he was, would she be as comfortable with him? Would she go out with him? I can tell by your expression that you're not certain. Neither's he. I promised I'd keep his secret, and you promised you'd keep mine."

"About Colton West." Clearly she didn't think that Rick was included in her bargain.

Marsh took her by the shoulders, turning her to face him, dislodging a grumbling Fargo from his new leaning post. "Let Rick be the one to tell her. It should be news that comes from him, not from us."

"If he hurts her…"

Marsh nodded. "I'll help you beat him up."

"Mrs. Patterson! Dr. Winslow! Look at what Walker found!" Jordan came running down the beach toward them. He waved his arm, signaling them to hurry.

Marsh looked beyond Jordan. Walker was bent over, prodding at something with a stick. Vivienne stood back a ways, looking with disfavor at whatever Walker had discovered.

"I think we should go rescue whatever the kid has," Marsh said as he started walking, pulling Abby along. He glanced down at her. "You will let Rick tell her, won't you?"

"Let's just say I won't say anything unless some major catastrophe arises."

"Good enough." He squeezed her hand. "I'll tell him he's heading for trouble if he doesn't level with her." He gave a rueful snort. "Secrets separate. I learned that lesson."

"Just so you learned it," Abby said, smiling.

"Stop smiling like the Mona Lisa. It makes me feel like I just lost and you just won."

Another seraphic smile. "Good. But I think we both won."

As they drew close to Walker, they saw that he was poking a jellyfish. He was being quite gentle for a seven-year-old boy, though Marsh thought the jellyfish might argue the point.

"Isn't it cool?" Jordan asked.

"There's lots more in the water," Walker said.

Marsh turned to the water where the creatures bobbed just below the surface. "Looks like a colony of them is passing through."

Vivienne shivered in disgust. "How can we go in the water with those horrible things? They sting."

"I hate to bump into them," Abby said. "Or step on them. That's when they sting."

"I want one," Jordan said, tired of vicarious appreciation of Walker's treasure.

"You can have this one," Walker said generously. "I'll get me another one."

"Wow! Thanks!" Jordan squatted beside his jellyfish, poking it with his finger.

"Jordan," his mother squawked in her usual dulcet tones. "Don't do that!"

Jordan, of course, ignored her, just as Marsh had known he would.

Walker waded into the water, swinging his stick first at one jellyfish, then another.

"What do you think you're doing?" Vivienne advanced to the water's edge, hands on her hips. "I told you not to go in the water. A shark might get you."

Marsh looked at Vivienne. Was that worry he heard in her voice?

Walker ignored his mother with the same practiced ease as Jordan. He was up to his shorts when he slid his stick under a jellyfish and lobbed it into the air. It flew straight at Jordan who ran screaming to hide behind Marsh. The poor jellyfish hit the sand with a splat mere inches from Abby.

"Walker!" Abby put on her sternest teacher face. "Get out of that water this minute and leave those poor creatures alone. Do you hear me?"

"Yeah," yelled Jordan, sticking his head out from behind Marsh's legs. "Or she won't save you from drowning this time. She'll let you float to China."

"That's Europe over there, sport." Marsh pointed to the horizon.

"Europe, China, who cares. He'll float there or drown!" He yelled the last two words at his older brother.

"That's okay," Walker yelled back as a wave hit his stomach. "Dr. Winslow can save me this time."

"Not me," Marsh said. "I'm not swimming with the jellyfish. They're slimy."

"She won't save him again?" Vivienne, confused and distressed, looked from Jordan to Walker to Abby to Marsh. "What do you mean, save him? What are you all talking about?"

"It was the first day we were here, the day you told us not to go in the water." The ever-talkative Jordan pointed at Walker. "He went in anyway, and it got over his head. He couldn't touch bottom." He pointed at Abby. "She ran in and pulled him out. Just swam right out to him. It was neat."

"Tattletale!" A livid Walker raced out of the ocean. "Tattletale!" His fists were balled, ready to pummel his little brother.

Vivienne reached out, grabbing Walker as he flew past. She held his squirming body against her, wet shorts and all, but her attention was on Abby. "You pulled him from the ocean?"

"She scared me to death," Marsh said. "I saw it all from my porch."

Vivienne stared at Abby. "You saved my son's life?"

"I don't think he meant to be disobedient," Abby said. "I think the water carried him out before he realized what was happening."

"It'd still be carrying him if she hadn't come along." Jordan hopped around Walker who couldn't reach him because of his mother's firm hold. "He was halfway to China."

"Europe," Marsh said.

"Europe. Then Dr. Winslow ran all the way across the beach. He was mad."

"At her," Walker yelled, still twisting and squirming. "Not me."

"You saved my son's life," Vivienne said again. Her face had lost all its color, and she looked like she was suffering from shock. "I don't know what to say."

Abby shrugged. "There's nothing to say."

"You saved my son's life," Vivienne repeated, clearly disturbed. She stared at Abby for a few seconds before grabbing Jordan with a shaking hand. Without another word, Walker still held close and Jordan squirming to break free, she walked across the sand to her lovely new home.

Thirty-four

ABBY, MARSH, and Fargo walked back from the beach just as Dad pulled into the driveway. Abby merely sighed when she saw him. If Mom insisted on staying with her, Dad might as well too. At least she wouldn't feel so guilty when she wasn't home. Mom would have company, and since the green shelves were now hanging in the bathroom, there was enough room for all their toiletries.

"Hello, baby." Dad enveloped her in a big hug, a somewhat difficult feat since Fargo insisted on pushing between them. "Marsh." Arm still around Abby, he offered his hand.

Marsh took it. "Mr. MacDonald. We didn't expect you until the weekend."

Abby watched her father. If he caught the *we* in *we didn't expect you*, he didn't show it. He bent and patted Fargo on the head.

"There's nothing wrong at home, is there?" Abby asked, belatedly aware that there must be some reason for his coming in the middle of the week. "You didn't lose your job or anything?"

Dad smiled at her. "Let's just say I was lonely and decided to do something about it. Why don't I go up and say hi to your mother?"

"One thing I'll say for them." Abby watched her

father hurry upstairs. "They love each other. I hope I feel the same intensity for my husband after I've been married as long." She blinked as she became conscious of what she'd said. Even after three years as a widow, there were still times when out of habit she thought or spoke of herself as a wife. Usually the realization saddened her. This time it embarrassed her. Would Marsh think she was throwing out hints?

She bent, petting Fargo to smooth what she felt was an awkward moment. When she straightened, she gave Marsh a small smile. "I'd better go up."

He nodded. If he heard anything untoward in the wife slip, he didn't show it. "You'll be fine, Abby." He gave her a quick, fierce hug. "You're stronger than you think."

Yeah. Right. But his belief in her did help.

He placed his hands on her shoulders. "If they get to be too much, just come down and sit on my porch anytime day or night. Feel free to read whatever manuscript pages you find."

She recognized the first offer as evidence of his kindness, his heartfelt concern, his understanding of her difficulties. She knew the second was a sign of his trust and confidence in her. She couldn't decide which offer touched her most.

He walked her to the stairs, giving her hand a quick squeeze before he released it. His warm smile and those devastating eyes with their gold flecks encouraged her, made her feel she could manage the days ahead with at least a modicum of grace. She went upstairs, pulled the sliding glass door open, and stepped into the apartment.

The first thing she saw was her mother's packed suitcase.

She looked at her parents. Mom's eyes were red, as if she'd been crying. "What's going on here?"

"Well, ba—no, Abby, your mother and I have been talking." Dad went to Mom, putting his arm around her shoulders. "We think we need to apologize to you. We were very pushy to decide Mom could stay here without an invitation from you. This is your house."

Abby knew her jaw had just dropped. She could feel it resting on her sternum.

"So," Dad continued, "we're going to spend our vacation at a motel downtown."

Mom tried hard not to look upset, but it was obvious she was struggling. Abby tried not to look too happy, but she was struggling too. She also didn't know what to say. "Oh, good," sounded almost cruel, like she rejoiced in getting rid of them—which in a way she did, but she didn't want to hurt these people whom she loved. On the other hand, "Oh, no," sounded like an invitation for them to stay here after all, which she definitely didn't mean. So she said nothing. She just kept winging lots of thank yous heavenward.

Dad carried Mom's suitcase and assorted paraphernalia to the car. Mom followed with obvious reluctance, Abby bringing up the rear. Puppy sat at the top of the stairs and watched through sleepy eyes. Her tail flicked from side to side like a black-and-white furry ribbon on a wand.

"Len, are you sure?" Abby heard Mom ask. Her voice quivered.

"Trust me, Han." He placed a hand on her cheek. "Trust me."

Mom nodded, turned, and climbed into their car.

Knowing Mom's feelings about Marsh, about her breaking free, Abby understood she was being granted a glimpse of the depth of her mother's commitment to her father. To trust him when everything in her screamed in disagreement had to cost Mom dearly.

Hearing the voices in the drive, Marsh came back out, Fargo trailing. He walked toward Abby, and she automatically moved toward him, the two of them drawn, she thought, like a magnet and filings. He stopped behind her, his hand resting on her shoulder. She leaned lightly against his chest.

"Mom and Dad are moving to a motel downtown."

"God answers before we even ask," he said, his voice quiet in her ear.

Dad stood in the door of the car, looking at Abby. "We'd like to have dinner with you once or twice while we're here, if it's okay with you. We can meet at some restaurant so we're not a burden to you."

How very difficult this letting go is for them. "That would be fine, Dad. I'd like that very much."

"Not just you, ba—Abby. We'd like to have both of you come." He smiled at Marsh.

"Oh, Daddy!" Abby ran to her father and hugged him. Marsh followed her, holding out his hand. "Thanks, Mr. MacDonald. I'd love to join you."

"Len," Dad said as the men shook. "Call me Len."

Abby went to the passenger side of the car and bent to kiss her mother through the open window. "I'll be all right, Mom. Honestly I will."

Mom didn't look convinced, but she tried to smile. "We'll call you—"

"—in a couple of days," finished Dad. "Maybe Monday."

Mom closed her eyes. It was obvious that four days seemed an eternity to her.

Abby's heart broke. She didn't want to be Alvild the pirate, losing her family forever. "Why don't we go somewhere after church on Sunday?" she suggested. "We're all going to be there anyway, and we all have to eat." She looked at Marsh for his opinion.

He nodded. "Is that an all-right time with you, Len? Mrs. MacDonald?"

Mom looked brighter. "We'll save you seats. You know your father, early for everything."

"We'll meet them after the service, Han."

"But—"

Dad looked at Marsh. "We'll meet you out on the front walk after the service."

Abby stood beside Marsh, his hand once again on her shoulder, and watched her parents drive away. Her chest was tight and she didn't know whether to laugh or cry.

Marsh leaned forward, giving her a quick kiss on the cheek. "Free at last."

She spun, grabbing him around the waist, burying her face in his chest. He held her, saying nothing, just gently rocking her.

"I feel like such an idiot," she told his T-shirt. "I wanted them to go, and now they have and I feel...lonely? Uncaring? Thoughtless? Mean? Ugly? All of the above? It's ridiculous!"

"You love them, and you're afraid you hurt them."

She straightened. "I love them, and I *know* I hurt them, or at least Mom."

"When two people who love each other disagree, one if not both of them are bound to get hurt, at least for a time."

She sighed. "Family relationships are so complex!"

He gave a half laugh. "Tell me about it. You'd think, wouldn't you, that since parents and kids are connected by DNA, heritage, and life experiences, that the members would be similar to each other when just the opposite is often true."

"I hate seeing us as dysfunctional. Somehow it sounds like we're not spiritual enough to overcome or something."

"All families are dysfunctional to some degree. How could it be otherwise when families are made up of sinners? I don't think, though, that disagreeing means you're failing in relationships. It just means you disagree. How you handle the disagreement determines how warped the fabric of your family becomes."

She was sure he was right. Still… "Did you see how red Mom's eyes were? I did that to her. When she cried over me when I was ill, I didn't feel guilty. I hadn't done anything on purpose to make her cry. It was just life happening. But this is different. I chose to make her sad."

"No, you chose to be your own woman."

"It comes down to the same thing, doesn't it?"

"Not really." He wrapped his large hand around her smaller one. "Motivation makes the difference. The outcome of your choice may be the same, but the reason for making your decision wasn't to injure your mother."

"So why do I feel so selfish?"

"'For we are God's workmanship, created in Christ Jesus to do good works, which God prepared in advance for us to do.' Do you want to be free of your parents' domination to do what you want regardless of their feelings or because you know God has special things for you to do?"

"I want to do whatever it is that God wants me to do. I want to be whoever it is that He wants me to be."

Marsh nodded. "That's why I'm not in politics, but was I wrong to choose as I have? It cost me my father."

"Your choice sounds so noble and godly. You chose seminary and teaching future pastors. It's so spiritual. But being a kids' librarian? Moving to the seashore?"

"Have you changed your mind then? Do you want Len and your mom to come back? I think they'd come at the drop of a hat."

She was silent for a few seconds, thinking back over the past three years with the constant protecting, cosseting, choosing on her behalf. "No." She squared her shoulders. "I don't want them to come back. I need to find my own path, wherever it takes me. I do want to remain close to them, so I'm glad we'll see them Sunday. But I'm also glad I won't see them for three days."

She could hear the smile in his voice when he said, "Good for you."

"Think so?"

"Sure do." He walked her to the steps. "Now you get a good night's sleep."

Abby was almost to her porch when she heard Marsh call, "Come on, Fargo." He slapped his side. Apparently the dog wasn't close at hand because the volume of Marsh's call increased. "Fargo! Come here, boy!"

Abby stepped onto the porch and stopped, frozen at the sight before her. Puppy stood on the end of the chaise, her body rigid, the hair on her back at full attention. She was nose to nose with Fargo, whose entire hind end vibrated due to the enthusiastic wagging of his stubby tail.

Abby called, "Marsh, he's up here. Come. You've got to see this."

Marsh took the steps two at a time. "He's not eating Puppy, is he?"

She shook her head. "I think Puppy's about to shred him."

Fargo whuffed, the loud noise replacing the whines of delight he'd been making deep in his throat. The noise startled Puppy so much that she jerked back, flattening her ears. Quick as a flare of heat lightning on a hot summer's night her paw flashed, catching the unwary Fargo in the nose. This time his whuff was one of surprise as his hind end collapsed and he sat, stunned by the attack.

"No claws," Abby assured Marsh as she hurried forward to save Fargo from further insult. She gathered Puppy in her arms where the cat promptly became boneless. Abby studied Fargo's black nose. "No blood." She held out her hand to him. "I apologize for Puppy's terrible manners." He licked her palm.

Marsh scratched Puppy behind the ears, and the cat began to purr. The noise fascinated Fargo, who risked putting his nose in harm's way to investigate. Puppy, eyes closed, was too mesmerized by the pleasant sensation to notice.

"So you're looking for a friend, not a meal?" Marsh took hold of Fargo's collar. "You can try again another day. Right now, heel."

With a sad look at the lounging Puppy, Fargo followed Marsh. At the top of the stairs, Marsh looked back. "Pleasant dreams, Abby. Things will look better in the morning."

Marsh turned out to be right. The next morning the apartment echoed a bit without anyone in it except her and Puppy, but it was wonderful to know that no one would be telling her how, what, and when she should eat, or check up on her when she came home. She left for work with a light heart.

The first thing she did was go to Nan.

"Do you have the envelopes that came with the letters about me?"

Nan nodded.

"May I see them? Marsh, my—" My what? What should she call him? Was he her boyfriend? Or was he just a good friend? Now that she thought about it, they'd never even been out on a date. She'd gone more places with Sean than Marsh. "Marsh, my friend, had an idea that might exonerate me."

Nan got the letters from her desk.

"See the date on the second letter, the false accusation one?" Abby put her finger on the postmark. "It was mailed on Tuesday, my second day here, in the morning. I spent most of my first day with you, right? So there was no time to get into trouble."

"No time to get into trouble!" Nan cried. She threw her arms around Abby, hugging her. "What a relief. I knew there was something wrong with this whole mess, besides the anonymity. I just hadn't been able to put my finger on what it was." She grabbed the phone. "I need to go call Mr. Martindale at once."

Abby smiled and drifted to her own desk where she was hard at work when Nan appeared again. "Abby, what was done to you is so wrong. Do you have any idea who would do such a thing or why?"

That was the one dark stain on Abby's brilliant horizon, that and her amnesia. As she and Nan discussed the accusations, the venom behind them seeped into her heart, poisoning even the joy of exoneration. Strange as it seemed, neither she nor Nan could think of anything except the hit-and-run that would account for the enmity of the letters.

"I guess they were to discredit me so I'd be a suspect witness."

"Despicable."

Abby agreed. She also agreed to call Greg Barnes of the Seaside police and report the letters. Perhaps there were clues there that neither she nor Nan could decipher due to their lack of forensic training.

"I don't think my serial reading loads of mysteries qualifies me," Nan said with a smile.

Greg had just left the library, taking the original letters and envelopes with him, when Sean Schofield stopped by unannounced to take Abby to lunch again, this time in his new car.

"Got it yesterday," he said. "Isn't she a honey?"

"Why are cars feminine?" Abby asked. "Why aren't they its?"

"That's easy," Sean said. "They are the loves of men's lives." He ran a caressing hand over the BMW's green fender.

The seats were wonderful, the ride was smooth, and she knew she should feel more flattered by Sean's attention than she did. Any number of women would give their eyeteeth for a chance to streak through Seaside beside him and to eat lunch with him, this time at a hole in the wall at the southern end of the boardwalk. Try as she would, she couldn't whomp up any feelings for him beyond a generic appreciation for him as a handsome, intelligent man. Still, he was a source of medical information she could plumb while she had the chance.

"In your experiences, have you ever met anyone with amnesia like mine?"

Sean shook his head as he automatically gave their waitress a huge smile when she delivered their food. The young woman colored a brilliant red and couldn't take her eyes from him. Abby had to grab her BLT on whole wheat toast, extra mayo, when the girl set it so close to the edge of the table that it started to tilt. She had to wave her empty Coke glass in the girl's face to get her to notice that she needed a refill.

"Don't feel guilty about the amnesia, Abby," Sean said, oblivious to the bemused waitress. "Many times a victim never remembers."

"But I wasn't a victim," Abby protested. "Karlee was. And she remembers more than I do!"

"In your own way you were as much a victim as that little girl." He drenched his hamburger with so much ketchup that

Abby questioned his ability to pick it up without dripping all down his front, making him look like he'd spent hours in emergency surgery and was wearing more of his patient's blood on his person than the patient had left in his veins. He took a huge bite, and somehow the ketchup remained where it belonged. "Do you remember the accident that killed your husband and daughter?"

It was obvious he expected a no, but Abby said, "Very clearly. I never lost consciousness, and I remember every horrible moment." Snapshots flickered through her mind. "I saw the car approaching because I was looking at Sam. I knew we were going to be hit at full speed. I remember the impact, the horrendous grinding noise of metal on metal, the ghastly silence after everything stopped moving, and the crying of the driver of the car that hit us. I remember knowing that Sam and Maddie were both dead and I wasn't. I remember thinking they'd never get us out of such a mangled corpse of a car, that I'd bleed to death before they got to me, and wondering if that would be so bad."

Sean looked shocked, his hamburger poised halfway to his mouth. "Oh, Abby." A huge blob of ketchup dripped onto his plate.

"With the accident last week, I remember Karlee skipping down the sidewalk. She wore pink overalls and had her ponytail caught up in a pink scrunchie. She must have just learned to skip because she could only do it with one leg, you know?"

He nodded.

"Of course you know. You work with kids all the time."

He smiled at her. "Go on."

"I even remember a car speeding down Thirty-fourth Street. It scared me. I remember telling myself that I would be fine. I wasn't in the intersection. No one could hurt me where I was. I remember Karlee checking the light, even looking both ways on Central. Then I remember waking up at the hospital."

"You remember the car?" Sean looked amazed. "Have you talked to the police?"

"I remember that there was a car, but I have no mental image of what it was like. It was just a black blur."

"A black blur?"

Abby nodded. "But even Karlee knows it was black. So do the cops from paint they found on the parked cars it struck."

"I wonder if the police can tell the make of a car from the paint they recover." Sean chomped on a potato chip, then looked at it in disgust. "It is so hard to get a crisp chip around here. They wilt as soon as they hit the sea air. It drives me crazy."

Abby grinned. She had been thinking the same thing. She'd also been thinking how grateful she was that he didn't dip his potato chips in the ketchup that had dripped onto his plate. It would have been more than she could stomach.

"Can you trust TV shows?" she asked. "I remember a TV show in which they caught the bad guy through tracing the paint, but I don't know how accurate that was."

"Well, I sure hope they get whoever it was. The police here are quite competent." Somehow it didn't sound like a compliment. "Now let's talk about something more pleasant. How do you like your new job? How do they like you?"

"Oh, Sean, it's great. I love what I'm doing. I like it better than teaching, and I liked teaching. I think they like me, too."

"No glitches after four whole days? Sometimes the first few days can be terrible until you're acclimated."

She thought about the letters but decided not to talk about them. They had become a nonissue. "Smooth as a new baby's bottom. You should have seen how responsive the little ones were to StoryTime yesterday All those bright little faces watching, laughing in the right places, getting worried in the right places."

"It must be nice to have them smiling at you. I get them in tears much of the time. Either they're sick or hurt, or I have to give them a shot. Makes one very unpopular."

Abby laughed, and they talked about her job all the way back to the library. She was reaching for the handle to climb out of the spiffy new convertible when Sean asked, "How'd you like to go out for dinner tomorrow night?"

Abby's breath caught. She had been hoping these lunches were just friendship visits with no further plans on Sean's part. She hated male-female complications. She'd never known how to handle them, and she'd been out of the dating loop so long, she'd lost what little skill she had.

"Thanks so much, Sean, but I can't." She tried to sound regretful.

"Saturday?"

Abby shook her head.

He studied her a minute. "Any time?"

"Not for a date, Sean. I like you, but—"

He put up a hand. "It's okay. I get the hint."

"I'm sorry. I really am. You're a great guy."

He looked grim. "Which one is it?"

"What?"

"Marsh or Rick? Which one?"

She thought about denying it but knew the truth was best. "Marsh."

Sean shrugged. "Your loss."

Taken aback by the towering ego that comment suggested, Abby nodded. "Okay." She climbed out of the car. "Thanks for lunch. I enjoyed it." *In spite of the ketchup.*

He didn't bother to acknowledge her comment, just drove off without a glance, leaving her standing in the street.

Someone doesn't deal well with rejection, does he?

Thirty-five

WHILE SEAN HAD no use for a specific woman and never had, he reveled in his popularity with all women. They fawned over him. From the nurses to the harried mothers of his patients to the girls in the checkout counters at the grocery store, they loved him. One smile was all it took.

Except for her.

He wasn't used to being turned down, and he knew he had let his pique show. It was not very polished of him, an educated, urbane man who oozed refinement and who had cornered the market on charm. It angered him that he'd allowed her to bother him, to remind him that a residue of life in that blue-and-white trailer still lingered just below the surface no matter how much he struggled to bury it, that he was a Piney no matter how hard he worked to acquire the polish that made him king of the hill, the soon-to-be-appointed chief of staff.

As he scribbled notations on patient charts in his crisp white lab jacket, he pondered her treachery. That she had no idea of the struggles she was putting him through was beside the point. She was the bane of his existence.

He heard McCoy's insidious voice in his ear. "Kill her, Sean. Take her out before she takes you out."

Sean's heart began to pound. Should he do that? Could he do that?

"Coward, Sean? A man takes charge and does what's gotta be done. A man protects his back."

Sean batted at his ear and rubbed over his right eye. He rarely got headaches, and he had little tolerance for them when they came. Too bad all his medications were at home.

"Excuse me, Dr. Schofield."

He raised his eyes to the worried face of a mother with a child dying of cancer.

He forced Abby and his headache to the back of his brain for the moment, smiling his trademark I'm-listening smile. "Mrs. Zelinski."

"Dr. Schofield, Joni is so weak." Tears pooled in the woman's eyes. "While that worries me, her pain breaks my heart."

Sean stood and placed an arm across her shoulders, hugging her gently, just enough to comfort her, not enough to make her uneasy. "Not five minutes ago I entered the order for more morphine. In no time, she'll be more comfortable."

The gratitude he read in her eyes was pure oxygen to the parched lungs of his ego. After Abby, Sada Zelinski was just what he needed.

"Oh, thank you, Dr. Schofield. I don't know what we'd do without you."

When he left the hospital, he decided to pick up takeout. He didn't have the tolerance for restaurant pleasantries tonight. A quick call on his cell phone, and his order for flounder, fries, and coleslaw was waiting for him when he drove up. The smell teased him all the way home, a tantalizing counter aroma to the new leather–new car smell of his BMW.

It was a nice car, a comfortable car, a car to draw the stares and envy of others, but it wasn't his beloved Jag. It lay, wounded and dying, far from home, far from the one who cared. His eyes narrowed. Everywhere he turned, she was there, the cause of all that was wrong.

He realized as he pulled into the garage and parked beside his cycle that he wasn't questioning McCoy's basic philosophy anymore. Somewhere between the hospital and home he'd concluded that she did indeed have to go. The question was how?

Drown her? She did live on the beach, and accidents happened.

Help her fall down the steps and break her neck? She did have that gimpy leg.

Feed her something laced with poison? Even she had to eat sometime.

He dropped his flounder on the kitchen counter and went straight to the master bathroom. He poured a pair of his magic little pills from their bottle into his palm. With a quick jerk, he tossed them down his throat, swallowing them dry. When he got back downstairs, he chased them with a glass of Scotch. Before the flounder was half gone, the headache had entirely disappeared. In a rosy cloud of well-being, he sat back on his leather sofa and plotted Abby's demise.

One thing for certain: There wasn't much time.

Thirty-six

WHAT DO you think?"

"What?" Marsh looked up from deep contemplation of his pumpernickel toast. His hand was locked around his orange juice glass, but he made no move to drink from it.

Rick looked at him with exaggerated patience. "I asked first."

Marsh groaned. "I'm sorry. What did you ask?"

Before Rick had time to answer, Marsh was staring with glazed eyes at the cabinet behind Rick's shoulder. It was there, whole in his mind, the crucial escape scene he'd had to skip earlier because he couldn't visualize it. Now he saw Marguerite, face pale with pain from her broken arm and the terrible blow she'd suffered when she fell off Maggie. She lay on a crude wooden bed, its mattress a piece of cloth resting on ropes laced from side to side. He saw Craig sitting on the floor, hands behind him, tied to the foot of the bed. His legs stretched out in front of him, crossed and tied together at the ankles. He saw their guard, a filthy man who with great pride wore the dirt of the ages upon his person.

Muttering to himself, Marsh left the table and grabbed his laptop. He was barely seated in his Adirondack chair before his fingers began to record the images his brain created.

The man smelled worse than any barn at high noon on a summer's day. When he had last had a bath Craig could only guess. Probably when he was small enough for his mother to wrestle him into a tin tub sitting on the floor before a wood stove in some kitchen somewhere.

He glanced at Marguerite. She lay on the narrow bed in the barren little room, her face ashen. He could only imagine her pain. The men who had surprised them and taken them at gunpoint had not been gentle with her. When silent tears had rolled down her cheeks, the men had remained unmoved while Craig died a bit inside.

Marguerite struggled to a sitting position, wincing as by accident she put pressure on her bad arm. She leaned against the wall that formed the head of the bed.

"What are you doing, girlie?" The malodorous guard glared but made no move to rise from the straight-backed chair he sat in, resting it on its two back legs as he leaned against the wall.

"Just sitting up." Her voice was a mere whisper as if talking took more strength than she had.

The guard smirked. "Well, don't try nothin' like you think is clever." He rubbed his hand over his gun, strapped to his waist by the sorriest looking holster Craig had ever seen. "I don't take well to people tryin' to fool me."

"I won't," she whispered. "I'm in too much pain. But if I did try to trick you, what would you do? Shoot me?"

The guard pulled his gun, aiming it at her. She didn't flinch.

"Because if you shot me, Snelling would shoot you, if my father didn't get you first."

"Like I'm afraid of your father." The scorn in his voice rubbed Craig raw. "He's a sick old man who's lost his hold on this here valley."

"Abner Frost is anything but washed up," Marguerite said calmly. "I can't say the same for your boss though. Of course, you'll go down with him."

The guard moved his gun slightly. The barrel flashed, and the bullet ripped into the wall inches from Marguerite's head.

"I missed on purpose," he explained as he reholstered his weapon. "Next time I won't aim so careful."

The door of the little cabin burst open, and Snelling barreled in. He could give the guard a run for his money in the slovenly department, his gray hair and beard wild around his head and face, his shirt held together by one button, his pants held up by a piece of rope. His saving grace was that he didn't smell as bad. Still, Craig would give a lot to always be upwind of both men.

"What's going on here?" Snelling demanded. "Skunk, what do you think you're doing?"

Skunk, huh? How appropriate. "He's threatening Miss Frost," Craig said, his voice as indignant as he could make it in his ignominious position. "See the bullet hole beside her head?"

"She was saying bad things about you, boss."

When a big, smelly man whines, it is a pathetic thing to witness.

With a steely look, Snelling jerked his finger to the door. "I just sent Tweed and Marks to check the new watercourse. Go join 'em. Make sure there are no collapses in the banks. We don't want that liquid gold pouring uselessly onto the desert."

Skunk clomped his chair back onto four legs and rose. Shaking his head at the unfairness of life, he left, but not before he shot Marguerite a venomous glare. She smiled sweetly at the man, then turned to Snelling. She gave him the most woebegone expression Craig had ever seen.

"Mr. Snelling, if you could open that back window and leave the door open for a bit, we'd be very grateful." Marguerite sounded for all the world like she was at a Sunday School picnic asking the church pianist if she would please pass the potato salad, not like she was asking her captor for a favor he had every reason to deny. "Some cross ventilation would be very much appreciated after our incarceration with Mr. Skunk."

Snelling snorted and shuffled his feet, but in the end he did as Marguerite asked. It was that imperious manner of hers. How did she manage that arrogance when you had to strain to hear what she said?

While Snelling wrestled with the warped window, Marguerite slid off the bed. With a stealth and surefootedness that made Craig blink, she moved to his side. She bent quickly, her hand touching his. He grabbed the cool metal she laid upon his palm. He blinked again. She had given him a small knife.

She stepped away from him and to his surprise slumped, her whole body falling in upon itself as she grasped her bad arm. She shuffled slowly, hesitantly toward Snelling and the window.

"Can I help?" she asked in a pathetic voice. "I feel like I'm going to be sick if I don't get some fresh air soon." She made a gagging sound that had Snelling redoubling his efforts. When she reached Snelling, she put out her good hand to help him press against the recalcitrant window.

Snelling scowled at her. "I can do this faster without your help. Go back and sit down."

"Oh." A world of hurt feelings echoed in that single word. "I didn't mean to get in your way." This time she sagged against him, forcing him to support her weight as he pounded his fist against the window frame.

As he sawed at the ropes behind his back, Craig watched Marguerite with reluctant admiration.

Fargo dropped his chin right on Marsh's keyboard. A line of nonsense letters and symbols appeared to the accompaniment of a beep, beep, beep.

"Dog, what are you doing?" Being pulled from his imaginary world made Marsh testy. He pushed at Fargo, but Fargo pushed back. He wasn't going anywhere. Quickly, before anything else could go wrong, Marsh reached over Fargo's head and hit save.

It wasn't until he dropped his feet to the floor and Fargo knew the writing was on momentary hiatus that the animal stepped back. He sank to his haunches, fixing his unblinking eyes on Marsh.

"What? You know better than to butt in to my working time."

Fargo licked his chops, catching a stream of drool just before it broke loose for a free fall to the porch.

"Ah." Marsh rose. "I forgot to feed you."

Feed touched some neural chord in Fargo's furry mind. He rushed to the sliding door, his hindquarters wagging with abandon.

As Marsh scooped some Alpo into a yellow plastic dish, Fargo scooted his huge red bowl across the floor with his nose.

"Thank you for your help." Marsh bent to pick up the red bowl. He walked to the lower cabinet by the sink and pulled out a great bag of dry dog food. He tipped the bag, letting the kibble fall. He glanced at Fargo who sat, eyes steady on the yellow bowl on the counter. Dry food might fill in the holes, but the canned food was the meal of Fargo's heart.

Fargo was inhaling his Alpo when Rick walked into the kitchen.

"I thought I heard you talking." He opened the refrigerator, pulling out an orange juice container. "Want to go play some pickup basketball?" He poured a glass full.

Marsh was torn. He looked at the man who had become his best friend and with whom he'd spent very little time since his arrival, thanks to Abby and Celia. He thought of Craig and Marguerite captive in Snelling's abhorrent cabin. The real world versus the imaginary but no less real one: the writer's eternal dilemma.

Christ didn't die for Craig and Marguerite, Marsh reminded himself. He didn't include them in His command to love others as yourself. All the "one another" verses in the New Testament didn't include fictional characters living in late nineteenth century New Mexico. Real people were who counted, even for something as mundane as basketball.

"There are hoops on the playground at Thirty-fourth Street," Marsh said.

"Good." Rick put the juice back in the refrigerator. "Ready when you are. I'm feeling sluggish without my regular gym work-outs."

Marsh stuck the dog food back in the cabinet. "I'm ready."

Rick looked him over from head to toe. "Okay, so you slept in that T-shirt last night and you haven't shaved. I can handle that, but you might at least comb your hair and brush your teeth."

Marsh looked down at himself. Sure enough, he hadn't done one thing hygienically since he rolled out of bed. "I'm turning into Skunk."

Rick shrugged. "I see no white stripe down your back, and you don't smell all that bad. Maybe a little halitosis, but that's all. Still, I do suggest that you roll on the deodorant for everyone's comfort."

Twenty minutes later at the basketball court Marsh and Rick found themselves facing eight boys, aged ten to sixteen. The kids were playing with equal enthusiasm but greatly varying levels of expertise when the two men arrived. The older boys were all on one team, strutting their stuff as they wiped the little guys' noses in their ineptitude.

The older boys ignored Marsh and Rick as they strolled to the edge of the court. Make believe the old men weren't there, and they'd go away.

"Here, Hank, I'm open!"

"What's the matter, Jase? You can't beat a ten-year-old?"

"I'm twelve," came the indignant reply. "Mike's ten."

Basketball sass. Marsh sighed with pleasure. Some things never changed.

At that moment Mike yelped, "Yipes!" He stopped cold, and the one good pass thrown his way all morning went sailing by him. "It's Duke Beldon!"

Rick rolled his eyes. Marsh grinned.

Soon they were surrounded by all the boys, the younger ones so excited that they couldn't stop hopping about, the older ones trying to be blasé but staring wide-eyed.

"I want to be on Duke's team!"

"No, I get to be on Duke's team."

"My name's actually Rick."

"Yeah," mumbled the one called Hank, if Marsh had gotten the names straight. "Rick Mathis, right?"

"This is my friend, Colton West." Rick's smile was fiendish.

Marsh started, never having been introduced by that name before.

The little boys looked unimpressed, but a flicker of interest sent the gazes of a pair of older boys Marsh's way.

"The writer?" Jase asked. "*Shadows at Noon*? *Rocky Mountain Midnight*?"

Marsh was impressed. "You've read them?"

"Oh, yeah." He studied Marsh. "You're good."

"You mean he wrote that book you gave me last week?" Hank asked Jase, who nodded.

"He writes all my movies," Rick added.

"Does he write Duke Beldon?" asked the twelve-year-old whose name Marsh hadn't heard yet.

"No," Rick said.

"Oh."

Marsh smiled to himself. What little cachet he might have gotten from his books and movie scripts counted for nothing with the younger crowd. "Okay, guys. Line up by height, and we'll pick teams." He held up a hand to suppress the I-want-Duke comments. "I want you to know that I played on my university's championship intramural basketball team for four years. I may not be Rick Mathis, but I'm not a slouch either."

The boys muttered phrases like *so what? yeah, right,* and *big deal,* but they looked at Marsh with less disfavor than before. By counting by twos down the height line, then flipping a coin to see which group got the privilege of playing with Rick, they quelled most of the complaints about being relegated to Marsh's team.

"Great play, Duke!"

"Over here, Colt!"

An hour and a half later when Marsh picked up little Mike, holding him high so he could dunk the ball and tie the score, everyone decided it was time for lunch.

Panting, red-faced, and pleasantly aching, Marsh and Rick climbed into Marsh's car. A chorus of "Bye, Duke," and "Bye, Colt," saw them off.

"Nothing like being imaginary people for a while to relieve tension," Rick said.

"Here I thought it was physical activity that alleviated stress."

Rick just grunted.

"What do you have to be stressed about anyway?" Marsh reminded himself to ease up on the gas. The posted limit was 25. "Oh, wait. Stupid question. I bet it's Celia."

Rick studied his nails intently. "How could anyone be foolish enough to walk out on her?"

Marsh frowned. "You're thinking of walking out? Going back to California?"

"Are you kidding? Not me! I was thinking of her idiot ex-husband."

"She's getting to you, isn't she?"

"She's real."

"To say nothing of beautiful, pleasant, fun, gutsy, capable, and strong."

Rick smiled, an indulgent look spreading over his face. "She's all of those things, all right. But it's the real I like best, that and her commitment to the Lord. I'd forgotten how nice it is to talk with someone who doesn't have a hidden agenda, someone who says what she thinks, someone who likes me, Rick Yakabuski."

"You haven't told her yet, have you?"

Rick didn't answer, but he began to frown.

"You need to, you know." Marsh pulled into his drive.

Still Rick said nothing, but the frown deepened to a scowl.

"She should hear it from you before she learns it some other way."

Rick climbed out of the car and slammed the door. "I'll tell her about Rick Mathis when you tell Abby about Colton West."

"Abby already knows," Marsh called. Rick ignored him, stalking onto the beach. When Marsh sat down to write again, he could see Rick striding to the south.

Snelling pulled his hand back and threw it forward against the window. The whole cabin shuddered under the blow. He drew his fist back again, and Marguerite gave a cry of agony.

"My arm! You knocked my arm." She whimpered as two tears slid down her cheeks. She grabbed Snelling's arm like only he could keep her on her feet. Snelling grimaced.

Craig watched in fascination as he sawed on the ropes with Marguerite's knife. He couldn't decide if Snelling had actually hit Marguerite's arm or if she was acting. If it was the latter, she should go on the stage. He twisted his hands every way he could, straining against the ropes. He could tell there was more give than before, but they still held him firm. He went back to sawing.

Where had she hidden the knife? Maybe in her boot? Strapped to her thigh? Though they had patted him down with an impressive thoroughness, no one had thought to search her. After all, she was just a woman. He couldn't help but grin. Woe to any man who underestimated Marguerite Frost.

Three things happened at once, each occurrence of major importance.

Snelling rammed his fist against the window sash again. It slipped on the wood and flew through the glass, which shattered with a great cracking noise. A jagged shard slashed across the base of his palm. Blood spurted in a crimson fountain.

As the window exploded, Marguerite grabbed Snelling's gun from its holster. She had stepped away from him before he even pulled his gushing hand back into the room. As she cocked the weapon, the click reverberated in the little room.

Craig's ropes parted. He pulled his cramped hands forward, his shoulders protesting as he did. His wrists were chafed and raw, marred with nicks from the knife, but compared to Marguerite's arm and Snelling's hand, the wounds were minor. With clumsy fingers he worked at the bonds that held his feet.

When he was free, he climbed to his feet, hurrying to Marguerite. His hand closed over hers, and she surrendered the gun.

Snelling stood by the window holding his hand away from his body, staring in horror at the laceration. Blood flowed in a red river over his hand, dropping to the floor like a ruby waterfall plummeting from a high mountain meadow to the valley below.

Marguerite stepped to Snelling, taking hold of his arm. She raised it as high as it would go. "Hold it there." She stepped away, ignoring his whimpers of pain and distress.

She walked to Craig. With her good hand she raised her skirt high enough to reveal her petticoat. He blinked in surprise.

"Don't get any cute ideas," she said, her voice tart enough to curdle milk. "Just tear off a strip. He needs bandages and a tourniquet."

In minutes, Snelling had his hand wrapped and a

moderately tight pressure cuff wound about his upper arm. Craig pulled a nail from the wall near the door, probably placed there to hang a coat or hat on.

"Come here," he ordered Snelling. He waved the gun to encourage obedience. Snelling came, all fight gone for the moment. "Raise your arm."

A question in his eyes, Snelling did as told. Craig noted where his wrist reached and drove the nail into the wall again. He grabbed the cloth that covered the bed, tearing it into strips. With fingers again agile he plaited three strips.

"Let me see that hand again," he said to Snelling. The man held it out. Quick as quail seeking cover, he tied the cloth about Snelling's wrist. "Now raise that arm again."

As Snelling watched Craig tie his raised arm to the nail, the man began to hyperventilate. "You can't tie me up like this!" Pant, pant. "I'll bleed to death!" Pant, pant.

"No, you won't. Between the tourniquet and the height, you'll be fine, at least until your men return and find you."

"But it hurts!"

"I didn't see you show any sympathy toward Miss Frost in her pain, and believe me, hers is more serious than yours."

"Are we finished now?" Marguerite was sitting on the edge of the bed, her good arm holding her broken one. She looked fragile, a glorious bloom shattered by a powerful wind.

Craig nodded. "We're ready to go back to the ranch."

"Good." She rose with obvious difficulty. "Because I don't feel too well." With that her eyes rolled back and her knees gave way.

Craig caught her just before she slammed into the floor.

Marsh closed his weary eyes, resting his head against the chair back. He was spent but pleased. Snelling would live to fight another day with more reason than ever to hate the Frosts. Craig and Marguerite were free to make their way back to Frost Spring Ranch where they could continue their sparring and sniping at one another.

He wondered how Abby would like the escape scene. It

seemed to him he'd done a fine job of balancing the part both Marguerite and Craig played in the action. He knew that the careful weighting of the action into equal contributions was a reflection of how he saw his growing relationship with Abby.

She needed him to help her at the hospital.

He needed her to challenge him about coloring outside the lines.

She suggested he use Colton West to ease the breach with his father.

He told her how to fix the problem of the letters.

She made him want to rise to great heights as a godly man as he watched her stand straight and with courage in spite of her damaged leg.

He encouraged her to believe in herself.

He opened his eyes and saw the glass of iced tea sitting on the table by the chair. The ice cubes were long gone, but who cared? It was wet. He gulped it down.

Perhaps the best thing about Abby was the rapport he felt with her. They understood each other, due in large part to their shared faith. With her he found that soul amity he would never have found with Lane, that oneness of heart.

Lord, am I reading things correctly? I made a mistake before with Lane, though You in Your grace rescued me. If I'm wrong about this growing bond, please let me know. All I want is what You want.

A car pulled into the drive. He went to the edge of the porch and smiled. Abby's hair was rumpled and she looked weary, but her smile made his day.

"Hey, tiger."

"Hey, yourself." She stopped in front of him. "Tiger?"

"You don't mind, do you? Tigers are feisty and beautiful, full of character and great courage."

She blinked. "Wow!"

"Yeah," he said. "That's what I was just sitting here thinking."

Thirty-seven

O<small>N THE WATERFRONT</small> was a restaurant fancy enough to make Celia's breath catch. If it weren't for Rick's hand on her waist, she would have felt like bolting. Celia Board Fitzmeyer had never in her life been to such a place. What's more, she had never expected to be. McDonald's and Burger King were more her style with a big night on the town being an evening at Olive Garden or Red Lobster. She hadn't even realized that classy places like this actually existed outside the movies and New York City. Maybe Paris, too.

"No wonder you told me to dress well," she whispered as they followed the maître d' to a table that sat in front of a great window overlooking the bay. She smiled at the man as he held out a chair for her.

"Like it?" Rick asked when the maître d' left.

She looked around the room, not wanting to appear gauche but wanting to take it all in. She smiled at the soft lighting, the real flowers in crystal vases on all the tables, at the crisp linens, gleaming silver and stemware, at the beautifully dressed women. Her royal blue rayon felt woefully unsatisfactory compared to the beautiful and obviously expensive dresses and pantsuits of those dining about her, but it was the best one of two dresses she owned. The other was a well-worn denim.

"What's not to like?" She grinned at him. "I could

get used to Saturday night dates like this much too easily. Why, I bet you don't even have to stand in line at the cash register to pay your bill."

Rick laughed loudly enough for the surrounding tables to turn and look. She saw them all look a second time as they thought they recognized him. Hopefully in a restaurant as upper-crust as this one, people didn't ask for autographs. She wanted an evening free of that conflict for him, an evening when he could relax, escaping public scrutiny and wearying explanations.

She looked out the window. The sun was beginning to fall toward the west, gilding the water of the bay a luminous gold. Seagulls swooped and soared; a family of mallards, ducklings paddling furiously behind their parents, floated past; and an osprey rocketed from the sky to scoop up a fish for dinner in his talons, his deep brown back and cream breast a beautiful blur.

"Did you see that?" Celia turned excited eyes to Rick. "He's so fast! What are those little black birds with the white beaks?"

Rick shook his head. "I'm a California guy. I don't know."

"American coots, miss," said a waiter as he put fresh, crusty rolls and a pot of butter on the table. "Over there in the marsh grass is a blue heron."

"I don't see anything." Celia squinted.

"He's fishing, so he's standing still. There. He moved. Did you see him?"

Celia watched, enchanted, as the large blue bird pulled a fish from the marsh water and lifted his head, dropping the fish down his gullet. His neck bulged where the fish slid down. "Oh, Rick, did you see? Wasn't it wonderful?"

She turned and found him watching her.

"Wonderful indeed."

Celia blushed and became very interested in arranging her cutlery. "Aunt Bernice wouldn't have to use her napkin to polish the silver here. No leftover food would dare cling, and water spots would be forbidden."

When the waiter took her napkin, shook it open, and laid it in her lap, Celia tried not to giggle. When the headwaiter made a Caesar salad from scratch on a cart wheeled to their table, she tried to look blasé instead of captivated. When the flambé dessert burned itself out, she gave up on blasé and sighed with pleasure. When the bill came, she was glad she couldn't see the total.

"I knew it," she said. "No line."

As the waiter hurried away with Rick's credit card, Rick reached across the table, taking her hand. "Thank you."

She blinked. "I'm the one who's supposed to thank you."

He gave her that smile that turned her heart over every time. "You have no idea what a joy it is to spend time with someone who is real."

"Are you sure you don't mean someone who's so much of a hayseed that she can't stop staring at it all? I've probably embarrassed you several times with my realness."

He rubbed his thumb across the back of her hand, sending little shock waves racing up her arm. "In my business I meet a lot of poseurs trying to be what they think is expected of them. Some of them are cynics, some act the life of the party, some become flirts or wheeler-dealers. I value honesty and authenticity, to say nothing of natural beauty." He looked at her, his gaze steady. "I value you."

Celia looked at her lap, bewildered and scared. Why would he pay her, Celia Fitzmeyer, extravagant compliments like that? *Don't say such things. Please. They mean too much.*

"Celia, look at me."

She raised her eyes to his, then lifted her chin, feigning confidence. If she could handle Aunt Bernice, she could deal with Rick. The only difference between the two was that Celia neither expected nor wanted anything beyond a place to stay from Aunt Bernice. From Rick she could so very easily want it all.

"I mean what I say," he said.

"Thank you," she whispered, lifting her coffee cup to hide the hunger his lightly given compliment aroused. To be valued by someone like him. To be loved by someone like him!

Oh, Lord, I'm in deep trouble here. Keep my heart safe. Having it broken once was more than enough.

The waiter appeared for Rick's signature. He automatically scribbled his name, but his attention was still on her.

"You don't believe me, do you?"

"About what?" Her coffee cup clattered as she set it down. She put her shaking hand in her lap, but he still held her other one. Undoubtedly he could feel her nervous quaking.

"About how beautiful you are. About how much I value you."

"Rick, I—"

"Excuse me, Mr. Mathis." The man from the next table stood at Rick's side. "I hate to bother you, but my boys think you walk on water. May I have your autograph for them? Their names are Jason and Tommy." He stuck a piece of paper under Rick's nose, holding out a gold pen for him to use.

Celia sighed. *Here we go again.*

As automatically as he'd signed the credit chit, Rick wrote "To Jason and Tommy," then signed "Rick Mathis" in large, splashy letters. He handed the paper back to the man.

"Thank you. I'm sorry to have disturbed you."

Rick smiled and nodded. "No problem." The man walked away smiling, holding the paper like it was a large denomination stock certificate for original shares of Microsoft. Rick turned back to Celia. He froze.

She wasn't sure what he saw in her face, but she knew what she saw in his. And she felt the total fool.

"You *are* him," she whispered as her heart plummeted to her feet. She'd made the mistake of trusting a man again. She shook her head. "Talk about naïve!" She threw her napkin onto the table, grabbed her purse, and bolted for the door. She was aware of another patron stopping him, but she kept on going. By the time she hit the front door, she was running.

He caught up with her as she stalked along the bay front, heading for the marina and a phone to call Abby or Pinky to come get her. A strange combination of anger and disappointment swirled through her. As she heard him bearing down on her, she swatted at the tears that streamed down her face. She couldn't let him know how much his deception hurt.

He spun her to face him. "Celia, let me explain!"

She heard desperation in his voice, but she steeled her heart against him. She lifted her face to him, trying to look like Aunt Bernice when she was displeased, which was 99 percent of the time, so Celia had seen the expression with great frequency.

"Don't," she said. "Whatever line you're going to feed me, I don't want to hear it." She began to walk again, wishing with all her might that she could hate him. Then his dishonesty wouldn't matter as much.

He grabbed her hand, pulling her toward him. "You can't just walk off like this."

"Just watch me!" She struggled briefly. "Let go."

"No." He tightened his grip on her hand. "I can't let you go."

She looked at him, knowing he would see more than she wanted him to but unable to think of anything else to do. "Rick, let me go. Please."

"On one condition." He pointed to a bench under a tree. "Sit with me for a minute. Let me explain."

She looked at the bench. If she sat, she was a goner. She knew it. She tended to believe the stories people told her as her years of hoping for the best with Eddie proved. Whatever Rick told her, she'd want desperately, too desperately, to believe. He was an actor. He could conjure up any emotion on demand. How would she ever be able to discern between his lies and the truth? "I–I can't."

He grabbed her other hand. "Celia, you've got to. Please."

She studied his red-rimmed eyes in surprise. Tears? From Rick Mathis? Real distress or alligator tears?

"Please, Cely. I'm begging you."

She closed her eyes. She felt herself falling, falling under his spell, sinking into the soft, sweet dream of who she had thought he was. She couldn't decide whom she despised most: herself for being so weak or him for making her that way. She pulled her hands free and stalked over to the bench. He followed. Before she sat, she skewered him with a malevolent look. "Think of this as what I owe you for tonight's dinner. I don't want to be indebted to you." She sat.

I want to be loved by you, she thought as she worked at keeping the nasty expression in place. "All right. Say whatever it is you have to say. Then call me a cab."

He reached for her hand again. She thought about pulling it back, but this was the last time he'd touch her, and she wanted the bittersweet experience.

"My name is Rick Yakabuski."

She stiffened.

"It is." He looked at her, imploring her to believe. "I was born in a little town named Barry's Bay in Ontario, Canada."

She frowned, uncertain. "You're Canadian?"

He nodded.

She was interested in spite of herself. "That's a long way from California. How'd you end up in Hollywood?"

Her question seemed to release some of his tension. He sat back, sliding an arm along the bench until his hand came to rest on her shoulder. His fingers began to toy with her hair. "When I was in college, I worked summers as a guide at Algonquin Provincial Park, a hour or so down the road from Barry's Bay. I guided parties on canoe trips on the many lakes pocking the park, places accessible only by canoe. I was the one that cooked them dinner, that kept them from losing their gear, but I made them portage their own supplies."

She could imagine him as a guide, paddling through the bush, pitching pup tents, cooking over a campfire, taking his party to places most people would never visit.

"One party was a group of ten, three men and their sons. All I knew was that they came from California. After one of the sons finally understood that I wasn't his servant and he had to work on this trip, we had a fine time. At the end of their two-week trip, one of the men asked me if I wanted to be on television."

"Just like that?" Celia grimaced. *I'm believing him.* She hardened her heart, trying to be skeptical, but it was hard with his fingers tickling the back of her neck.

He nodded. "Just like that. The man's name was Mike Rosko, and he was about to begin a search for someone to play a cowboy named Duke Beldon for a new series. I was twenty-two. Playing Duke Beldon sounded like a lot more fun than getting a real job, so I said I was game. Mike flew me to California, put me up in his home, and gave me a screen test. It was a great lark."

Screen tests, Hollywood producers, TV shows. Poverty, Aunt Bernice, Seaside Spa. They hadn't a thing in common, she thought with a deep sorrow.

"Then it dawned on me that I'd have to ride a horse." Rick laced his fingers through hers, folding them to clasp her hand possessively. Automatically she gripped him back.

"Never ridden one before?" She stared at their meshed hands, felt the fingers of his other hand comb through her hair.

"Never. I'd been too close for comfort to moose and bear in the Algonquin back country, and it never fazed me. Horses scared me for some reason. The whole deal almost fell apart over that one fact. Mike made me take riding lessons every day for a month until I at least looked comfortable in the saddle."

Celia thought about the Duke Beldon episodes she'd seen. She couldn't remember much horseback riding. But she'd watched a Rick Mathis TV movie with Poor Uncle Walter last year. "Do you mean that was a double in that Colton West adaptation on TV?"

He shook his head, amused at her outrage. "No, that was me. Horses and I do very well together now. It was just a matter of getting used to each other. I even own a horse ranch in Montana."

"A ranch?" Celia couldn't imagine such a wonderful thing. "A big one?"

Rick's eyes turned dreamy. "It's wonderful. Wide skies and open range." He smiled at her. "You'd love it."

She didn't respond. She was certain, though, that she would love it, mostly because he would be there. "Why did you lie to me, Rick? I feel like an idiot."

"I didn't actually lie," he said. "I just told you I was Rick Yakabuski, and that's true. All my identity papers say Yakabuski. It's only on the marquee that I'm Mathis."

She could see the obvious reasons why Yakabuski had been changed to Mathis professionally. "Still you lied by implication."

He watched a sailboat coming into the marina under power, its sails packed in a blue boom cover, and nodded. "I did. When I left California, I was so sick of the fawning, of the pretense. I wanted to be a real person again. I told Marsh that I didn't want anyone to know who I was professionally. I was just his friend Rick. I–I never counted on meeting you."

Celia studied the sailboat too, its white hull glistening under the lights along the docks. He'd wanted to be just a guy, not Duke Beldon, famous cowboy. He wanted to have people respond to him, Rick Yakabuski, not to Rick Mathis, star. She could understand that, sort of. She had to admit that his little identity misdirection wouldn't have been an issue at all if she hadn't been so taken with him. Well, that was her fault, not his.

"Besides, Cely." He slid closer. "Would you have felt comfortable with me if you'd known about my other life?"

That question was easy to answer. She shook her head. "Never. I know my limitations. I'd have been too overcome to even talk to you, let alone spend time with you alone."

"The minute I saw you, I knew I wanted to spend time with you alone."

She looked at him, confounded. She knew why she'd want to spend time with him, but why would he seek her out?

"You have no idea how beautiful you are, do you?" He ran a thumb down the side of her jaw.

Given the responses of the previously important people in her life—her mother, Eddie, Aunt Bernice, and Poor Uncle Walter—she had no reason to think herself notable in any way. "I've not had caring people in my life, Rick. I'm not used to people, especially men, saying nice things to me. If it weren't for the fact that God loves me, I'd be convinced I have no value at all."

"Your relationship with God is part of what makes you so beautiful to me," Rick said. "His love anchored you when no one cared, and your dependence on Him has given you a depth that reaches out to me."

"Rick," she began, but she didn't know how to express her thoughts.

"Believe me, Cely, I would never feed you a line about something as important as God's love. It's saved me too, from the falsity and hype of the industry in which I work. When Marsh first shared Jesus with me, telling me how I could find real love and real relationships through Him, I was skeptical. It was bad enough when I found out the writer of my movie was a seminary professor, but when he began to talk about the Lord in such a personal way, it made me squirm. I'd been in Hollywood so long that it was hard to remember what authenticity was. But his faith is so real, and his knowledge so vast that I came to the point where it was harder not to believe than it was to believe. It was during our second movie together that I accepted Jesus as my Savior."

The lights of Seaside winked at Celia from across the bay. The scents and sounds of the salt marshes whispered. Her heart yearned to believe him, to trust him.

Rick stood, pulling her to her feet. "Come on. I'll take you home."

She nodded. That was what she wanted, wasn't it?

They walked hand in hand back along the road she'd run down such a short time ago. She stole a glance up at him and found him looking at her. He smiled that devastating smile.

"All I ask, Cely, is that you don't shut me out. Let me keep seeing you while you make up your mind about me."

She wanted to tell him he could keep on seeing her forever, but she managed to restrain herself. She needed time to pray, to think when he wasn't beside her, his mere presence turning her mind to mush. "How long are you going to be in Seaside?"

"Marsh and I have lots still to do on the screenplay for *Shadows at Noon,* and I don't need to report for work for another month and a half. I've been thinking of spending the whole time here, assuming Marsh doesn't kick me out."

A month and a half. Long enough to fall completely under his spell and have her heart broken, smushed, crushed to pulp.

Why don't you just say no? You know it's not going to work out. Two different worlds. Haven't you been hurt by enough people? Do you need to ask for more?

But what if it could work? What if she said no, and all the time there had been a real possibility for—for something.

Lord, I want to learn if he's all he seems, all he says. Is it okay if I leap off the cliff?

She felt an ease at that thought, and she made her decision. She'd leap. And she knew just the way to see if he was indeed as serious as he said he was about her, about them. As they walked up to his little red sports car, she turned to him, holding out her hand, palm up.

"Can I drive us home?"

Thirty-eight

"ARE YOU READY up there, tiger?"

Marsh's voice was rich and deep. Abby shivered at the sound of it. *Idiot*, she chided herself. *You are not sixteen. You have been married and widowed. Now behave yourself. Act your age.*

What? My age can't fall in love?

"Be right there." She grabbed a sweatshirt and hurried to the stairs. She looked down at the man who had become so important to her that it scared her, especially since it happened so fast. Tonight was Saturday. She'd only been in Seaside a week and a day. "Do I need my cane?"

Smiling, he shook his golden head. "You've got me."

Oh, boy. Her heart tripped double time. She turned and waved good-bye to the glowering Puppy who stared at her from inside the sliding door. "I'll be back before too long." Puppy was not impressed.

She made her way down the stairs with care. Marsh held out his hand, and she took it for the last few steps. He tucked it in the crook of his arm as they walked the few feet to his car.

"Is Fargo as unhappy as Puppy at being shut inside?" Abby asked.

"Ah." He lifted his index finger like he was about to make an important point in a lecture. "It's all a matter of timing. I didn't feed him dinner until I was ready to leave. He was wolfing down his Alpo when I slipped out the door. By the time he discovers he's alone, he'll be fat and sleepy."

"You hope."

"At least I won't be around to hear his piteous whines."

"Hey, you two."

Abby and Marsh turned to find Rocco deMarco waving to them as he loped over to the car. He grinned as he shook hands with Marsh.

"You look pleased with yourself," Marsh said. "Life going well?"

"Much better than it was a couple of days ago, let me tell you."

"Really?" Abby studied him. He looked like a different man. Gone were the scowl, the angry eyes, the belligerent set to his mouth. He looked carefree, satisfied. "I take it you and Vivienne are doing much better?"

Rocco glanced back to his house. "Couldn't be better, believe me."

"I'm so glad." Abby caught sight of Vivienne on the deck fronting the beach and waved. Vivienne waved back. She looked beautiful as always in a brilliant blue top and white shorts, her hair pulled back in a ponytail. She also looked uncertain. Strange, that, Abby thought. If ever anyone seemed to rule her world, it was Vivienne.

Rocco caught sight of his wife, and his eyes lit. He touched the tip of his thumb and forefinger together in an okay sign, and Vivienne nodded. She moved out of sight behind the house.

"I'm sort of here on Vivian's behalf," he said.

"Vivian?" Abby couldn't help it. "Not Vivienne, accent on the last syllable?"

"Plain old Vivian," Rocco said. "Viv, really. She sort of went overboard when I sold my business." He grinned with a boyish enthusiasm that made Abby smile back. "She wasn't used to being rich, and she didn't do too well with it. All she did was make people angry. When she tried to act like a rich lady might, her girl-friends got jealous and gave her a hard time. They kept telling her I was in the Mafia, and that's how I made my money."

"I'm assuming that's not true," Marsh said, "or you wouldn't be telling us."

"Not true," agreed Rocco. "I had a dot-com and sold it before the bottom dropped out. Thirty million."

Abby blinked, surprised that Rocco would mention a figure. She looked at Marsh. "I bet that beats Colton West."

"By a mile."

"Hey, I'm reading Colton West's book right now," Rocco said. "It's the one with that cowboy in it, right?"

"I think they all have cowboys," Marsh said.

"There's more than one?" Rocco leaned in like he was about to share a confidence of major proportions. "I don't read all that much, but if they all got cowboys, maybe I'll read another some day."

"Do that," Abby said. "I think Mr. West would like that."

Rocco nodded. "I started reading when Viv wouldn't speak to me. I had to do something, you know? I was going nuts."

"You can only take so many game shows and soaps, right?" Marsh edged Abby toward her seat.

"Wait." Rocco cleared his throat, then cleared it again. "I got something to tell you." He opened his mouth, then closed it, stalled.

Abby and Marsh both leaned their heads toward him. "Yes?"

He looked at Abby, words rushing out in so rapid a stream that she almost didn't understand him. "Viv wanted me to tell you she's sorry."

"Me?" She poked herself in the chest.

"Yeah. She didn't mean to upset you, not really. She was just sort of mad. The guys liked you better, you know?"

"The guys?" Abby thought of Walker and Jordan. If they were hers and they liked another woman better, she'd be upset too.

"You know." He gestured to Marsh. "Him and that Rick guy."

"That's what upset her? That Marsh and Rick liked me better?" *I think it was more that they disliked predators.*

Rocco nodded.

"And she's not mad now?"

He shook his head, a smile lighting his face. "She's wonderful now."

Curiosity ate at Abby. Why was Vivian wonderful all of a sudden? Why did she all of a sudden long to be friends? Why did she reconcile with Rocco? "What made her change her mind?"

"You saved Walker's life."

"Oh."

"When she learned that, she felt so bad. Here you'd done something so huge for us, and she was making your life miserable."

Was there just a chance that Vivian was overinflating her importance in the scheme of things? "Then tell her everything's fine. We all have bad days." Of course Vivian's—or Viv's—bad times had lasted a lot longer than a day, but she didn't say what she was thinking.

"Thanks." Rocco glanced toward the porch. "That'll mean a lot to Viv. She'd feel real bad if you were hurt. Just in case, she said to tell you she'd make it all better."

Abby looked at Marsh. Whatever did that mean? "Tell her thank you."

Rocco nodded, turned to leave, then stopped, looking over his shoulder. "Did they ever find that car and the driver who hit the kid?"

Abby sighed. "No, and I still can't remember what I saw either."

"Don't worry," Rocco said with a flick of his hand. "It'll work out."

"That was interesting," Abby said as Marsh stuck the key in the ignition.

"Old Viv is something, all right." Marsh put the car in reverse. "Imagine asking your husband to apologize for your temper tantrums."

"Imagine him doing it!"

They drove the dozen or so blocks to the southern tip of the island and the small state park there. Houses that had been vacant for months teemed with life as summer people and vacationers arrived. Lights shone in windows, kids played tag, teens stood with studied nonchalance.

"Nan told me today that the population goes from 10,000 off season to 125,000 during the summer." Such numbers staggered Abby.

"That means we won't be able to find a parking place downtown for the next three months."

"Personally, I think it's a miracle the island doesn't sink under all the added weight."

Marsh grinned. "If Manhattan Island doesn't sink under the weight of New York City, I think Seaside's safe."

Abby rested her head against the headrest, turning slightly so she could see Marsh. As always just looking at him pleased her. "Did anyone ever tell you you're a handsome man, cowboy?"

He glanced at her, surprised. "Did anyone ever tell you, you have good taste?"

She blew a raspberry.

He slowed, searching for a parking place. "Just think. A night at the shore with the humidity blown away by a cool front, a night when we can actually see the stars."

Abby tied the arms of her sweatshirt around her neck. "You know, I think I've seen about two shooting stars my whole life."

"Tonight will up the number considerably." Marsh slipped into a spot. "The predicted meteor shower should be spectacular."

They climbed out of the car, Marsh reaching into the rear seat for a quilt, an electric lantern, and a can of heavy-duty bug spray. He set the quilt and lantern on the hood of the Taurus while he sprayed his head and neck, arms and ankles. Then he turned to Abby.

"Shut those beautiful eyes and don't breathe." When she did as told, he sprayed her also. He stuck the can into his back pocket, tucked the quilt under one arm, and let the lantern dangle from his fingers. It wasn't dark enough to need the light at the moment, but it wouldn't be long before full night fell. He reached for her and laced his fingers through hers. She made believe his touch didn't make her feel all warm and cozy. They walked to the entrance of the park.

They started up the sandy path that led through the dense scrub that made up about half of the five-acre park. In an instant they were surrounded by bands of marauding mosquitoes, gnats, and sand fleas. Even sprayed within an inch of her life, Abby was all too aware of the insects flying reconnaissance missions of her face and neck, looking for that one millimeter untreated, that one tiny spot where they could dive in and draw blood. To her relief, their sorties failed. The smelly repellant was working. Still the presence of that many insects was disconcerting.

"This is what the island must have looked like when God created it, before people cleared it," Marsh commented as the soft deep sand pulled at their feet. Shoulder-high shrubs Abby couldn't identify made a dense tangle about them, broken occasionally by clumps of what looked like bayberry bushes. Marsh ducked under the reaching limbs of a shrub and waved their joined hands at a particularly thick cloud of mosquitoes. "Imagine being ship-wrecked here and having to fight your way through this snarling mess and these bugs. You wouldn't have any skin or blood left by the time you got help."

"Robinson Crusoe managed."

"But not on Seaside."

The silky, shifting sand that formed the path through the park made walking a challenge for Abby. Intensifying her problem was the rapidly fading light that threw deceptive shadows, making it all the more difficult to judge her footing.

"Not so fast, cowboy." She pulled back against Marsh's forward motion. Her foot slipped as a pile of sand resettled itself under her tread. "Oops!" She lurched in an effort to regain her balance, scraping her arm against an encroaching shrub. A broken branch scratched its way down the fleshy underside of her upper arm.

Hissing at the pain, she pulled her hand free of Marsh's and clapped it over the injured area.

"Are you okay?"

"I'm fine," she said through gritted teeth. She tried to twist her arm so she could see if she was bleeding.

"Let me see." Marsh took her arm, examining the angry welt. "No blood. Just a nasty scratch. You'll want to put antiseptic cream on it before you go to bed tonight. We can wash it off in the ocean. The salt water will cleanse it."

"To say nothing of sting," she said, relieved she hadn't punc-tured the skin.

"A little pain is good for your character."

She laughed without humor. "Then I should have character coming out my ears."

He looked at her, and she could see the admiration in his eyes. "You do, you know. You have integrity and strength like few I've ever met."

She gazed back at him, moved by his comment. "Thank you," she managed to whisper.

"Um." He looked at her, his mouth cocked at one corner.

She'd seen that look in his eyes before, and it meant trouble.

"What?" Before she realized what he intended, he bent and kissed her sore arm.

She shivered. "Marsh."

"Just making it all better," he said as he straightened.

Oh, boy. Her heart beat triple time. "It doesn't hurt much," she managed, ignoring both the continuing sting and the hot brand of his lips.

"It shouldn't hurt at all if I do it right." He smiled. "I'd better treat it again." He did. When he straightened, he shoved the quilt into her hands. "Here, hold this." The lantern followed. "And this."

"What?" Automatically she took the items, thrown from the romantic to the mundane in a wink of time. How in the world was she to keep her balance with these things in her arms?

As she contemplated her burden, Marsh bent and caught her under the knees. His other arm went around her back, and just like that she was cradled against him. She gasped in surprise and pleasure. The very next second she began to cough violently. She wheezed, coughed some more, cleared her throat and tried not to make gagging noises.

He set her on her feet, holding an arm to balance her as she continued to choke. "Is my holding you that bad?" he asked, half in jest.

"A bug!" She shuddered and coughed again. "When I gasped, I inhaled a bug, maybe a whole colony of bugs. They went straight to the back of my mouth. I swallowed them!" She shuddered again.

Marsh looked interested. "What kind?"

Abby scowled at him. "How should I know? Why should I care? Bleh! It tasted awful."

"Doubtless biting the inside of your stomach right now," Marsh said as he bent and lifted her into his arms once again. He walked the shifting sand with a surefooted ease that Abby envied. When he abruptly turned sideways to pass an overgrown shrub, Abby grabbed his shirt to keep from tumbling out of his grasp at the sudden movement. When she felt certain she wasn't going to fall, she released the fabric and patted at the wrinkles. Then she slipped her arm about his back for a more secure ride.

The gathering darkness wrapped around them, and Abby

leaned back into Marsh. What she wanted to do was lay her head on his shoulder, but somehow she lacked the courage.

"Could you shine the light at my feet?" Marsh asked. "It's getting difficult to see in here."

Abby reached for the switch on the lantern, which rested on the quilt that rested on her lap. The beam of light cut through the gloom, illuminating a wide-eyed raccoon hiding from them beneath a bayberry bush. It made little chirruping noises as it backed away.

Abby swung the light to the path. "Poor baby. I bet we scared years off his life. How long do raccoons live?"

"I have no idea." Marsh wasn't even straining under her weight. "Why don't you go to the library tomorrow and ask about it? I understand that children's librarians know how to find out all kinds of information like that."

She gave him a little punch in the kidney with the hand behind his back. He grunted, grinning as they emerged from the scrub onto a wide expanse of beach. Here in the open, the night darkness wasn't yet deep.

"You can put me down now," Abby said. "I'll be able to walk better here in the open."

"What if I don't want to?" Marsh kept walking at the same steady pace.

Abby flicked off the lantern, leaning back into him again. "Then don't. I sort of like being cared for so well." She took a big gulp and laid her head against his shoulder. It felt just right resting there. She was surprised and pleased when he bent to press a kiss on her temple.

He walked all the way to the edge of the water, then lowered her to her feet. He pulled a handkerchief from his pocket and bent to swish it in the water. "Let me see that arm again."

Embarrassed, Abby held out her hand for the wet cloth. "I can do it."

He batted her hand gently. "But I can see what I'm doing. You can try all you want, but you'll never see this part of your arm without a mirror."

Acknowledging the truth of that remark, Abby offered her arm. With care he blotted it with the cloth. As Abby had expected, the salty water stung. She flinched.

"Hurt?"

"A bit."

When he was satisfied with his ministrations, he rinsed the handkerchief once again, wrapping it about her arm, tying a knot in the ends to secure it. "To keep out any sand."

She nodded. "You're a very nice man."

He grinned. "Ready?"

"For what?"

He picked her up again, holding her close. "I don't want you choking on any more giant bugs."

"There aren't many down here by the water." She wrapped her arm around his neck this time. "The breeze blows them away."

"Okay," he said a few minutes later. "How's this?"

Abby straightened and looked around. They were standing at the demarcation line between the soft beach and the tide-scrubbed sand. The park was several yards behind them, the ocean ahead, and above were more stars than she'd ever seen. The nearest people, a family with two young children running circles around their parents as they sat on a blanket, were several yards away. "Perfect."

Marsh lowered her until she was standing, but he kept his arm around her back. They stood for a long moment, sides touching from shoulder to hip. Again she laid her head on his shoulder, and again he bent to kiss her temple. The air around them thrummed with intimacy and an unnerving intensity. One of them had to move, to break the tension. But which one and move how? Apart? Or into a full embrace? She dropped the quilt and lantern, sliding her other arm about his waist.

He smiled down at her, and something in his glance made her feel beautiful and desirable instead of skinny and scarred. He leaned down, kissing her on the crown of her head. Then with a sigh, he released her and picked up the quilt. With a grand flourish he shook it out, spreading it on the sand.

Abby sat, drawing her legs up, resting her chin on her knees. Marsh came down beside her, close but not quite touching. He glanced at the sky.

"Any time now," he said.

Abby looked up and swallowed. The vast canopy of the heavens glittered with stars beyond number. "I can't get my mind around the sheer size of it all, let alone the idea of other galaxies. It's a hard enough struggle to comprehend the extent of our own."

"'The heavens are telling the glory of God,'" Marsh sang.

Abby turned to him in surprise.

"It's a chorus from Haydn's "The Creation," one of the all-time great oratorios. It was first performed in 1798 and is still sung today."

"Ah."

He cast her a look. "No name of the female musician who sang the soprano solos?"

She laughed. "No, but I certainly agree with the thought. The heavens do testify to God's glory."

"I don't understand how people can look at the night sky and not believe in God."

Abby nodded. "At the very least God as Creator. All those brilliant suns up there sure don't stay in place by some cosmic accident. That stretches credibility too far."

"It takes more faith to be an evolutionist than it does to be a creationist, as far as I'm concerned. The laws of probability alone defy anything as complex and immense as this." He swept his hand.

"There!" Abby pointed out over the water. "Did you see it? A real falling star!"

"A real one, huh? So much better than a fake."

She was so pleased to spot the first one that she didn't even bother commenting on his teasing. He lay back, hands behind his head, eyes skyward.

In a few minutes, her neck aching from looking up, she lay back too, close but not touching.

"There." Marsh pointed to the northwest. "Did you see that one? That's twelve for me."

"I saw it, and I'm at thirteen. Oh, look! I mean fourteen."

When a trio of meteors flared, then died in the southern sky, Abby turned her head to Marsh in delight. "Did you see?"

He turned to her, grinning his slow grin. "I did. Beautiful." But he wasn't talking about the sky. That's when she realized that they were definitely touching, shoulders pressed together and hands linked. All at once even breathing became difficult.

Thirty-nine

$\mathcal{M}$ARSH RAISED himself on his elbow and leaned over Abby. Her mouth went dry. Slowly he lowered his head, giving her plenty of time to pull away. But she didn't move. She wanted his kiss.

His lips were soft and warm, and her blood began to sing. She wrapped her arms around his neck and kissed him back, pulling him down to her. Tears pooled behind her closed lids. She'd forgotten how wonderful a kiss from a man you loved could be.

She'd also forgotten how intense the longings could be, longings she had soothed regularly during her marriage. Appetites once sanctified now coursed through her without God's blessing on their appeasement. In the words of the old King James, she burned and with an intensity that scared her.

Her hands moved from Marsh's neck to his chest; she gave a gentle shake. "Marsh. Marsh!"

"Um?" He kissed her nose, her eyes. His hands held her face.

It felt so good! "Marsh, we have to stop." She turned her face, burying it in his neck.

He stilled, dropped his hands, and sat up, his back to her. She could hear his labored breathing. "I'm sorry," he mumbled. "I–I'm sorry."

She sat up, resting a hand on his back. "I'm not

upset. It's all right. It wasn't you who scared me. It was me."

He turned to her. "What?"

She wrapped her arms about her knees. "I was married, Marsh. I know what it's like to love a man and be loved. It's like nothing else, and your kiss reminded me of how wonderful it can be. Should be. Would be." She laid her head on her knees. "I wanted us to continue too much."

They sat in silence as meteors continued to rain above.

"Desire's a funny thing," Marsh finally said. "One minute it's 'you're beautiful,' emotional but controlled, and the next it's fire in the blood." He reached out, running his fingers down her cheek. "But it's more than mere desire with you. I want you to know that."

It's more here, too. Tears burned her eyes once again. "I'm glad."

"When I became a Christian in college," he said, looking back to the sea, "I entered what I've always referred to as my second virginity. I knew I couldn't go back and undo what was already done, but from that moment on, I could be chaste. And I have been. It's been hard at times, but I don't regret that decision." He got to his feet and reached for Abby's hand. "I think that for our own protection we'd better go."

She let him pull her up, then bent for the quilt. They each took two corners and shook it. Then she walked her corners to him. He grabbed not only them, but her hands as well. He searched her face. "You're certain you're all right?"

She leaned forward, brushing a light kiss over his lips. "I'm certain." She slipped her hands free, and he finished folding the quilt. She bent for the heavy flashlight and the bug spray. She glanced at the park. "Do we have to walk back through the bugs?"

He shook his head. "We'll just walk along the beach until we get beyond the park. If we have to walk back a block or two for the car, it'll be better than providing a living feast."

Nodding, Abby turned to walk along the water's edge. As she did so, she stepped in a slight depression. Her weak leg buckled. She lurched, and Marsh reached for her.

A great crack of sound shattered the air. Abby jumped in reaction. "What was that?"

Marsh didn't answer. Instead, he groaned and sank to his knees, his hand going to his left shoulder.

"Marsh?" She grabbed for him. Unable to support his considerable weight, she went down with him.

"I think I'm shot," he managed as he hunched in on himself.

Her stomach lurched. "What?" How could that be? "Where?"

"My left shoulder." He stared at the hand clamped over the area.

Abby knelt in front of him, her back to the sea. She grabbed the lantern and turned it onto his shoulder. She swallowed against panic as she saw blood seeping between his fingers.

"Turn that off," he hissed. "Don't make us any bigger a target than need be."

Abby flicked the switch on the light. "Someone shot you on purpose?" The hair on the back of her neck prickled. She searched the night, but the dark had become impenetrable, denser, full of unspecified, unseen terrors. "You mean he's still out there?"

Marsh sat, stunned and sweating. "Yeah."

"Then lie down so he can't get you again!" She pushed him down onto the quilt, throwing herself down beside him. She stared up the beach toward the park with all its low-growing trees and shrubs, the perfect hiding place for someone evil enough to gun down an innocent man. She saw nothing except blackness. She looked up and down the beach, but there was no one except them. No enemy, thank goodness, but also no one to help. The family with the little ones had left when she wasn't paying attention, but she thanked God they had. Of course if they hadn't, maybe the shooting wouldn't have happened.

She grasped the knot in the handkerchief wrapped about her arm—how trivial that scratch now seemed—and worked it loose. She folded it into a square, pressing it against Marsh's shoulder. He grimaced.

"Sorry," she whispered even as she saw the square become black immediately with his blood. What else could she use to staunch the hemorrhage? The quilt was too bulky. She pulled her sweatshirt over her head, folded one sleeve, and pressed it as hard as she could against the front of Marsh's shoulder. She folded and pressed the other sleeve against the back. He groaned at the pain but didn't complain.

Some sense of another near made the hairs on Abby's neck rise. She looked up. She gave a choked scream at the sight of a man dressed entirely in black, wearing both a black ski mask and night vision goggles, standing a few yards away. He held a handgun pointing down his side.

"Wha—?" Marsh tried to rise.

"Shh. Don't move. You'll make it bleed more."

The man in black stared at them. At least Abby assumed that's what he was doing. His face was toward them, his stance never changing, but the protruding goggles made him look more a movie alien than a man. He muttered a curse under his breath and began to raise the gun.

"I won't miss this time," he whispered.

Marsh twisted to see who was speaking even as Abby tried to hold him still. He groaned at the movement but persisted. When he saw the nightmare standing mere feet from them, he tensed. Then he sagged back against her in a faint.

"Marsh!" She bent over him, the man in black forgotten. *Oh, God, help me help him!* When she touched his cheek, she was surprised to hear him whisper, "The lantern."

Of course. She reached for it as she watched the shooter raise the gun.

"Don't," she pleaded, trying to infuse all the desperation she felt into her voice. "You don't want to do this."

He laughed. "Ah," he whispered, "but I do."

As he brought his arms straight in front of him to steady the gun, Abby hit the switch on the lantern. The strong beam of light, aimed straight at the night goggles, cut the darkness.

"What the—" The gunman, blinded as the bright light caused the phosphorescent screen of the goggles to shut down, dropped his gun and grabbed at the goggles.

As he did so, Abby surged to her feet. She rushed toward the man. *Oh, Lord, make my footing sure!*

She swung the heavy flashlight with all her might. The dull thud as it connected with his skull made her nauseous. The man sank to his knees, then fell forward onto his face. She snatched the gun from the sand where he'd dropped it. She aimed it at him but knew there was no way she would ever be able to pull the trigger.

"Shoot him in the leg," Marsh prompted. "That will disable him."

She threw an agonized glance at Marsh. "I can't! I just can't."

She heaved the weapon as far as she could, wishing like never before that she didn't throw like a girl. She heard the faint plop when it hit the ground. He'd never find it in the blackness. She would tell the police the general direction that she'd thrown it, and they'd come get it first thing in the morning before anyone else found it. They had metal detectors like Clooney's, right?

Marsh sighed. "The one time in my life I need a Colton West hero, and I have a softie, a beautiful softie."

"I just couldn't do it. I'm sorry." But she wasn't, even though she knew she had put them back at risk.

"It's all right. But we need to get out of here before he comes to." He tried to pull himself to his feet, got as far as his knees, and couldn't go farther. He looked at Abby. "Run, tiger. Get help."

She knelt beside him. "I'm not leaving you here." She wasn't leaving him ever, as far as she was concerned. She draped his uninjured arm over her shoulders. "Come on. Up you go. You can do it." She struggled to her feet, pulling him with her.

Marsh tried to support himself, but his body wouldn't cooperate. He could do nothing but lean against her.

Abby gazed in despair across the wide beach to the park and their car beyond that. Never could she manage Marsh's weight for even a quarter of that distance. She looked in the opposite direction. The water.

She wrapped one arm about Marsh's waist, pushing her shoulder into his uninjured armpit. She took a firmer grip of the uninjured arm draped across her shoulders. "We're going swimming, guy. Help me get us into the water."

"What?" He lifted his head, staring at her, his eyes unfocused.

She began her unsteady move into the sea. "Help me, Marsh. Help me!"

He tried. He took several small steps before he fell to his knees in the shallows. She glanced back at their shooter. He was almost invisible in his black, but she could just make him out, kneeling in the sand, his head hanging. Any minute he'd stand and come after them again. He wouldn't even need his gun to do in a wounded man and a lame woman. She dropped to her knees in front of Marsh.

"Come on, sweetheart." She put her hands on either side of his face, forcing him to look at her. "Come on. Just a little deeper.

Then I can take care of you." Tears ran down her cheeks. "Can you hear me? Marsh?"

He blinked at her, then leaned forward and placed a sloppy kiss on her cheek. "I hear you, tiger." His voice was so weak it frightened her.

"Don't you faint on me," she hissed. "I need you to walk a bit farther." A wave washed softly around their thighs. "Feel that? Just a little deeper. Come on now. Up you go!" She pulled both of them to their feet. "Come on, love. Step. Step. That's the way. I knew you could do it."

Slowly, painfully, they made their way into the surf. Every other step Abby glanced back, expecting to find their pursuer crashing into the water behind them. She could just make out a deeper black form rising to its feet, staggering about. He was looking for his gun.

Oh, God, help!

A wave broke over Abby's waist. At the same time Marsh collapsed. She grabbed at him as he went down, catching his collar. She lifted his face above the water, then tugged him close. She wrapped her arms across his chest, pulling his back against her front. She continued to back into the surf, dragging him with her. She needed to get beyond the breakers so they could move with greater ease. Thankfully undertow was not a consideration on a clear, calm night like tonight.

When she was in water almost to her chest, she decided she was far enough beyond the breaking waves. She turned and began making her way parallel to the land, using the far-off streetlights as her guide. Marsh hung in her arms, his head resting on her shoulder, his legs trailing in the water.

Suddenly the figure in black ran toward the water, arms flapping like a mad scarecrow. Abby's heart stalled, then jump-started itself at a frantic pace.

"I'll get you!" he roared. "Don't think you can escape me!" He plunged into the water until he stood knee deep, scanning the waves, looking for them.

Forcing herself to remain calm, she turned her head so her white face wouldn't show, wishing for the first time that Marsh's beautiful golden hair was a common, muddy brown. Thankfully his head rested against her shoulder farthest from land, but still, that golden head gleamed in the starlight like burnished bronze.

The gunman turned and raced back to the beach. He fell to his knees, hands raking through the sand, searching for the gun again.

May it take him forever! She continued their slow but steady progress through the water. Judging by the house lights she now saw, Abby thought she and Marsh had gone at least one block. How far should she go in the water? Three blocks? Five blocks? Ten? How long before she ran out of strength? That would undoubtedly decide for her how far she would go.

A roar of triumph sounded above the breaking of the waves, and their pursuer ran to the edge of the water. He fired two shots, making Abby flinch, but they were wasted. He had no idea where she and Marsh were. He began walking along the edge of the water, searching for them.

He would find them with his night goggles, wouldn't he? He'd found them once before; surely he could do it again. Unless the phosphorescent screen was damaged somehow by the bright flash she'd shined into it or by the sand when he'd dropped it. Or maybe he didn't know how to restart the device. She strained to see if he was still wearing the goggles, but she couldn't tell at this distance.

In her focus on the goggles, Abby didn't see or hear the large wave bearing down on them until it broke early and over their heads. She managed to turn in time to avoid the worst of the water, but it broke full in Marsh's unprotected face. He wrenched away from her, coughing and spitting.

"No, Marsh!" she screamed as he slid from her grasp. She reached for him and felt only water.

Forty

OH, GOD, HELP! Oh, God, help! The same prayer screamed through her mind over and over as she swung her arms wildly, trying to locate Marsh. The opaque green-gray water of daytime was an impenetrable black at night. There was no way she'd ever see him. All she could do was dive, praying that she would literally run into him. Six minutes without oxygen before brain damage began: Wasn't that what they said? Of course if you breathed in lots of water and filled your lungs, the six minutes meant nothing.

She dived and swam the way she thought the water'd pull him. She flailed her arms, reaching, grasping. Once she bumped into something and felt a surge of joy that turned in an instant to agonizing disappointment. It was only a jellyfish.

Lungs bursting, she came up for air. Taking a deep breath, she dived and slammed into his body. Overwhelming relief poured through her, dulling the pain in her shoulder where she had rammed him. She found his head, grabbed his hair, and stood, praying she could still touch bottom. The water came to midchest, a little dicey with the swell of the unbroken waves, but manageable.

Thank You, God!

Yanking on his hair, she pulled his face out of the

water, rolling him onto his back. She let the next wave float them a bit toward shore. She pulled his back against her chest once again, only this time she kept her back to the waves. She'd walk sideways all the way to Atlantic City if she had to, but she couldn't let any more rogue waves break in his face.

She stood perfectly still for a minute, her hand resting over Marsh's heart. She leaned her head over his shoulder, listening. At first there was nothing, and she felt sick. *Oh, God, You can't take another I love! You can't!*

Then she felt the beating of his heart against her palm, heard the faint intake of breath, felt its exhalation against her cheek. She buried her face in his neck, sobbing in relief.

But they were far from safe. Marsh still had his wound, and she could only assume it was still bleeding. Blood in the ocean. All kinds of unpleasant shark stories flashed through her mind. It was all she could do to begin crab-walking northward toward town and help, but if she panicked, they'd both be lost.

She searched the beach. Where was the man in black? Shouldn't she be able to see him silhouetted against the lights on the far side of the beach?

Right foot, together, right foot, together. She was amazed at how stable her footing was, thanks to the weight-bearing property of the water. Right foot, together, right foot, together. The man in black was nowhere to be seen.

Or more accurately, she couldn't see him. That didn't mean he wasn't out there, gun at the ready, waiting for her inevitable exit from the sea. Or maybe he somehow knew where they lived. What if he went there and was waiting, ready to jump them when they got home?

If there proved to be any truth to that scenario, it meant two things: He knew who they were, and this was not a random crime.

Right foot, together, right foot, together. But why was someone after them? It was as confusing as those horrible letters. Why? And who? Was it *them* he was after or just her? She had lurched right as the shot was fired. What if he had been aiming for her and gotten Marsh when he reached to help her?

Now there was an idea to assure her a lifetime of guilt.

But why her? What had she done? Right foot, together, right

foot, together. There was only one possibility. If it was just her, then it had to have something to do with the hit-and-run. Nothing else made sense. Probably the letters were involved somehow too.

Marsh stirred, and she leaned over him. "I'm here, Marsh. We're all right."

"Cold," he breathed as he shivered. "So cold."

Shock, she thought. *He's suffering from shock.* She felt sick to her stomach. *Can't shock kill you?*

He shivered again like one convulsing, and she had to clutch him to her so he didn't slip from her grasp. Not just shock, she realized. Hypothermia too.

"You're going to be okay, Marsh. You are. Just hang on." Who was she trying to convince, him or herself?

"Love you," came in the merest whisper. "So sorry."

She kissed his temple. "I love you too. And I'm the one who's sorry."

But he was gone again, unconscious, as the water continued to steal precious body heat from him, and his blood flowed away with the tide.

"Don't you leave me," she sobbed at him through gritted teeth. "Don't you dare leave me!"

She had to get him out of the water. At this point the gunman could be no more a threat than their present situation. She turned, pulling Marsh toward shore with the same crablike steps. Right foot, together. Right foot, together. She had to have come several blocks. The darkness that represented the park seemed a great distance, too far for the gunman to have tracked them. *Oh, Lord, please. Too far!* It would be safe here.

She was standing in shin-deep water, bent double and thoroughly winded from pulling Marsh, when she realized that none of his weight was being borne by the water anymore. His head and shoulders were above water because she held them there, but his body was resting on the bottom.

She reached up an arm, swiping it across her face to get rid of the seawater and tears that blurred her vision. She bent again, pulling and tugging with all her waning strength, and fell with a splash when her bad leg gave way. The jar of the landing clinked her teeth together and stole what little breath she still had. Pain streaked across her lower back and up her spine.

Marsh! She jerked to her knees, ignoring the biting agony the movement caused, grabbing for him, pulling his head above water. She tried not to think about the way he had sunk like a stone in water less than a foot deep, but she knew he'd still be lying there breathing in the sea instead of oxygen if she hadn't lifted him. She sat with him cradled against her, her legs spread like parentheses down his sides, waiting for the worst of the pain from her fall to subside.

When she thought the twisting movement wouldn't send her into spasm, she looked back over her shoulder at the houses no more than fifty or sixty yards away, houses with their lights still on, probably some with people sitting on their decks.

They might as well have been miles away for all the good they were doing her. No one could see her sitting in the water, so low to the ground, and no one would hear her scream for help over the noise of the water.

She scootched a few inches toward shore on her bottom, straining to drag Marsh with her. Her back complained about the abuse to the already ragged nerves and muscles. Tears fueled by fatigue and frustration ran down her cheeks and into her mouth.

"Oh, God," she sobbed. "Please help us!"

An almost spent wave purled in, lifting Marsh momentarily from the sand. She tugged and he floated a few inches closer to shore before he sank once again. Maybe all she had to do was be patient, moving with each incoming wave. Soon they'd make it to a place where she could safely leave him while she ran for help.

Ran for help. That was a laugh. She was so weary that she'd be lucky if she could crawl across the beach. Her breath came in jagged gasps, and her hip was on fire. She rested her cheek against Marsh's head for a minute, hoping, praying for a second wind. Her arms felt so weighted it was all she could do to keep them wrapped around his chest. Her legs were cramping from their awkward position and their prolonged immersion in the chill water. Her back began to spasm from all her tugging and lifting of the dead weight of Marsh.

Oh, Lord, more. We need more help!

The prayer had barely been thought when she heard splashing. She turned her head, and there stood the man in black, gun pointed at her head.

Forty-one

Sean RUBBED at his eyes. They stung miserably from that light she shined at him. One minute the two of them were there, eerie green aliens folding a quilt on the Seaside beach. Then *boom!* It was like the world exploded in a flash of white. The goggles shut down quickly just as they were supposed to, but that left him blind, the darkness total, punctuated only by brilliant flares where the light had burned his retina.

He'd wrenched the goggles off, throwing them aside, rubbing his eyes, trying to get decent natural night vision. That was when she hit him.

She hit him! That skinny, crippled girl hit him! As he pitched forward onto his face, the blackness swamping him, his one thought was that McCoy was laughing.

Finally he came to. His head ached fiercely, but it was his ego that had taken the greater hit. One thing he knew: Before the night was over, she would pay for that attack.

You think you're clever enough to get her if you couldn't manage it when she was right in front of you? You are such a loser, Sean! Just like your mom and dad.

McCoy! Sean took a deep breath. *The night's still young, McCoy. Just you watch! And I am not my parents!*

After endless minutes, he found his gun, half buried

in the sand where she must have thrown it. Why hadn't she used it? McCoy would have. He would have. She just threw it away. Idiot woman. She deserved whatever happened next.

He stood at the waterline and stared at the waves. They were out there somewhere. He fired a couple of random shots just to put the fear of God in them, then began moving down the beach toward town. She had to get out of the water sometime. She'd try and get to help, to the lighted houses filled with sympathetic people who would call 911 for her. But she had to cross the unlit beach before she found people, and he'd be there when she tried it.

We'll *be there when she tries it.*

Sean stiffened. For years he'd kept that voice stilled. *McCoy! Go away! I'm doing fine on my own.*

Sure you are. That's why you have a car buried in the Pines, an aborted letter-writing campaign, and the wrong person injured.

Sean closed his mind and refused to respond. He raced along the tide line, eyes scanning the water. Where were they? Shouldn't he be able to see their dark forms against the white spume? He paused, caught by a new thought. Maybe they had drowned. Now there was a happy thought, a solution that would save him lots of time and trouble. It'd save him from becoming McCoy too.

The more he thought about them drowning, the more enamored he grew with the idea. They would just sink to the bottom and rot or float off to wherever corpses floated off to. He didn't know that much about how the sea dealt with its victims. The best part of drowning would be that he wouldn't be the killer. The Atlantic Ocean would be the culprit.

Squeaky clean Sean M. Schofield, gentle physician, charmer of women, about-to-be-appointed chief of staff. In spite of McCoy's strident mockery, that was the person Sean wanted to be once again.

What price are you willing to pay, Sean, old boy-o?

Any price, McCoy. Any price. The prize is worth all.

McCoy's shout of triumph filled his mind. *Just what I needed to hear.*

He felt the shift, the breaking, the reforming. He felt both ripped apart and recreated as the splintering he had fought for years came to pass.

He was still shuddering from the cataclysmic event when he spotted her sitting in the shallows, holding the man out of the water.

He raised his gun in anticipation. S. McCoy Schofield was not going to lose this round.

Forty-two

ABBY RESTED HER cheek on Marsh's head, releasing a groan that came all the way from her toes. All that work, and here he was again.

Lord, this isn't the help I wanted at all!

"You won't get away this time!" Their pursuer, his voice shaking with his intensity, assumed a position just like the cops on TV shows.

Abby looked at him, too weary to feel fear. "Why?"

He ignored her at first, standing tense, poised to pull the trigger. Then he eased his stance. The gun was still at the ready, but he wouldn't shoot her this second.

"Why do you think?" he asked.

"The hit-and-run."

He nodded.

"What about the letters?"

"I want you to know that I never wrote them." He sounded defensive.

Great. He was going to murder her, but he wouldn't dirty his hands by writing nasty, damaging letters. What a skewed sense of ethics, morality, whatever. She was so tired she couldn't think what the right word was.

"The letters were to put you under a cloud of suspicion as far as your character went. Then, if you remembered the accident, your word would be suspect."

She nodded. "I see." Clever in a warped way.

"It was too bad it didn't work out," he said. "If it had, I wouldn't have to protect myself like this."

Ah, the whole situation was her fault. She should have known. "Your letter writer made a mistake by accusing me of things I couldn't have done. Bad sense of timing."

"Why did I ever think she would do it right?" he muttered, his voice full of disgust. "I should have done it myself."

She? Abby caught the pronoun, but her mind was too foggy for her to think it through at the moment.

"Do me a favor, will you?" She wrapped her arms more closely about Marsh as a dog began to bark in the distance. She thought wistfully of Fargo. "Pull Marsh out of the water after you shoot me? Call 911 anonymously. There's no reason he should die. He didn't do anything."

"I meant to shoot you, not him."

She nodded. "I figured that out."

"I didn't mean to hit Karlee."

"Of course you didn't. Everyone knows that."

"Now my whole future's on the line."

"How so?" She wanted to understand his motivation. If she had to die, it would be nice to know why.

"I should be appointed to the governor's panel on ethics in medicine next week. I'm also due to become chief of staff at the hospital."

He was going to sit on a panel on medical ethics, but he was going to murder her to guarantee the honor. He was going to oversee the saving of lives at a hospital of reputation but only if he took hers.

"My whole life is at stake here," he said, apparently seeing no irony in the situation.

"So's mine." She rested her head against Marsh's again. Just holding him like this was somehow comforting. Her fingers sought his carotid. *Still beating, thank God.*

"Hey, bracelet lady, isn't it a bit cold to be sitting in the water?"

Abby and the man in black, equally startled, looked at the vision who walked off the beach to stand beside Abby.

"Clooney!" His baseball cap was on backward, and his raggedy sweatshirt cuffs fell over his hands, but when he moved, his diamond stud glittered in the starlight. What was he doing here? How could she keep him from getting hurt?

"I was hunting stuff." He held out his detector toward the gunman, moving closer to show him his expensive toy. He seemed to see nothing sinister in a ski mask in summer or a gun in hand. "Didn't find too much tonight."

Clooney turned to Abby. "No pretty bracelets to give to pretty ladies." He shrugged. "So I lay me down to watch the meteors." He talked to her with ease, like it was everyday common to converse with a woman sitting fully clothed in the water, an unconscious man draped over her legs like a limp lap robe.

Clooney turned back to the masked man. "Did you know that there were meteor showers tonight? Great stuff. I watched for a while, then fell asleep." He shook his head. Abby could just make out his ponytail swinging beneath the bill of his cap. He yawned and stretched, his hands reaching for the sky, his detector wobbling over his head. "I just woke up."

"We watched the meteors," Abby said.

"We?" Clooney asked.

Abby nodded. "Marsh and me."

For the first time Clooney seemed to see Marsh. "Yo! What's wrong with him?" He started forward to help.

"It's okay! Don't bother!" Abby yelled at the same time the masked man ordered, "Don't move or I'll shoot!"

Clooney froze, then turned, arms held away from his body so the man could see he had nothing but the detector dangling from his right hand. "You shouldn't do this, you know. It's not very nice."

"Oh, but I will anyway. And you're first." He aimed at Clooney and pulled the trigger.

Abby screamed as Clooney went to his knees. As he fell, he threw himself forward, swinging his detector in a broad arc. It curled behind the man, catching him behind the knees. He staggered, almost falling, swearing violently.

Abby watched, sick with horror as the man struggled to regain his footing. He pointed his gun at Clooney for a second shot.

"Don't!" she screamed. "That's murder!"

"Shut up!" He swung the gun toward her, then back to Clooney. "You're both as good as dead."

He assumed the position, arms straight ahead of him, when a black shadow appeared out of the night, launching itself at him, growling deep in its throat. The gunman screamed in genuine, well-founded fear as Fargo sent him to the ground and stood growling over him, saliva dripping onto his vulnerable throat. The gun dropped into the sand as the man pushed vainly against Fargo's chest.

"Get him off me! Help me!"

Clooney looked over at Abby, a hand gripping his arm where blood ran red. "Like we're going to call off that beast so the man can try to do us in again." He shook his head. "We're not that stupid."

Sirens sounded, growing louder by the second.

"That should be the cops and an ambulance. I called 911 before I showed myself. Always have backup if you can."

"Clooney!" Tears of relief streamed down her face and clogged her throat. "You're wonderful!"

He glowed, patting his fanny pack. "I carry a cell phone. You never know when you'll need it."

Abby's tears turned to hysterical giggling. Something about an iconoclast like Clooney carrying a cell phone hit her weary sense of humor dead on. "Are you hurt badly?" she wheezed between giggles.

"Nah. Small stuff, especially compared to your man." Walking on his knees he came to her side. "Here. Let me help."

Using Clooney's good arm and Abby's waning strength, they inched Marsh out of the water. She slid beneath his upper torso to keep the wound out of the sand and stared at his shoulder. Blood still oozed, but the cold water had slowed it.

"Must be vascular if it's still pumping," Clooney said. He pulled his shirt over his head. "Use this for applying pressure."

She took the shirt and did as he said to both the front and back of Marsh's shoulder. She looked up. "Thank you for everything. You saved our lives."

Suddenly they were surrounded by people. Abby watched in a daze as the policeman who talked to her after the hit-and-run— her fuzzy brain would not call up his name—took charge. EMTs appeared and began working on Marsh, hollering things like hypotensive and 60 systolic. Abby didn't know what it all meant, but she knew that Marsh was now receiving good care. She was dimly aware of Rick standing behind her and Celia crouching beside her.

But her attention was directed to the man on the ground. She laid her hand on Marsh's cheek and stroked, careful to stay out of the EMTs' way. She had to touch him. She had to. If she touched him, he was here, not gone, and he had to be here. He had to be! *Oh, Lord, save him!*

The medical team also helped Clooney, who had been grazed in the arm. "I knew he was going to shoot," he told the police. "I've had lots of experience with pistol-toting folks a lot scarier than him. I was an MP in Nam. I threw myself before he pulled the trigger. Is my detector okay?"

Other men tried to take the man in black prisoner, but Fargo's growls kept them at bay as he loomed over the prone figure, fangs bared.

"Can anyone do anything with this dog?" Greg Barnes—yes, that was his name—asked. "I don't want to have to call the animal control guys."

Abby looked at Marsh. He was unconscious, no help with Fargo. Then she remembered the animal leaning against her thigh when she and Marsh were arguing.

She staggered upright and was relieved when Rick's hand was there to steady her. "I might be able to talk to the dog."

She went to Fargo but didn't touch him. "Hello, guy. It's me, Abby. Puppy's mom. Remember? You are such a wonderful doggie. I'm sorry I ever doubted you." She talked to him in a gentle, soft manner, telling him over and over how wonderful he was. He remained frozen in position, but his ears twitched as she talked. The growling slowly lessened, then stilled. His tail trembled.

"Come here, Fargo, baby." She went to her knees, holding out her hand. "Let the police take care of the bad man. You just come to me and let me hug you." He looked at her, his eyes filled with emotions she couldn't decipher. "Come here, guy. I'll take you to Marsh."

Whether it was the magic of Marsh's name or just Fargo's tiring of guard duty, she didn't know, but he stepped away from the whimpering man in the sand and came to her. She wrapped her arms around his warm, solid body and hugged him. He rested his chin on her shoulder, hugging her back.

The man in black was hauled unceremoniously to his feet. Greg ripped his ski mask away. There were gasps all around when they saw who it was, gasps from everyone but Abby, who had known.

She stared up at him. "I probably would never have remembered, you know."

"We couldn't take that chance."

"We?"

"This is about the hit-and-run?" Greg Barnes asked, astonished.

Abby nodded. "Ironically it was him chasing us tonight that jogged whatever was blocking my recall. I do now remember that black car." She looked into Sean McCoy Schofield's face. "And the vanity license plate. KID DOC."

Forty-three

ABBY STEPPED BACK as Sean was cuffed and read his rights. As she did so, she lost her balance, strained with Fargo's great weight resting against her. Rick reached out and grabbed her arm, steadying her. She smiled her thanks automatically, her eyes seeking out Marsh once again.

"It's all your fault!" Sean suddenly screamed at her.

Abby flinched but didn't acknowledge the hit.

"Shut up." Greg grabbed him, pulling him across the sand.

Sean struggled, twisting and turning, bucking and kicking. He screamed over his shoulder, "I was just protecting myself. It's self-defense! It's all her fault!"

"I'd like to see him sell that to the judge and jury," Rick muttered in Abby's ear.

"It is my fault." Abby wrapped her arms about herself, trying to get warm. Her shivers made her voice sound wobbly. "He wanted to shoot me, but I lost my footing. Marsh reached for me, and he got shot." A harsh sob closed her throat. She swallowed. "It really is my fault." Her voice was a mere whisper.

"Abby, look at me." Rick took her by the shoulders and turned her to face him. She could feel the heat from his large hands through her shirt. "It is *not* your fault. *He* chose to break several laws. You did not make him do that." He searched her face. "Do you understand? It's not your fault."

Abby sniffed and nodded. "I know, at least up here." She touched her temple. "But here." She laid her hand upon her heart. "Here it feels like it is my fault."

Rick pulled her close and hugged her. His concern, his bulk of body offered her a sense of protection. She wrapped her arms about him and began to sob in reaction to all that had gone before.

"Rick!"

Abby straightened and turned with Rick. Celia stood nearby with Fargo, a piece of rope attached to his collar for a leash. The dog was straining after the paramedics as they carried Marsh to the ambulance. It was all Celia could do to restrain him.

Rick took the rope, and though Fargo still pulled, Rick was a match for his efforts.

"Marsh!" Abby felt her heart wrench. They were taking him away from her. "Wait for me! I have to come along." She tried to hurry over the sand, but her feet were leaden with fatigue. When the treacherous surface rearranged itself beneath her, she fell to her knees. "Marsh!"

The medics kept walking.

Celia dropped to the sand beside Abby, wrapping her arm about Abby's waist. "Shush, honey. It'll be all right."

Abby turned to Celia, uncaring of the tears wetting her face. "I have to go with him," she whispered. "I have to. What if…?" She shuddered. She couldn't finish. The what-if was too terrible to articulate.

"You can't do anything for Marsh right now, honey," Celia said. "He needs the hospital, and the faster they get him there, the better. We don't want to hold them up even for a minute."

Abby both saw and heard the doors of the ambulance slam shut. The siren whirred once as the vehicle disappeared down the street, red strobe washing the houses as they passed.

"Come on, Abby." Celia pulled her to her feet. "Let's get you home and into dry clothes. Fargo needs to go home too. Then Rick and I will take you to the hospital. We'll make sure you're there when he wakes up."

Abby nodded, knowing Celia was right, letting her and Rick lead the way home. *Oh, God, please let him wake up!* Fargo walked beside them, turning frequently to look at Abby, his brown brows arched in question.

She reached for him, running her hand over his soft fur. "I wish I knew what to tell you, old man. We'll just have to wait and see."

When they reached the house, Abby welcomed Celia's arm around her waist as they climbed the stairs. First there was a quick hot shower to wash the ocean out of her hair, and then warm clothes. They came downstairs to find Rick sitting in Marsh's Adirondack chair, Fargo resting his head on Rick's knee, Rick's fingers fondling the dog's ears. Abby thought Fargo looked as forlorn as she felt.

"Fargo." Abby took the dog's head between her hands. "You are a hero, guy. You saved our lives." She gave him a great kiss between his eyes. He gave her a great slurp over her entire face. "Marsh'll be okay, boy. Just you wait and see."

Fargo whimpered, his confusion and hurt sounding clearly. She fell to her knees, wrapping her arms about him and burying her face in his neck.

"How did he get free to rescue us?" Abby looked up at Rick and Celia though her hands continued to caress Fargo's head. "I know he was in the house when Marsh and I left to see the meteors."

"When we got back here after dinner," Rick said, "he was scratching frantically to get out. He was up on his hind legs, his forepaws clawing the glass. The door was coated with saliva where he had drooled in his desperation. Somehow he knew something was wrong." Rick gave a solid couple of thumps to Fargo's chest, and the dog's tail managed a small wag.

"When Rick opened the door," Celia continued the story, "Fargo burst out and shot straight off the porch. I've never seen anything like it. He hurtled down the beach, barking and snarling and whining." She shivered. "I hope he never has reason to come after me."

Rick stood and put the reluctant dog inside the house. Fargo stared out at them, decidedly unhappy. Lauded as a hero one minute, discarded like a chewed-up bone the next. He gave a snort that clouded the glass.

Abby spent the trip to the hospital wedged between Rick and

Celia, trying still to get warm. She struggled to beat back her panic, but if she was this hypothermic, what about Marsh? And how did his body temperature complicate his injury?

Abby let her head rest against Celia's shoulder. "I'm so scared."

Celia swallowed. "I know, honey. Me too."

"If he dies, I don't know what I'll do." Abby paused a minute to swallow the threatening tears. "This is worse than Sam. I haven't even known Marsh long, and already losing him would be worse than losing Sam. Oh, God, please!" Her voice broke on the last word.

Celia stroked Abby's hair. "Shh. It'll be all right."

"I love him so much. And he loves me. He said so."

They spent the rest of the trip in silence. When they arrived, Rick drove directly to the emergency room. Abby and Celia climbed out and hurried inside.

"Marsh Winslow," Abby told the woman at the desk.

"He's being treated now."

"Can I see him? Please?"

The woman looked dubious. "Let me check." She slipped through a door at the back of her cubicle, returning a few minutes later. "I'm sorry. Let me take you to the surgical waiting area."

"Not until I talk to somebody." She could be stubborn if she had to. She could lie down on the floor and kick and scream if she had to. "I need to talk to somebody."

The woman heard Abby's implacable desperation and excused herself again.

"We'll wait right here until someone comes," Rick assured Abby, slipping a comforting arm across her shoulders.

Abby blinked at his kindness. "You need to see him too. You love him too."

Rick cleared his throat. "Yeah, I do." His voice was rough.

After what seemed forever to Abby, a nurse in green scrubs came into the emergency waiting room. She smiled at Abby and Celia and did a double take when she saw Rick.

"How is he?" Abby demanded, having no patience for any Duke Beldon nonsense.

"When the paramedics brought him in he was in shock from blood loss and hypothermia, to say nothing of the bullet wound. We're warming him and giving him packed RBOs."

"What?" Rick asked.

The nurse smiled. "Blood. We've also cleaned the area around the wound where cavitation occurred." Seeing their blank expressions she explained, "When the bullet entered, the tissue expanded, then collapsed on itself. It sucked in clothing and other debris, in this case sand. Further debridement will be necessary during surgery. We're waiting now for a surgeon to come in. As soon as one arrives, it's up to the operating room for Mr. Winslow. Would you like to sit with him until we move him?"

"All of us," Abby said.

The nurse nodded. "I'm sure we can find three chairs."

She led them back into the emergency room, to a cubicle closed off by curtains. Marsh lay on a table, pale, unmoving, blood and saline flowing into his arm. A warming blanket lay over him.

"Can he hear us?" Abby asked the nurse, who shrugged an I-don't-know. "Can you hear me, Marsh?" She brushed back his hair, stiff and sticky with salt water, and kissed his forehead. When he made no response, she sighed and took her seat. She reached under the blanket for his hand and squeezed it. She looked at Rick and Celia and shook her head. No response. It was a good thing the monitors behind him kept up their steady record of his vital signs, or she'd have been in agony.

The three sat in the uncomfortable plastic chairs they were given. Mostly they sat in silence, staring at Marsh's unconscious form. Every so often, Abby leaned forward and spoke, telling him what a hero Fargo had been and how Sean Schofield was the villain of the piece. Several times Rick stood and leaned over Marsh, talking quietly about *Shadows at Noon*. Other times, Rick prayed aloud. After one joint vocal amen from the three of them, Abby froze. "I think he squeezed my hand!"

When Marsh was whisked away, they were shown to the surgical waiting room where time dragged and anxiety thrived.

Oh, God, please!

Abby was eating a stale doughnut and downing her third Coke when Vivian deMarco walked into the room.

"Vivian!" Abby stared in astonishment. "What a surprise."

Vivian looked terrible, something Abby would never have

thought possible. Her eyes were red from crying and had dark circles beneath them. Her uncombed hair was pulled back, caught carelessly with a rubber band that made little knotted clumps stick out. She wore a wrinkled T-shirt that must belong to Rocco if size was any indication, baggy jeans, and plastic flip-flops.

"I had to come." She looked at Abby and began to sob.

Abby reached for her and held her, sharing a bewildered look with Celia and Rick. She would never have thought Vivian cared that much. "He'll be all right." Abby led Vivian to the sofa. "It's okay."

Vivian sank into her seat. "I'm so sorry."

"Aren't we all." Rick ran a hand back and forth over the nape of his neck.

Abby watched Vivian and in that instant knew she wasn't talking about Marsh. "What are you sorry about?"

"Sean. I believed him." Her face turned ashen, then red. "He used me. He played on my jealousy, and I was too stupid to see what he was doing." She swiped at her tears with a shaking hand. "'Just think of how dangerous it is to have an unstable woman with a psychiatric record like hers in charge of our children.' That's what he told me. He made me feel so important, like he trusted me enough to confide something important, you know? 'Imagine what she could do to sweet kids like Walker and Jordan,' he said."

Abby nodded. She now knew what was coming, and she finally understood what Rocco had been talking about as she and Marsh left last evening. She didn't interrupt Vivian though. She knew the woman needed to talk. That was why she had come, unkempt and disconsolate, in the very early hours of a summer morning.

Vivian searched through her pockets for a tissue. When it was obvious she would find none, Abby held out one of several boxes placed around the waiting room. Vivian took a handful and blew her nose. Then she continued with her story.

"When I told Sean you needed to be stopped, he asked how would I recommend stopping you. Like I was smart and I would know the answer. I didn't, of course, so I asked him what he would suggest. Maybe a letter, he said, written to a person's boss telling her how unqualified or dangerous the person in question was. 'Why don't you do that?' he said, and the next thing I knew, I did. And then I wrote the one that I knew was a lie."

Rick spoke for the first time since Vivian began her confession. "You know that slander is against the law? Abby could make things very tough for you."

Vivian paled again but said nothing, merely nodded, wide-eyed.

"Mrs. Winslow?" a woman called from the doorway.

Abby knew the woman meant her. She rose.

"Mr. Winslow is fine. The surgeon is finishing up now. Then it's into recovery. He should be back in his room in an hour or two."

Abby grabbed the nearby chair back to hold herself up as relief turned her legs suddenly nerveless. *Thank You, Father!*

"Do you wish to wait?" the woman asked.

Abby, Rick, Celia, and Vivian nodded as one.

The woman smiled. "The cafeteria will be open in an hour for breakfast. Maybe you can eat and then see Mr. Winslow. He'll be in Room 215."

Everyone nodded again. The woman turned away, and for a moment those in the waiting room were quiet. Then Rick gave a great wah-hoo! and swung first Celia, then Abby around in great circles. Laughing and crying at the same time, Abby hugged Celia. Rick grabbed the hands of both women and said, "Father, we thank You for Your great mercy and kindness!"

"Amen!" yelled Abby, kissing both Rick and Celia on the cheek. Then she spotted Vivian, lost and forlorn, sitting on the sofa. As Abby walked to her, Vivian gave a tentative smile. "I'm glad Marsh is going to be all right."

Abby nodded. "Thanks."

"I sent a note, you know."

Abby was confused. "You just said you sent two."

"I mean another one. I told them that what I wrote before was all lies. I told them I was sorry. I said you were nice and wonderful and they were lucky to have you." Vivian was all earnestness and yearning to be believed.

"What made you decide to write that?"

Vivian looked at her clasped hands. "You saved Walker's life."

"Ah."

Vivian looked up, tears once again streaming. "How could I say such things against you when you saved my baby? I'm sorry, Abby. I even signed my name."

She twisted her tissues into a rope. "Can you forgive me?"

Abby felt so relieved over the good news about Marsh that she would forgive anyone anything, but she held her tongue for a moment. Absolution too quickly given can seem too easy.

"Rocco forgave me," Vivian said, like this fact would make Abby more inclined to do the same. "I told him what I did, and he told me he loved me."

"Rocco's a nice man."

Vivian actually smiled. "He told me I hadn't done anything worse than he had when he ignored me and the boys."

Abby wasn't certain she agreed with that assessment, but she wasn't about to debate it with Vivian.

"What I did wasn't right," Vivian said as she rose. "The one good thing is that Rocco proved his love by offering to talk to you for me. Then when I saw them taking Sean away tonight—we saw the lights and stuff when we were sitting on the deck and went to investigate—I knew I had to talk to you too. Please, Abby. Say you'll forgive me."

Abby looked at Vivian so long the woman began to squirm. "I forgive you. But I want you to promise me you'll never do anything like that ever again, no matter how mad you get."

"Oh!" Vivian bounced on her toes, a beautiful smile lighting her face. "I won't. I won't. I learned my lesson. Oh, thank you!"

Two hours later, Abby sat alone beside Marsh's bed. Vivian had left when Rick, Celia, and Abby went to the cafeteria. After they ate, Rick and Celia left to reassure Jess and Karlee, who had spent the night with Mrs. Winsky.

"We'll come back after church," they said.

Abby leaned over Marsh and brushed his hair off his forehead. Then she ran her hand lightly up and down his day-old beard. It rasped and pricked, and the sensation caused Marsh to open his eyes.

"Hey, tiger." He croaked and managed a lopsided smile.

"Hey, hero." She leaned in and kissed his cheek.

He looked down at himself, one shoulder all bandages over stitches, the other arm full of IVs. "Can't hug you right now."

"I'll take a rain check. And there's nothing wrong with my arms." She wrapped them carefully about his middle and, resting her head on his chest, squeezed gently. He dropped a kiss on her head.

She straightened. "You scared me."

"I scared myself."

"I don't know what I would have done if you'd died." Tears gathered in her eyes.

His face creased in concern. "Don't, Abby. I'm going to be fine." He turned his palm up, and she gripped his hand. "We have years and years to love each other."

"Years," she repeated. She stood, leaned over, and kissed him again. "Years."

He fell back to sleep.

As Abby sat, she knew it was time to make the call she dreaded. She picked up the phone by the bed and dialed.

"Hi, Mom."

"Abby! What's wrong?"

"Why do you think something's wrong?"

"It's seven o'clock on a Sunday morning. Why else would you call, especially when we're supposed to see you at church in a few hours."

"Um. It's Marsh." And Abby braced herself.

"Marsh? What happened?"

Abby had to hand it to her mother. She sounded concerned. "He was shot."

"What?"

Abby could imagine her mother's thoughts. *What kind of man gets shot? Good people don't get themselves shot. They don't even know people to shoot them. But my daughter's new boyfriend gets shot. Maybe he was hurt in a robbery. Innocent people could get shot in a robbery.*

"Was it a robbery?" Hannah asked

"No, no. The shot was meant for me. It hit Marsh instead."

Mom said nothing for so long that Dad grabbed the phone. "Hello?"

"It's me, Dad. I was just telling Mom that Marsh got shot last night."

"Is he all right?"

"He's banged up a bit." She looked at his much loved face and thought that an understatement. "But he came through surgery well. The prognosis is good."

"What hospital?"

"Mainland Memorial."

"We'll be there as quickly as we can make it."

"Thanks, Dad."

It was almost an hour before her parents arrived. Abby spent that time dozing in the chair by Marsh's bed. She awakened when she heard her father's voice just outside the door.

"You will be gracious, Hannah. Remember, the shot was supposed to be for Abby. That's what she told you."

"Who would ever want to shoot our Abby?"

"How should I know?" Dad said. "All I know is he got Marsh instead."

"You mean like he jumped in front of her?" Mom sounded floored by the idea.

Len nodded. "I can see him doing that. He's a fine boy."

Mom made a disgusted sound. "I don't even like him, and I've got to be thankful to him?"

Abby closed her eyes and rubbed her forehead. *Lord, will it ever change?*

A new voice entered the conversation in the hall. "Hello." Rick was back.

"I'm glad to hear Marsh is going to be fine," Dad said.

"Thanks. I'm glad for Abby that she doesn't have to suffer any more loss. She and Marsh are so good together."

Mom made a choking sound.

Rick kept talking, just like he didn't know he was pouring salt on Mom's wound. "He's so good with her. He's the one who figured out why the accusations against her were bogus."

"What accusations?" Mom's voice bristled.

"You'd better talk to her about it," Rick backpedaled. "But Marsh was definitely the hero. And if it weren't for him, I wouldn't know the Lord."

Abby had to smile. Poor Mom. She was hearing so many nice things about Marsh.

"How did you ever get to meet Marsh?" Dad asked. "Don't you live in California?"

"When I got the lead in the first Colton West film—"

"Aha!" Dad said.

"What?" Mom asked.

"Marsh met with me to talk over the character and his vision for the film. We hit it off. He was sanity in an insane world.

Working with him on the next three films proved his faith to me, and I knew Jesus was real."

"Why in the world would you and Marsh have anything to do with Colton West?" Mom asked, her voice still too acerbic.

"You *are* Rick Mathis," Dad said triumphantly. "Duke Beldon. I knew it."

"And Marsh is Colton West." With that bit of news, Rick walked into the room, smiling in satisfaction. He had actually silenced Mom.

But not for long. "Aha!" she cried. "Spoiled celebrities! I *knew* something was wrong. We've got to protect her, Len."

But Dad had followed Rick into the room and didn't respond.

Abby glanced at Marsh. His eyes were open and twinkling. He'd heard the whole conversation. She rolled her eyes, and he dropped one eyelid in a wink. He gave a little come-here toss of his head. She leaned over him.

"I don't call you tiger for nothing, you know."

She nodded. "I love you."

He smiled sweetly and went back to sleep.

Epilogue

Two Years Later

"IT'S GOING TO rain tomorrow," Marsh said as he stared up into the beautiful deep blue sky of a late July evening in Seaside. He gently rubbed his shoulder, shifting it forward and back to ease the twinges it sent every time the barometer fell.

Abby nodded, aware of the dull ache in her hip. "I was thinking the same thing."

They grinned at each other.

"At least," Marsh said, "we know when to take umbrellas."

They stood in the drive next to the beach house, watching Senator and Mrs. Winslow leave after their annual one-day summer visit. Marsh stood slightly behind Abby, and she leaned back against him, delighting as always in having him next to her. Her husband. Her beloved.

"We're safe from another visit until Christmas," Marsh said, but Abby heard the wistful sound in his voice.

"I'm sorry you'll never have the closeness you deserve with you father." She reached up and kissed his cheek.

Marsh shrugged. "Nothing I can do about it." But she knew it hurt him deeply.

"At least your father's proud of Colton West."

"And he's delighted with the prospect of becoming a grandfather." Marsh put his palm on Abby's slightly rounded tummy. "Almost as pleased as I am at becoming a father."

"And me at being a mom again."

"Does the pregnancy bring back painful memories?" She understood that this was his greatest fear for her.

"Once in a while. Mostly I remember the precious times: Maddie sleeping through the night, Maddie rolling over, Maddie standing on her chubby little legs—sweet memories. And I look forward to making a whole new collection with you and Little Whoever."

He wrapped his arms about her in a protective and comforting cocoon. "We'll make them the best and most extraordinary memories the world has ever seen."

They laughed softly at the exaggeration, but it seemed a worthy goal nonetheless.

The driver of the limousine honked, and Marsh and Abby waved.

His hand dropped to her shoulder. "I'm glad we waited to tell them about the baby until this visit. In person was much nicer than over the phone."

"You just wanted to see Lane's face when she learned she was going to be a grandmother!"

He grinned, totally unrepentant. She smiled back. He had a right to be pleased with life. *Shadows at Noon* had earned him an Emmy nomination for writing and Rick one for best actor in a drama. Marguerite and Craig of Frost Spring Ranch had been a great success in book sales, and Rick's take on Craig, now in editing, was proving the richest performance of his career to date.

They walked onto the porch and took their accustomed seats—he in his red Adirondack and she in her matching one.

"You realize that it won't be long before you're going to have to haul me from this chair, don't you?" Abby snuggled into the deep V of the seat. "I'll never be able to get myself out."

"Hey, are they gone?" Rick and Celia and the girls stood beside the porch, all sunburned and smiling. They had arrived for a month in the upstairs apartment, fresh from their ranch in

Montana. Celia was even further advanced in her pregnancy than Abby.

When Marsh nodded, Rick beckoned. "Come with us. We're going to the boardwalk for some popcorn and french fries."

Celia held up a hand. "Not me. I'm just going for the exercise."

"I want to ride the roller coaster," said Jess. "You promised, Dad."

Rick beamed. "I did."

"I want some cotton candy, the blue kind," Karlee announced.

"It'll turn your lips blue," Celia protested.

Karlee looked at her blankly. "So?"

Viv and Rocco appeared, trailed by Walker and Jordan. Walker immediately went to stand beside Jess. She ignored him as usual.

"Can they go?" Rocco asked Rick, who shrugged. "Can you go?" he then asked Marsh.

"Let's," Abby said, her aching hip forgotten. "It's our last free night before Mom and Dad hit town."

"Are they staying here?" Celia asked in surprise.

Abby shook her head. "But we have plans to do several things with them."

"That's just because Colton West is Len's favorite writer," said Rick, laughing.

"Len's not my problem." Marsh didn't have to spell out who was. He pulled Abby out of her chair.

"But Mom frowns less every time she sees him." Abby slid her arm around Marsh. "That's because she sees how happy I am."

"That's because she knows she doesn't have a choice," said the ever-practical Marsh. "It's be nice to me or...." He didn't finish the sentence.

Abby smiled somewhat sadly at Marsh's joke. There was just enough truth in it to hurt. Why a smart and devout woman like her mother couldn't understand that Marsh was Abby's top priority was a mystery. Why she felt Abby wasn't smart enough or godly enough to make wise choices was another puzzle.

However, they were making progress. Mom appeared to be trying, at least most of the time. Certainly boundaries had to be drawn and redrawn, and the coming baby would necessitate much negotiation. The last thing either she or Marsh wanted was the tension of a long visit from Mom when the baby arrived. By the same token, they didn't want her to miss the joy of the event either.

Abby sighed. It would never be easy. Without a doubt the distance they lived from each other made things less complicated, but it still took much thought and prayer, and Abby suspected it always would. Still she knew she and Marsh were able to honor her parents with sincere hearts.

Arm in arm the two of them walked to their car.

"We'll meet you in front of the merry-go-round," Marsh called, knowing the three families might not get parking places near each other.

"I'm going to ride the white horse with flowers in its hair," Karlee said.

Jordan looked at her in horror. "I'm riding the dragon with the big claws."

"Scaley boy." Karlee climbed into her car, leaving Jordan staring, trying to decide if he'd been insulted.

Marsh and Abby held hands as they drove into town, as they walked to the boardwalk, and as they waited for their friends at the merry-go-round.

"Hey," said a teenager near them. "Isn't that Rick Mathis?"

"With a pregnant lady and two little kids?" his friend said. "Are you kidding? He's way too cool for that. Next thing you know you're going to tell me Colton West is a family guy too."

Marsh and Abby looked at each other and laughed until tears came.

Dear Reader,

What an influence family exerts over each of us.

When God blesses us with strong, healthy, caring relatives, He bestows a favor of sweet richness. We see not only a picture of our loving Father but also of how the brothers and sisters who inhabit the Body should interact and care.

When we are raised in a family where stress and contention, perhaps even abuse, are a way of life, God had granted us one of those severe mercies. We learn that the only way to survive, to grow, to become whole, is to cling to our Savior and draw on His boundless love and strength.

"Yet I still dare to hope when I remember this: The unfailing love of the LORD never ends! By his mercies we have been kept from complete destruction. Great is his faithfulness; his mercies begin afresh each day. I say to myself, 'The LORD is my inheritance; therefore, I will hope in him!'" (Lamentations 3:21–24, NLT).

Gayle Roper

Multnomah Publishers ®

The publisher and author would love to hear your comments about this book. *Please contact us at:*
www.multnomah.net/seasideseasons

TEARS ARE FALLING LIKE SPRING RAIN...

Spring Rain **by Gayle Roper**
Seaside Seasons, Book One:

Leigh Spenser, a young teacher and single mother of ten-year-old Billy, is thrown into conflict. Clay Wharton, the boy's estranged father, comes home to Seaside, New Jersey, to await the passing of his twin brother, Ted—now dying of AIDS. Threats against Billy's life ratchet the tension tighter, as Leigh wrestles with both tough and tender feelings for her old flame. Clay's own conflict, as he seeks to come to grips with his brother's lifestyle choices and the needs of the boy he fathered, underline the issue of God's forgiveness in the hearts—and lives—of this modern-day family. An emotionally gripping read!

ISBN 1-57673-638-5

Spring Rain

TEN-YEAR-OLD BILL has rushed into the night and onto the jetty to rescue Terror the terrier before high tide claims him.

"It's okay, Terror," he called again and again. "It's okay. I'm coming."

He glanced up and saw a huge wave, crest white with spume, about to break over Terror's rock. It would definitely wash him out to sea. Bill jumped the last crevice and grabbed just as the wave broke.

The wave caught him full in the face as he bent over the pup. He coughed and sputtered and tried to lift the very wet and frantic Terror, but he couldn't. The wave receded, pulling him down on his knees beside the terrified dog. His toes hooked over the edge of the rock toward land and held on. Water now covered the rock with no relief, lapping partway up his thighs as he knelt.

He felt rather than saw the rope about the animal's neck. At first he didn't realize what it was. He squinted at it through water-spotted glasses, puzzled. Then it hit him with all the force of the line drive that had clipped him in the nose last year. Someone had tied Terror to the rock!

Anger burned in Bill, hotter than he'd ever known in his life. Who would have done such a terrible, terrible thing? He grabbed the rope and pulled. It wouldn't budge. He pulled again harder. Nothing. It was wedged firmly in a crevice, and with all the water, he couldn't see where and how.

Moving quickly, he put himself, still on his knees, his back to the sea, behind Terror. When the next wave broke, it struck him in the middle of the back, but his body protected the dog, at least a little bit. He began working his hands around the rope at Terror's neck. He found the knot quickly, and his cold fingers began to pick at it.

Come on. Come on!

Whoever the guy was who tied Terror up had used the slip-knot that boaters use to tie up to a dock, loop inside loop inside loop. He'd tied it himself lots of times when he'd gone out on Uncle Ted's boat with him. Bill stood, gave a brisk tug, and the loops fell apart. The rope dropped away just as a wave struck him in the back of the knees. He felt himself stumble and grabbed Terror.

As the wave receded and pulled at him, he braced himself. When the sickening sensation was gone, he picked up the dog and held Terror against him like a mom did a burping baby. He was relieved and surprised that they were both still solidly on the rock.

Thanks, God. Just a little bit longer, okay?

He cradled Terror, cooing to him as the dog lay shivering against his chest, his wet little head pressed against Bill's neck.

"Just stay still, okay? We'll be back on land real soon."

He looked back the way he had come, and in that moment Bill knew fear like he'd never experienced before. The houses were so distant, their lights little pinpricks, like stars. The night was so dark, and the water swirled wildly over the rocks in front of him. He couldn't see where to step. He just couldn't see.

CAN THE LIVING FIND GOD'S FORGIVENESS FOR THEMSELVES AND JUSTICE FOR THE DEAD?

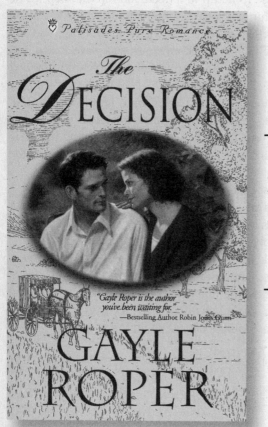

> "If you're looking for a contemporary mystery with wit and romance, Gayle Roper is the author you've been waiting for."
>
> —ROBIN JONES GUNN

Rose Martin, fearless young nurse, cares for the critically injured. But when a car bomb explosion kills her cancer patient—rich widow and beloved mentor Sophie Hostetter—Rose faces a difficult question: Who could have done this? Was it Peter, Sophie's financial risk-taking son? Rose escapes into the arms of Jake, a man struggling with his past and his Amish heritage, yet decisions come hard in matters of love and forgiveness. Can the living find God's forgiveness for themselves and justice for the dead?

ISBN 1-57673-406-4

The Decision

I HAD JUST witnessed a car bomb and was finally on my way home. I hadn't gone very far when my mind, never very quiet at the best of times, exploded. Images flashed through my mind with the relentless pulse of the light strip on a police cruiser. Fire, crushed impatiens, sirens, static, yellow police tape. Surviving brothers with sunglasses. Firefighters with Mercurochrome. Polite detectives with fine brown hair that floated every time they turned their heads.

And rushing white water, swollen and angry, creaming over rocks.

And the inevitable, "Rose, what happened?"

It didn't take much intelligence to realize just how close to the edge I was.

"I'm fine. Really. I'm fine." I repeated it to myself like a litany. Maybe if I said it often enough, it would become true.

But coming out of the house and seeing those lights and hearing that static had brought such a rush of agony, I was unlikely to feel fine for quite some time. I hadn't had this strong a flashback in years.

You're being stupid, I told myself. You're a nurse and an EMT. You deal with emergencies much too frequently to be spooked like this.

But that's when I'm the healer, the helper. I fix the problems. I don't cause them.

But you didn't cause the problem today.

No, I didn't, but I didn't prevent it, either.

Like you could have. What are you, prescient?

I shrugged away that bit of logic and went back to the real crux of my distress.

But I was the cause then.

The little voice that had been answering me back was uncomfortably quiet.

Suddenly I knew I wasn't going to make it home. I felt the bile rise in my throat and swallowed desperately against the impulse to vomit. I felt the tears begin, blurring my vision until I could barely see the road. I felt the shaking start deep in my stomach, and I knew it would radiate outward until my whole body shook.

Oh, God!

I blinked madly, desperately.

Oh, God! I have to get off the road before I fail again, before I'm the cause again.

And I saw the answer to my prayer loom out of the darkness, a white farmhouse with green trim, clean and orderly and known. I pulled into the Zooks' drive, shoved the car in park, and fell to pieces.

SOMETHING'S GOT TO GIVE—AND THIS TIME, IT'S NOT GOING TO BE HER!

Often moms feel their kids getting beyond their control. Through the genre of fiction, *Enough!* humorously presents patterns for dealing with the situation. In this comical novel, Molly Gregory realizes that her three teens have gotten away from her and goes on a two-week strike to remind them to honor her—with chaos as the result.

ISBN 1-57673-185-5

www.letstalkfiction.com

Let's Talk Fiction is a free, four-color mini-magazine created to give readers a "behind the scenes" look at Multnomah Publishers' favorite fiction authors. *Let's Talk Fiction* allows our authors to share a bit about themselves, giving readers an inside peek into their latest releases. Published in the fall, spring, and summer seasons, *Let's Talk Fiction* is filled with interactive contests, author contact information, and fun! To receive your free copy of *Let's Talk Fiction* get on-line at www.letstalkfiction.com. We'd love to hear from you!